PRAISE FOR *USA TODAY*
BESTSELLING AUTHOR
LYNN KURLAND

"Kurland surprises and enchants with each turn
of phrase and page."
—*Publishers Weekly*

"Kurland reveals a remarkable talent and
a delightful sense of whimsy."
—*Affaire de Coeur*

"Kurland's special brand of humor and delightful
storytelling always gives . . . fans a 'must read.' "
—*Romantic Times*

"Ms. Kurland has moved to the head of the class as one
of the top scribes of historical drama by demonstrating a
talent that many writers would kill to call their own."
—Harriet Klausner for *Painted Rock Reviews*

"Lynn Kurland is a welcome new voice in romance."
—Susan Wiggs

"Keep them coming, Ms. Kurland."
—*Rendezvous*

continued on next page . . .

The Very Thought of You

"[A] masterpiece . . . this fabulous tale will enchant anyone who reads it."　　　　　*—Painted Rock Reviews*

"Outstanding and imaginative. Lynn Kurland gives her fans another time-traveling treat to savor."

—Romantic Times

The More I See You
A *ROMANTIC TIMES* TOP PICK

"Delightful and humorous."　　　　　　　　　*—Booklist*

"The superlative Ms. Kurland once again wows her readers with her formidable talent as she weaves a tale of enchantment that blends history with spellbinding passion and impressive characterization, not to mention a magnificent plot."　　　　　　　　　　　　　*—Rendezvous*

"Lynn Kurland is a literary magician. . . . Her special brand of humor and delightful storytelling always gives time-travel fans a 'must read.' *The More I See You* is just one more jewel in Ms. Kurland's crown!"　　*—Romantic Times*

"Entertaining . . . The story line is fast-paced and brings to life the intrigue of the era . . . wonderful . . . Lynn Kurland is definitely a writer whose star is on the rise."

—Harriet Klausner

continued on next page . . .

This Is All I Ask

"In this character-driven medieval romance that transcends category, Kurland spins a sometimes magical, sometimes uproariously funny, sometimes harsh and brutal tale of two people deeply wounded in body and soul who learn to love and trust each other. . . . Savor every word; this one's a keeper."

—*Publishers Weekly* (starred review)

"Both powerful and sensitive, this is a wonderfully rich and rewarding book." —Susan Wiggs

"A medieval story of stunning intensity. Sprinkled with adventure, fantasy, and heart, *This Is All I Ask* reaches outside the boundaries of romance to embrace every thoughtful reader, every person of feeling."

—Christina Dodd,
bestselling author of *A Knight to Remember*

"Sizzling passion, a few surprises, and breathtaking romance . . . If you don't read but one book this summer, make this the one. You can be assured of a spectacular experience that you will want to savor time and time again." —*Rendezvous*

"An exceptional read." —*The Atlanta Journal-Constitution*

A Dance Through Time

"One of the best . . . a must read." —*Rendezvous*

"Lynn Kurland's vastly entertaining time travel treats us to a delightful hero and heroine . . . a humorous novel of feisty fun and adventure." —*A Little Romance*

"Her heroes are delightful. . . . A wonderful read!"
—*Heartland Critiques*

"An irresistibly fast and funny romp across time."
—Stella Cameron

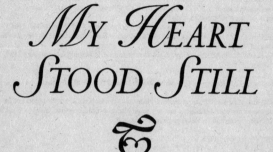

MY HEART STOOD STILL

LYNN KURLAND

BERKLEY BOOKS, NEW YORK

THE BERKLEY PUBLISHING GROUP
Published by the Penguin Group
Penguin Group (USA) Inc.
375 Hudson Street, New York, New York 10014, USA
Penguin Group (Canada), 10 Alcorn Avenue, Toronto, Ontario M4V 3B2, Canada
(a division of Pearson Penguin Canada Inc.)
Penguin Books Ltd., 80 Strand, London WC2R 0RL, England
Penguin Group Ireland, 25 St. Stephen's Green, Dublin 2, Ireland (a division of Penguin Books Ltd.)
Penguin Group (Australia), 250 Camberwell Road, Camberwell, Victoria 3124, Australia
(a division of Pearson Australia Group Pty. Ltd.)
Penguin Books India Pvt. Ltd., 11 Community Centre, Panchsheel Park, New Delhi—110 017, India
Penguin Group (NZ), Cnr. Airborne and Rosedale Roads, Albany, Auckland 1310, New Zealand
(a division of Pearson New Zealand Ltd.)
Penguin Books (South Africa) (Pty.) Ltd., 24 Sturdee Avenue, Rosebank, Johannesburg 2196,
South Africa

Penguin Books Ltd., Registered Offices: 80 Strand, London WC2R 0RL, England

This is a work of fiction. Names, characters, places, and incidents either are the product of the author's imagination or are used fictitiously, and any resemblance to actual persons, living or dead, business establishments, events, or locales is entirely coincidental.

MY HEART STOOD STILL

A Berkley Book / published by arrangement with the author

PRINTING HISTORY
Berkley edition / October 2001

Copyright © 2001 by Lynn Curland.
Cover art by Theresa Falsalino.
Cover design by George Long.

ISBN: 0-425-20869-9

BERKLEY®
Berkley Books are published by The Berkley Publishing Group,
a division of Penguin Group (USA) Inc.,
375 Hudson Street, New York, New York 10014.
BERKLEY is a registered trademark of Penguin Group (USA) Inc.
The "B" design is a trademark belonging to Penguin Group (USA) Inc.

PRINTED IN THE UNITED STATES OF AMERICA

15 14 13 12 11 10 9 8 7

To Ashley and Molly,
who actually use the word wench *in everyday conversation,*
for their friendship and laughter.

The more complicated my life becomes, the more I realize just how many people contribute to making my dreams a reality. First and foremost, thanks go to Ashley and Molly, who organized my business and entertained my little one so I could finish this book. Innumerable thanks to Lynn, with whom I've had many vital conversations about Studs in Pain. Thanks also to: my Scottish cousin-in-law, Claire, who gave me obscure and fascinating historical tidbits, and her brother, David, who rated British vulgarities for me without so much as a flinch; my English cousin-in-law, Julie, who graciously introduced me to a vast array of idioms and slang; and to Harry L., a veritable font of information, humorous anecdotes, and unforgettable rhymes. Heartfelt thanks also to my publisher, Leslie Gelbman, for her unflagging support.

And a simple thank-you is completely inadequate for my editor, Gail Fortune, who is not only a fabulous editor but a truly lovely person as well. She lets me follow my heart.

And, as always, Matt and Elizabeth, who very patiently made the time for me to write. I love you both.

Prologue

THE BORDER
FALL 1382

They had betrayed her with a promise of the sea.

Go with the English-man, and he will show you the strand, her half-brother had said. *Father has traded you to make an ally, but you'll have a keep on the shore as your recompense,* her half-sister had said.

Trust us, they had said.

Liars both.

The woman stood in a cold guard's chamber and stared out the small slit of a window before her. The only thing she could see was darkness, but perhaps that was a boon. It obscured the bleak, endless stretches of land that surrounded the keep in which she found herself captive—land seemingly so far removed from the sea she wondered if the villagers even knew that such a thing existed. 'Twas almost a certainty she would never see the like now.

She was tempted to weep, but she knew it would serve her nothing, so she forbore. After all, she was a MacLeod, and MacLeods did not weep with fear.

Despite how desperately she wanted to do so.

That she found herself in straits terrible enough to warrant tears was difficult to believe. Was it possible that just a fortnight ago the English-man had come to her home? She had stirred herself only long enough to determine that he held no interest for her, then thoroughly ignored him. 'Twas odd to see an English-man so far north, true, but her father often had men from many foreign places at their keep. She'd had much to occupy her and had paid little heed to one more unfamiliar fool loitering at the supper table.

A pity she hadn't, for the next thing she'd known, she had been given to the English-man. That her father would think so little of her that he would send her off with a stranger didn't surprise her. That a stranger would take her surprised her very much indeed. What value she had to him, she couldn't imagine.

Perhaps she should have refused to go. She would have, had she supposed she had had any choice. But she'd been but one lone woman in a press of half-siblings who hated her, with a father who had forgotten she existed until that moment when he'd needed her. The whole lot had no doubt been rejoicing that they would soon be well rid of her. Defying them all had been unthinkable.

Besides, she had contented herself with their promises of a keep by the sea.

More the fool was she for having believed them.

Of course, it wasn't as if she'd continued on the journey willingly, once she'd learned the true character of her buyer. Her struggles had earned her naught but heavy blows that had set her ears to ringing. The farther south they had traveled, the less often she had tried to escape. By now, she supposed she had traveled so far south that she stood on English soil—a place she had never thought to find herself.

She had certainly wished for a different life than the one she suddenly faced. Since her mother's death, she had dreamed of a man who would come to take her away. Aye, he would have been a braw lad with a mighty sword. He would have arrived at her keep and demanded that she be given to him. Where words might have failed, his sword would have spoken meaningfully. Her miserable life at her father's keep would have been over and a new life begun with a man who loved her.

Such, she supposed, was the stuff of dreams only. She had been carried from her keep, true, but only to face a fate she suspected was far worse than her life at her sire's keep ever had been. There would be no rescue now by a man who would love her. She knew with dread certainty that she would meet her fate where she stood, and she would meet it alone. The only choice left her was to do so with courage.

The door opened behind her, and she closed her eyes

briefly. Then she drew herself up, put on her fiercest expression, and turned to look at her captor.

The man stood just inside the door with a torch in his hand. He set it in the sconce, shut the door behind him, then bolted it. He put his hand on the hilt of his sword.

Ah, so that was how it would be. Whatever the man wanted from her, he intended to have his answers one way or another, so it seemed. But there was one thing she would not endure. She lifted her chin.

"I'll not bear rapine."

He wrinkled his nose. "Think you I would bed a wench of Scots breeding?"

"What do you want, then?" she asked curtly. Perhaps if she spoke strongly, he would find her not worth the trouble of harming. It had worked countless times with her half-brothers. This fool could be no more intelligent than they.

"I'll have the secret of your keep," the man said.

"The what?" she asked blankly.

He looked at her coldly. His was not a handsome face, and the determination there did not improve the visage. "You know of what I speak. Your brother himself boasted of it. He spewed out bits and pieces of the tale as we sat in an inn near Edinburgh. He said there was a magical secret in the MacLeod keep that would bring a man riches beyond belief and that you, best of all, knew that secret."

Ah, so that was why the English-man had taken her so readily. Damn Angus, the blabbering fool who could scarce hold a thought in his head, much less any wits with his ale. She shook her head in disbelief. A pity her father couldn't have chosen someone else to forge his alliances. For some reason, and one beyond her comprehension, her father seemed to find his son trustworthy, for he sent him on all manner of journeys to far-flung places to woo and befriend powerful men who might become allies. It shouldn't have surprised her that the selling of her soul had much to do with one of Angus's foolish acts.

She looked at the man whose name she hadn't bothered to pay heed to when she'd heard it. She could scarce believe he'd gone to such lengths to uncover the truth of Angus's tales. Then again, with the state of his keep, perhaps he had need of the gold.

But to give him what he asked?

Never.

"Your journey was wasted," she said flatly. "I have nothing to tell you."

"You lie!"

The sudden violence in his voice made her jump. Fear stole over her in spite of her fine vow to remain calm.

"My brother is the liar," she managed.

"But he said you knew—"

"He is a boastful, foolish boy who should have remained at home and passed his time mucking out the stables," she said. "My father is the greater fool for having let him leave the keep."

The man cursed fluently and at great length. Then he looked at her. "You're of no use to me then."

A desperate hope bloomed suddenly in her breast. "Then you'll release me?"

"And have you return to your sire and snivel out your sorry tale?" He shook his head. "I think not. I was the fool for thinking your sire would have entrusted you with knowledge of any value." He laughed shortly. "He didn't even give you a name. What does he call you? Gel?"

She pursed her lips. 'Twas true her father could never remember her name. Being that she was his eldest girl-child and the only girl sired on his first wife, *girl* was what he called her. But her mother had given her a name, one that her father was too feeble to wrap his tongue around. Her mother had never used it save for her ears alone. She supposed now that no one remembered what it was. Certainly her half-brothers didn't. Nothing they called her was worth repeating.

Nay, her true name she would keep as hers alone, until she met a man worthy to share it with. And that man would not be the one standing before her.

Her other secret was indeed the secret of her keep, but neither would she give that. Not upon pain of death, for so she had sworn herself. Her grandfather had entrusted it to her, and she would not betray that trust.

Though she had to admit that giving her grandsire her word when they were together on the side of a mountain was one thing; keeping that word when she alone was looking at death was another.

"If you let me go," she said, trying mightily to keep the quaver from her voice, "I will not return home." There was no sense in not trying to free herself. She hadn't given her word not to do that.

"The promise of a Scot means nothing."

"But—"

"Nothing," he interrupted shortly.

"My brothers will come to see how I fare," she warned, though she knew in her heart that wasn't true.

The man grunted. "They seemed rather happy to see the last of you. I doubt anyone will come after you." He folded his arms over his chest. "This choice I will at least offer you. Will you starve, or will you be put to the sword?"

Her heart felt as if it might shake the very walls surrounding her with the force of its pounding. A slow death or a less slow one. Where was the choice in that? She looked at the man facing her and could scarce believe she found herself in his clutches.

"You," she said, "are an honorless whoreson."

"Perhaps. But at least I am giving you a say in your end."

"And I am to be grateful for it?"

" 'Tis more than your sire offered you."

There was truth in that. She took a deep breath, then attempted a swallow, which she found to be a futile exercise. She'd seen men starved to death in her father's pit, and it wasn't pleasant. Perhaps there would be pain with the other, but it would be over much sooner. And it seemed a braver way to die, if one had to die.

But, by the very saints of heaven, she didn't want to die. She wanted to live. She wanted with every bit of her soul to continue drawing breath long enough to have her heart's desire.

She wanted to see the sea.

And she wanted the man of her dreaming to look at it with.

The man facing her drew his sword. Perhaps he thought

she wasn't able to choose. Perhaps he thought he offered her the more merciful death. She suddenly found her thoughts less on what she would never have and more on not shaming herself by falling to her knees and weeping. She was, after all, a MacLeod, and a MacLeod always died well if he could.

So she lifted her chin, stared her murderer full in the face, and let his sword do its foul work unhindered.

And then Iolanthe MacLeod knew no more.

Chapter 1

Thomas MacLeod McKinnon was a man with a problem.

Not that problems bothered him usually. He generally viewed them as challenges to be solved, heights to be summitted, obstacles to be climbed over and outdone. That was before. This was now, and his current problem was the sight before him.

There were—and he couldn't really call them anything else—mouse ears poking up from behind his rhododendron.

He blinked, drew his hand over his eyes for good measure, then looked again.

Now the ears were gone.

He shifted his last sack of American junk food to his other arm, then crossed his porch to look more closely at the bush in question. He bent down and studied it, trying to judge what the angle of his vision had been a moment before and how such an angle might set a particular configuration of leaves into an earlike pattern. He pitted all his skills of observation and his considerable stores of logic and ingenuity against the problem. After several minutes of effort, he came to a simple conclusion:

He was losing his mind.

"Okay," he said aloud. "There are plenty of reasons for this."

The rhododendron didn't offer any opinions on what those reasons might be.

It would have been something he could have dismissed rather easily if it had been the only sighting. Unfortunately, he'd just about run off the road on his way home from the store thanks to the same delusion. He'd been innocently driving along when he'd glanced in his rearview mirror and seen those same black orbs attached to a beanie hat floating quietly in midair in his backseat.

All right, so he was driving an old Wagoneer that hadn't been washed all that often. It hauled stuff for him, and that's all he cared about. It was possible, he supposed, that some dust particles left over from his last trip to the dump had coagulated into a beanie-and-mouse-ear configuration. It was possible that the sun had reflected off something else and cast a shadow where you wouldn't have thought one should be.

It was also possible that his first conclusion was right and his mind was really starting to go.

He turned away and let himself into his house before he did anything else stupid, like discuss his hallucinations further with a plant. He dropped his keys on the entry hall table and walked back to his kitchen. Could an ultra-unhealthy meal of eggs, spicy sausage, and extremely processed cheese spread cure delusionary states? He wasn't sure, but he was willing to try.

He emptied his groceries onto the counter, pulled out a frying pan, and dumped his sausage into it. He turned the burner up to high and listened with satisfaction to the sound of saturated fat sizzling happily. This was the life for him. Uncomplicated. Unfettered. Uncluttered by visions of things that belonged in theme park gift shops.

Thomas tilted the pan to roll the sausages to one side, then cracked a handful of eggs into the freed-up space. With what the immediate future held in store for him, who knew when he might get a decent meal again?

He turned the heat down, then began to walk around the kitchen, looking out the windows at the sea rolling ceaselessly against the shore and enjoying the smell of a late breakfast filling his kitchen. The more he prowled through the kitchen, though, the more unsettled he began to feel. He supposed it had a great deal to do with the fact that he was standing in a house he'd built with his own two hands, yet he planned to leave it behind and spend a year in a strange, foreign land.

He shoved aside the temptation to speculate further on the condition of his mental state.

The feeling of nostalgia, however, was a very unfamiliar one. He'd never been prone to it before. He'd always done what he needed to do, then moved on without a backward glance.

His education was proof enough of that. He'd gotten his degree in history at twenty, decided it wasn't for him, then moved on to law school. Three years and a degree later, he'd dumped that idea as well. He hadn't wanted to teach either history or law. He hadn't been able to stomach the thought of spending his days litigating either. He'd walked away from both degrees without remorse.

He'd turned to the stock market with hopes of making enough money to do whatever he wanted to without worrying about funds. In two very hectic years, he'd parlayed a fifty-thousand-dollar loan from his disgustingly wealthy grandmother into five million. He'd paid her back with interest and by a month of being her packhorse through France, then he'd taken the rest, rounded up a number of other serious investors, and started his own brokerage firm. Nine years later, he'd sold that firm and added the price of that sale to his already staggering list of assets.

He'd moved on to create an elite securities management firm, but it was at that point that he'd decided he'd had enough. He still owned the company, but he'd given over the day-to-day running of it to a college buddy. After all, it was just money. He'd made buckets of it, and what did he have to show for it?

Nothing.

Well, except his house. Looking back on it now, he wondered how he'd managed to build a house in Maine, yet run a multimillion-dollar business in Manhattan at the same time. He'd spent every weekend, holiday, and vacation day for three years commuting north to work on his house, that's how. Standing there now, just the thought of it made him want to go take a nap.

If he'd been a nap-taking kind of guy, which he most definitely was not.

Of course, his life hadn't been all business—not by a long shot. Even early on, he'd always surrounded himself with trustworthy partners who had left him free to pursue his true passion, the one that made his father roll his eyes and his mother wring her hands.

Mountains.

Short ones, steep ones, tall ones, ice-covered ones; he didn't care. As long as he could climb them, he was happy. And when he wasn't climbing, he was either training to climb or working like a fiend to make enough money so he'd have time to climb.

All of which left him wondering why in the world he was putting his entire life—his house and his mountains—on hold to chase after something that seemed less like an obsession and more like Fate.

He finished his prowl by winding up where he started. He reached over and jiggled the pan, then turned to look at his refrigerator. It was fairly uncluttered as far as fridge fronts went, but there, in unmistakable clarity, were the two things that had utterly changed his life.

One was a picture of a castle. His sister had taken the photograph last Christmas, well after he'd bought the place, sight unseen. He'd noticed the auction in the *New York Times* a couple of years before that. Apparently, some titled Brit had been dumping some of his assets, and the castle had come up on the block. Without fully realizing why he was doing it, he'd forked out the money, then promptly put it out of his mind because something else had captured his attention.

He looked at the other photograph and sighed. Mt. Everest stood there in all its stark beauty, with the trademark plume of white cloud adorning its summit. He supposed pitting himself against it had been inevitable. He'd been awash in a particularly satisfying rush of making a fortune when a buddy had dropped a picture of a mountain on his desk and dared him to climb it.

Everest.

Why not?

Well, there had been plenty of reasons why not, but he'd

ignored them. He'd packed up his office, packed up his place in the city, closed up his house in Maine, and moved to Utah. He'd hired a trainer and used both the desert and the mountains to physically make himself into a kind of climbing animal he'd never been before, even with the impossible heights and sheer rock faces he'd managed in his past.

But it hadn't come without cost. He'd missed his sister's wedding in January because he'd gone the extra mile (well, extra three hundred to be exact) and hiked in to Everest base camp instead of flying in like the rest of his team. He'd been determined to make the summit and was willing to do whatever it took to get there. He was not a man accustomed to losing.

He stared hard at the picture on his fridge. He had no trouble locating the precise point at which he'd begun to wonder if the altitude had fried his brain. It had to have been the lack of oxygen. One didn't hear voices at 27,000 feet, did one?

Thomas, there's more to life than climbing. Turn around and go home.

He shook his head at the memory. Five hundred feet from the summit, five hundred feet from conquering the most impossible challenge of his life, and he'd begun to hear voices. It had probably been his late grandmother haunting him. She had never minded a good hike now and then, but she never would have approved of him climbing to the top of the world.

Of course, he'd ignored the voice and gone on to make the summit, just as he'd planned. Anything else would have been unthinkable. But the rush he'd expected to feel, the feeling of triumph, the bone-deep satisfaction he'd anticipated had been missing.

There was more to life than climbing?

He scowled as he turned back to the stove. What the hell was that supposed to mean? That conquering challenges wasn't everything? That there was more to life than achieving goals? That making a fortune, climbing peaks, being the best wasn't all there was?

He couldn't deny that something along those lines had begun to occur to him as he built his house. When he'd been working on the kitchen, he'd imagined it serving a wife and children, being filled to the brim with family on holidays and birthdays, full of laughter and conversation. When he'd worked on the bedrooms, he'd taken special care to see they were strong and sound, so they would safely shelter children in the future. The master bedroom had been made with a woman's comfort in mind, as a retreat from the rest of the house. The house was full of nooks and crannies just perfect for children to use in playing their games of hide-and-seek. Thomas had three sisters, and he had very fond memories of doing the like with them.

All of which had very little to do with making millions of dollars or climbing mountains that were capable of killing even the most skilled.

And it was those kinds of thoughts that had led him to continued speculation during the ensuing months about the adverse effects of altitude on his common sense.

The phone rang, and he jumped in spite of himself. Maybe he wasn't sleeping enough. Yeah, that was it. He needed more sleep. He'd get some, just as soon as he got off the phone with whoever was calling to make his last day at home hell. It was probably his dad, trying to talk him out of his current obsession, which in light of his usual obsessions, seemed fairly tame.

His father hadn't done much more than roll his eyes when Thomas had bought the castle. The grumbling had begun when Thomas had sent his sister to investigate the site, and she'd wound up marrying a Brit. The true roaring had ensued when John McKinnon had learned that Thomas, too, intended to cross the Atlantic. Not even assuring his dad it was just a year-long do-it-yourself project had soothed him. His father was convinced he had lost it.

Thomas wasn't so sure his dad was wrong.

The phone continued to ring. Thomas turned off the fire under his meal, then grabbed the phone.

"What?" he demanded.

"Well," a sultry feminine voice drawled, "isn't that a pleasant greeting."

Ah, Tiffany Amber Davidson, the beginning of his love life's downfall. Not that it had been much of a love life to begin with, but she'd certainly decimated what there'd been of it.

Damn, this was all he needed. When compared to what he was certain would be a very unpleasant few minutes with this woman, listening to his dad gripe at him sounded like a vacation. If he'd only known a year ago where a simple smile in Tiffany's very expensive direction would have led him, he would have kept frowning.

"Tiffany," he said, "I told you—"

Her sigh was a thing of beauty. Thomas found himself almost in awe of the subtle shades and nuances of disappointment, despair, and guilt-inducing reproach that layered a simple exhalation of breath. A lesser man would have been moved.

"Thomas, can't we let bygones be bygones?"

"Sure," he said easily. "It's gone. Let's leave it there."

"No," she said, sounding as if it was an enormous effort to be patient. "I mean, let's start again."

"Where? When?" he asked politely. "Two months ago? On that particular afternoon in June? Should it be before or after I walked in on you displaying your assets to my former friend on his desk during his lunch hour?"

"You weren't supposed to be back from your stupid trip to that stupid mountain until July!"

He had to admire her ability to completely ignore the bigger issue. "I suppose I should apologize for that," he said dryly.

"I'll forgive you," she said magnanimously. "Now, should I catch a flight up tomorrow?"

"I won't be home."

He could feel her eyes narrowing over the phone.

"You won't?"

"I won't."

"Some other stupid quest?" she asked acidly.

"Something like that." He wasn't about to tell her where he was going. The last thing he needed was Tiffany haunting him in England while he was trying to remodel.

"When are you coming back?"

"Next year, probably."

"What?" she screeched. "Thomas, you *can't* go anywhere.

I *love* you. No one will ever love you like I do."

Heaven help him.

"Good-bye, Tiffany."

"I'll do anything!" she said, sounding decidedly frantic all of a sudden.

"Good-bye, Tiffany."

"But my ring!"

Thomas smiled grimly as he clicked off the phone. Her name was appropriate, as all she had ever seemed to be interested in had been trips to that particular jeweler. It had cost him a bundle. That might have left him permanently grinding his teeth had Tiffany not done him the favor of taking his ring off along with her clothes to accommodate his former friend Robby Saunders. Thomas had picked up the ring, nodded politely to the two, then taken a cab to Tiffany's, where he'd sold the ring back at a substantial loss. He didn't care. The ring and Tiffany were out of his life.

As were a very long string of women who just weren't right for him. Thomas didn't consider himself a failure, but when it came to women, he suspected he needed to start.

Ten minutes and a cube of butter deposited on all food surfaces later, he was walking into his den with a roll of paper towels tucked under his arm, a pop in his other hand, and nothing more complicated on his mind than watching some preseason football. He frowned at his couch, covered as it was with last-minute gear to stuff in his suitcase, then settled for an uncomfortable straight-backed chair that Tiffany had insisted he buy. He sat down gingerly, balanced his plate on one knee, the can of pop in his lap, then reached for the remote. He had almost made thumb contact with the On button when he heard something behind him. Well, perhaps *heard* wasn't the right term for it. He *felt* something behind him. Damning every Scottish ancestor he could think of for passing on such unpleasant flashes of intuition in the gene pool, he turned his head as slowly as he could and looked behind him.

And then all hell broke loose.

Out of thin air, a pair of mouse ears materialized, sitting prominently upon the head of a flame-haired, ruddy-complected Scot in full battle dress.

And then the phone not six inches from his left leg started to ring.

Thomas jumped, apparently hard enough that the back right leg of the chair gave way. He wondered absently as he was falling if Tiffany had been at the damned thing with a nail file for just such an occasion as this. He landed flat on his back with egg literally on his face, and pop sloshing all over his jeans and a very expensive Aubusson rug. He rolled to his feet, then whipped around to gape at the apparition behind him.

Which was, he found as he managed to remove grease and fried egg from his eyes, no longer there.

And still the phone continued to ring. Great, more distress from his former fiancée. Couldn't she just leave him alone? Thomas dragged his sleeve across his face and grabbed the receiver.

"What?" he snapped.

"What? It's your father calling, that's what."

"Oh, sorry, Dad," Thomas said. "I'm a little indisposed at the moment."

Thomas could feel his father's frown traveling through the airwaves as if it possessed a life of its own. "I don't approve of these premarital relations going on—"

"I'm not in the middle of sleeping with Tiffany, Dad," Thomas said in exasperation. "I just fell out of that damned chair she made me buy, and now I'm wearing what was supposed to be my last decent meal!"

His father grunted. "Then you'd best whip up something else. I'm the first one to tell you that that inn of your sister's will ruin your appetite."

"Megan said the place was wonderful."

"Your sister's opinion in these matters is not to be trusted."

Thomas pondered just what that might mean for his immediate future. Given that he'd based his plans for that future on Megan's judgment, that could spell serious trouble for him. At the time, she'd seemed like the logical choice to do his castle reconnaissance. She'd been between jobs the year before—which unfortunately for her always seemed to be the case—and, with time on her hands, had been happy to do his investigating for him. The results of her journey had been the acquisition by some means he still wasn't clear on of a reportedly lovely little inn down the way from his castle. She'd taken a couple of pictures of both his castle and the Boar's Head Inn, then up and married some big-shot CEO who'd been vacationing at the inn with her.

Thomas's father, having stayed at the inn for the wedding, had been less than impressed by the little hotel, but would say no more than the place gave him the willies. Thomas's mother had told him that he would really find it interesting, and she'd said it with a wicked twinkle in her eye that left him wondering if he might have been better off to accept his father's conclusion. The inn could be draped with cobwebs, lack basic necessities like running water and toilets, but if Megan had heard rumors of a love story having happened there, she would have called it fabulous. All of which led him to wonder how reliable her opinion of his castle was.

Needs a little work could mean so many things.

". . . Your mother thinks you'll enjoy it," his father was saying with a grumble. "I think she's wrong."

"Primitive?" Thomas asked, not for the first time.

"That isn't the half of it," his father said, also not for the first time.

"Come on, Dad. If there's something I should know, don't you think you should tell me now?"

His father was silent.

"That bad?" Thomas asked finally.

"You wouldn't believe me if I told you, so there's no point in discussing it. Just don't be surprised by anything that goes bump in the night."

Thomas laughed uneasily. Immediately the memory of a Scot in his living room came to mind. He looked over his shoulder, sincerely hoping he wouldn't see anything there. "Ghosts?" he asked absently.

"All I can say is that I know what you'll find at the inn. Heaven only knows what you'll find up at that pile of stones you threw your money away on."

"I doubt I'll be seeing anything unusual." *Other than mouse ears stalking me,* Thomas added silently, turning his back on the rest of the room.

"Don't say I didn't warn you. And another thing: Don't

plan on staying over there permanently. We fought a perfectly good war two hundred years ago so I didn't have to cross the Atlantic to see my grandchildren."

"I'm not moving there. I'm just taking a little time off for a fix-up project."

"There are plenty of ramshackle ruins over here on American soil."

"I know," Thomas said with a sigh. "It's just—"

"It's just that damned MacLeod blood you get from your mother," his father groused. "She gets these kind of harebrained schemes as well."

"Thanks, Dad," Thomas said dryly. "I'll think of you fondly while I'm remodeling."

His father made a few gruff noises, then cleared his throat. "Well, I just called to say good-bye. And, well"—more throat clearing ensued—"call me if you need help."

"I will."

"Your mother's already bought tickets for Christmas. She's planning some kind of damned Dickens celebration."

"Dickens celebration?" Thomas asked suspiciously. This didn't sound good.

His father grunted. "I'll probably have to wear some damned costume."

Thomas had very vivid memories of his sisters coercing him into all manner of costumes in his youth. "Put your foot down, Dad," he said with feeling. "Save yourself if you can."

"I intend to. See you soon."

His father disconnected. Dickens would mean cravats, and Thomas was going to avoid any kind of neckwear at all costs. Maybe he could come in Scottish dress and avoid the whole tie issue. Either that or maybe he could find himself called away for a last-minute bit of skiing in the Alps and be regrettably unable to dress up for the holidays. On the whole, that might be the safest course of action.

He put down the phone and looked at the ruins of his final meal spread out in glorious disarray on his floor. The sausages could be washed off and nuked, but the eggs were past redemption. He looked at the carpet and wondered what it might look like in a year if he didn't do a good job of cleaning it now. Then again, Mrs. Murtaugh would be coming in to clean in a day or two. Maybe he could scrape a bit, then leave the rest for her. He'd hired her to come in once a week and air out the house, anyway. He'd give her a bonus for this last little bit of dirty work and call it good.

He rescued what could be eaten, then headed toward the kitchen. He cooked up more eggs, then stood at the counter and ate them. The kitchen floor was far easier to clean up than the carpet in the den, and who knew what else he might see that afternoon?

Not that he was planning on anything else. He'd seen enough already.

Once he was finished, he found himself prowling around his kitchen again. He tried to avoid the pictures on the fridge, but time and time again he found himself standing in front of them. Everest he could put behind him. He'd conquered it, no matter how unsatisfying it had been.

The castle was another matter entirely. Just looking at it sent chills down his spine. The minute he'd touched the envelope his sister had sent him, the chills had begun. He remembered vividly sliding the photographs out and feeling himself go still.

He had, after all, dreamed of the castle.

With perfect clarity.

A year before he'd ever seen the piece in the *Times*.

He stood there, frozen again, and wondered if he truly was losing his mind. Was it stress? Poor diet? Too much time on his hands? Permanent brain damage from his trip to Everest?

He didn't believe in ghosts. He didn't much believe in a sixth sense, though in all honesty, he had to admit to possessing more of it than was good for him. He didn't want to believe in a Fate that sent a poor hapless human careening inexorably toward a destiny he never imagined. He didn't want to think that something chaotic was tinkering with his life plans.

So why did he feel as if the roller coaster ride had just left the gate, and there was no getting off now?

He sighed. Much as he liked to find some kind of order in the universe, perhaps there was little to be found of rational thinking in his current actions. The best he could do was to keep things as simple as possible and duck—to escape any stray arrows Fate might be winging his way, of course.

There was, actually, a very logical reason for his compulsion to get to northern England. Though his ancestors had been Scottish, it was conceivable that they could have scattered themselves all over Britain at some point. The castle had seemed like the perfect place to really start tracing the branches of his family tree. Restoring a castle might bring all sorts of people out to see what he was doing, and who knew whom he might meet because of it? He didn't like to delve too deeply into why he felt such sudden compulsion to dig around for his roots. He suspected it was perhaps the same reason he'd built his house: so he'd have something to leave behind him, something that showed evidence of his passing.

He shook aside his thoughts; they didn't serve him. Fresh air, a little remodeling, and possibly finding a few cousins he didn't know about was what he needed. So it wasn't glamorous. He'd had enough of glamour. He'd also had enough of pushing himself past the limits of his physical endurance, swimming with the sharks in Manhattan's business pools, and negotiating the minefield of a social life where the women were more concerned about the size and quantity of his assets than they were about him. Fixing up a castle. What could be more pleasant for a fall project?

Just the same, he reached out, took the castle picture, and turned it so it faced the fridge. No sense in rattling his nerves unnecessarily.

He opened the French doors off his kitchen and walked out onto his deck. He stared out over the ocean and felt the endless ebb and flow of the waves begin to ease the tension from him. Maybe he was crazy to leave his house. The castle was completely landlocked. He felt sorry for the people who'd lived in it over the years. Although he'd grown up in the Midwest, he'd always loved vacations on the beach. When the chance to buy land on the coast of Maine had come his way, he'd leaped at it without hesitation. As sappy as it might have sounded, the home behind him had become the home of his heart.

He grasped the railing and let out his breath slowly. He would stay in England for a year and get whatever was in his system out of it. Then he would come home and make a conscious effort to date the right kind of women. Hearth and home were sounding better all the time. But first the castle.

He hesitated. If he was seeing mouse ears in his den, what would he see in an eight-hundred-year-old pile of stones?

He went inside to look for a sponge to clean up his carpet before he could give that any more thought.

Chapter 2

THE BOAR'S HEAD INN, ENGLAND

Ambrose MacLeod stood at the end of the drive and looked up at the inn nestled so cozily against a small hill. The house had been built during the Tudor era and boasted the original leaded glass windows and timbered beams. Ancient vines of wisteria and rose clung to the sides of the house with admirable tenacity. The shadows of twilight lay softly upon the grand variety of late-summer flowers that covered every available bit of earth in the gardens, and a soft rain blanketed it all. Ambrose closed his eyes and sniffed deeply. He wished, with a brief flash of regret, that he actually could have enjoyed the fragrance.

The problem being, of course, his no-longer-mortal nose. He was a ghost, after all.

Ah, but with that ghostly status had come many other advantages, and he wasn't a man to discount whatever blessings came his way. After all, he'd led a rich life. One didn't count among his accomplishments being the laird of a powerful clan, a statesman of the most diplomatic proportions, and a wily sixteenth-century lad as well without having lived hard and well.

And now such a long afterlife to look forward to, with all the matches there were to be made! It was almost enough to induce him to indulge in a little capering about, but there was no telling who might see that. He did, after all, have his dignity to maintain.

So he continued on his way up the path and ducked in out of the rain by walking through the front door. The receiving desk was currently empty, but that wasn't unexpected. The handful of boarders who had arrived that morning were all settled, and no one else was expected that evening. With one more to come on the morrow, no doubt the staff was recovering with a good rest.

Ambrose strode to the desk and looked it over critically. There was naught out of place, and, look as he might, he could think of no fault possessed by the woman who manned the post. Even so, he would have preferred to have had the inn run only by family. It was, after all, owned by his American granddaughter (several generations removed, of course), Megan. Though she came north as often as possible, her husband's business interests were in London, and 'twas there that her duty lay. That left the inn in the care of hired help, but there was nothing to be done about it. Ambrose was never shy about instructing the staff, which often left them looking for new workers, but that, he supposed, was simply what Megan would have called the cost of doing business.

Ambrose walked through the door into the dining room only to come face-to-face with several of the inn's occupants telling tall tales. He paused and listened with great interest.

"Haunted," a young woman said in hushed tones. She shivered. "That castle up the way is haunted. It was, like, spooky. You know?"

"Dude," her male companion agreed with a vigorous nod. "One minute the flowers in the garden were there, the next— *poof!* Gone. I tell ya, dude, it was spooky!"

"I already said that," the girl said, frowning at her companion.

"I was just agreeing with ya, babe."

Ambrose shuddered at the unabashed slaughter of the Mother Tongue. He looked at the couple's audience, three older mortals whom Ambrose knew belonged to a rather radical preservation society. They wouldn't be using the warm, lilting tones of his beloved Highlands, but at least he might count on them for a few crisp consonants and a bit of proper grammar.

"Anything else?" one of the three asked. He was a thin, rodentlike man whose nose twitched eagerly, as if he scented a particularly tasty treat.

"I was asking the questions, Nigel," a gray-haired, nononsense woman said briskly. She pinned the couple to their seats with a steely gaze. "Did you witness anything else untoward?"

"Duuude," said the male Colonist, "isn't that enough? What kinda special effects do ya want out here?"

"What we saw was enough," the girl agreed with a shiver.

"Note that, Gerard," the gray-haired woman said, elbowing a plump man sitting next to her. "We've definitely a ruin in pristine condition."

"I am endeavoring," the scribe said, dragging his forearm across his perspiring brow, "to note things as quickly as I can, Constance!"

The man named Nigel slapped his hands on the table and stood. "I daresay we need no other evidence," he said enthusiastically. "The castle must be preserved in its natural state. Come, Constance! Come, Gerard! Let us away to plan our strategy!"

Ambrose lifted one eyebrow. So these three were bent on preserving the castle up the way. An interesting idea, but he wondered how the souls loitering in the keep would feel about their home being chosen for such an honor. He watched as the trio rushed from the dining chamber, their petards mightily hoisted. Ah, well, if nothing else, they would provide a chuckle or two for those who would be watching.

He left the Colonists to their tea and uneasy whispers and made his way to the kitchen. A flick of his wrist lit candles and lamps and stoked a hearty fire in the stove. He pulled out a chair, sat, and prepared to pass a pleasant evening pondering his next matchmaking task. He had just returned from a lovely pair of months at his home in the Highlands, but he couldn't deny the pleasure he felt at being back at the inn, ready to turn his considerable energies to the task at hand: a task that he suspected might tax even his substantial stores of cunning.

He had just settled back in his chair with a hefty tankard of ale when the back door blew open. Lamps flickered wildly, and several candles extinguished themselves altogether. Ambrose looked up with a faint bit of annoyance and relit the abused tapers with another flick of his wrist.

"Wet out," the other man said as he stomped the water

from his boots and cast aside his cloak. He slammed the door behind him. "Never should have left France."

Ambrose looked at Fulbert de Piaget and couldn't help briefly agreeing with the last sentiment. But the man was, after all, his own sweet sister's husband, so Ambrose forbore any nasty remarks.

"Lovely holiday?" he asked politely.

"Could have been longer," Fulbert grumbled. "But I heard that the McKinnon lad was set to arrive soon, so I knew I'd best come back and lend some good sense to this venture."

The McKinnon lad in question was Thomas, Megan's brother. Megan herself had found very little favor with Fulbert before she had married his nephew (many times removed, mind you). Unfortunately, not even her marriage to Gideon de Piaget had improved Fulbert's opinion of her much. Even with his own wife having been a Scot, Fulbert never seemed to find much to recommend anyone related to anyone who had ever sported a plaid.

"Should have *never* allowed me nevvy Gideon to have wed with young Megan," Fulbert grumbled.

Ambrose ignored the expected slander and placidly took another drink of his ale.

Fulbert scowled. "I can scarce wait to learn what poor lass you have found to foist your grandson off upon."

" 'Tis a bit of a tale—"

Fulbert reached out and grasped a suddenly materialized mug of ale and downed it in one long pull. "Leave me to me fortifying before you begin—"

The back door burst open a second time, and Ambrose felt his jaw slide down of its own accord.

"Foolishness," Fulbert said, choking on his ale.

Ambrose, for once, had to agree with him. He looked at the newest arrival, who currently struggled to balance all the paraphernalia he was holding and shut the door behind him at the same time.

"What," Fulbert managed in a very strangled voice, "have you done to yourself?"

The third man beamed a rather gap-toothed smile at them and placed his burdens most carefully on the worktable near the door. Ambrose glanced at the pile and saw all manner of souvenirs there, things a body might have acquired in a . . . nay, he couldn't bring himself to think on where they had been acquired.

Then the man turned back to them and held open his arms wide so they could admire his clothing. Gone were Hugh McKinnon's manly plaid and rugged boots. Gone were the well-wrought saffron shirt, the sword buckled around his waist, and the cap tilted with a goodly amount of jauntiness atop his head. In its place were mouse ears, a red shirt, suspenders, blue trews, and, the most appalling of all, a tail.

"California," Hugh said proudly.

"Southern region?" Fulbert asked in horror, his hand to his throat.

"Aye," Hugh said, nodding enthusiastically and causing his ears to bounce wildly about. "Passing pleasant there. No rain. A goodly amount of sunshine."

Apparently the lack of clouds had caused Hugh's brain to catch fire. Ambrose could find no other explanation for his cousin's (by way of several intermarriages) sudden departure from good sense. He'd had his own trip to the Colonies and loitered where no sensible shade ever should have found himself, yet he'd returned home as quickly as he could, hoping none of his proud and illustrious ancestors had been watching what he'd been forced to do.

For he, too, had made that harrowing journey to the western coast, and he, too, had ventured inside that theme park's gated enclosure.

But he certainly hadn't gone so far as to *wear* any of the cartoon creatures he'd found there.

"Hugh," Ambrose said, feeling faint with dismay over what he was seeing, "what have you done?"

Hugh suddenly shifted from foot to foot uneasily, causing his tail to sway in a most unsettling manner. "Nothing I shouldn't have," he said.

"I meant your clothing . . ."

"Ah," Hugh said, looking vastly relieved. "Well, you see, I saw them being worn so nicely there, and I couldn't resist obtaining a set for myself—"

"Hugh," Ambrose said sternly, realizing they had been speaking about far different things, "what have you been doing? Other than dressing yourself as a mouse? I sense something else is afoot."

Hugh ducked his head, looking very guilty. "He is my grandson, after all," he muttered.

"Hugh . . ."

"Several times removed, of course."

"Hugh!" Ambrose exclaimed.

"And a fine, braw lad he is. Strong, clever—"

"You were to leave him be!"

"I didn't say anything to him," Hugh said defensively.

"Did he see you?" Ambrose demanded.

Hugh suddenly seemed to find the footwear he was sporting enormously interesting, for he studied it with great intensity. And remained silent.

"A disaster," Fulbert said grimly. "I could have told you that before we even started."

Ambrose was tempted to agree, but he was, after all, a MacLeod, and MacLeods did not give in so easily. It made no difference what Hugh had done, for Ambrose greatly suspected that young Thomas would chalk whatever he'd seen up to a sour stomach. He would never believe he'd seen anything resembling a ghost.

Which left them in something of a quandary concerning Thomas's future bride, but that was something to be solved later.

Ambrose cleared his throat purposefully. "What's done is done," he said.

Fulbert shook his head with a grumble. "This feels all too familiar for some reason."

"As you both know," Ambrose said, ignoring the dissention in the ranks, "we've a grand work set here before us."

Fulbert took a long pull from his mug and refrained from comment.

"Assuming," Ambrose said, casting a stern glance Hugh's way, "that things haven't been befouled already."

Hugh gulped and looked horrendously guilty. Ambrose could only hope that his cousin hadn't done irreparable damage to the scheme. Then again, if Thomas's own father hadn't been able to convince him to remain in the Colonies,

Ambrose was quite certain no chance sighting of Hugh would do the like.

Ambrose could only hope his cousin had been sporting a kilt and not his current costume.

He put that thought aside and turned his mind back to the task at hand.

"Thomas arrives on the morrow," he continued.

Fulbert yawned. "Just thinkin' on it is wearying."

"Then mayhap ye should think on somethin' else," Hugh growled.

Fulbert paused and glared at Hugh. "What is it you mean by that?"

"'Tis Scots' business," Hugh said, sticking out his chin stubbornly. "Ye'll only set the plans awry."

"I'll not leave it all to you two," Fulbert said stiffly. He stood and cast his mug into the fire. "You'll have need of my good sense at some point. See if you don't."

And with that, he vanished.

Ambrose sighed. He looked at his cousin, the former laird of the clan McKinnon, and waited for his thoughts on the matter. Fulbert would no doubt return at the worst possible moment, but there was nothing to be done about it. They would simply have to press on as best they could.

"Herself up at the keep'll be passing furious," Hugh offered with a shudder. "No matter what we do."

"Very likely."

"Don't like it when she's passing furious."

"Then I suggest," Ambrose said, "that we keep ourselves busy here and let those who venture up to the castle do so at their own risk."

Hugh nodded heartily in agreement, downed the last of his ale, and vanished with all his newly acquired gear.

Ambrose sat back, crossed his feet at the ankles, and contemplated the next pair of days. Of course, he had no intention of remaining behind when there might be a show up the way, especially when Herself caught wind of what was up. *Passing furious* was likely a very mild approximation of the fury that would explode when his kinswoman learned she was going to have a permanent houseguest.

Or landlord, as the case might be.

Well, that would likely sort itself out in time as well. Ambrose finished his own ale and stood up. Rest was likely in his best interest. He would need all his wits about him if he was to be of any use to either Thomas or the lass up the way.

He extinguished the lights and left the kitchen.

Chapter 3

T homas turned the car's ignition off, then very carefully leaned his head against the steering wheel. He should have listened to his sister. He would tell his father that the next time he talked to him. Megan gave good advice. At least when it came to advising those befuddled by jet lag and too much ego.

It had all started with a bumpy commuter flight to Kennedy, followed by an evening flight to London on which he'd chosen to travel coach. He'd come to several conclusions from that alone. A man who was six foot two had never been meant to sit in a seat in which his knees were actually partway into the seat in front of him. There was also something very unwholesome about having strangers sitting on either side of him fall asleep and use him as a pillow. No, the next time he would fly business class. At least that way he'd arrive at his destination without feeling crunched and drooled on.

He'd called Megan once the plane had landed bright and early five hours into another time zone. Megan told him to take the train to Thorpewold. She'd promised that her husband Gideon could find any number of people willing to pick up the car he'd bought in London and drive it north for him. But had he listened? Of course not. He'd taken a taxi to the car park and picked up his keys. He'd gotten into the car, buckled up, then reached for the steering wheel.

Only to discover it was on the other side of the car.

That should have been a sign.

His subsequent drive-on-the-left baptism-by-fire had come in morning rush-hour London traffic. Nine hours and numerous stops for map deciphering later, he'd thought he might have gotten the hang of things. Even despite his jet lag, he was managing to keep on the correct side of the road,

and he'd only had a handful of near misses with curbs and
the side mirrors of parked cars.

And then the sky had suddenly opened up and poured out
a kind of rain he was sure hadn't been seen since the Flood.

He'd ignored the deluge and pressed on. A close encounter
with some sheep and another with a pair of angry bicyclists
had left him seriously doubting his skills.

Thank goodness the most dangerous stretch of road he
would have to negotiate in the near future would be the one
between Megan's inn and his castle—and he suspected the
morning light might reveal the distance to be quite manage-
able on foot. Even if he got soaked to the skin, it would be
better than creaming any of the natives before he could introduce himself.

He peeled himself out of the car, retrieved the luggage
necessary for the next twenty-four hours from the trunk, then
trudged doggedly toward the front door. He let himself inside
the house, grateful to be out of the inclement weather. He
noticed out of the corner of his eye that the place was indeed
as old as Megan had said it was. Well, he'd have a good
look later. At the moment, all he wanted was a hot shower
and a bed. It didn't have to be a comfortable bed. It didn't
even have to be a flat bed. He wasn't even sure he needed
a mattress. He'd slept in enough strange and/or precarious
places over the years that the amenities really didn't matter.
He just needed someplace to crash.

He shut the door with his knee, then turned around to face
the entry hall. His immediate impression was of age and
patterned wallpaper. Then he blinked. There was the registration desk, obviously. A woman of substantial stature and
soldierlike carriage stood at attention. But that wasn't what
was so startling.

To her left, leaning against some kind of sideboard, was
an older gentlemen in full Scottish dress. Plaid, sword, spor-
ran, snowy white shirt with no frills, and an enormous silver
brooch pinning the plaid to his shoulder. The man's face was
rugged, but a twinkle in his eye spoke of good humor.

Thomas gaped at him. The man folded his arms over his
chest and looked back just as boldly. Thomas dropped his

bag, rubbed his eyes, then blinked away the residual fuzziness.

Now the man was gone.

Thomas paused to consider. Jet lag? He didn't think so.

He looked at the woman behind the desk.

"Who was that—" he began, then shut his mouth. Yes, that would certainly make a good impression. *Hi, I'm your guest, and wasn't that a ghost I just saw leaning against one of your antiques?*

Maybe he was just more tired than he thought. Shower. Bed. Or maybe just bed. He could clean up later. Unconsciousness was probably the safest place for him right now.

He grabbed the strap of his bag and stumbled toward the desk. "I have a reservation," he managed.

"Yer name?" the woman asked crisply.

"Thomas," he said. "Thomas McKinnon."

"We've been expecting ye," she said. She thrust a sheet at him and slapped a pen down next to it. "Sign in. I'm Mrs. Pruitt. I'm in charge whilst Lord and Lady Blythwood are in London."

Ah, Lady Blythwood. That was his sister. She'd married Gideon de Piaget, Lord Blythwood. Thomas shook his head wryly. Megan, an honest-to-goodness titled person. She really should write all those people who had fired her over the years and let them know. It would have been very satisfying.

Then Thomas frowned. Something was not right. He looked at Mrs. Pruitt and realized that she was Mrs. Pruitt. When Megan had first come to the inn, the proprietress had been a Mrs. Pruitt, but that Mrs. Pruitt had decamped for some unknown reason, signing the title over to Megan on her way out the door. Had that Mrs. Pruitt returned? Or had another come to take her place? Thomas looked at the woman, wondering if his bafflement was because of the time change or if hugging his knees to his chest across the Atlantic had cut off important blood flow to his brain.

"You're . . ." he trailed off.

"Mrs. Pruitt," she said firmly.

"But," he said, "I thought Mrs. Pruitt had gone."

"My sister," Mrs. Pruitt announced.

He frowned. "Your sister? Don't you mean sister-in-law?"

"I don't," Mrs. Pruitt said.

"But," he said, wondering if arguing with a woman who held her pen like a sword was wise given the torrential downpour outside and the potential for finding himself once again in it, "you have the same last name."

"We married brothers," Mrs. Pruitt said, looking as if her previous estimation of his intelligence had been a sore disappointment to her.

"And your husband . . ."

"Dead, like the other one," she said with pursed lips. "Weak constitutions."

Given the apparently robust constitution of the woman facing him, Thomas could well understand why she found that so objectionable.

"Should have wed me a Highlander," she said, lowering her voice and stealing a glance or two around the hallway. "Now *there* are lads worth the effort."

Thomas found himself with absolutely no desire to investigate further Mrs. Pruitt's matrimonial regrets and preferences, especially since she seemed to be looking around purposefully for someone Thomas was just certain wasn't there.

"Sleep," he slurred. "I'm starting to hallucinate."

"Hmmm," Mrs. Pruitt said, with a disapproving glance. "Well, best hie yourself up the stairs. Don't want any bodies littering me entryway."

Thomas made one final stab at getting an explanation. "But your sister—"

"Deserted her post without a backward glance," Mrs. Pruitt said with a disgusted shake of her head.

"And you don't regret—"

"That she left the place to yer sister Lady Blythwood, and not me? Not at all. I've full command of the area without concerning myself with funding the operation."

Thomas suspected the British Navy would have been proud to call this woman one of its own. He was ready to surrender already, and he was sure he hadn't forced her to pull out her big guns yet.

"Besides," she said, lowering her voice and looking about with another purposeful, if not covert, glance or two, "this leaves me plenty of time for me investigations."

"Investigations?" Was this really something he wanted to know?

"Of the paranormal kind," she whispered. "And believe me, the place is ripe for 'em."

Thomas was certain now that he had crossed some kind of line. Maybe it had to do with lack of sleep. Maybe it had to do with too much motorway stress. Maybe it had to do with the fact that he'd just signed in at a place where the proprietress was running her own Ghostbuster squad, be-kilted Scotsmen were appearing and disappearing near side-boards, and he was beginning to take both very seriously.

No wonder Megan had laughed so hard when he'd told her he was looking forward to a few days of quiet contemplation in the inn before he took stock of the situation up the road.

Mrs. Pruitt shoved a key at him. "Be off with ye," she said briskly. "Up the stairs and down the hallway. Go lie down before ye fall there."

He frowned as he took the key. Was he supposed to find some kind of hidden meaning in her last words? Was he supposed to give up before someone forced him to? Or was the woman really just trying to get him out of her way so her entryway remained tidy?

Maybe it was better not to know.

He made his way to the stairs, then paused and looked back over his shoulder. No bekilted Scotsmen loitering there. No ruddy-complected Scotsmen wearing mouse ears either. Maybe those were good signs.

He dragged himself up the stairs and down the hallway. He checked his room number against the number on the key, let himself in, and found that a bed did indeed await him. He dumped his stuff on the floor and considered a shower. No, sleep was more attractive. He stripped, crawled into bed, and sighed gratefully over something beneath him that didn't move.

As he tried to wind down, he wondered absently if the carpentry tools he'd sent over earlier had made it. He'd also sent his Everest gear. Though he supposed he could have stayed indefinitely in Megan's inn, he'd planned for the pos-

sibility of wanting to camp on his own soil. And he suspected, based on the pictures Megan had taken, that the castle
wasn't all that hospitable. At least not yet. He hoped he was
equal to the task of making it so.

After barely surviving the trip north, he was beginning to
have his doubts about that as well.

He blew out a deep breath and consciously made the effort
to stop thinking. Sleepy thoughts were generally unreason-
able thoughts, and he wasn't served by entertaining them.

But even so, he couldn't resist a last bit of speculation.
What would he find up at the castle? That he owned a castle
at all was remarkable, no matter its condition. But could he
turn it into something useful? Would he find it beyond redemption?

Would he find it empty?

That last thought came at him from out of nowhere, and
it was almost enough to rob him of any notions of sleep. His
father had basically told him Megan's inn was haunted.
Thomas had seen with his own eyes some sort of apparition
in the entry hall.

What did that bode for the castle up the way?

He rolled over, punched his pillow a couple of times, then
settled back in. He closed his eyes determinedly and concentrated on sleep. Either his castle would be just a pile of
stones, or it would be home to all sorts of ghosts. He'd just
have to go up as soon as he'd slept off his jet lag and see
what he found.

Which, he was certain, would be nothing. His sister had a
very active imagination. His mother even more so. They were
toying with him, those two, and had somehow brought his
father in on their little scheme. He snorted as he kicked the
blanket off him. The castle was just a castle, and that was
that. His biggest worry would be keeping his hands warm
while he rebuilt. Maybe his survival gear would come in
handy more than he'd hoped.

With any luck, he'd have some of his keep habitable before really nasty weather descended. That was a worthwhile
goal and one he could easily achieve.

But first, sleep. He sighed a final time, turned his mind

away from plans and schemes, and considered the fact that there wasn't a mountain in the entire United Kingdom higher than five thousand feet.

So what was he doing there?

He certainly didn't have the answer.

He could only hope Fate didn't, either.

Chapter 4

The woman stood on the parapet and looked out over the windswept moor. She stared up at the early-morning sun and wished that it could warm her. The heaviness of her heart weighed upon her so that she felt as if she'd almost become part of the stones beneath her feet, stones that had been standing for centuries. She felt as if she'd been standing atop those stones for centuries.

Which she had been, actually.

She sighed deeply. Normally, she wouldn't have allowed herself to wallow in such misery, but today she was powerless to rise above it. What a miserable existence she led with no fine form to enjoy the sunshine, yet all her wits about her to wish for the same. Who would have known that losing her life so unwillingly would have brought her such grief?

She had long since resigned herself to her condition, of course, but that didn't make things any easier. She had kinsmen about her now, aye, 'twas true, as well as others who had sought refuge at her crumbling keep, but that didn't ease her heart. She couldn't look at mortals without longing for what they had.

If only she'd had more time during her life. If only she'd found what her heart sought before her untimely demise. If only the bloody stones beneath her feet had been near the seashore, instead of deposited in the midst of what was surely the most uninspired landscape along the entire Scottish border!

That would have been misery enough had that been all she was forced to contend with. More was the pity that along with her regrets, she'd found herself bothered for over six hundred years by unwanted ghosties who seemed as determined to haunt her castle with her as she was that they not.

"You'd be miserable without us, my dear."

Iolanthe MacLeod gritted her teeth; should she ever manage it, this one would be the very first to go. She turned her head and scowled at the man standing next to her on the parapet. He currently stuffed some sort of disgusting substance up his nose.

"Snuff," he said, with a sniff.

"Dinnae lose it in yer cuffs," she grumbled. 'Twas indeed a very likely possibility, what with the yards of lace floating gracefully over his wrists.

"My dear girl, must you lapse into that primitive Scottish dialect?" he asked, continuing to poke foul weed up his nose.

" 'Twas guid enough fer me grandsires," she said, "so 'tis guid enough fer me—and a far sight too guid fer ye!"

The man shuddered delicately. "It's just so barbar—eeek!"

Iolanthe watched as the man was hoisted from behind by shirt collar and trouser band, lifted entirely overhead, and, without ceremony, flung over the wall.

"An' keep off tha roof, ya frilly bugger!" the thrower called down into the bailey. He brushed his hands briskly and looked at Iolanthe. "Good morning to you, lady."

Iolanthe smiled benevolently at one of her father's cousins. Duncan MacLeod was a formidable warrior, and she was ever grateful for his aid. He had looked after her as best he could during her lifetime, teaching her how to wield both a knife and a handful of curses in various tongues. After her death, he had come to her and volunteered to be captain of her guard. She hadn't argued with him. How ridiculous her father would have found such a thing—she being a mere woman, of course.

That she was didn't seem to bother Duncan MacLeod any. He seemed happy to guard her peace and defend her honor when the need arose. Perhaps she couldn't rid herself permanently of her other hangers-on; at least Duncan saw to them whenever required.

"Ever you come when I most need you, Duncan," she said pleasantly.

"You're powerful jealous of your broodin' time," Duncan said. "A pity we canna rid ourselves of the bugger once and for all."

"Aye," she said, with a nod.

"I never cared for those Victorian lads," Duncan said with disapproval. "Too much time 'afore the lookin' glass, seeing to their shirtfronts. Ruins a man for anything useful."

Iolanthe nodded and turned back to her contemplation of the moor. Lord Roderick St. Clair of Herefordshire was now off her roof, and she could turn her attentions back to her grim thoughts. She did her best, then realized her cousin was still standing beside her. She turned to him with a frown.

"Is something amiss?"

"Aye," he said slowly. "I've tidings."

"Tidings? Of what sort?"

"There's a group headed up the way."

Iolanthe frowned. "Tourists? Still? Is it not autumn yet in truth?" They had been coming, the gawkers, for what seemed like decades. Though her keep had fallen in and out of fashion, and the accompanying stream of visitors ebbed and flowed accordingly, there had always been a number of mortals about, peering into her nooks and crannies. But the summer was waning, or so the leaves had begun to tell her, and she supposed it was beginning to grow cold out.

"Nay," Duncan said carefully, "they're not tourists."

"What, then?" she asked.

"A small collection of English, with papers and quills for writin'. They've a look about them that bespeaks serious business."

Iolanthe sighed. What, by Saint Michael's sweet soul, could anyone want with Thorpewold? Not only did the keep proper lack the most basic of comforts, it lacked a bloody roof! No one had dared live in the place for what had seemed like centuries.

But papers and quills. That was unwelcome. For all she knew, the fools had come up to purchase the keep. Would that she could have sold it to them and been on her way. She would have gone. Gladly.

Not that it was anything but habit and her own foolish dreams that kept her where she was. Mayhap if she'd been faced with a permanent resident, she might have stirred herself to dwell somewhere else.

"How long has it been, Duncan?" she mused, trying to

distract herself with thoughts of a less troublesome nature. "Since we had houseguests?"

Duncan squinted up into the sky, as if he used the clouds to help him count.

"One . . . two . . ." he began, then shook his head. "Nay, perhaps 'tis three . . ." He began to use his fingers now, so truly it must have been a very long time. "Nay, 'twas some two hundred odd years back. You remember. 'Twas after that bloody awful spell with the English when they outlawed the wearing of the plaid."

Iolanthe nodded. "Aye, you have it aright, Duncan." She thought back to the houseguests in question. It seemed but a moment ago, but apparently it had been decades, no, centuries. She could still remember the lieutenant who had commandeered her keep as if he actually had a right to do so.

"Ruddy arrogant wretch," Duncan said, as if he knew of whom she thought. "Comin' in here and takin' over . . ."

"Ah, but for how long?" she asked, smiling in spite of herself. "Do you not remember, my friend, how we paraded about before him in our best colors? Saints above, how many times was it he came at us with a sword, only to find himself thrusting at nothing?"

"Aye," Duncan agreed with a smile. "Fine sport, indeed."

The lieutenant hadn't stayed but a fortnight, thanks to their efforts. Thereafter, there had been very few mortal souls indeed who arrived with intentions of staying for any length of time. Apparently, rumors of the castle being haunted had been believable enough to keep them at bay.

Aside from mere visitors, there had been the odd exorcist and the occasional ghost hunter come to test his mettle against them. Iolanthe had taken a great deal of pleasure at not providing those sorts with any bones to take away and gnaw on, as it were. Each had left, disappointed.

She'd had peace for longer than she could remember, and likely longer than Duncan's fingers could aid them in counting. She'd known it couldn't last. It never did.

"Well," she said, straining to see along the road, "we must divine what mischief is afoot, Duncan. Let them pass unhindered. After you've given the word to the rest of the garrison, meet me in the hall."

"Aye, I will."

And, with that, he was gone. Iolanthe glanced again over the countryside and allowed herself a final regret that the ruins of her keep did not rest along the seashore. How pleasant a view that might have been over the past six hundred years.

And that was, in truth, the reason she remained where she was. The seashore was meant to be walked along while holding hands with the love of one's heart. Or so her greatgrandmother had told her. Iolanthe had never had cause to disbelieve her. Megan MacLeod had known of what she spoke, being an undisputed authority on all things tender and ardent. Even after all these centuries, Iolanthe still hadn't found the heart to view the strand alone. So she remained at Thorpewold, landlocked and miserable.

She sighed and turned away. She walked down the stairs, stepping across thresholds that had once sported doors, down steps that were worn and grooved with the passing of countless feet. Thorpewold had not always been so poor a keep. It hadn't been much to speak of when she'd arrived and lost her life there, but there had been lads over the next pair of hundred years who had put the place to good use against the English. She'd been happy to aid them in that cause whenever possible.

But keeps had ceased to serve their original purposes, and border keeps even more so. She'd watched her adopted home fall into disrepair and been powerless to stop it.

Had the souls walking up the road come to change all that?

She contemplated what that might mean for her—the annoyance of having mortals underfoot at all hours—and decided that she wasn't for the idea. She'd send them back the way they'd come without hesitation.

Iolanthe entered the great hall and stopped to admire the fine view of sky afforded by the lack of roof. She glanced about her and saw two dozen Highlanders standing against the walls, their swords bare in their hands and their eyes glinting with the light of battle. She wished, as she wished each time she saw the men who were loyal to her at the ready, that she'd somehow managed to escape her fate, had gathered such men about her, and returned to father's keep to give him her thoughts on his matrimonial plans for her. She suspected he might have noticed her long enough to listen to her with these lads at her back.

But there was no time now for regrets. She could see the hapless mortals coming toward the great hall, thanks to the lack of a front door. Now was the time to listen to them spew forth their plans, then convince them that such planning was in vain when the fate of her hall was at stake.

Three was their number; a woman and two men. Iolanthe immediately identified them by their miens. There was the Gray Lady, whose hair greatly resembled a helmet; the Fat Scribe, with all manner of pens and paper tucked under his arms and held in his hands; and another man whom she instantly compared to a rat. She was quite sure she saw his nose begin to twitch.

"Marvelous," said the Rat.

"Perfect," said the Gray Lady, patting her hair affectionately.

The Scribe said nothing, but arranged his things so he could more easily scribble upon his papers.

"Cannot be touched," said the Rat firmly. "Look at the walls, the window openings, the stairs! No, no; it cannot be touched."

"We'll have to stop the sale," said the Gray Lady, elbowing the scribe in the side. "Make a note of that, Gerard."

"Well," said the Scribe, squinting down at his paper, "I daresay the sale has already gone through."

"We'll stop it," the Gray Lady said, raising her fist to the sky.

"Too late for that, I shouldn't wonder," argued the Scribe. "Pesky Yanks."

"When is the Yank in question set to arrive?" asked the Rat, his nose quivering fiercely.

"On the morrow." The Gray Lady shook her head sadly. "All these fine ruins, ruined."

"Restored," said the Rat. "Redone."

"A Do-It-Yourselfer," the Scribe offered. "As if being an American wasn't insult enough."

"What about those rumors of the castle being haunted?"

the Gray Lady asked with a look of cunning on her face. "Would that deter him?"

"The American couple was certainly affected by what they saw," the Rat agreed.

Iolanthe held up her hand to stop any of her men from moving. She could scarce believe what she'd heard, and she knew she should take a moment to digest it all before she took any action.

A Yank?

He'd bought her hall?

And he intended to restore it?

She hardly knew what to think. She stood there and struggled to find her wits. A man in her keep? A man with hammer and nails and the saints only knew what other kind of modern creations, fouling up her unlife and making himself at home in her home?

It was a calamity.

Iolanthe looked around the hall at her men.

"Give these souls something to recount," she said clearly, then let her hand fall.

Two dozen Highlanders made themselves quite visible, bellowing their war cries and charging the little group of three with merciless expressions and upraised weapons.

The Rat fell over in a dead faint.

The other two screeched and fled for the door. There was a great commotion there, and Iolanthe hopped up on the ruins of a table to get a better view. And she couldn't help but smile just a bit.

Roderick was there, plain to the eye, doing his best to keep the two cowards just inside the doorway.

"Better fetch your fellow," he reprimanded. "Shame on you for leaving him."

The Fat Scribe pushed past Roderick and ran screaming down the way. The Gray Lady took a deep breath, then turned back inside the hall. She hoisted the Rat over her shoulder, staggered, yet managed to keep her feet. Roderick gallantly encouraged her as she hastened from the keep. Iolanthe could hear him keeping up a steady stream of chatter as the poor woman struggled down the way.

"Should someone help the auld wench?" one of the clansmen milling about said.

"Dinnae fash yerself, Douglas," another said with a hearty laugh, clapping his fellow on the back companionably. "She heaved him into the grass down the way, didna ye see it?"

"Ach, weel, a brave one, that," Douglas conceded.

Iolanthe let their conversations drift over her as she made her way to the back of the hall. She nodded to the men she passed, smiling to let them know she was pleased with their performance.

But inside, she was trembling.

From fury, not fear.

By the time she reached what was left of the battlements, she was seething. How dare some strange man, who she'd never met and who she knew already that she wouldn't care for in the least, think to overrun her home? Not that she cared overmuch for the place, given the circumstances, but 'twas her home, and she'd paid a dear price for it.

Well, no matter what the Yank thought, he would not be spending any nights in her hall. Her men would see to that and enjoy the doing of the deed.

Aye, there would be no intruders in her home.

She wouldn't allow it.

Chapter 5

Thomas struggled to find the demarcation between dreaming and waking. His dreams had been full of Everest, of snow and wind and desperate weariness. He wondered at times if he would ever escape the shadow of that experience and the way it consumed him. Then again, with the number of ghosts he kept seeing serving as a distraction, maybe he just might.

He forced himself to be fully aware of where he was. He wasn't camped on the side of a mountain; he was in a comfortable bed in his sister's inn. Once he'd convinced himself of that, memories of the day before returned with a rush, though he studiously avoided mentally reliving any scarcely avoided encounters with sheep, pedestrians, and other vehicles he'd had on his journey north.

He looked at his watch, determined that he'd slept until almost ten, then rolled out of bed and stretched, feeling remarkably like his old self. He was mentally alert, physically restored, and ravenous. All very good signs. The past few weeks of packing up his gear, seeing it sent, closing up his house, and getting to England seemed like nothing more than a bad dream.

He shaved, showered, and dressed in record time. With any luck, General Pruitt wouldn't have closed down the mess hall. If so, he'd have to fend for himself. Would foraging in the fridge result in a court-martial? He wondered if she preferred an old-fashioned hanging or the firing squad. He could easily see her executing either.

There was no one at the registration desk as he trotted by, so he started opening doors. He found the library, a sitting room, an office of some kind, a gathering room of another kind, and then finally the dining room. It was occupied, which came as a relief. At least he hadn't come too late for some kind of meal. He smiled politely at the group there, then looked for an empty seat at the long table.

And then he noticed the reception he was getting. He paused, halfway to sitting down.

"I'm sorry," he said, wondering if he'd stumbled in on some private breakfast. "Am I interrupting?"

The other three occupants of the room were giving him looks of complete disgust.

"I should say you are!" said one man, who threw down his napkin, shoved away from the table, and got to his feet, all the while glaring at Thomas.

Thomas sat down, baffled.

"I couldn't agree more, Nigel," a rather portly man said, standing up and throwing down his napkin as well.

"Thank you, Gerard," Nigel said with a sniff in Thomas's direction.

Nigel? Gerard? Who were these yahoos?

"Just like a Yank," Gerard continued, "without a thought in his head for loyalty to the Crown!"

Thomas wondered if his hearing had gone right along with his mental stability. "I beg your pardon?"

"Romantic, *historic* ruins are not to be tampered with!" Nigel stated.

"Oh, I see," said Thomas. And so he did. Clearly. He was facing a preservation group taking exception to his remodeling plans. Somehow, it just figured.

"Leave him to it," said Gerard with a knowing look at Nigel. "He'll have his just deserts up the way, I'd say." He looked at the older woman. "Coming, Constance?"

"When I've finished," the woman said placidly.

The two men left the dining room without further ado, leaving Thomas looking at the woman named Constance. She had gray hair that looked so solidly plastered in shape that Thomas doubted even the fiercest of storms could move a single strand. She looked neither indignant nor flustered. She merely finished her breakfast, then dabbed her napkin to her lips. Without comment, she pushed back from the table and stood.

Thomas could hardly wait for her assessment of his character, nationality, and/or ripeness for receiving just deserts, all of which seemed rather ironic to him. He'd always prided himself on the ability to blend in with the natives. His dark hair and blue eyes allowed him to pass for several nationalities, and his gift for languages allowed him to pick up accents easily. In addition to that, he went out of his way to be unobtrusive and excessively polite. That usually took care of what his looks and tongue didn't. It looked like all his skill and charm would do nothing to win over this group.

Constance cleared her throat. "We're from the National Trustees Concerned with Preserving Ruins," she announced.

Thomas heard all the capital letters there, and he was impressed.

"We understand that not only have you purchased Thorpewold, you intend to restore it."

No sense in denying it. "Actually, yes. I have. And I do."

"As it was in the Middle Ages?"

He paused and considered his answer. He actually hadn't finalized his plans where the remodel was concerned. He needed a place to live, and he needed a challenge. But he'd purposefully left the specifics for when he'd reached England.

"Honestly," he said slowly, "I'm not quite sure. I don't intend to tear it down and start over, if that's what you're worried about."

"We worry about progress, young man."

"I'll probably try to restore it to as original a state as possible," he conceded. "With a few modern conveniences, if that won't incite riots."

She pursed her lips. "The castle is a national treasure, young man."

"Is it?" he mused. "Any decisive battles fought here? Any famous occupants? Any legendary trysts? I don't think so."

"It is the age of the structure that makes it important."

"I'll give you that, but I imagine Thorpewold was built for function, not beauty."

"Nevertheless—"

"I don't see a good reason not to make it habitable."

"There are many good reasons why not."

"I think we're at an impasse," he offered with as much of

a smile as he could muster. He had no intention of not trying to live in the place he'd bought, so making it habitable was definitely in the cards. But he had to admit that, not having examined the castle at close range, he wasn't all that sure what would need to be done. "I am," he said finally, "going to make a home of it."

"We'll not give up so easily," she said, waving her napkin at him in challenge.

"I'm sure you won't," he said with a sigh.

"Then war it is!" she exclaimed, tossing her napkin down with a flourish. "Steel yourself for a long siege, young man. We're very good at this."

"I'm quite sure you are."

She walked to the door with a spine so stiff a two-by-four would have been impressed. She paused, then slowly looked back at him. She stared at him for several moments in silence, then spoke.

"Why did you buy it?" she asked.

Now if that wasn't a question for the annals. He didn't really want to answer with the truth, but if there was one thing he wasn't, it was a liar, so he took a deep breath. "Because I had to."

She looked at him for a moment or two longer, then turned and left the room. Thomas didn't even have time to mull over the answer that had come from deeper inside him than he would have liked before Mrs. Pruitt was bustling in, carrying a hearty breakfast.

"Heard them declaring war on ye," she said, setting down the plate in front of him. "Passing irritating, that lot."

"I'm sure they do some good," he offered.

"Hrmph," she said with a sniff. " 'Tis private property now, that keep. Ye do with it what ye like. 'Twould probably be better torn down, anyway."

"Really?" he asked, surprised. "Why?"

She chewed on her answer for a moment or two before she shook her head. "Just rumors, and likely better left unsaid. I daresay ye'll know more about the whole affair than I in the end."

He wasn't sure he liked the sound of that.

"And by the by," she said, clearing up a plate or two, "all

yer woodworking things ye sent from the States are in the back shed. I cleaned ye out a right proper place out there. Campin' gear is there as well."

"Thank you."

"Ye aren't planning to sleep up there, are ye?" she asked sharply.

"If the weather holds, I might."

"I'll be plannin' on ye for supper each night. Just to make sure ye've survived the day."

He only smiled and dug into his eggs. He looked up as she made for the kitchen door.

"Mrs. Pruitt?"

"Aye?"

"Thanks for breakfast."

"Late as it is," she agreed. " 'Tis nothing, me lad."

"Are they staying long?"

"Them's as have it in for ye?" She snorted. "Aye. Indefinitely."

"I was afraid of that."

"I thought ye might be. Mind yer back, me lad."

He watched her go and wondered if he'd just gotten himself in for more than he'd bargained for.

Well, it wasn't as if he wasn't used to people being irritated by what he did. He'd acted on unpopular ideas before and survived the fallout. He'd also survived climbs in incredibly inhospitable environments and come away the victor. A few grumpy Brits weren't going to faze him. If the number of people he annoyed remained at three, he was going to be damned lucky.

Besides, he wasn't going to go home. He'd come to accomplish something, and accomplish it he would. He didn't have a thing to show for twelve years of work. He'd never left any permanent traces of his passing while climbing. His house in Maine was the first tangible thing he'd left behind in his life. He wasn't about to leave another indiscernible reminder of his passing if he could help it.

A half hour and a very full belly later, he was walking out the front door. He looked neither to the right nor the left, on the off chance he might see something he didn't want to. No sense in tempting fate, despite his earlier determination that his mother and sister were loony. His dad had always said Megan was the one with the overactive imagination. Maybe his dad had been neglectful in not applying the same label to him.

No, it was the past that was full of ghostly visions. Today he felt marvelous, and he was just certain his hallucinations were behind him.

He walked through the garden and down to the road, enjoying the lack of clouds in the sky and the crisp smell of a late-summer morning. The road was well paved, but definitely a one-laner. It was deserted, though, so he supposed driving wouldn't have been that big a stress. But the walking suited him, so he enjoyed the route as it meandered along through fields and up and around a small hill.

And then the path began.

It was dirt and gravel and broke off from the road, heading to the right. Thomas stepped onto its surface and then felt a chill go through him.

Why did you buy it?

Because I had to.

He looked up and shivered. He would have liked to have blamed it on the weather. Unfortunately, there wasn't a cloud in the sky. Even if there had been, that wouldn't have been what unsettled him.

It was that he'd been to this place before.

It was as if some strange permutation of déjà vu had overcome him. He found himself powerless to keep from walking up the road. As he walked, the feeling increased until he wasn't sure any longer what century he was in or how many times he'd walked along the same path.

And then he rounded the little copse of trees and found himself facing his castle. For a moment he could see it with perfect clarity—

As it must have been centuries ago.

The outer walls were intact, the drawbridge down, the road hard-packed and well used. The trees were gone, and the rest of the surrounding countryside stripped of all vegetation. That made sense. No enemy would sneak up unnoticed with only that pitiful bit of foliage to hide behind. He could hear faint noises of hammer on anvil, men shouting, horses neighing.

Then he blinked, and the vision was gone. Trees surrounded the castle, ones that had certainly sprung up in the past couple hundred years. The castle walls were crumbling, and no drawbridge protected the keep from invaders. A stone bridge spanned what had perhaps been a moat in times past but was now nothing but a filled-in ditch.

Thomas made his way along the path until he was staring at the gatehouse. It was in good shape, along with the walls, if you could overlook the missing masonry. The gatehouse still stood firm, and the four corners of the outer walls still boasted guard towers. Thomas walked over the stone bridge that spanned the distance from a grassy expanse to the gatehouse itself. The enormity of his task began to sink in. He was no mason. Even with his unwavering belief in his ability to tackle anything, he had to concede that perhaps this was beyond him. Never mind his lack of knowledge of stoneworking. The repairs would take months just by themselves. He'd have to hire help.

He walked under the gatehouse and looked up at the portcullis hanging above him. He was almost certain he saw spikes in the shadows, but when he blinked, they were gone.

It was really starting to drive him crazy. He wished that if true madness was going to overtake him, that it would do it in a rush instead of in annoying bits and pieces.

He shrugged aside his visions, then walked out of the gatehouse and back out into the open—

And back again, seemingly, into medieval England.

He froze at the sight that greeted him. Men milled about the inner bailey. One or two were dressed in rough peasant garb, but the majority were obviously Scots going about their business in their plaids either with mighty swords hanging at their sides or strapped to their backs. He looked quickly at the keep itself, expecting to see it functional as well.

It was, oddly enough, a wreck.

The hall had no roof, nor a front door for that matter. He realized absently that it would take him years, not months to put the hall to rights and that, too, would take a mason's skills. But that wasn't the worst of it. There were men milling about in his inner bailey—men who looked like they belonged quite firmly in the past.

Yet here they were in the present.

And that led him to believe quite firmly that they were anything but mortal.

"Hell," he said with feeling.

All right. So the castle needed a lot of work. So he was likely going to be harassed by a preservation society for the duration of his stay in England. Those he could handle. But ghosts? In his bailey?

Somehow, he just knew he shouldn't have been surprised.

The men seemed to be ignoring him, so he took the opportunity to stare at them. They argued, laughed, and talked loudly about things he couldn't divine. He supposed they spoke in Gaelic. Well, that was something he should look into learning. Best to know what his castle mates were saying about him if he could.

He looked around the bailey, trying to see past the paranormal activity within his view. To his left were two guard towers on the outer wall. One was so perfectly preserved, it was startling—and unsettling. Just looking at it gave him the creeps. No, he would not be spending any length of time there until he knew its history. He suspected that once he knew what sorts of things had been done inside those circular walls, he'd be even less likely to visit it.

He looked at the far corner tower. It was much larger than any of the others, and it was crumbling in a few places. Maybe that would be a good place to start work. The stones looked sound. Maybe all it would take was some carpentry work to make it habitable.

To his right, the inner bailey stretched for some distance, based on what he could see from the walls and guard towers there. He suspected that in the past, such a space might have housed stables, a smithy, or other workaday buildings. A wall now separated him from that part of the castle, a wall taller than he, but there was an arched wooden gate there.

He turned away from it. That could be explored later. He wanted to see the inside of the great hall and examine the damage time had wrought.

He stepped inside the doorway and jumped in spite of himself. The place was packed with Scotsmen, even more numerous than the group he'd seen outside. There was no doubt in his mind that he was facing men who were no longer flesh and bone. They stood at attention, with their backs against the four walls of the great hall. Thomas gave up trying to convince himself he was having stress-induced hallucinations. He'd had a great night's sleep, a substantial breakfast, and a brisk walk up the way. The only thing he could surmise was that this kind of sight was something he'd inherited from his mother. It was certainly nothing he would have gotten from his father.

Well, there was a decision to be made. He suspected that these unexpected fixtures in his house might be very reluctant to leave. For all he knew, they had been there for centuries. So, he supposed the best thing to do was pretend to ignore them. Maybe they would be just as busy ignoring him.

He walked around the great hall, looking up at the roof— or lack thereof—and examining the fireplaces. There were two, one on either side of the hall. They were large enough that he could walk inside them. He did, then looked up and hoped to see sky. He heard the chatter of birds instead and saw nothing but black. Not good signs, but perhaps Thorpewold's village had a chimney sweep.

He stepped back, then found himself face-to-face with a ghostly Scot. The man was huge. Thomas was tall, and he considered himself quite fit. But this guy was taller than he was and definitely broader. His sword had to be almost six feet long if it was an inch. Thomas was almost blinded by the brooch on the man's shoulder that held his plaid to his shirt. He was so startled by the complete picture of power and menace that he stared right into the man's eyes.

The man blinked in surprise, then a scowl of formidable proportions came over his face.

"So, ye can see me, can ye?" he growled.

Thomas found himself without a single coherent thing to say.

The man drew his sword with a flourish. Thomas stepped back instinctively.

"To me!" the man roared. "Clan MacDougal!"

Thomas waited to be assaulted, but only a handful of men drew their swords, and it was done with less enthusiasm than he would have suspected from that kind of bellow.

"Ach, damnation," the man groused. "All right then, ye great bunch of women, to Herself! The MacLeod!"

Thomas had several thoughts running through his mind as he found himself tripping backward over something he was sure hadn't been behind him moments before—or maybe he'd been so distracted he hadn't noticed it—and those thoughts came to him in no particular order.

First, it was one thing to keep out of the way of one sword; it was quite another to try to avoid the flashing blades of three dozen angry Scots.

Second, it was extremely embarrassing to go sprawling and land, sans his dignity, on his backside with his head still traveling at a velocity high enough to render him unconscious when that head apparently struck a rock.

And as he surrendered to the blackness, actually quite grateful that he would be spared the humiliation of listening to said Scots laughing themselves sick over his poor performance, his final thought was perhaps the most disturbing.

Were the swords real?

At least he would be unconscious when he learned the truth.

Chapter 6

Iolanthe walked down the flat stone pathway between her roses, plucking off a diseased leaf here, removing a spent blossom there. She paused and looked down doubtfully at a rose she'd been just recently given, which bore the dubious name of some Colonial rock legend. The only king she knew of resided in London, or at least he had the last time she'd stirred herself to make note of him.

She stood in the midst of her garden and breathed deeply, imagining how it would have smelled had she possessed a mortal nose to smell it with. Lavender, rose, mint; aye, they would have mingled with the aroma of sun-warmed earth and the hint of greenery from the forest.

The sight at least was something she could enjoy. She looked over the plants that made up the large expanse of her unlife's work and named them all in her head. The majority of them had been gifts from a handful of ghostly monks who had happened upon her digging in her illusionary dirt in some century or other. They had brought her cuttings from their travels and taught her the names for things she'd never seen before. It was the single pleasure of her existence, her garden with its strange and marvelous collection of plants.

Of course, they weren't plants from the physical world, but perhaps that was even better. In life, she had gardened for survival, to feed herself and her kin. In death, she had the luxury of growing what she pleased merely for the joy of seeing it all in glorious array around her. No pests, no weeds. Nothing but what she chose to see.

"What a lovely garden, um, Patience?"

Iolanthe gritted her teeth. Perhaps her garden had a pest after all, and it was surely the man who had just come up behind her. A pity she couldn't squash him under her heel like a bug. She turned and glared at him.

"My name, you bejeweled peacock, is not Patience."

She brushed past him and made for her bench near the wall.

"Well," Roderick said, following hard on her heels, "if you won't give me your name freely, I suppose I must continue to try to guess it." He tidied up his immaculate suit of clothes, then sat next to her. "Let's see. We've eliminated the fourteenth and fifteenth centuries—and what doing that took!—so I suppose that leaves us turning to the sixteenth. Perhaps one of those charming Puritan names. Charity? Humility?"

"I'm a Scot, you simpleton."

"Tribulation? Mercy?"

Ach, but she'd been through the former and had little enough of the latter.

"Fly-fornication?"

She glared at him. "Have you nothing better to do than trouble me?"

He examined his perfectly tended fingernails, then looked at her and smiled. "I'm afraid not."

"Why did you come to Thorpewold?" she demanded. "What foul fancy possessed you to come here?"

"Well," he said with a smile, " 'tis quite a tale, and I'm more than happy to relate it. Now, after my untimely demise—"

"At the hands of an angry, cuckolded husband, no doubt," she muttered.

"Quite so, my dear. As I was saying, after my untimely demise, I was visiting my club, as one does you know, and I heard tell of a beauty in the north that was simply not to be missed."

The Highlands. Aye, she could understand that. Iolanthe sighed in spite of herself. She rarely allowed herself to miss her homeland, but there were times that the longing rose up so sharply in her that she could scarce bear it. She turned her face away, lest the Victorian fool see her tears.

"Then you stopped too soon," she said. "You missed your journey's end by many miles."

"But, my dear, you were my journey's end."

She had to look at him, she was so surprised by his words. "Me?"

"Word does get 'round, you know," he said, digging into his waistcoat pocket. He produced his snuff case and began to lighten it of its contents.

Iolanthe could hardly believe anyone would think her beautiful, much less take that tale all the way to London. She knew her limitations. She was too tall. She was too old. By the saints, she'd been almost a score and five when—

She jerked her mind away from the memory and glared at her companion.

"You would be," she said sharply, "far more attractive if you did not poke that foul weed up your nose. I scarce know how your scores of women bore watching you do it."

He stretched lazily. "I had other attributes that more than made up for any aversion to snuff a woman might have had."

She had no desire to learn any more about his attributes. He was fair enough, she supposed, if you wanted a man who was more concerned about the length of his eyelashes than he was about whether or not he could wield a sword. But he was certainly not for her, especially with his incessant prying into things he was not entitled to know.

"Would you care to examine my attributes . . . Virtue?"

Iolanthe would have sharpened her tongue on him, but just at the moment when she might have begun such a thing, Duncan came hurrying around the corner. He came to an abrupt halt in front of her.

"Bit of a battle," he announced.

Iolanthe was unsurprised. She thought she'd heard a goodly amount of noise a while back, but she'd certainly had no desire to interrupt it. Men were men, she had decided several hundred years ago, and were best left to their games when it suited them. Besides, the men of her keep were a more vigorous lot than most and had need of their exercise. Fighting passed the time most pleasantly.

She waved her hand dismissively. "Ever they bicker amongst themselves, Duncan. No harm done."

He shook his head. " 'Twould have been nothing of note had it been merely amongst themselves. They're trying to heave a man out of the hall—"

Iolanthe was on her feet before she knew she intended to rise. "Him? The Yank?"

"Oh, delightful," Roderick said, rubbing his hands together enthusiastically. "Let us go examine him, my dear. It seems decades since last I saw one."

Iolanthe glared at him. " 'Twas but a pair of days ago, you fool. The lad and the lass ran screaming from the garden, or don't you remember?"

He opened his mouth to no doubt spout some sort of foolishness she had no desire to listen to, so she turned and walked away, not caring if he followed or not. She couldn't spare Duncan to dispatch him at present.

"How are the men?" she asked Duncan.

"Debating how best to kill him," he said, striding alongside her.

"Awfully unsporting of them," Roderick said, catching up on her other side.

Duncan growled at him. "Shut up, ya frilly fool. We've no need of yer judgments."

And Roderick, who had spent his share of time being heaved by Duncan off battlements and being run through by Duncan's great sword, apparently decided silence was more prudent than speech. He shut his mouth.

"We cannot slay him," Iolanthe said firmly. "It will only bring his kin upon us, as well as no doubt the king's—"

"Queen's," Roderick corrected.

Iolanthe blinked in surprise. "Queen? Another one?"

"Another Elizabeth," Roderick informed her with what she could only term a bit of smugness. "She's been on the throne for quite some time now."

Iolanthe scowled. "Queen's men, then. Those we want even less banging on our gates."

Aye, that was all she needed. She'd had freedom from the interventions of the outside world for, what had it been? Decades? Centuries? Visitors were one thing, either of the mortal or not-so-mortal kind. Those she could ignore readily enough. But trouble from the Crown? Nay, that she could not have.

And then there was the man inside her gates to consider. If this Colonist was determined enough to give his hard-earned gold for her keep, then he was likely not a man to be ignored.

Perhaps it would have to be death for him after all.

She walked through the inner bailey to find a gaggle of men clustered there. As she approached, she heard their spirited conversation.

"Slit his throat," one offered.

"Poke him repeatedly with a sword," offered another.

"Put out his eyes," chortled yet another.

"Nay," said another. "Heave him full into the ditch and let him drown. It'll rain soon enough and choke the life from him."

Iolanthe tried to see over the men, but that was a futile exercise. She tried to politely make herself a path, but apparently the thought of a bloody battle had left the men quite unwilling to give up a good spot for watching any possible sport. Iolanthe was forced to push, shove, and make a nuisance of herself before she was grudgingly allowed a place at the front of the group. She glared at the men she had most recently displaced, then put her shoulders back and turned to see what the fuss was all about.

She looked down.

And her heart stood still.

She remained there, mute and unmoving. She wondered, with what poor wits remained her, how the man lying before her had been rendered senseless. Had her garrison actually taken a blade to him, or had he struck his head fleeing from her great hall? He surely didn't look the part of a coward. She judged him to be rather taller than she, perhaps even almost as tall as Connor MacDougal, who wielded a six-foot broadsword that even he topped by a hand. A man so large wouldn't be intimidated by much.

She considered his clothing. He was dressed in those denim long-legged trews that she occasionally saw mortals wearing. She had to admit that he did them justice. His shoulders were wide, but that apparently came from his build, not the excess fat that Roderick's pampered, corpulent visitors sported when they came to visit. She looked at his long fingers resting over his belly and wondered absently if they grasped a sword readily or if his were other kinds of tools.

Hammers and saws most likely, damn him.

His face was a wonder of planes and angles with a finely shaped nose, a handsome mouth, and attractive ears. His hair was dark, far darker than hers, and fell back from his face in pleasing waves.

None of which truly mattered, she supposed. However he looked, whatever his business, it didn't change the fact that beyond all reason and logic stood the single fact that set the hairs on the back of her neck on end.

It was him.

The man she had dreamed about for centuries.

She had dreamed of him while walking through the meadows, sitting under trees during the rain, snugly holed up in the warmth of the hay during the winter. She had dreamed of him in spring, hoped for him in fall. He'd first come to her heart during her tenth summer and never left it since.

The man who would come to rescue her.

She stared at him in silence for several minutes before another thought occurred to her.

If he was the man who had been destined to rescue her, then where had he been? Where had he been six hundred years ago when he could have saved her life? Where had he been for the past six centuries?

He was late. If his being that late wasn't reason enough to feed him to the wolves, she wasn't sure what was.

"Damn the man," she muttered.

"Aye," Connor said, rubbing his hands together purposefully, "let us slay him and send him to his foul rest."

Iolanthe found the thought suddenly very appealing. As for recognizing the man, perhaps her wits were addled. She had likely seen him before, and that was what unsettled her so.

But the only Colonists she'd seen in the past two hundred years had been tourists, and this one certainly hadn't been amongst them. She'd never seen a man so handsome. More was the pity that his face wasn't covered with pockmarks, that his nose wasn't broken from too many encounters with another man's sword hilt, that half his teeth weren't missing thanks to another's fist in his mouth.

She knew the last because he was snoring with his mouth quite widely open.

"Attractive," Roderick said, peering over her shoulder. "But not nearly as handsome as I—"

Iolanthe elbowed him in the belly and he ceased speaking with a great whoosh of air and a tiny squeak. She turned her attentions back to the man lying just inside her hall. Recognize him she might, but that was beside the point. He had come too late. To her, he could only be a Yank bent on destroying her home. Perhaps 'twas best for all if he did just disappear.

"Cut off his head and be done with him," a man behind her grumbled.

"Och, and where's the sport in that? Open his belly and pull out his intestines. There's a goodly bit of entertainment in that for the afternoon."

Iolanthe considered the last. 'Twas Connor MacDougal to suggest it, and she had to admit that he had a fine head for thinking when it came to meting out gruesome revenges. A pity that was his only redeeming quality.

"Carry him to the woods, and let the beasties finish him," Duncan said. "Herself'll be well rid of him, and no murder will be laid at our gates."

Iolanthe listened to the men argue first over whether or not they could manage the feat of carrying a mortal such a far distance, then they began to discuss what could be done to make the man more palatable to whatever animal might be haunting the woods. Several ideas were fine ones, and when the men looked at her expectantly, she was fully prepared to agree and commend them on their resourcefulness. She opened her mouth to speak.

"I'll parley with him," she heard herself say.

"What!" thundered Connor MacDougal. "Have ye gone daft?"

She was wondering that herself. "I—" she began.

"Ye've no head for thinkin', ye silly twit! What need have we to surrender to some spineless coward from across the sea? Why, he couldn't even stand up to me blade, and that was naught but illusion!"

Iolanthe agreed heartily, but apparently her mouth didn't.

"I said I'll parley with him, and that's what I'll do," she said firmly.

"Ye'll do nothing of the sort," the MacDougal snarled.

Iolanthe glared at him. He was not her lord, and she had no intentions of having him wrest the chieftainship of her little clan from her. "Who's to stop me?" she asked haughtily.

In answer, he drew his sword.

She had to admit that it was a fearsome weapon indeed. Add to that the ferocious Highlander glaring down at her from his great height, and she found herself nigh onto intimidated.

Until he spoke.

"What think ye of that, *girl*?"

That was truly more than she could bear. Not that she'd ever given her name to any of the men surrounding her. They mostly called her *Herself* or *Lady MacLeod*. No one called her *girl*. It reminded her of all the times her father had done the same, uncaring that she had a name. Iolanthe folded her arms over her chest and looked stonily back at the Mac-Dougal.

"Is this your ancestral keep?" she asked coldly.

"Nay, but I'll take it just the same—"

"Have you a right to it through battle? Were you slain here?"

He chewed on that one, then spat out a curt nay.

"The keep is mine," she said. "I paid for it with my own blood."

"Your virgin's blood?" he sneered.

She was certain none save Duncan knew the truth of her murder, and perhaps even he didn't know the precise way of it, but the men fought as if they did. Connor rallied a handful of his own lads about him, but the rest of the keep's inhabitants were demanding justice for the insult to her. Even Roderick had pulled forth his sabre and was looking at it carefully, as if trying to decide how the obviously unfamiliar weapon might best be wielded.

Iolanthe stepped back several paces and considered where she might go now. The battle would likely go on all day. There would be many mortal wounds inflicted, though obviously none would die from them nor feel the pain of them.

It made for a very long day on the field.

Besides, it was beginning to rain—perfect weather for a fine day of fighting. 'Twas best that she leave them to their business. They would enjoy their play and have a great deal to talk about around the fire that night.

In time, Connor would give her a gruff noise and a curt nod that would pass for his apology. She would accept and put his words behind her.

But she wouldn't give him her keep.

And she *would* parley with the man lying in the mud.

She passed the afternoon standing on the parapet. She supposed she had the skill of the stonemasons to thank for even that small place to stand. Unfortunately, haunting the walls didn't soothe her. She forced herself to wait until dusk was falling before she made her way down to the great hall, ignoring everyone she saw on her way there. She went to stand on the front steps and looked out into the bailey.

It wasn't as if she wanted to look.

But she couldn't help herself.

The man was stirring. As she watched, he heaved himself to his feet, sneezed heartily, then slowly made his way out through the barbican and down the road, rubbing the back of his head. Perhaps that was all she would see of him. He would likely hie himself back to his beloved Colonies and be grateful to be returned.

Somehow, though, she had the feeling that wouldn't happen.

Change was in the air. She stood and examined the feeling. It was like . . . She closed her eyes and let the memory wash over her. It was like the Highlands at the end of summer, when suddenly out of the north came a breeze with a hint of chill clinging to it.

Aye, a mighty change was in the air, and she was as powerless to prevent it as she would have been to hold off autumn.

A mighty change.

She could only hope it would be a good one.

Chapter 7

Thomas pulled his shirt over his head and winced as it made contact with the back of his skull. It certainly wasn't the worst concussion he'd ever had. He'd had a couple of bad falls over his long career of climbing up things he probably should have let alone, and his head had paid the price. He wondered if it was just more than his thick skull that was wounded. It was pretty damned embarrassing to have passed out because of a cluster of ghosts coming at him with fake swords.

He had come to the conclusion that the swords couldn't have been real. If they had been, he would have either woken to find himself cut to ribbons or never woken again at all. The next time he was faced with a blade almost as tall as he was, he wouldn't flinch.

Which was all good and fine for the future, but it didn't help his gargantuan headache or the sharp sting to his pride. He supposed that in all fairness, getting back to the inn under his own power had been something of an accomplishment. But two days in bed afterward? Never mind that he'd been drugged against his will. His performance was pitiful.

He left his room and made his way gingerly down the stairs, feeling several decades older than the thirty-four years his driver's license claimed he was. He paused to stifle an enormous sneeze in his sleeve, then started across the foyer.

"I'd be remiss if I didn't tell ye that ye don't look up to any walking about today."

He turned to look at Mrs. Pruitt with narrowed eyes. She'd been the one to do it, the traitor. How could she have so calculatingly crushed up painkillers and slipped them into his juice? It had to have been the juice. It had tasted a little on the bitter side, hadn't it?

"I'm fine," he said, "thanks to all that rest you provided for me."

She didn't look in the slightest bit guilty. "Ye needed it."

He only grunted and wondered what kind of damage would result from asking her for an aspirin.

"They'll do worse than leave ye out in the rain the next time," she said ominously.

Why she couldn't have warned him before his first trip up to his castle, he didn't know. Then again, perhaps he should have known better. This was the woman who worked at the inn so she could keep up with her paranormal investigations.

"They?" he asked.

"Ye know of whom I speak." She nodded wisely. "Them's that's up the way."

"I don't suppose you'd care to enlighten me further?"

She only puffed herself up, resettled her girth, and began buffing anything remotely shiny on the reception desk.

Apparently, no further enlightenment was forthcoming.

"Breakfast?" she asked, scrutinizing an inkwell.

"No thanks."

She frowned in displeasure.

Who knew what he would find in his eggs, put there by his well-meaning innkeeper? No, it was better that he escape while he could.

He turned toward the door, putting all thoughts of aspirin behind him. He'd lived through worse headaches than this without the aid of drugs. Besides, with Mrs. Pruitt at the dispensary, who knew what he'd get to dull his pain or how long it would put him out for?

"I'll be back for supper," he said over his shoulder.

"One could hope," she said darkly.

And with that cheery send-off, he let himself out the front door. He stood on the stoop and stuck his hands in his pockets. He rocked back on his heels and examined the day. No rain; that was a bonus. He supposed maybe he should have taken another day of rest, but he just couldn't. At least the past couple of days he'd been unconscious, except for that brief period of misery when someone had woken him every hour on the hour to make sure he hadn't slipped into a coma.

He'd had little time to think about his ignominious defeat at his own castle.

Scared by ghosts. It was pathetic.

In all fairness, he hadn't been scared, he'd been surprised. He'd stumbled backward, like any man with any sense would have, then tripped and gone down and into unconsciousness. The rest of the day had passed in something of a haze. He vaguely remembered a lively discussion of how he should be finished off, then the sounds of an enormous battle raging around him.

He wondered absently if his mother had had any idea what he was getting himself into. Did his sister?

Thomas set off toward the castle before he could give the true ridiculousness of his situation any more thought. He'd been looking forward to something of a repeat of his house-building experience. He'd planned to get in touch with the rocks that made up his castle. Rekindling some of his interest in history had seemed like a bonus as well.

He just hadn't been expecting to have history come alive in quite this way.

What he'd anticipated was a year of hard physical labor with no distractions, a year to get his head together and decide what he most wanted from life. He was thirty-four, and it was past time he settled down. He was wasting his life chasing after the almighty dollar and finding himself dating expensive, unpleasant women. A year of introspection with something to show for it in the end had seemed like such a good idea at the time.

He really hadn't planned on having company while he was doing it.

It took far less time to reach the castle than it had before. Maybe it seemed that way because it had taken him so long to get back two days ago. He ignored the eerie feeling he got every time he put his foot on the gravel road. Maybe the bump had taken more out of him than he thought.

He had almost reached the castle when he looked up, then sighed. First it was ghosts. Now it was the preservation society with pickets.

He halted several yards away and read the signs: *Damn Yankees, Let Our Ruins Remain, Hammers Harm Our Her-*

itage were the best of the lot. When they saw him coming, the protestors broke into a spontaneous rendition of "God Save the Queen."

The peace and quiet of his house on the coast sounded better by the minute.

Thomas jammed his hands in his pockets and continued doggedly on his way toward his tormentors. "No power tools today," he announced as he approached.

The three stopped with their screeching, but they didn't look convinced.

"I'm just here to look around," he said.

"But you'll return another day to render our ruin remodeled!" exclaimed one.

"Without a doubt," he agreed pleasantly.

They hoisted their signs and looked like they meant to do business with them this time.

"Want to come along to the castle?" he asked politely. "Just to see the ruin in its ruinous state before it's restored?"

The ratlike leader sat down and put his head between his knees. The other two looked so unsettled by the prospect that Thomas began to wonder if they hadn't seen more than they cared to themselves. He frowned thoughtfully. It looked like his choice was either ghosts or preservationists. If he had to choose at the moment, he would take the ghosts. At least having a few restless spirits around would spare him from any more patriotic songs being warbled his way.

He walked away, still leaving the trio in various stages of collapse. One hurdle overcome, one to go. He sighed as he walked toward the little stone bridge. There were two dozen Scots standing guard at the barbican. Thomas recognized the leader immediately. Even knowing the sword was just for show wasn't all that comforting. Maybe his imagination was too good. He could easily imagine having faced that in battle and subsequently having found himself without any guts. Literally.

He stopped a few paces away and sized up the other man. The Scot glared back at him.

"Good morning," Thomas said politely.

The man snarled a curse at him. "A good mornin' would be *you* dead with yer head on a pike outside me gates."

Thomas realized immediately that he was in over his head. Bonding with the guy by discussing the Lakers was out, as was inviting him to toss the old pigskin around for awhile. What would the village barkeep say if he came in for a pint or two with a local ghost carrying a huge sword?

Get out, and don't come back, was Thomas's guess.

Well, he'd faced down some fairly nasty individuals in the business world and found the best way to deal with them was to be brief and direct. He suspected the man before him might understand that. After all, what could be briefer or more direct than cutting off your enemy's head and displaying it outside your front door?

"Thomas McKinnon," he said, not bothering to extend his hand. "And you are?"

The man drew himself up and looked incredibly insulted. "Connor MacDougal," he said stiffly. "*The* MacDougal."

"Ah, Laird MacDougal," Thomas said, inclining his head just the slightest bit. "A pleasure."

"A pleasure would be opening ye up and pulling out yer innards whilst ye watched."

All right, so pleasantries were going to be wasted on this one. "You'd enjoy it, I'm sure, but I doubt I would. Is this your castle I've bought?"

"Aye," he said. But his eyes shifted.

Several of the men standing near him shifted as well. Ah, a liar. Thomas filed that away for future use.

"I thought the MacDougals were Highlanders," Thomas said easily. "I wouldn't think you would find your home so far south."

"He has it aright, my laird," one of the men near him began miserably.

"Shut up, Donald," Connor MacDougal snarled. He glared at Thomas. "The keep'll be mine in the end. Believe all ye like that ye'll stay here, but I swear I'll see that ye don't. If what's awaiting ye inside doesn't have the spine to rid us of ye, *I* will."

And with that, he vanished. Thomas had no idea if he was really gone or if he was still hanging around beyond Thomas's ability to see him.

Which was, oddly enough, an ability he'd never suspected he would have.

Thomas took a deep breath, squared his shoulders, and walked up the path the remaining men left for him. He felt their eyes on him, but he ignored them. If they weren't blocking his way, that was enough for him. Whoever wanted to make trouble for him later could, when he'd had a chance to work out a good strategy for dealing with it.

That would come later. Now, as he made his way into the inner bailey, he focused all his mental energy on what potentially awaited him inside.

A grumpy, grandfatherly ghost who would need a little buttering up, a listening ear for endless stories of battle, and a guarantee that the keep wouldn't be changed too much? Or perhaps it was a man even more fierce than Connor Mac-Dougal, and Thomas would spend the next year of his life constantly fighting for supremacy. There were myriad possibilities between those two polar opposites, so maybe there wasn't any use in speculating further. The bottom line was, he owned the castle now, and he intended to make it habitable. He would do his best to be cordial and pleasant, but he wasn't going to leave. The sooner the ghost inside realized that, the better off life would be for both of them.

He walked briskly across the courtyard, his purpose and determination energizing him. He'd already faced down one extremely unpleasant Scot. Another man of the same temperament wouldn't faze him.

He stepped over the threshold of the great hall, his loins girded for battle, his tongue practically tripping over all the things that were on the verge of coming out of his mouth.

He came to a sudden and very unexpected stop.

Well, the hall was definitely occupied. And it was occupied by a single person.

But that person definitely wasn't a man.

Thomas very rarely found himself without something to say. He could always come up with something clever or disarming or inoffensive. But right then, he found himself absolutely speechless.

The morning sunlight streamed down into the hall, thanks to the lack of a roof. It fell in soft strands of light onto the dirt and stones of the floor. He could even see the swirling motes dancing, thanks to the faint hint of breeze that blew through the crumbling hall, bringing with it a hint of fall.

That same sunlight fell softly upon a woman who stood in the center of the hall, unmoving, unspeaking. Her hair was dark, almost as dark as his, and it fell down past her shoulders in a riot of curls. Tall and slender, she was dressed in a simple peasant's gown of dusty purple that looked as if it had been dyed the color of heather.

He looked at her face and found himself rendered motionless. All he could do was gape at her and grope mentally for words to describe what he was seeing.

Lovely? Yes, she was, but in a wild, reckless way that probably would never have graced the cover of a fashion magazine. Beautiful? Perhaps, but in the same way an unyielding, unforgiving mountain was. He felt, looking at her, the same way he'd felt when he'd had his first up-close look at Everest. It had been overwhelmingly beautiful. And at the same time, it had scared the hell out of him.

This woman did the same.

She was . . . haunting.

There was a stillness about her that immediately became his stillness. The longer he stared at her, the more he found he couldn't look away. She was simply stunning.

He felt stunned. He stood facing her and wondered, absently, if he would ever move again.

This was not at all what he'd expected, but somehow, he suspected this was why he had come.

She was looking at him, but she said no word, made no move to indicate that she was even going to say anything. Thomas wondered how it was you began a conversation with a woman who was, well, standing alone in the middle of a great hall dressed in something that was likely fairly fashionable several hundred years ago.

All his preconceived notions of how the next year of his life—hell, the *rest* of his life—was going to proceed went straight out the window. He'd planned on restoring his castle. He imagined that he would probably hike up whatever England had to offer, then maybe take a little time during the winter and head toward the Alps. He'd envisioned a final year of selfish living before settling down and beginning to look at a more mature way of life. He hadn't expected to find his castle occupied by the most arresting woman he'd ever laid eyes on, who was, from what he could tell, a ghost.

He strove manfully to gather his wits about him. The game had changed, drastically, and he was scrambling for a plan. What he wanted to do was ask her for a date, not tell her that he'd just bought her castle out from under her. It was for damned sure that he had no lines in his very exhaustive supply of lines to use on the woman in front of him to make her find him charming and unthreatening.

Introductions. Introductions couldn't go wrong. He cleared his throat.

"I'm Thomas McKinnon," he said.

She didn't reply.

He frowned. Couldn't she hear him? Was he imagining her? Was he fighting not to go down on his knees and profess undying devotion to a woman who couldn't even understand anything he said?

He tried again. "Thomas McKinnon."

No response.

"Can you hear me?"

She lifted one eyebrow. "Aye, I hear you well enough."

His palms were sweaty. He could hardly believe he was talking to someone who might or might not have been real, and just the sound of her voice had made his palms sweaty. Thirty-four years of maturity had been inexplicably stripped away to leave a gawking, sweaty-palmed sixteen-year-old in its place. He hadn't been a geek at sixteen. What had happened to him in the past thirty seconds?

And if sweaty palms weren't trouble enough, his head had begun to pound again, and he found himself suddenly quite desperate for somewhere to sit down.

"Let's try that again," he said absently, looking around for a chair. "I'm Thomas McKinnon." He saw nothing but rock and dirt. Not useful. He looked at the woman, wondering if she could be prevailed upon for a seat.

She had tilted her head to one side. "Shall I fall to my knees and praise the saints for giving you such a lovely name? Or shall I merely clasp my hands to my bosom and thank you kindly for seeing fit to share such a name with my unworthy self?"

Thomas had to appreciate the comeback, even if her words were less than polite. A smart-ass. He never would have suspected it, given how peaceful she looked, but apparently still waters still ran deep. He certainly hadn't expected her to blurt out that she'd been waiting all her life for him, but a polite *Nice to meet you* would have been sufficient.

His head began to throb with a very annoying rhythm.

"I thought," he managed, forcing himself to keep his hands in his pockets and not clutching his aching head as he so fervently wanted to, "that I should come up and introduce myself."

"Why?"

"Why?" he repeated. "Well, because it's polite. Maybe you'd like to introduce yourself."

"Would I?"

Was that a star swinging through his field of vision? And another? Great, was he going to pass out in front of the most incredible woman he'd seen in his life?

"Could we knock this off?" he asked, wishing she would just cut him some slack so he could leave very soon and go faint in peace. "I think we have some things to work out."

"Do we?"

"Yes," he said shortly, more shortly than he would have under normal circumstances. "Apparently you're not aware of this, but I own this castle."

"Do you?"

This was going nowhere fast. "Yes, I do."

"Is that so?" she said, sounding exceptionally unimpressed.

"Yes, it is so," he said, exasperated. His head was starting to feel like a blacksmith's anvil. Pound, pound, pound. The stars were starting to swim in front of his eyes like dust motes. "I'm the one who paid for it," he managed.

"With what? Your hard-earned gold?"

He closed his eyes. "Yes," he said, wincing. "My hard-earned gold."

He realized she was silent only after he noticed he'd been standing there for several moments silently himself, just trying to breathe like a man who wasn't in agony. He took a deep, steadying breath and opened his eyes. One more try at coherent conversation.

"The castle was sold—" he began.

"By those who didn't have the right," she said flatly.

"They certainly thought so."

"They were wrong. It wasn't theirs to sell."

"And you think it's yours?" he began, then shut his mouth abruptly when he noticed that she was coming toward him. Even he, in his present state, which included a blinding headache, a complete lack of manners, and an apparent lack of common sense, could see that she was shaking with fury.

Fury was bad.

Even in his impaired state, he knew that.

"I paid for this keep," she said in a low, tight voice, "with my blood."

"Ah . . ."

"My blood, you fool!" She thrust out a trembling arm and pointed back behind him. "There, in that cursed guard tower chamber. My lifeblood was spilt there, mercilessly, and my murderer didn't even accord me the courtesy of lingering so that I might not die alone."

And then her fury changed into something else.

Tears began to stream down her face. Thomas found himself reaching out to her only to find there was nothing to hold on to. *Please not tears.* Not a headache so bad he was ready to puke and the sight of tears, too. He wasn't good with tears. His sisters had used them on him mercilessly to get what they wanted, and he'd inevitably caved in. Tears were bad.

"Ah . . ." he tried again.

"So you see, Thomas McKinnon," she said, "I have paid indeed for this poor pile of stones you think is yours."

There was absolute silence for the space of several of the longest minutes of his life.

He was desperate for something to say, but all he could do was stare at her tear-ravaged, angry face and wish that he'd done something besides make a complete ass of himself. He struggled to find something that might be adequate to express his regret.

"Um," he managed.

She looked at him with contempt. "Well put."

"Ah—"

She leaned her face close to his. "Damn you for wringing the truth of it from me," she snarled.

And then she vanished.

Thomas stood alone in the middle of the empty hall. He wondered if he would ever again take a normal breath. He looked around and saw nothing. No ghosts. No witnesses to his idiocy. The place was empty, empty but echoing with the words of a woman he had never expected, a woman he had pushed much harder than he'd intended to.

And then he realized he was either going to pass out or be heartily sick. He left the hall before he could spread any happiness, joy, or what he'd eaten that morning. There was, unsurprisingly, the usual cluster of Highlanders congregated by the gates. Thomas was even less surprised to find Connor MacDougal waiting for him, a sneer on his face.

"Well?" Connor demanded. "Did Herself give it to ye proper?"

Thomas looked up—as if having to look up at an adversary wasn't unpleasant enough in itself—at the MacDougal. "This is the thing, Laird MacDougal," he said, wondering how the ghost would feel if he puked at his feet. "You don't have any more right to this place than I do, so why are we arguing over it?"

He had the momentary satisfaction of seeing Connor MacDougal speechless, but that interval lasted long enough for him to sidestep the man and continue on his way down the road. He'd gone only about thirty yards before he heard the angry response from behind him.

"Don't think yer fancy words will win ye the day!" Connor bellowed. "I've still a sword, and you've a neck to be severed!"

Thomas held up his hand in acknowledgment and continued on his way without turning around. He nodded to the picketers, all of whom were swiveling their heads from his direction to the keep and back, their mouths hanging open in astonishment.

He made it to the road before he dropped to his knees and was heartily sick.

And when he found he could crawl to his feet, he did so

and made his way back to the inn. Maybe he could sleep the headache off. Maybe he could find the key to Mrs. Pruitt's liquor cabinet and drink himself into a stupor. It really didn't matter that he didn't drink. He suspected that the combination of the havoc he'd just wreaked on an innocent woman and the blinding headache he was suffering merited some kind of dive into the swamp of vice.

Maybe it would erase the memory of what he'd just seen.

He'd made that beautiful, proud woman cry.

It wasn't exactly how he'd intended to meet the neighbors.

Chapter 8

The tidings spread like fleas in wet, humid grass. She'd known they would the moment she'd made the mistake of blurting out the truth. Never mind that most of the men had been at the gates, keeping a respectful distance. There were always several professedly innocent eavesdroppers loitering about in case she needed aid. Damned nosy old women, the lot of them. She had no doubts Roderick was at the heart of all the gossipmongering.

The only good to come of it was that Connor MacDougal had not only grunted at her and nodded his apology, he'd doffed his cap and made her a little bow.

But that was poor recompense for the loss of her privacy.

She supposed, though, that she only had herself to blame for her temper that had led to such loss, but how was she to have done anything else? She hadn't been able to remain silent. It had been all she could do to keep her wits about her when faced with Thomas McKinnon in the flesh.

She'd decided to wait for him in the hall because she thought it might make her seem more powerful. She also hadn't been hiding herself. She had fully intended that he see her immediately.

But she hadn't anticipated how the sight of him would affect her.

He'd been taller than she had supposed, tall and broad and so beautiful she had been scarce able to look at him without wanting to sigh in appreciation. His voice had been deep, a soothing sound that washed over her and left her wanting to close her eyes in pleasure. His eyes were a pale, unearthly blue that had been so mesmerizing, she'd struggled to find wits enough to give him the uninterested responses she'd planned.

Ach, that such a lad had actually come for her.

That *he* had come for her.

It was so unjust—to finally find the man she had waited for all her life some six hundred years after her death.

The thought of that injustice had been enough to harden her resolve and sharpen her tongue. Perhaps it wasn't his fault that he hadn't arrived when she'd wanted, but it was far easier to be angry with him than to be desperately regretful that he'd come too late. So she'd been aloof and curt. To her mind, he'd been passing unpleasant and astonishingly disrespectful. He certainly hadn't lingered to beg pardon for his poor behavior. He'd stammered out a few apologetic noises, then walked off, ceasing, no doubt, to give her another thought.

But would he return?

Now, that was the question that plagued her—and that it plagued her infuriated her. Why should she care what a mortal did? She was unmoved by his broad shoulders and strong hands. He'd trampled over her heedlessly, and for that he should have been forgotten and thought well rid of.

And it was the thought of ridding herself of him that was driving her out of her keep and down the road to the inn, notwithstanding the lateness of the hour. It wasn't that she didn't frequent the inn, and at whatever hour suited her. She had, on more than one occasion. She had kin down the way. Every decade or so, there rose up in her a longing to be with family. Or, rather, family that she cared to see.

Fortunately, there were at least a few decent men in her family tree, and she found that quaffing a companionable cup of ale every now and again with one or another of them was a pleasure she could allow herself. And 'twas Ambrose MacLeod she sought that night, and not just for the pleasure of speech with him. He was a wily old warrior with unlimited ideas on how to rid oneself of annoyances.

An annoyance such as Thomas McKinnon, for instance.

She walked through the inn's immaculately tended garden and permitted herself a small flash of envy for the gardener. It reminded her too much of her own garden in the Highlands. How many happy hours had been passed there, tending herbs, plucking out weeds, growing things that could actually be eaten? Perhaps 'twas a simple thing, that tending of things the earth nourished, but she had loved it.

She paused at the back door that led into the kitchen, feeling suddenly that she might be making a very great mistake. Perhaps Thomas McKinnon would simply go. Would it not be better to consider him beneath her notice? Then again, perhaps 'twas too late to turn back now. Besides, there would be those awake and happy for a bit of conversation.

She took a deep breath and walked through the door.

A single candle burned low on the table. The simple light fell on the drooling visage of the man she suspected she might come to loathe, given enough time. He was rude, aye, but not only was he rude, he was a drinker as well. She glared at him in disgust. Could this not be any more undesirable a houseguest? He would pound away with his hammer all day, then drink himself into a stupor and snore all night.

Nay, 'twas far better that she got rid of him before he disturbed her peace any further.

"Tommy, my lad, if you want to drink yourself senseless, you'd best fill up your glass."

Iolanthe looked quickly to her right to find that another soul had entered the kitchen. Either she had been concentrating so hard on her thoughts that she'd not marked him, or he'd walked through that dining chamber door as easily as she could have.

Which, given the identity of the man, was entirely possible.

The man took no note of her but sat himself down at the table. A tankard of ale appeared in his hand, and the kitchen brightened considerably when a flick of his wrist lit candles and stoked the fire in the hearth.

Thomas McKinnon didn't lift his head. "I couldn't bring myself to open the bottle."

The older man facing him clucked his tongue sadly. "Ach, but what a sorry state you're in."

Iolanthe watched Thomas lift his head, stare at the man facing him, then close his eyes. He swallowed with apparent difficulty.

"Tell me I'm hallucinating."

The man facing him laughed heartily. "Poor lad. Rough go of it?"

Thomas opened his eyes. "You have me at a disadvantage, I'm afraid. You obviously know who I am, but I have no idea who you are."

"Ambrose MacLeod," the older man said. "Chieftain of your clan during the glorious sixteenth century."

Thomas took a deep breath, then put both his hands on the table as if to steady himself. "Why is it I seem to be seeing so many Highlanders so far from home? What is it with this place? Everyone seems to congregate here."

"We've business hereabouts, if you like."

Iolanthe snorted before she could stop herself. The only business the old fool before her had was befouling the lives of all those about him with marriage and other such undesirable unions. He'd grown soft and sentimental in his death. In life, he had been notorious for hatching wild and impossible plots to mete out revenge and rid himself of troublesome enemies. Would that he would use some of that kind of stratagem for her benefit.

She cleared her throat purposefully. If Ambrose marked her, he didn't show it. Iolanthe folded her arms over her chest and leaned back against the door. She glared at Ambrose, but apparently he was more skilled at ignoring others than she'd given him credit for. He merely concentrated on the lout facing him.

Then something struck her, something she'd heard but not truly listened to. Ambrose was chieftain of Thomas's clan?

Thomas was a MacLeod? How could that be?

"I saw you in the hallway that first day." Thomas looked anything but bleary-eyed now. He was sitting up, bracing himself with his hands on the table.

"Aye."

"And you're a ghost."

"Aye, lad. That, too."

Thomas seemed to chew on that for quite some time. "My mother is a MacLeod," he said finally. "She sees things others don't."

"As do you, apparently."

"Unfortunately."

Iolanthe pitied the poor woman, with such an ill-mannered son as this. Well, at least the mystery of his lineage was solved. She wondered how she should feel about having this lout as a kinsman.

"You'll accustom yourself to it all in time," Ambrose said. " 'Tis a blessing, actually, that seeing."

"I think the jury's still out on that." He frowned suddenly. "Speaking of seeing, do you know anyone who wears mouse ears and travels?"

Ambrose sighed heavily. "Hugh McKinnon. Sorry to say it, lad, but he's a laird back in your father's line—"

Hugh appeared next to Ambrose, beaming. "A good e'en to ye, grandson," he said, bobbing his head a time or two. "Now, Tommy lad, forgive me that I couldn't present myself to ye, understand, for at the time—"

"Hugh," Ambrose said with a sigh, "we've business to attend to."

"Aye, I can see that," Hugh said, sitting down and making himself comfortable. "I'm sure you'll want me in on it."

"And I'm just as certain we won't," Ambrose said.

"But—"

"Perhaps you and Thomas can share a cup of ale at a later time," Ambrose said.

"But—"

"A much later time."

Hugh looked as if he planned to protest again, but apparently something in Ambrose's eye convinced him he shouldn't. He grumbled something under his breath but rose just the same. Iolanthe watched as he bowed with a flourish and popped his cap back onto his head. "I'll come to ye later, grandson. When we have some peace for speaking," he said, giving Ambrose a pointed glare.

"Well . . ." said Thomas.

Hugh disappeared.

Iolanthe looked at Thomas. Well, at least the man was still breathing normally. She'd come to find that most mortals upon seeing a ghost gave in to a mighty case of hysterics. Then again, this man here seemed passing arrogant and excessively full of his own words. Perhaps he was too stupid to be afraid. Either that, or he'd seen so many ghosts already that day that he was impervious to being further startled.

Thomas rubbed his hands over his eyes, then looked at Ambrose and took a deep breath.

"You know my sister, Megan?"

"Of course," Ambrose said. "I arranged her marriage to young Gideon de Piaget."

"Of course," Thomas said faintly. He toyed with his glass and the bottle on the table for a moment or two, then looked at Ambrose. "If I ask you a few questions," he began, "will you answer them?"

"Ask all you like," Ambrose said easily. "I've naught but time on my hands and a love for a goodly bit of talk."

Iolanthe caught herself before she snorted again. Ambrose always told the truth, and never more than when he said he loved to talk. She sat down on the little boot bench by the door and settled in for a long evening.

"Who is she?"

"Who is whom?"

"Herself up the way."

Iolanthe pursed her lips. Ah, here was the question indeed. Perhaps he intended to have answers as to how to rid himself of her so he could be about his work with his accursed tools.

"And why, lad, would you be wanting to know that?" Ambrose asked.

"Well," Thomas began slowly, "I met her today. And I have no idea what came over me."

All the fatal flaws in your character? she wanted to ask.

"She does have that effect on men," Ambrose murmured into his cup.

Iolanthe glared at him. She was quite sure he felt the heat of it because he rubbed the side of his neck absently.

"Well, actually I do know what came over me: a gargantuan headache. It wasn't much of an excuse for how rude I was to her, but—"

Aye, "but," she thought sourly. *Here comes the excuse, indeed.*

"I looked at her, standing there in the sunlight, and . . . well . . ."

My wee brain caught fire and left me with no wits, she finished with a snort. She almost wished he could hear her thoughts and know just what a reprehensible oaf she found him.

"I read this poem once," he said. " 'Loveliness shone around her like light/Her steps were the music of songs.' " He looked up at Ambrose. "Do you know it?"

"I don't, lad."

"It's Lachlan MacDonald," Thomas said. "I couldn't think at all when I was looking at her, but that's what came to me once I could think straight again. It's a fair description of her, don't you think, those lines of verse?"

Iolanthe couldn't have cared less if Saint Michael himself had been wielding the pen when those words had been put to parchment. She could only gape at Thomas in surprise. He was using such to describe her?

"Then you found her beautiful," Ambrose prompted.

Thomas shook his head. "No."

Iolanthe was almost relieved to find that she hadn't misjudged his character. He was simply without redemption. Flawed. Unpleasant. Besides, why would he have found her beautiful? She knew the truth. She'd seen her own visage—

"Beautiful is too tame a word," Thomas said, interrupting her thoughts. "She was . . . stunning."

Iolanthe was sure she hadn't heard him aright. Stunning? What meant he by that foolishness? That she was so ugly that she left him gasping with horror? She looked at him narrowly. He wasn't gasping in horror now. In truth, he was smiling—and the sight of that was almost her undoing. By the saints, he was a handsome man. When he smiled, she could almost forget his lack of character.

"I'd walked into that hall expecting to find another Connor MacDougal, or perhaps a dozen of him, facing me, so when I saw her, I was, well, speechless. Which for me is a rare condition."

Would that it afflicted you more often, she thought, but she couldn't muster up any venom to go with the thought. If he wanted to think her beautiful, poor fool, then he could, she supposed. She was too surprised that such a thing would occur to him to do much but stare at him, dumbfounded.

"And then what happened?" asked Ambrose. "I take it you found your tongue."

"I told her my name, and she wasn't exactly impressed. Things get fuzzy from there, and I'm not sure quite what I said. My head was killing me, and it was all I could do to stand up. I'm fairly sure I was very rude."

He paused. Iolanthe supposed a more foolish woman might have thought he looked almost repentant.

"I made her cry."

"I daresay they were tears of rage, not hurt," Ambrose said placidly. "Herself has a fiery temper."

"I owe her an apology."

"I'd say you do."

"If she'll listen."

Ambrose shifted a little uncomfortably. "Well, I daresay you may not have her full attention the first time. I'd keep at it, were I you."

Thomas looked at him closely. "Then you know her? You know her name?"

"I know her," Ambrose said.

"What's her name?"

"Don't know it," Ambrose said evasively.

Thomas blinked. "You don't?"

"It's something of a secret of hers," Ambrose said.

"Hmmm," Thomas said with a frown. "Well, then what do you know about her?"

Ambrose smiled into his cup. Iolanthe saw him do it and knew he was about some kind of mischief. She was half tempted to urge him on. Perhaps he would startle the fool into some sort of fatal heart condition.

Then again, perhaps she should bid Ambrose cease with his games. If he chatted Thomas up long enough, the oaf would spout more of that ridiculous nonsense he'd been blathering on about before.

About her being lovely, and all.

"I know her father," Ambrose was saying.

"And?"

Ambrose only smiled.

"Are you going to make me beg?" Thomas asked.

Ambrose stretched with his cat's smile, and Iolanthe shook her head. Here came the killing blow. The man hadn't held the chieftainship for so long without having a mighty head for strategy. She could scarce wait to hear what he was going to say to destroy Thomas.

"Are you sure you want to know?" Ambrose asked.

"I'm sure."

Ambrose paused dramatically. "Well, lad . . ."

Thomas waited. Then he frowned. "Yes?"

"Well, she'd be your . . . aunt."

Thomas stood up so fast, his chair went crashing back onto the floor. He slapped his hands on the table.

"My *what*?" he shouted.

"A wee bit removed," Ambrose said calmly. "Trace your mother's line back to the fourteenth century and the laird Malcolm. You'll find that he has a pair of daughters. The younger was Grudach. The elder is your vision up the way."

Thomas leaned on his hands and hung his head. "My aunt."

"Your half-aunt, if you want to put a finer point on it. Your mother's ancestor and the lass up the way had different mothers."

"Oh, that's a relief." Thomas looked calculatingly at the bottle, then shook his head. "I'm going to bed."

"Best place for you. Rest your head."

"My aunt," Thomas muttered as he walked around the table. He paused at the door. "Well, outside of that news flash, it was a pleasure talking to you, my laird."

Iolanthe watched as Ambrose preened like a peacock. He beamed a smile over his shoulder at Thomas.

"My pleasure, grandson."

Thomas left the chamber with a shake of his head. The door closed behind him. Ambrose drank deeply from his mug, as if he hadn't a care in that white-capped head of his. Iolanthe rose to her feet.

"You old fool," she grumbled.

He looked at her and winked. "Auntie."

"Be silent," she said in disgust.

Ambrose laughed as he rose, crossed the room, and pulled her into a ferocious hug. "Come and have a tankard of ale with me. It seems years since last we did so."

"It has been years," she muttered, but she didn't protest

when he tugged on her hair affectionately, nor did she decline the offer of a chair before the fire next to his and a hefty mug of drink. She sat and drank, then found that she couldn't ignore his assessing gaze any longer. "What?" she demanded, looking at him.

He only smiled. "A father's worry, my girl. Nothing more."

How was it when he called her *girl,* it was full of affection and concern? Would that her father could have shown her the like. Would that she'd had a father such as Ambrose.

"You know," Ambrose said slowly, "there are many men who are not good."

"Stop reading my thoughts."

" 'Tis difficult not to, when you think them so strongly. Your father, I daresay, was less of a man than he might have been."

"You've been talking to Duncan."

"As it happens, I have. He is my kinsman as well, you know, and he has a fine head for thinking. But that isn't how I knew of your sire. Unlike you, my dear, I get out and travel about. There is much to be seen in this world, and you've no reason to lock yourself away in that keep."

The reason she stayed was such a foolish one, she could scarce bear to think on it. To think she remained confined simply because she didn't want to travel about without a man to share the view with her.

A particular man.

And a particular view.

"And whilst I was out traveling about, I visited your sire," Ambrose continued.

"You didn't!"

Apparently he had no fear of her temper, for he only looked at her placidly. "Raging and roaring like a stuck boar, as you might imagine." He shivered. "Don't know as how anyone gets any sleep in that keep with him howling at all hours."

"And he stopped bellowing long enough to talk to you?"

"I am a MacLeod as well, my girl, and I can shout as long and as loudly as the rest of them."

"And what did the wretch have to say for himself?" She knew no words would excuse him, but 'twas an idle curiosity she had.

"It was more what he didn't say." Ambrose looked into the fire. "You were but a wee thing when your elder brother was murdered and your mother wounded so grievously."

"I had passed ten summers already in his hall," she interrupted.

Ambrose sighed. "I cannot answer for his actions. Perhaps your sire went mad from his grief."

"He didn't. He'd been whoring about for years. He certainly had no trouble taking a mistress and siring other children on her—and that years before my mother was wounded."

"As I said, he was not himself."

"And I am to forgive him for that?" she exclaimed, then she shut her mouth with a snap, horrified by how plaintive her question sounded. She threw her mug into the fire. "That doesn't excuse him."

Ambrose merely looked at her. "I think you need to forgive him more for yourself than for his own absolution. Whatever neglect, whatever injuries he did to you are in the past."

"They feel as fresh as if 'twere yesterday."

"Aye, and they bind you to those stones up the way as surely as if by chains."

And with that, he turned away and contemplated the fire. Iolanthe had nothing else kind or polite to say to him, so she stomped from the kitchen in a fury.

Her anger lasted all the way back along the road and almost all the way to the keep. It failed her just before she reached the barbican. She looked at the castle in front of her and cursed it. Aye, 'twas her prison, as surely as her father's was in the north. And, just like him, she wasn't sure she would ever free herself from it.

Then she realized just what she hadn't done. She'd gone to the inn to seek Ambrose's advice on how to rid herself of a man who had offended her so deeply, only to listen to that same offensive man describe her in glowing terms she was certain no one had ever used on her poor self before. She'd left without any ideas on how to rid herself of him.

Of his bad-mannered self.

Of his astonishing compliments.

"Oh, by the saints," she said in disgust.

Mayhap she would go back down on the morrow and consult with Ambrose on how she could be about her business. She wasn't about to go down again that night. Perhaps on the morrow Thomas would come back to the keep, and Connor MacDougal would push him off the parapet and save her the trouble of having to do it.

Or perhaps he would come and say to her face what he'd said to her kinsman.

She sighed, called herself a dozen kinds of fool, and went back into her prison.

Chapter 9

Thomas stood at the bend in the road where he could just begin to see his castle. He stared at it thoughtfully, trying to firm up his plans in his head. He had wanted to spend the night thinking about them, but after his conversation with his grandfather heaven only knew how many generations removed, his head had been pounding so hard that he'd gone straight to bed and passed out. His head was better today, but his plans were no closer to being thought out.

Would she be there again? Would she even speak to him?

Would he get a chance to give her what he held in his hand?

He smiled wryly and started up the road to his—or was that her—castle? Whatever the deed said, he could hardly deny that the person who really had a claim on those stones was that nameless, beautiful woman who haunted them.

Who haunted him.

His half-aunt, no less.

He trudged along, sincerely hoping he wasn't on his way to making a colossal fool of himself. He bypassed the protestors, who carried new signs and pelted him mercilessly with words. Ignoring them was no trouble. Ignoring the other souls who loitered about the gates would be a different story.

He sighed deeply. It seemed like he'd done this a thousand times before. He wondered if that was because he had the only flowers he'd been able to scrounge from the garden clutched in his hand like a five-year-old ready to present them to his mother.

Only he wasn't going to see his mother.

And he had a damned large audience.

The usual suspects were loitering at the front gates. Thomas fixed a serious look on his face. These were bribery flowers. Anyone with any business sense at all knew that the best way to get your foot in the door was to come bearing gifts.

At least that's what he told himself as he watched the entire group of Scots look at what he was holding in his hand, then, as if on cue, erupt into gales of hearty laughter. Well, all except Connor MacDougal, who only regarded Thomas with his customary look of malice.

"Come a'wooin', have ye?" he demanded.

"I'd say it isn't any of your business," Thomas answered easily.

"Won't work," Connor said.

Thomas raised an eyebrow. "You've tried?"

"With that acid-tongued wench?" Connor said with a huff. "Who'd want her?"

All right, so Thomas didn't know her all that well. So she was actually his half-aunt quite a few generations removed, and that should have been enough to give him pause. None of that mattered. First off, she was a woman and, as old-fashioned as it might have seemed, he made it a point to treat women with more respect than he would have his buddies in the locker room. Second, she was without a doubt the most arresting creature he'd ever seen, and that alone should have made up for whatever other flaws she might have reportedly had. Third, and lastly, he was quickly acquiring an intense dislike for the former laird of the Clan MacDougal.

"You and I, my laird," he said looking up at the man coldly, "will someday come to blows, I think."

"She won't want yer pitiful blooms," Connor sneered.

"Maybe not." Thomas smiled briefly and walked around him and past the suddenly silent group of men that watched.

"She won't want ye either!" Connor bellowed.

Thomas didn't deign to answer.

"Witless mortal! I'd say ye couldn't tell one end of a blade from the other!"

Well, the MacDougal had a point there, but Thomas wasn't going to concede it to him. He'd never considered learning swordplay, but maybe it wouldn't be such a bad idea. That led him to uncomfortably speculate on the reasons why that seemed like such a good idea. Was it because it would be a handy thing to know how to do or because it would impress *her*?

As if she would even be impressed by anything he might do! He imagined he could take down an entire squad of Scots, and she probably would just yawn. He could only guess how quickly he would find his flowers thrown back in his face. Though he couldn't deny that he would deserve it, maybe he could plead having had a migrainelike headache on the afternoon in question and hopefully receive a bit of mercy.

He tried not to wonder why it mattered to him.

He also tried to ignore any more self-initiated probes into the condition of his mental state. He'd considered that far too often of late. The truth was, he was so completely out of his element that he hardly recognized himself anymore.

Take last night, for instance. He'd gone down the kitchen, helped himself to a bottle of whiskey and a glass, then found himself completely unable to ingest the vast quantities of it any rational man would have, given the circumstances. Instead, what had he done? He'd had a conversation with his four-hundred-year-old ancestor about a woman who just happened to be his six-hundred-year-old aunt.

And both of them were ghosts.

And if that wasn't bad enough, now he was bringing apology flowers!

He clapped his hand to his forehead in an effort to bring some sense back. It only hurt, which made him wonder if it might not be a good time to go back to bed where he would be safe.

He understood ice and snow and sheer mountain faces. He understood staying alive outdoors in all kinds of weather. He understood business and how to survive all kinds of attacks from within and without. He understood construction and tools and finish work.

He didn't understand women.

He especially didn't understand medieval women who were ghosts.

He walked into the bailey, then caught sight of the garden to his right. It was the part of the castle he'd missed the two times before. There was a wall there, probably seven feet tall, but he knew it wasn't part of the outer defenses. It seemed to enclose some kind of space, and he could see from where he stood that the area was filled with a riot of flowers.

He walked under the arched entrance, then found himself unable to proceed further. It was the most amazing thing he'd ever seen. The garden was huge, and he supposed that in times past it might have included a small training area or perhaps stables and other buildings necessary to the running of a medieval keep.

Now all it contained were flowers. Thomas could hardly take in the scope of what he saw. Not that he was much of a horticulturalist. He knew some of the plants around his house—such as that uncomfortable familiarity with the rhododendron outside his front door—but past a few rosebushes and pansies, he'd couldn't put a name to much.

It probably would have taken him a month of poring through reference books to have looked up everything he saw. The flowers bloomed madly, riotously, and unnaturally, given the time of year. Those realizations passed through his mind, but he didn't stop to consider them. All he knew was that the castle had to have one hell of a gardener to produce this kind of beauty at this time of year. The flowers he held in his hand were simply weeds in comparison.

And then he saw her.

She was sitting alone on a stone bench placed against the wall. As before, her stillness reached out and touched him. And as it did, he understood how quickly and heedlessly he tramped through life. Though he didn't consider his pace unusual, he certainly pushed hard when he needed to. Even climbing mountains, he usually made a quick business of it. Rarely did he linger at his summits.

But to sit and be still?

With her?

It was overwhelmingly tempting.

He started down the path toward her, trying out different kinds of apologies and wondering which would be the most effective. He could dazzle her with semantics, excuse himself with a dozen clever explanations, bowl her over with enough justifications to weary a judge. But would it make a difference?

She sat still, her hands in her lap, dirt on her dress and on her fingers. Her hair was pulled back in a braid, and it fell over her shoulder in a fat, heavy tail. Thomas cleared his throat as quietly as possible, but she looked up just the same.

And the flowers in the garden disappeared.

Thomas looked to his right and gasped. Nothing but dirt and stone. He looked back at the woman. She brushed her hands off on her gown.

But she said nothing.

Thomas could scarcely put two words together. He gestured helplessly toward the former garden.

She merely looked at him.

"But," he managed, "it was so . . . so incredible."

She still didn't offer any comment. The only thing that he found even marginally reassuring was that she wasn't weeping anymore. Maybe she wasn't wearing an exactly welcoming look, but she wasn't weeping, and he'd take that any day. He held out his flowers.

Well, weeds.

"I'm sorry," he said.

She didn't move.

He tried again. "I'm very sorry."

"About what?"

"About what I said the other day."

"Yesterday?"

"Yes. Yesterday. I went too far."

"Did you?"

He wondered if she was torturing him on purpose. "Yes," he said firmly. "I did. And I'm sorry."

She looked at him appraisingly. "Are you?"

He suppressed a sigh. "Do you always answer a question with another question?"

She looked down at her hands thoughtfully. "It gives away fewer answers that way, I suppose."

"I'll give you that," he said. He held out his flowers again. "This is my peace offering. It doesn't compare . . ." He gestured toward the dirt and rocks. "But it's the best I could do."

She stared at the flowers for several moments, then looked up at him. "Thank you."

He waited. And he waited a bit more, but she made no move to take his flowers.

"They're yours," he said finally.

"Aye, I understood that."

He wondered if he could survive a year living in the same place with this woman without her wearing what patience he had down to nothing. He smiled briefly.

"You're supposed to take them."

"And how is it you suggest I do that?" she asked, looking at him solemnly. "With hands that cannot hold them? With arms that have not the strength to lift them?"

Thomas found, for the second time in as many days, that he had absolutely nothing to say. Obviously, there were some things he was going to have to figure out. But he'd never had dealings with a ghost before, so he could hardly be blamed for a few faux pas. With any luck, by the time he'd figured it out, he wouldn't have completely destroyed any possibility of a relationship with her.

He set the flowers down on the bench next to her, finding himself very relieved that the bench was actually of a temporal nature.

"I'm sorry," he said quietly. "I didn't think."

She folded her hands in her lap and leaned her head back against the wall. Thomas wanted to believe that she had almost smiled, but that was probably wishful thinking. He cleared his throat.

"Could I sit next to you?"

She shrugged. "If you like."

Damn, there went his palms again. How was it possible that a grown man of thirty-four very well-lived years could be such a geek around a woman who wasn't even real?

But she looked real.

And since sitting seemed preferable to falling, and he suspected that if he thought about his present circumstances any longer he would probably fall down from the complete improbability of them, he sat.

He stared out over the dirt. He burned with questions he hardly dared ask. But a coward he wasn't, so he plunged ahead.

"Will you tell me your name?" he asked.

She looked him full in the face. The full force of her gaze made him light-headed.

"My name is mine," she said quietly.

Fair enough. He tried another tack.

"Where were you born?"

"You're determined enough, aren't you?"

"What do you think?"

She sighed and looked away. "I was born in the Highlands. My sire was Malcolm MacLeod, my mother Moira Mac-Donnell. The year of my birth was 1358. Does that satisfy you?"

"No, but it's a start." In reality, he could hardly believe he'd gotten that much out of her. He wondered how much more she would talk if he got her to do something besides sit and parry questions with him. "Would you show me your castle?"

"*My* castle?" she asked with pursed lips. "I thought 'twas your castle."

"Your payment came at far greater cost than mine."

She considered, then looked at him. "Why will you see it? So you can decide where 'tis best to first wield your implements of destruction?"

He shook his head. "I won't do anything you don't want."

"Is that so?"

"It is."

"And if I want nothing done at all?"

Well, she had him there. Damn. He'd have to be very careful what kind of mouthy promises he made in the future. He took a deep breath. "I'll have to do something with at least a part of it. I need a place to live."

"The inn looks passing comfortable to me."

This was not going as well as he'd planned. He took another deep breath. Hell, at this rate, he was going to be hyperventilating before long.

"I don't want to live at the inn."

She shifted on the bench to look at him fully. "Why did you buy this keep?"

There was no answer but the honest one.

"I was compelled," he answered.

"By what?"

"I have no idea."

She looked at him searchingly. "In truth? You had no reason at all in mind?"

"I had no reason that makes sense. It came up for sale, and I bought it without having seen it, without knowing anything about it. My sister sent me a picture, but I'd already dreamed of it before I saw it." He looked at her and smiled. "I climb mountains. I make money with other people's money. I never thought to own a castle."

"I see," she said thoughtfully.

"But I have no regrets about it," he said quickly.

"Don't you?" she asked, looking up at him with a half smile. "The MacDougal doesn't give you pause? Your friends with the songs outside the gates don't deter you?"

"I can ignore what's outside in favor of what's inside."

"Do you expect me to keep the garden blossoming for you, then?"

He shook his head with a smile. "I wasn't talking about the garden."

She looked vaguely perplexed, then her eyes widened and she looked at him in surprise. Then she stood up abruptly.

"I'll show you the keep," she said, walking away.

Thomas was no expert when it came to women. He'd spent years being baffled by his sisters. Even his mother made him shake his head now and then. That he was bewildered by this woman shouldn't have come as that big a surprise. Whatever he'd said had apparently sent her running. Maybe he should can the compliments until he was sure how they would be received. It was a good thought, one he'd consider later, after the tour.

"This was where they have, at times, kept horses, a garden, a poor wooden chapel, and the mews," she said, waving at the area to her left.

"Would you rather it be a garden?" he asked, but she had already turned and walked purposefully away.

"I'll show you the great hall," she said over her shoulder.

All right, so conversation would have to wait. He followed her under the arch in the gate and toward the great hall. There was a cluster of Scots loitering nearby. He looked at them and smiled. Several of them scowled in return, but a handful looked at him with what might have approximated pleasant expressions. At least Connor MacDougal wasn't there, brandishing a sword.

Thomas followed his guide obediently. Her explanations were limited to brief namings without elaboration.

First came the great hall, with its missing roof, then the alcoves built into the outer walls where men had, he supposed, first stored arrows, then munitions for use in keeping an enemy at bay. She showed him where the garrison hall had been at one time, then the kitchen with its modern marvel of a cistern to store clean rainwater for use in cooking. The well was still there, too, covered over but apparently not polluted.

There was a very large tower in one corner of the outer wall. Thomas stepped inside and looked up three stories to the still sound stone roof. He could see where the wooden floors had been, with niches in the walls to use for scaffolding. There were hearths with flues. The second floor was accessible from the parapet, and he could see where a set of stairs on the outside of the tower led one up to the third and final floor.

It was by far the largest and most usable space he'd seen so far. And it had a very pleasant feel to it. He looked to his right and saw his companion staring off into the distance. He clasped his hands behind his back in what he hoped was a nonthreatening pose.

"I really won't do anything if you're completely opposed to it," he began slowly, "but if you don't mind, I think I'd like to start here."

She sighed. "I suspected this might suit you."

"Would that bother you?"

She shook her head. "Nay. Nothing untoward ever happened here."

Thomas stepped back out into the sunshine and looked at the one corner of the keep where they had not been.

And a chill went through him.

"I will not go there," she said.

Thomas looked at her and felt the answer to his unasked question resonate in his soul. That was where she had lost her life. Hadn't she said as much the day before? It was also, oddly enough, the only part of the castle in perfect condition. It was as if that section of the keep had been sealed against the ravages of time.

"Have you never been back inside?" he asked quietly.

She shook her head.

"I imagine he's dead by now, don't you?"

She looked at him bleakly. "Does it matter?"

Well, he wasn't about to tell her how to deal with her past, which was apparently very much the present for her. He smiled grimly.

"I'll see how bad it is."

"I don't want to know."

"I understand."

But he also knew he had to see for himself, so he walked across the courtyard. He spent a brief moment considering the fact that his unwilling hostess had spent the better part of the morning showing him around her castle. She easily could have told him to take a hike. That she hadn't, and that she was even speaking to him in brief sentences, was significant.

He came to a halt in front of the guard tower. Now that he was standing in front of it, he could completely understand why his guide hadn't wanted to come. There was something exceptionally unpleasant about the vibes he was getting from the place in front of him.

Well, standing there uncertainly wouldn't dispel any uneasiness he had, so he took a deep breath and stepped through the dark doorway. And as he made his way up stairs that were impossibly small and incredibly claustrophobic, the déjà vu that overwhelmed him was staggering.

He'd been up these steps before.

He felt as if the past had somehow layered itself over his present in such a way that it was he and an echo of himself that crept up the stairs together.

It was, on the whole, an extremely unsettling experience.

He stopped at the landing. There was a torch in a sconce there. He pulled a lighter from his pocket—he didn't smoke but he had been a Boy Scout and he was nothing if not prepared—and lit the thing. He was almost surprised that it caught.

He put his hand on the wood of the door and the two worlds of past and present shuddered together with an almost catastrophic collision.

He gasped as he pushed the door open. He couldn't breathe. He wondered if he might ever again suck air into his desperate lungs. He hunched over with his hand on his thigh, gulping in great breaths of air and trying to keep the torch aloft at the same time. It seemed forever before he managed to stand up straight. He leaned against the doorway and looked inside the guardroom.

And for an instant, he saw a man there with his sword bared, standing before a woman who refused to cower.

The woman he'd left standing in the bailey.

He blinked. And the vision was gone.

He walked into the tiny guardroom with its stone floor, ceiling, and walls. He jammed the torch into another sconce and walked to the window slit. As he stared out over the countryside, he felt the effects of the almost surreal events of the past ten minutes recede, leaving him weak. He put his hands on the walls on either side of the window and bowed his head. There was something going on, something far larger than him, something he had never expected.

Did she relive this every day that dawned? Was this what she lived with each one of those days?

" 'Tis a small place."

He turned around at the sound of her voice. She stood just inside the room, hovering on the edge of the light like a shadow. Thomas waited, perfectly still, as she took a step or two inside. She looked down at the floor for several minutes, then she looked up at him.

"I remember it being bigger."

He nodded carefully. "I think we do, with things that frighten us."

She shivered and wrapped her arms around herself. "It was all for foolishness, you know. All for the sake of a secret that would have had no meaning to him."

"Your name?"

"Nay, the secret of my home."

"Your home has a secret?"

"Several of them, or so the tales go." She looked back

down at the floor. "He wanted my name as well, but I wouldn't give him that either."

"What did your family call you?"

She was silent for quite a while, then she spoke. "My father called me *girl*. My half-brothers called me various things. Most of them not pleasant."

"What names?" he asked gently.

"Old woman," she said with a half shrug. "Heather-gel."

"Because of your eyes? The color?"

She looked up at him then. "Because they were fools," she said shortly, "and there was an abundance of the stuff surrounding our hall."

He walked across the chamber until he was standing in front of her. He looked down into her eyes and felt himself on the edge of knowing something. It was that damned intuition again, but it was only nagging at him, not providing him with answers.

He racked his brains for something that made sense. He considered the word *woman* in all the languages he knew. He spoke German and French, knew a smattering of Japanese, Italian, and Greek, could ask for the nearest bathroom in Russian and Dutch, and could haggle for a yak and a cup of Sherpa tea in Nepali.

None of that was helping him at the moment.

Heather. Violet. Lovely.

And then a word popped into his mind, a word he was certain he must have read somewhere in some obscure spot on some far-flung travel.

Violet.

Greek.

"Iolanthe," he said.

She couldn't have looked more surprised if he'd slapped her. Her mouth worked for several moments, but no sound came out.

"How did you . . . how . . . who told you . . ."

He was so surprised—no, in reality, he wasn't surprised at all. Once her name had left his lips, he realized he'd always known it, just as he'd always known dozens of other impossible things. He looked at her helplessly. "No one told me," he said. "I just . . . knew."

She started to cry.

Damn.

"I'm sorry," he offered desperately. "I never meant . . . it's a lovely name—"

But she was gone.

"Please come back," he said earnestly. "I never meant to upset you!"

There was no answer.

"I won't tell anyone!"

There was only silence in response.

He closed his eyes briefly, then leaned back against the wall and opened his eyes. He looked around him and let the past and present swirl around him in dizzying eddies. He wanted to call out to her again, but he suspected it was futile. He had no sense of her being near.

And if she had any sense, she would be far away.

Well, perhaps he had once again done enough damage for the day. He looked at the torch and had no idea how to blow it out. Rubbing on the floor seemed like a good idea, so he did so until even the embers were extinguished. Then he felt his way down the stairs, across the courtyard, and out the front gates. No Highlanders lingered at the barbican to heckle him. No protestors lined the road to sling slander at him.

Ambrose was, however, waiting for him, leaning casually against the outside of the crumbling castle wall.

"Finished, grandson?" Ambrose asked.

Thomas didn't bother to ask why Ambrose had come. Maybe he had heard Thomas shouting from the inn.

They started off down the road.

"I guessed her name," Thomas said.

Ambrose's jaw slipped down. "You did?"

"Didn't you hear me yelling for her to come back from out here?"

Ambrose shook his head. "I just came out to enjoy the evening and thought I'd wait for you." He looked closely at Thomas. "How did you guess? How did you even know where to begin?"

Thomas looked at him helplessly. "I have no idea. I just knew it. I just know things."

"She couldn't have been happy about it."

"She cried again."

Ambrose opened his mouth to speak, but the bellow from behind him stopped all hope of conversation.

"There he goes! After him! To me, lads! The MacDougal!"

Thomas sighed. "My friend, Connor MacDougal." He turned to face the Highland chieftain bearing down on him. "Can I help you?"

"So," Connor said, his chest heaving, "ye thought to escape 'afore I could see to ye, eh? Not this time, ye wee—"

"Connor," Ambrose said wearily, "shut up."

"Shut up?!" Connor drew his sword with a flourish. "I'll be avenged for that, ye wee silly woman! Bring out yer blade, unless ye've forgotten how to wield it."

"You're the bloody woman, MacDougal," Ambrose said, drawing his blade with a great whoosh.

"And ye're a field faery, MacLeod!"

Ambrose looked at Thomas. "You can stay if you like, grandson," he said conversationally. "This won't take long. . . ."

It was amazing how swords that were seemingly made of nothing but thin air could ring so truly. Thomas had the feeling that sword lessons might have to be bumped up on his list of priorities. Just in case the odd laird decided that his head really would make a fine gate post adornment.

He walked down the path, leaving the sounds of battle behind him. He turned at the bend of the road and looked back at the keep. Was she watching? Would she ever speak to him again?

Iolanthe MacLeod.

It was a beautiful name. No doubt it had been her mother to give it to her. One thing puzzled him, though. How could a girl live out a good portion of her life in the close quarters of a Highland castle without anyone knowing her name?

Well, that was a mystery indeed. He suspected that the story would provide him a great many of the answers to the questions he still had about her.

Assuming he could ever pry the story from her. After today, he wondered if she would ever show herself to him again. Maybe the next time, if there was a next time, he could just keep his big mouth shut. Not everything he thought had to come out in words. He could grunt and shake his head. He could just smile and nod.

It would probably be safer that way.

Or maybe he should just get to restoring the castle, keep his hands busy, and his conversation to a minimum. He wondered if it would be too late to root around in Mrs. Pruitt's shed. It was past time he got to work. It would be nice to have at least some part of the castle put together before it got really cold.

He could only hope that the chill would come just from the climate.

He sighed. It looked like another apology was in the offing.

Chapter 10

I olanthe knelt in the midst of her herb garden, pulling
weeds. That she had allowed weeds to grow there in the
first place should have given her pause, but she steadfastly
ignored any hidden meaning that might have been found in
her actions. What she did know was that if she'd had the
sense given a thistle, she would have been anywhere but
where she was. She would have left the keep the night before
and never returned. She would have at least ensconced herself in some bloody nook somewhere to keep herself out of
eyesight of any prying soul who might happen by.

A pity that she wasn't so wise, for there she was out in
the open, kneeling with her hands in dirt that wasn't real,
tending flowers that weren't real, and dreaming of things that
could never be real.

Such as a man to love her.

She savagely yanked a particularly nasty interloper out.
How much more wise she would have been to have spent
her time regretting the moment of weakness she'd had when
she'd agreed to let Thomas McKinnon ruin what was left of
her poor keep.

Well, should he be bold enough to return, she would
merely ignore him. If he spoke to her, she would give him
no answer in return. If he approached her, she would give
no indication of having marked him. He would be less than
nothing to her.

That man who knew things he shouldn't.

"Iolanthe is a lovely name, you know."

She was up on her feet with her hands at Roderick's neck
almost before she realized what she was doing. She shoved
him, tripped him, and took him down to the dirt, all with her
hands still clutching his throat.

"Don't you ever," she said, banging his head smartly against the ground, "*ever* use that name again!"

"But—" he gurgled.

" 'Tis not yours to use! I did not give it to you."

For all his preening, he was still a man and still stronger than she, notwithstanding their ghostly status. She found that much as she protested, her fingers were still pried away from his flesh and she was still pushed back until he could sit up. She jerked away from him and staggered to her feet. She stood, glaring down at him, her chest heaving.

"Eavesdropper," she accused.

"I wanted," he said, rubbing his throat and straightening his ruffles, "to make certain he did not take liberties."

"With me?" she exclaimed. "You fool, I'm a ghost!"

"Be that as it may," he said, rising gracefully to his feet and brushing off his trousers, "I felt I had a need—"

"To eavesdrop, you despicable worm," she spat. "There is no term low enough to describe you."

"It's Greek, you know," he said calmly. "Your name."

"I know," she said haughtily, but in truth she hadn't. Her mother told her 'twas a special word that meant *violet*. She had no idea if it was a word for the flower or the color itself. As far as that went, she'd only ever seen heather, so she had been left to imagine another flower of even more brilliant cast.

" 'Tis quite a lovely name. But," he added hastily, "I won't use it, if you forbid me."

"I do forbid you," she snapped.

"But you'll let *him* use it."

She ignored him.

"You didn't give it to him, you know," he pointed out. "Not freely."

"I am," she said tightly, "finished having speech with you."

"He took it from you."

"I said, I am finished with you!"

"May I call you Violet?" he asked, persisting in that infuriatingly polite way he had, as if he merely asked for a cup of tea and it would have been ungracious of her to refuse him. "Violet is a lovely name as well. I once had a lover named Violet—though she wasn't nearly as beautiful as you are, of course—"

A sword suddenly appeared, protruding from his chest. Roderick vanished with a mighty screech. Iolanthe looked at Duncan as he resheathed his sword and made her a low bow.

"At your service, cousin."

Iolanthe's relief at being rid of Roderick was swallowed up in apprehension that Duncan had heard the conversation. She considered him. "Did you hear what he said?"

He merely looked at her, his expression inscrutable.

"Do you know?" she asked miserably.

Duncan was silent for so long, she began to regret her question. She shifted uncomfortably.

"Lady," he said finally, "I was there at your birth. I was passing fond of your mother. And, unlike your sire Malcolm, I wasn't afeared to try my hand at a name I'd never heard before."

"Oh," Iolanthe said, nonplussed.

"And I remembered it long after he'd forgotten it."

She could hardly speak. "I see," she managed.

"But I've never used it, out of respect for what I knew to be your wishes."

She took a deep breath, moved almost beyond words by his loyalty. She tried a smile, but failed.

"And what of the men?" she asked.

"They know it now," he said with a shrug. "But I daresay none will utter it. Save the MacDougal, of course."

"Of course," she murmured.

"I'll see to whomever dares."

She had no doubts he would. She tried another smile then and was much more successful at that one.

"Thank you, my friend. Your discretion means much. Much more now that I know how long it has lasted."

He only smiled briefly and inclined his head. "By the by, my lady, you'll be interested in what's coming up the way. I believe we've a guest preparing to assault the keep."

"A tourist?"

Duncan pursed his lips. "Nay, lady, not a tourist. I believe this one has come to stay for a bit."

She blinked. "He's come already?"

"This cannot surprise you."

Iolanthe looked back over the garden at the wilting flowers still sitting on the bench where Thomas McKinnon had placed them. Though she couldn't say she'd accepted his apology fully, she couldn't deny that she had given him permission to begin his work. Of course, that had been before that startling bit of business in the chamber of her death. She wondered if that might be reason enough to withdraw her consent.

"He is yet without the gates," Duncan added slowly. "Shall he remain there?"

Iolanthe looked up at the sky, took a deep breath, then shook her head. "Let him do as he wishes." Perhaps if he was concentrating on his work, he would leave her be.

Not that she cared either way. She fully intended to ignore him. He could bang away at all hours for all she cared. She would simply pretend he didn't exist.

"Kinswoman," Duncan said, "this is your home."

"I've given him leave to improve it as he likes," she said.

"Hrmph," Duncan said, sounding unconvinced. "Very well, then. But I'll watch him closely, lest he make a nuisance of himself."

She shrugged, as if she couldn't have cared less, and went back to her gardening. Duncan turned and walked off purposefully. There was a part of her that almost felt sorry for Thomas, what with Duncan and his lads watching his every move. Perhaps he wouldn't even see them. Most mortals didn't. They walked through spirits without realizing what they'd done until they'd gotten a nasty chill.

Then again, Thomas McKinnon wasn't most mortals. He saw very clearly indeed.

She sat staring at the dirt for another half an hour before she found herself getting to her feet, dusting off her dress, and looking about for something else to do. She was restless. Aye, that was it. She needed a bit of a walk to soothe herself. And if that walk took her through the bailey, who could fault her for it? She made her way from the garden, fully intending to continue on her way out the front gates. But the sight in the bailey made her pause.

Thomas was sitting in the dirt a goodly distance away from

the tower he'd selected for his work. Roderick stood next to him blathering on about the saints only knew what. How did the man concentrate with all that nonsense being spewed at him? She knew she never could, which was why Roderick so often found himself skewered on Duncan's sword.

She looked across the bailey, noting that the entire garrison was there, leaning against various walls and sharpening various bits of their gear. Connor MacDougal stood near the southwest guard tower, glowering. She was surprised neither by his choice of location—no one save him loitered at that place of evil if they could help it—nor by the expression on his face. She supposed Thomas was lucky Connor was a ghost. It would not have gone well for him otherwise.

She intended to walk straight toward the gatehouse without turning either to the right or the left. But instead, she found herself crossing the bailey and stopping behind Thomas. Who knew what sorts of mischief Roderick was stirring up? She felt she had no choice but to see for herself and stop it if need be.

"You're a poor artist," Roderick said with a sniff.

"Yes," Thomas said placidly.

"I could do much better."

"I'm certain you could."

Iolanthe watched Roderick scowl and couldn't help but wonder what he was about. Was he purposely trying to force a confrontation?

"Your manner of dress is highly questionable," Roderick said disdainfully. "I wouldn't be seen in such low clothing."

"I'm sure you wouldn't."

"And I suppose you think your hair is far less unfashionable than it truly is."

Thomas put his pencil down and looked up at Roderick. "Why don't you tell me what it really is you want to say? You're wasting your time trying to insult me."

"Leave her alone," Roderick snapped. "She doesn't want you. She doesn't want you here."

"You know," Thomas said evenly, "out of all the women I've ever known, the lady of this keep strikes me as the least likely of any to mince words. If she doesn't want me here, she'll tell me."

"*I'm* telling you."

"She can speak for herself."

Roderick drew his saber with a flourish. To Thomas's credit, he didn't flinch. Iolanthe watched Roderick fumble for a moment with the blade, poke himself sharply in the arm with it, then spew forth a torrent of curses at Thomas.

"I haven't finished with you," he vowed.

"You and the rest of the garrison," Thomas said with a sigh. "Take a number."

Iolanthe watched Roderick vanish with another curse. Indeed, the entire garrison seemed to have found other things to do, for she realized that she was alone in the bailey.

Well, other than the man who sat in the dirt, drawing.

The man she had vowed to ignore.

So he thought her more than capable of speaking for herself. Perhaps she would then, especially about the events of the day before. Powerfully cheeky of him to have blurted her name out without warning.

And powerfully unsettling that he'd known it.

Just how had he known it?

She turned that mystery over in her mind for a goodly while as she stood behind him and watched over his shoulder as he drew. Perhaps Roderick was more particular about his renderings than she, for what she saw looked skilled enough. She took a step closer and studied what Thomas had done.

He'd drawn the tower before them, yet it was as if it missed the front of its walls, for she could see inside the chambers. There were three floors, as it had had originally. She watched as he drew various bits of furniture in the lower floors. The top floor, however, soon began to have some changes made to it. More windows were added. Once that was done, things began to appear inside: a chair or two; a tapestry frame; a table for working. It was very luxurious, to her mind.

"Do you like it?"

She jumped when she realized he was looking over his shoulder at her. "How can you see me?" she demanded.

"How could I not?" he asked with a smile.

There was no useful response to that, for she suspected that if she told him that he could have used self-control to his advantage, he would have spouted some sort of nonsense about . . . well, about something foolish.

So she only grunted at him with what she hoped was a proper amount of disgust.

"Do you like this room?" He gestured to the topmost floor.

There was no point in lying. She suspected that he would know it anyway.

"Aye," she said grudgingly. " 'Tis fine enough, I suppose."

"Anything you would change about it?"

She shook her head. A chamber so luxurious would have been far beyond the reach of her or anyone else she'd ever known in life.

He tapped his pencil against the drawing. "I noticed," he began carefully, "that you didn't show me any place that was yours." He looked up at her. "When you showed me the castle."

She blinked at him. "Mine?"

"A room of your own. Where you go for peace, if you need it."

"Why would I need such a thing?"

"Don't you ever want to have somewhere to go to be alone?"

She almost said, *That's what the forest is for*, but then she began to wonder why he was asking the question. He was idly drawing odd bits in the topmost chamber, things that would be pleasing to a woman's eye. She could scarce believe that he might set aside a place just for her, something he would build with his own hands for her comfort.

A place of her own.

What an astonishing idea.

"A place for peace," she managed. "Aye, that would be nice enough, I suppose."

His smile was truly the most beautiful thing she'd ever seen. It made her want to smile. It made her want to wrap herself in its warmth. It made her want to do something else to cause him to grace her with it again.

It made her want to check her forehead for fever.

"Then this room will be yours," he said. He took off his coat and spread it out on the dirt next to him. "Will you sit with me?" he asked.

Damn him, even a hint of that smile was going to be her undoing. All her fine resolves to keep him at a distance were somehow lost in the beauty of that smile. She found herself, fool that she was, sitting down next to him on clothing, though she surely didn't need to protect herself from dirt that would never in his lifetime or anyone else's sully her skirts.

She sincerely hoped the MacDougal wasn't laughing himself ill. Then again, perhaps that would be a boon. If he were suffering in some corner of the keep, she wouldn't be forced to listen to him point out in words what a complete horse's arse she was being.

"Are you interested in the details?"

If it would mean more of his smiles, she supposed she was. "If you will."

"All right then. Laying the floorboards will be easy," Thomas said as he pointed to his drawing. "I'm hoping the fireplaces will work—or that we can make them work eventually. Electricity would be nice, but it may be impossible."

"Electricity?"

He looked at her. "You know, power. Current."

She looked at him blankly.

"Lightbulbs?"

She nodded uneasily, though she had no idea what he was talking about. There were those strange lights at the inn that seemingly had no flames, but she'd never thought to inquire as to what powered them. She'd assumed 'twas Ambrose or one of his lads about some mischief.

Thomas put his pencil behind his ear and turned to look at her more fully. "When was the last time anyone lived here?"

She stared at the sky thoughtfully. "Duncan could tell you with more exactness than I—"

"1746," Duncan said, materializing in front of them. "After the slaughter at Culloden."

She watched Thomas look at Duncan and blink a time or two in silence. Then he cleared his throat.

"I don't think we've met," he said, standing up.

"Duncan MacLeod," Duncan said, planting his feet a manly distance apart and putting his hand on the hilt of his sword. "Cousin to my lady. I will defend her to my dying breath."

Well, that was a bit much, but Iolanthe couldn't help but feel warmed by Duncan's loyalty. She looked at Thomas to make certain he was receiving the tidings with the proper amount of respect.

"I see," Thomas said, nodding. "I certainly don't intend to give you any reason to put me to the sword."

Duncan grunted. "See that you don't, lad." He looked at Iolanthe. "I'll be nearby, in case you need me, lady."

Thomas sat, watched Duncan move a goodly distance away, then looked at Iolanthe.

"The MacDougal wants to decorate your gates with my various and sundry severed body parts, and now your cousin is warning me not to hit on you."

She stiffened in surprise. "You would strike me?"

"It's an expression. It means—well, never mind what it means. No, I would never hit a woman. You're safe with me."

And for some reason she could not fathom—though she was certain it had come from the most ridiculous portion of her underused heart—she felt as if he spoke the truth.

Thomas looked around as if he expected another interruption. When none materialized, he looked at her with a smile.

"I was going to tell you about power."

"Aye."

"Well, there once was a man named Benjamin Franklin."

She shook her head. "I'm not familiar with him."

"I can tell you about him, if you like."

She wasn't about to admit the full extent of her ignorance, but perhaps it was so apparent that there was no need. But still it did not sit well with her to be possibly considered less informed than he.

"I know people as well," she said defensively.

"Do you?"

She looked at him closely but could see no mockery in his eyes. She lifted her chin. "Aye. I saw Queen Mary once."

He looked genuinely impressed. "Really?"

"And James I, as well. From a distance, you understand. They never would have come to stay at this hall."

"Fascinating," he said, putting aside his drawings. "I studied history, but I never thought I'd ever be hearing a firsthand account. Will you tell me more?"

How was it—and the saints preserve her, *why* was it?—that such a simple expression of interest was enough to set her heart to pounding in her chest? By the saints, he was but a man—and a mortal one at that!

But as he looked at her so expectantly, she found that she could do nothing but begin to tell him hesitantly about the people who had come her way over the years. Many were unimportant, but there had been a few before the troubles of '45. And during it all, he sat and watched her with rapt attention.

"Amazing," he said.

His frank regard made her unaccountably nervous. She had to force herself to sit still and not flee. She looked around frantically for some kind of distraction.

"What of that Franklin?" she asked, grasping for the first thing that came to mind. "I suppose he was loitering over in the Colonies?"

"Actually, he loitered quite a few places. He was quite instrumental in getting the Colonies away from George III."

"I imagine His Majesty was none too pleased with him."

"Probably not," Thomas agreed.

Iolanthe frowned. "Was that who was king then? This George you spoke of?"

"Yes," he said kindly, "that's who was king then."

"Then tell me more. About them both," she commanded, hoping she sounded a bit aloof.

And thus proceeded a very long afternoon for her. She heard all manner of tales about this Benjamin Franklin, then there was talk about currents and watts and other things she couldn't for the life of her fathom. Then came the illustrations with arrows and lines going in every direction.

It began to give her a pain between her eyes.

"Sorry," he said, flipping his page back to the one he'd begun at the first. "I get a little carried away with the whole construction business. Feel free to stop me if it gets to be too much."

"Stop."

He laughed as he folded up his book and turned himself to face her. Then his smile faded.

"I owe you another apology."

She wasn't sure what was more distracting: the lightness of his eyes or the darkness of the hair that fell down into those eyes. Or maybe it was that chiseled jawline that she found her fingers itching to touch. She'd never had such a thought in her life, and she could scarce believe she was having one now—especially given the fact that she could do nothing about it.

". . . apology?" he was saying.

She blinked. "Apology? For what this time?"

"For yesterday." He looked as penitent as she'd ever seen a man before, which hadn't been all that often, but he did indeed look sorry. "I didn't mean to take your name from you."

The surprise and panic she'd felt the day before came back in a rush. "How did you know it?" she whispered. "I've never told a soul. I vow I haven't."

"I just knew," he said, looking as baffled as she felt. "Sometimes, I just know things."

"You're fey."

That made him smile. "Actually, that's never a word I've applied to myself, but I guess it fits now and then." He tapped his book with his drawing pencil for a moment or two, then looked at her from under his eyelashes. "How did you come by your name?"

She sighed. There was no use in either being angry with him for knowing or refusing to give him any more of the details. He would likely pluck them out of thin air just the same to spite her. "My mother gave it to me. It wasn't as if she was learned," she added quickly, "for she wasn't. But she loved words and how they sounded against her ear."

"But it's a Greek word. Greece is a long way from Scotland."

"My father's hall is not easily reached, true, but it always seemed to attract the odd visitor."

"The secret of the keep and all that?" he asked with a smile.

"Aye, that."

"It must be a good one."

"Most secrets are."

He laughed. "Point taken. I won't ask for the details. Tell me instead of these visitors."

"Minstrels, foreigners, scribblers of tales," she said with a shrug. "My mother learned their words and gathered them up in her heart. 'Twas from one of them that she learned my name, for he said 'twas a word for violet. That was the color of her eyes."

"Which are your eyes."

She nodded.

He was silent for a moment before he spoke. "Will you," he asked slowly, "let me use your name?"

She found, suddenly, that she couldn't answer him. No one had ever used her name, save her mother, and only when they were speaking for each other's ears alone. She hadn't heard her name from the lips of another soul in over six hundred years. Did she want to start now?

With this man?

At least, she decided finally, he had asked permission.

"I won't use it in front of the others," he added. "I'll be discreet."

And that, for some reason, made her feel as if she were making more of it all than she should.

"You think I'm being foolish," she said.

"I don't. It was something you would have given your life for, wasn't it?"

"Aye," she agreed. "Likely so."

"Then it's important to you." He smiled easily. "If you don't want me to use it, I won't."

She found she couldn't speak.

"But if you don't mind me using it, would you give it to me?"

She closed her eyes and prayed for some return of her wits. After a moment, she opened her eyes and looked at the man sitting next to her, fully intending to give him a list of reasons why she couldn't do what he asked.

Then she looked at him truly, saw the strength in his face, the kindness in his eyes, and found her heart softening with a frightening swiftness.

By the saints, she was going to give it to him. She wanted to believe she was powerless to do anything else, but she couldn't even hide behind that weak excuse. She *wanted* to give it to him.

So she took a deep breath.

"My name," she said clearly, "is Iolanthe."

"Iolanthe," he repeated with a smile. "Thank you."

"You may use it," she added quickly, before she thought better of it. "Discreetly."

"Of course," he agreed. "But I don't think any of the men would use it even if they knew it, if that's what worries you."

She stood before she knew she meant to and wrapped her arms around herself. " 'Tis late. You should go."

He stood more slowly, took up his coat and put it on. He gathered up his book, then paused and looked at her.

"I won't abuse your trust."

"See that you don't," she said with as much haughtiness as she could muster. "It isn't given lightly."

"I'm well aware of that."

She looked at him and wondered what was possessing her to keep her talking to a mortal who had no means of understanding her sorry existence, who would likely hammer in his nails, grow bored, and then leave. She hadn't the time for this kind of foolishness.

"I'm going to Edinburgh for supplies tomorrow," he said quietly. "But I'll be back the day after to start work. If you have no objections."

"Would such serve me?"

"They would."

It was tempting to push him, just to see how far she could.

Then again, if he were there working, she might have a few more of his smiles.

"Daft," she muttered with a shake of her head. She was daft and foolish and likely deserved whatever heartache came her way, for 'twas a certainty she would have brought it on herself. She looked at him. "Off with ye, ye silly man. 'Tis no doubt growing cold out."

"Good night, Iolanthe."

He smiled, then made her a little bow and walked away. She watched him go, then realized the bailey had suddenly become full of others who were watching her watch him.

She swept them all with a glare and most of them suddenly found other things to do. A few hardy souls braved her look and continued to watch her with interest, but she took care of them with her most formidable scowl. Roderick was standing glowering against a wall, but she turned away before she had to listen to any of his babbling.

She walked up the stairs onto the crumbling parapet and looked at the tower where Thomas McKinnon would build her a place of peace. She wished mightily that the deed was already done, for she certainly could have used a bit of privacy at the moment.

She had just given her name to him freely.

After so many centuries, 'twas a noteworthy event indeed.

She stood there long after the garrison had settled in for the night. And once all was quiet, she sought out her accustomed place on the bench in the garden.

It was a very long time before she closed her eyes.

Chapter 11

A week later, Thomas sawed through the last bit of the floor joist he was working on outside, then set the saw aside, straightened, and arched his back in a stretch. He'd gained an entirely new respect over the past couple of days for men who had built things with their bare hands—literally. He was starting to miss his power tools.

Well, he'd made do with less in far more precarious places. At least the ground floor was done. Maybe the bottom floor had originally boasted dirt, but he'd decided on hardwood. The floor had taken him three days to lay, but it looked great. He and his help had since begun work on cutting the second-floor joists. Thomas knew he was pushing his lads probably harder than he should have, but he felt a sense of urgency about getting everything put back into shape as quickly as possible.

It probably had something to do with the look on Iolanthe's face when he'd told her he was building her a room of her own.

He laid down his saw and walked into the tower. The floor beneath him was solid. Now that the groundwork was laid, the scaffolding was going up for the next floor. He stood there and let the significance of it settle into his soul. It was a great deal like building a relationship. Groundwork, then construction of various levels, then the finishing touches.

He shook his head with a smile. Too many comparisons between the restoration of the tower and his relationship with Iolanthe MacLeod would give him nothing more than a headache—and he'd already had one of those that had knocked him flat.

Relationship?

He stepped back out into the open before his thoughts led

him down that path of no return. He saw the woman in question immediately, but he didn't do anything past dart a glance at her. It was probably safer that way. Even though she'd been watching him off and on for the whole of the day, he suspected it was more to make sure he didn't demolish anything rather than a desire just to watch him.

He looked up into the sky and decided that perhaps it was time to pack it in. A look at the hired help he'd found in the village revealed two young men who'd probably had just about enough of looking over their shoulder every two minutes to make sure no ghost was about to jump them.

Working on a haunted castle was hell.

"Burt, Charlie," he called, waving them over. "Let's call it a day, okay?"

They looked as if they'd been given a reprieve from the guillotine.

"Be here bright and early tomorrow," Thomas said. "With any luck, the rain will hold off and we'll get the next floor laid. I'd like to be finished before the end of the week."

Burt was looking about him nervously. "As ye will, sir."

Charlie only gulped and nodded, his face a pasty white.

Thomas smiled and clapped them both on the shoulder. "Take a deep breath, guys."

"But I've heard . . ." Burt began.

"Aye, so've I . . ." Charlie agreed.

Thomas pulled out a fat wad of notes and divided them between the young men. "Listen harder to my money than you do to pub gossip. The scariest thing around here are the protestors outside the gates. They aren't very fierce, are they?"

That seemed to distract the pair because they walked off, discussing whether or not they should have run over the three picketers who had stretched themselves across the entrance to the castle that morning. Thomas had been tempted, but had decided that perhaps protestoricide wouldn't look good on his record. He had to admit to dropping a chunk of wood or two on the men as he carted things over them, but could anyone really blame him for that?

He smiled to himself as he gathered up his tools and stowed them inside the tower. Once that was finished, he stood at the doorway and looked over the courtyard. Iolanthe was gone. Oddly enough, he found himself feeling surprisingly bereft.

And then it struck him just who he was missing.

A woman who was a ghost.

What in the hell was he doing? Looking for a woman who, for all intents and purposes, didn't exist? He leaned against the doorjamb and looked up into the late-afternoon sky. All right, so he could get used to seeing ghosts. He'd seen plenty of wacky things over the course of his life. He could get used to living with a bunch of Highlanders dogging his every step. He'd seen worse. Tiffany's tenacity would have left them in the dust.

But being interested in Iolanthe MacLeod?

The improbability of it all was almost enough to make him walk out through the barbican and go home.

He was a flesh-and-blood man. He needed the same kind of woman. What made sense, at least in his head, was for him to go get in his car, head to Edinburgh, and look up the business associates he knew. Surely there would be potential introductions to datable women as a result. Hell, if worse came to worst, he could think of a dozen women in New York who wouldn't be opposed to flying over for the weekend, or longer.

Get hold of yourself and walk through the front gates.

Yes, that was what his head was telling him. And it wasn't as if his head had often led him astray. He used it for thinking quite often and found it completely satisfactory.

Then again, his heart had led him to Maine and convinced him to build a labor of love there.

Head. Heart. Which was in charge?

He wasn't sure he wanted to find out.

He stepped out into the courtyard and turned himself toward the gate. His head would have the first shot at keeping him sane. It would certainly make the most self-preserving decision.

He was halfway to the gate when he stopped. Maybe he was being a bit hasty. After all, he wasn't committing to a lifetime with the woman. He was just going to be polite and say good-bye. For the evening.

Then again, maybe he should just go and count himself well rid of potential heartache. After all, he'd ended numerous things over the course of his life—climbs and businesses both—and never looked back with regret. Life was all about endings.

But, his heart argued, *the house in Maine is all about beginnings.*

He stood in the bailey and argued with himself so long over what he should be doing that when he finally gave up in disgust, he found he had an audience. A very large audience. One that was watching him with various expressions of humor, irritation, and pity.

He glared at them. "Got things on my mind," he said in his most manly fashion.

The men were, almost without exception, apparently unimpressed.

Thomas turned abruptly toward the garden. He was just going to be civilized—something Connor MacDougal would probably never understand. The rest of the men could think what they wanted. He would make nice with Iolanthe, then get the hell out of there before he really got in over his head.

He paused at the entrance and looked down the pathway that hugged the wall. The afternoon had waned, but there was plenty of light to see the woman kneeling near the path's edge, weeding. He closed his eyes and swallowed, hard. He wanted to tell himself that he was losing it. What he really wanted was for there to be some reason why he was losing it.

But all he could think of was a woman who tended something she loved and lived an existence that wasn't of her choosing. And if that wasn't enough to break his heart, he was certain he couldn't imagine what would.

He opened his eyes. Heart it would be, then.

He walked along the path, then came to a stop next to her. She looked up at him solemnly.

And he was forever and irrevocably lost.

It wasn't her beauty, because that was something that perhaps could have been argued about. It wasn't even her life status, because many could have made a case for leaving her alone based on that alone. It was the dirt smudged on her cheek. It was the way her hair fell down her back in a fat, heavy braid with little bits of it escaping all over. It was a simple dress that matched the color of her eyes. It was the stillness, her stillness, that drew him in and made him want to be still as well. That was why he climbed, after all. For that brief moment of stillness high up in the air where he could be at peace. That he had found the same with another person was nothing short of miraculous.

He knelt down next to her. "It's beautiful."

"The garden?"

"That, too."

She did smile then, and his heart broke a little at the sight. "It isn't much, but it passes the time." She returned to her digging. "Your lads survived the day."

"Barely. I'm sure they'll have incredible kinks in their necks from swiveling them around to make sure they weren't about to be attacked."

"I warned off the garrison," she said defensively.

"I never doubted it," he said. "Some people are just a little intimidated by what they can't see."

"And you aren't?"

"I am lucky enough to see fairly clearly."

"Is that lucky?"

He considered how it might have been, had he not been able to see her, and his heart gave a lurch.

"Actually," he said, "I think it is."

She looked at him for a moment, then turned back to her work. "You're going now."

"Well, no. I'd like to stay for a while, if you don't mind."

She shrugged and pulled out a particularly nasty weed.

"How do you do this?" he asked. "How do you make the garden?"

She sat back and looked at him. "It is but illusion."

"It doesn't look like illusion." He reached out his hand to touch a rose petal. He could almost smell it, and he was certain that if he'd tried hard enough, he could have touched it as well. Just the smallest bit more substance, and he could have felt it beneath his fingers. "It's amazing."

" 'Tis nothing more than you do," she said, reaching out to pluck a flower from a bush. "Do you not create your thoughts in your head before you speak them?"

He considered. "I suppose so."

"Your plans for the tower. Were those not created in your head before you drew them?"

"Definitely."

She shrugged. "So it is with my garden. I create it in my mind, and thus it takes shape here before me."

"It's pretty convincing."

" 'Tis centuries that I've practiced doing it."

He made himself comfortable next to her. "Did you garden when you were a girl?"

"Aye, I did."

She didn't seem inclined to elaborate, but he wasn't one to give up that easily. He was nothing if not persistent, so he pressed on.

"What kinds of things did you grow?"

"Herbs."

"What kind of herbs?"

"Medicinal ones."

He pursed his lips. "Are you enjoying yourself?"

She smiled as she rooted around another plant of indeterminate origin. "Aye."

"I'm trying to get to know you."

She sat back on her heels and looked at him then. "Why?"

"I'm interested."

"Why?"

"I can't help myself."

She looked at him narrowly. " 'Tisn't much of a reason."

"Would you rather hear that you're the most remarkable woman I've ever seen, and I want to know everything about you?"

"Fennel," she said promptly.

"Fennel?" Well, that wasn't so hard. "You grew fennel?"

"Aye," she said.

"It sounds useful."

"You would have no doubt found it quite so."

He smiled smugly. "A manly herb, then?"

"Actually, we used it to heal idiocy."

He blinked, then laughed out loud. "Well, I'll file that away for future use. Now, what else did you grow? And please leave out all the herbs you think I need to heal my flaws."

" 'Twill be a powerfully short list, then."

He scowled at her, but she only smiled, then began to tell him of her garden. He noticed that she paused often, as if she judged the depth of his interest. In reality, she could have been talking about the intricacies of defluking sheep, and he wouldn't have cared. It was enough that she was talking to him.

His heart was satisfied.

Of course, listening to the contents of her garden was fascinating as well. As was hearing all she didn't tell him. Judging from the time she spent either tending her plants or carrying them down to the village to heal the sick, he gathered she didn't spend all that much time hanging out with her family. She said nothing about her father nor did she mention any siblings, and he assumed she had all of the above.

"What did you do for fun?" he asked.

"Fun?"

"Amusement. Entertainment. Something other than work."

She looked off into the distance for a moment or two. "I went up into the hills," she said slowly, staring out over the garden, unseeing. "Or down the meadow in front of our keep. Where I could turn my back on the hall."

Ah. That was something to chew on.

"I see," he said quietly.

She brushed her hands off briskly. "It grows late."

Thomas looked around him and realized that it would have been pitch dark if it hadn't been for the full moon. He laughed uneasily.

"I think I was distracted."

"Gardening will do that to a body," she conceded. "You should go back to the inn whilst you can still see to get there."

He rose, then looked at her still kneeling at the garden's edge. And it struck him how completely wrong it was to leave her behind. Building her a solar was great, and maybe that would solve the problem in the future, but it did nothing to ease his mind for the coming night. Where would she go? Where would she sleep?

"Iolanthe . . ." he began.

She turned back to her garden. "Off with you, now. 'Tis a fair walk."

"I really think—"

"That you should hurry? Aye, I agree. I've work to do here and no need of further distraction."

This was not what he wanted to do.

"Will you—" he began.

"I've work to do," she said, not looking at him. "So do you. Morning comes early."

Well, it looked like there was no point in arguing with her. Today. But tomorrow was another day.

He jammed his hands into his pockets. "I'll see you tomorrow, then."

She nodded, but she didn't look up at him.

Thomas backed away, then turned and walked in a sideways kind of way that any crab would have proudly claimed. He just couldn't take his eyes from her. And he was quite sure that the sight of her kneeling in the dirt with the moonlight falling all around her would haunt him for the rest of his days. The desperate loneliness of it was almost enough to make him retrieve his sleeping bag from the inn and unroll it near the bench.

He paused by the garden gate and waited to see if she would look up. And if she had, he would have made good on his plan.

But she didn't.

He sighed, turned, and walked out into the bailey. He nodded to Duncan, who stood guard at the garden entrance, ignored the MacDougal and the Victorian Fop, and parted the large cluster of Highlanders loitering at the gate with almost no thought at all. His eyes were too full of what he'd left behind, and he vowed to himself that he wouldn't leave her behind again. It was clear to him that his head was no longer in control of his fate—and maybe that was for the best, because if he listened to logic at the moment, he probably would have returned to the inn, packed up his suitcase, and headed back to the States.

Instead, he went back to the inn, ate what Mrs. Pruitt had left for him, and went to bed.

He had the feeling he would need all his wits about him for the battle ahead, because he was just sure that wherever he wanted to lead her, Iolanthe wouldn't go quietly.

Chapter 12

Iolanthe watched as Thomas's workers went about their business. They were no less nervous than they had been the day before, nor since they'd come to work several days earlier for that matter. Her men circled about the lads like ravenous wolves harrying a hapless sheep, despite her having warned them off. They wouldn't show themselves, but she couldn't stop them from hanging about. The saints pity the lads should an all-out battle ensue between them and any number of indiscreet Highlanders.

She walked out into the bailey purposefully and called for Duncan. He dragged himself away from his post near the barbican and came to her.

"Aye?"

"Those are lads who need no encouragement to carry tales to the village. I've asked the men not to show themselves, but I'm worried they'll do it just the same."

"I'll see to it."

She watched him go and wondered if her word would be enough. She had been at the keep the longest, and apparently that was reason enough for hers to be the final say—at least at times. The MacDougal certainly would have been happier had things been different. She was a woman, after all. She looked over the men and couldn't help but be a little grateful that they respected her as they did. Perhaps it was that she was of their ilk. Why they found themselves at her keep, though, was still something of a mystery to her. Duncan, she understood. He was kin. Several other MacLeods had come south as well, and that she understood, too.

As far as the others went, perhaps their ancestral homes were too crowded either with the living or with their enemy dead raising a ruckus—like her father howling forever in the

Fergusson's dungeon—that a bit of peace wasn't unwelcome. The MacDougal was, as usual, a mystery as far as his motives went, but perhaps he was eternally spoiling for a good fight and thought he'd come to the proper place for it.

Thomas was coming out of the tower, looking very weary. She found herself, quite suddenly, meeting his gaze. He smiled, and she quickly looked down at herself.

He shouldn't have been able to see her.

Maybe he had it aright about seeing so clearly. She'd never known another man who had such a gift. Or a curse. She suspected it might be the latter as Thomas clearly saw the MacDougal sharpening his sword. Perhaps even a mortal blind to those things of the spirit wouldn't have missed hearing the insults Connor spewed forth. She had to admire Thomas's ability to ignore the man. She wished she could have done the same.

She found herself a quiet rock and went to sit upon it. It would have been a lovely thing to sit in the sunshine and be warm, so she pretended she could feel the like. It was a pleasant afternoon at least, with no rain and but a little breeze. It wasn't often that she had the peace to simply sit and look about her. Usually she was mediating some sort of dispute, listening to Roderick babble, or simply brooding her time away. In fact, she couldn't remember the last time she'd merely sat thusly and let her thoughts wander.

Perhaps she had Thomas to thank for that.

The night before had been something of a wonder to her. At first, she'd been bewildered by his interest in her garden. She'd thought that perhaps he'd had one of his own and needed suggestions for plants. That he would be interested in what she was doing simply for interest's sake had been a curious thing indeed. At first, she'd found herself rather uncomfortable talking about her past. But with time, she'd found it perhaps not easy, but possible to think on her memories. Indeed, she'd spent the rest of the night simply staring off over her garden, remembering the things about her life that she'd loved.

Her garden, surely. She'd claimed a little bit for her own and grown what pleased her. She'd tended the whole of it, especially when there was no friar to do the like, but that little patch of her own had been a joy to her.

As had been walking the hills behind her house. No one had ever missed her, save Duncan. She'd caught him keeping watch over her a time or two and eventually convinced him to teach her how to fend for herself. In time, she'd been able to escape alone for a handful of days at a time. Only during the summers, of course, but the peace had been welcome. Duncan had also taught her how to use a knife to protect herself, so she'd never feared for her safety. Besides, she was nothing at her keep. It hadn't occurred to her that someone might want to harm her simply because of who she was.

And that, she had decided sometime during the night, was likely why she hadn't taken the English-man seriously when he'd come to the keep. She'd never suspected that he would want her, whatever the reason. And when he'd taken her away, she'd been too surprised to snatch up any kind of weapon to aid her.

But perhaps the most startling revelation of the night had been that there was a man—albeit a mortal one—who found her interesting enough to ask questions of. She'd given Thomas many opportunities to yawn, stretch, and beg to leave. She'd fully expected him to suddenly announce that he was tired and would be going.

She hadn't expected him to stay well past moonrise.

Stranger still was that she was presently finding the sound of hammers and saws soothing. She leaned back against the wall and listened to the work going on inside the tower. Thomas was driving his lads hard, and for what reason, she couldn't imagine. To her mind, the longer it took him, the longer he would stay.

And that she wanted him to stay was difficult to believe.

Perhaps she should have been wed when she was young, before she'd grown so old that the passing attentions of a completely unsuitable man were enough to bring her to her knees with gratitude.

She looked up to find that same man standing in front of her, smiling down at her. And it was without difficulty that she understood why his attentions had undone her so.

He was, in a word, beautiful.

"May I sit with you?"

"Aye," she managed.

He sat down on a rock next to her and leaned back against the stone wall. "It's a nice day out. Not too hot. Not too cold."

"How lovely."

He smiled at her. "Yes. You are."

She almost wished he wouldn't say things such as that. "I've already given you leave to restore the tower," she said grimly. "You needn't try to flatter me anymore."

"Is that what you think I'm doing?"

She had no intention of answering that.

"Iolanthe," he said quietly, "I never lie, and I don't exaggerate. And I don't flatter to get what I want."

"Hrmph," she said.

"You're beautiful, a pleasure to talk to, and I can't get you out of my mind whether I'm here or at the inn. So sue me."

"Sue you?"

He smiled briefly. "It's something we say in the States. You would translate it as 'If you don't like it, take me out back and chop off my head.' "

That seemed a little drastic, even to her.

"The MacDougal would be more than happy to help, I'm sure," he added dryly.

"He has a sour disposition," she said. "I wouldn't take much note of him, were I you."

"I'll keep that in mind." He stood up. "I'm going to go get the lads taken care of, then I'll be back. Will you wait for me?"

"Ah . . ." she stalled.

"It won't take long."

She meant to tell him that she had things to do, pressing things that didn't allow her to wait on a man's pleasure. Of course she had things to do. Many things.

Which was why she said "Aye" as readily as a lovestruck twit and remained where she was. And, even worse, she watched him walk off and suspected that there might have been an almost pleasant expression on her face.

"I do not like him."

She looked at Roderick, who had suddenly made himself visible next to her. "Why not?"

"He's too glib."

"Perhaps he's in earnest."

Roderick snorted.

"He could mean what he says," she said stiffly. "About me."

He pursed his lips. "It isn't the subject of his praises I disparage. It is the delivery." He looked at her. "When I tell you you're lovely, you call on that devilish protector of yours and I find myself skewered on his sword."

"Mayhap 'tis because I find you less than sincere."

He looked so shocked that she began to wonder if she had misjudged him.

"Me?" he asked, his hand to his breast. "Insincere? My dear Io—"

She glared at him, and 'twas likely very formidably done, for he shut his mouth immediately and chewed upon his words. When he'd apparently mastered his errant tongue, he cleared his throat.

"I flatter, to be sure, but that is habit. With you, my lady, rest assured that the flattery is sincere."

She found that she had absolutely nothing to say to that either. Perhaps it would have been better if she had been accustomed to receiving compliments whilst she was alive. That men, admittedly only Roderick and Thomas, found something about her worthy of flowery words now was quite astonishing.

"I—" she began.

He scowled at her, then vanished.

Well. That was something.

Then again, sincere though he might have been, Roderick had been a thorn in her side for centuries, and she wasn't about to look on him with any more favor than she had in the past. The saints only knew what sorts of flatteries might result from that. Intended or not.

She turned her mind back to her day and realized that she actually had something to look forward to. Waiting for Thomas McKinnon should have been a silly thing, but she found that it seemed of great import.

Daft, she was. Perhaps she was the one in need of the fennel to cure her idiocy.

Yet even so, she sat in the sun and waited, as she said she would do. It was quite a bit later when Thomas and his lads emerged from the tower. She was surprised to see them come out through the door that led onto the parapet. Perhaps they had finished their upper floor after all.

Thomas dismissed his lads, then came to stand next to her. He looked up at the sky. "It's getting late."

"Aye, I suppose it is."

He took a deep breath, as if he steeled himself for some kind of battle.

"I was thinking," he began slowly.

Always a dangerous pastime, but perhaps he was more successful at it than most.

"Would you like to come back to the inn with me? The sitting room is usually fairly empty—"

"Och, and there'll be none of that!" Duncan exclaimed, standing suddenly in front of them. "She'll be well enough here, thank you just the same."

Iolanthe watched as Thomas very deliberately put his hands behind his back and looked at Duncan unflinchingly. "You are her cousin, and I feel quite sure that you have taken very good care of her over the years—"

"Aye, I have," Duncan said firmly.

"But I am a MacLeod as well—"

"Aye, through your mother," Duncan said, "or so I've heard."

Thomas blinked. "You heard?"

"I'm as capable as you of speaking with the laird down the way," Duncan said.

"Oh, I see," Thomas said, looking rather taken aback. "Well, I am trustworthy."

Duncan only grunted, sounding less than convinced.

"I promise I won't let anything happen to her."

"And how is it you'll protect her, hmmm?" Duncan asked archly. "With what?"

Thomas looked momentarily baffled, and Iolanthe couldn't blame him. But she also found quite suddenly that she wanted desperately to go with him.

The saints pity her for being three kinds of fool.

"Perhaps," Thomas said slowly, "once I've finished a bit of work on the tower, you'd teach me swordplay? I'm quite sure it will come in handy someday."

Duncan gave him the oddest look, but the look was there and gone so quickly that Iolanthe wondered if she'd imagined it. It had almost looked for a moment as if he'd been waiting for Thomas to ask something such as that.

Her cousin then cleared his throat and made a few gruff noises of pleasure. Iolanthe snorted silently. Thomas was wise, she'd give him that. Swordplay was Duncan's weakness, and teaching it to a willing pupil even more so. Duncan was, from that moment on, Thomas's man. With only one last piercing look, Duncan said he would go plan Thomas's training, and he went off, counting on his fingers.

"Where's he going?" Thomas asked.

"He's deciding the number of years it will take him to turn you into something useful on the field," Iolanthe said pleasantly. "He'll likely have to take off his shoes and use his toes soon."

"Thank you for the confidence in my abilities," Thomas said dryly.

"In building? Aye, I have confidence in you. Swordplay?" She looked at him and shook her head. " 'Tis never an easy task, no matter if you're born to it or not."

"I've done lots of impossible things in my life. This will be just one more."

She had to admire his complete arrogance, and she vowed right then to try not to enjoy it overmuch when Duncan ground him into the dust, as he most certainly would. She leaned back against the wall and looked up at him.

"So you have exploits?" she asked politely.

He considered her narrowly. "You sound unconvinced."

"You mortals lead a softer life now than we did then."

He cleared his throat and put his shoulders back. "I climbed the highest mountain in the world. And the steepest as well. And believe me when I tell you, they aren't one and the same."

She shrugged. "We have mountains in Scotland. They never seemed all that formidable to me."

His mouth had dropped open, and he seemed to be struggling to take in air. His look of complete astonishment was enough to make her wonder if she'd just insulted him thoroughly.

"Mountains?" he repeated with a gasp. "*Mountains?* You have *hills*. Bumps. Grassy knolls. I'm talking about *mountains*." He took a tiny rock and dropped it at her feet. "That's the highest mountain in England." He looked around him, then pointed to an enormous boulder. "*That's* the size of Mount Everest. It's *huge*. And the other, K2, is impossibly difficult. All right, so I admit that maybe K2 was pushing my skills a little—especially on the way back down—"

"You couldn't just sit down and slide?" she asked.

He was making those noises again, as if there simply wasn't enough air about him to aid him in breathing. She laughed at his consternation, and the look *that* earned her was enough to silence her abruptly.

"You laughed," he said, sounding as stunned as he looked.

"Aye, and I imagine I should be sorry for it."

"Well, you just insulted a big part of what my ego's based on, but I'll forget that. You laughed."

She shrugged with a smile. "I suppose so." She looked up at the sky and considered how long it had been since she'd done the like.

That she couldn't remember was the pity.

"Iolanthe, come back to the inn with me."

The depth of her good humor enveloped her with such agreeableness that she could hardly say him nay. But perhaps she was being too hasty. After all, she rarely left her keep. It was where she felt safe.

Not happy, but safe.

"I imagine they have an empty room as well, with a comfortable bed," he added.

Iolanthe sat there for what seemed to her a very long time, feeling the first chill of autumn brush across her soul.

Change.

The warmth of a comfortable house with family therein beckoned to her with a lure she found almost impossible to resist. There would be conversation there, companionship, laughter. No more haunting walls, keeping to the edge of the hall because she felt awkward with the men, wishing desperately for a place to sit that was hers alone and one where she was wanted.

"I'll stay with you," he said gently.

She looked at him, heard the earnestness of his words, and felt the strength and comfort behind them.

"You won't be alone."

Ach, but now the man was reading her mind. She looked up at the sky and considered how pitiful she was to wish for such simple things as those.

"You have family there as well," he added.

"Aye," she said, sighing, "but he's a blathering old fool."

"But he loves you." He smiled down at her. "That has to be worth something."

She rose. She could scarce believe the foolishness of her act, but she rose just the same.

"You're coming," he said, sounding pleased.

"If you like," she said with a shrug she hoped spoke volumes about her disinterest in the idea.

"Yes," he said. "I'd like very much. Besides, now I can give you a proper appreciation of just what I've climbed. You're not nearly as impressed as you should be."

And so she went with him, walked through the bailey and out her gates. She ignored the gapes of the Highlanders who lined the road as she passed, as well as the curses the MacDougal heaped upon Thomas's head. She ignored the fact that this was the second time in less than a se'nnight that she'd traversed these paths, when her usual visits never came more often than once a decade or so. And she most vigorously ignored the fact that she was walking along with a man at whose invitation she came.

A man she could never have.

But he was drawing her after him like a fey piper, and she followed with nary a thought in her head but for the pleasure of his company and the warmth that awaited her at journey's end.

"Who *are* you?" She stopped at the bottom of the road leading up to the inn and looked at him searchingly.

He only smiled and shook his head.

Fey and daft, that's what he was, she decided as she followed him.

And there she was, becoming just like him.

Chapter 13

Thomas sat in a comfortable chair in the inn's cozy little sitting room and savored both the fire at his feet and the company around him. It had been a remarkable evening, made all the more so by the people he had shared it with. He leaned back with a smile and replayed in his mind the events of the past handful of hours.

He had walked back to the inn with Iolanthe, almost surprised that she had come with him, yet not surprised at all. It had felt right. His heart had been content, and even his head had stopped shouting the impossibilities at him. He'd opened the front door for her, then walked with her into the entry hall, remembering vividly the first time he'd done the same thing and seen Ambrose leaning against the sideboard. He'd never thought to be walking through that door with Iolanthe at his side. She had seemingly thought nothing of it.

Mrs. Pruitt, on the other hand, had apparently thought a great deal of the occasion. She had taken one look at Thomas's companion, her eyes had rolled back in her head, and she'd started to slip toward the floor. Thomas had leaped around the counter and tried to catch her, but she'd stiff-armed him and dragged herself back upright. She'd put her shoulders back and produced her most businesslike expression.

Thomas had requested the inn's finest bedroom to be prepared—at his expense of course—and retained for Miss MacLeod's personal use for as long as she cared to remain. Mrs. Pruitt had said, manfully, that it would be done at once. She had only given Iolanthe another look of intense speculation before she'd made for the stairs. Thomas had invited

Iolanthe to sit with him in the library until dinner was ready. It had seemed the safest place to wait.

Dinner had gone off without a hitch. Iolanthe had sat next to him, looking as corporeal as he, but not touching a thing on her plate. The Preservation Trio, as he'd come to affectionately call them, had managed to down their dinner yet gape at her at the same time. Finally, one bold soul had asked her why she wasn't eating.

"Weel," she'd said, her accent as thick as pea soup, "ye ken hoo it is wit' a soor stoomach, aye?"

There had been no more questions, but Thomas hadn't had any trouble imagining what sort of speculation their strategy session that night would include. It was possible they could have thought her nothing but a simple village lass he'd picked up on his way home.

But how could anyone with two eyes in their head think that?

After supper, Thomas had retired to the sitting room with Iolanthe, promising her a thorough explanation of how far Everest was off the ground. Midway through trying to describe to her just how high 29,000 feet was, he remembered the pictures in his suitcase. He had grabbed them, then returned to the sitting room only to find that he was no longer alone with the woman of his dreams.

Ambrose and Hugh were there, chatting pleasantly with her. Thomas had found that his chair had been appropiated by Fulbert de Piaget, Megan's uncle-in-law—the usual generations removed. Thomas had spent a ticklish moment or two glaring at the man pointedly before the shade relinquished the chair with several uncomplimentary comments about Highlanders in general and their descendants in particular. Thomas had resumed his seat with satisfaction, then looked to his left at the woman whose company he'd intended to have all to himself. So he didn't have her undivided attention anymore. He could spend the evening looking at her, and maybe that would be enough.

She sat in an equally comfortable chair in the sitting room, with her long, slender fingers resting on the padded arms. Her dress was the same simple gown he'd always seen her in, but her hair tumbled freely over her shoulders and hung down in tight, heavy curls. The firelight played softly over her face, and he suddenly wished he had the talent to draw something besides very rough blueprints.

She should be painted, he decided. Just like this. With her features at peace and a soft light bathing her in an Raphael-esque glow. She radiated stillness and tranquillity.

"Why, ya bloody fool," she snapped suddenly, "what are ye blatherin' on about?"

Well, most of the time. Thomas put his hand over his mouth to hide his smile. Heaven help him if Iolanthe thought he was laughing at her. He'd already heard her give one of the other occupants of the sitting room the sharper side of her tongue.

"Ye silly girl," Fulbert said stiffly, "what would ye know about it?"

"I'm a Highlander!" she exclaimed. "And you and your bloody cohorts have been tryin' to steal my country for the past . . . um . . . How long has it been?" she demanded, turning to Thomas.

"Eight . . . nine hundred years?" he offered.

She looked unconvinced—and irritated.

"Maybe longer," he amended. "Much longer. I'm sure of it."

The discussion—if that's what it could be termed—only deteriorated from there. Thomas looked at the other members of their little after-dinner party. No one seemed to find the name-calling and shouting to be anything out of the ordinary. Then again, Ambrose was probably used to the bickering. Hugh was alternately wringing his hands in distress and glaring at Fulbert de Piaget as if he meant to do him intense bodily harm.

Fulbert, who was apparently Ambrose's brother-in-law by some unsavory quirk of fate (Iolanthe's characterization, seconded rather heartily by Ambrose himself), was an Englishman to the core and had no trouble defending his national pride. Every now and again, he would look at Thomas as if he expected some sort of aid to come from that quarter, then he'd mutter something about "bloody Colonists" and hop back into the verbal fray by himself.

It eventually came down to Hugh leaping up and unsheathing his sword with a flourish, Fulbert jumping to his feet and casting his mug into the fire before he drew his own blade, and Ambrose bidding them take their quarrel outside. Once they'd gone, Ambrose looked at Iolanthe.

"Nothing like a bit of stimulating conversation, eh, daughter?"

"Aye, my laird," Iolanthe said, stretching happily. "Stirs the blood quite pleasantly."

Thomas shook his head with a wry smile. Maybe after living in times where battle was the norm, a bit of enthusiastic talk was nothing but a diversion. Then he paused and frowned.

"You aren't her father," he said to Ambrose. "I thought—"

"She could use a father, don't you think?" Ambrose said. "Who better than me to take on the task?"

Thomas looked at Iolanthe. "Where's your father? Or do you know?"

"Or is that an ill-mannered question?" she asked.

He held up his hands in surrender. "You're right. Sorry. I'm just curious."

"Been bitten by the search-for-your-ancestors bug?" Ambrose asked with a twinkle in his eye.

"Well, as a matter of fact . . ." Thomas began, then he looked at Ambrose suspiciously. "How would you know?"

"Who do you think gave you your ideas?"

Thomas wondered how much of the remainder of his life he would spend with his mouth open, gaping in surprise at something this crowd said. Judging by the number of times he'd been left speechless already that afternoon, it would probably be a good chunk.

"You didn't," Thomas said. "You couldn't have."

"I whispered a suggestion or two whilst you slept."

"I thought those dreams were because of bad fish!"

Fulbert appeared suddenly out of thin air with his chest puffed out. "Now, if we wants to talk about dreams, let me recount me visit to that Dickens chap."

"Dickens?" Thomas repeated weakly.

Fulbert looked at him archly. "You think he came up with the idea for those ghostly visits on his own? 'Twere *me* visits that gave him the inspiration for his story. And if I'd had me way, *I'd* have had the credit for it."

Ambrose sighed deeply. "Leave off with your bragging, Fulbert. We've no stomach for it."

"Better bragging than casting about for matches to be made," Fulbert grumbled, heading for the door. "Why he thinks that's a proper activity for us, I *don't* know." He disappeared through the wood with a final grumble and curse.

Thomas looked at Ambrose. "Matchmaking?"

"Would you care to hear about your ancestors?" Ambrose asked pleasantly. "I'm certain between the lass here and me, we can provide you with all the names you'd like. Fetch something to write with, and we'll begin."

Thomas knew the subject was being changed, but maybe that was for the best. He wasn't sure he wanted to know anything more about Ambrose's dabbling in his dreams. Or his matchmaking activities. For all he knew, he was one of the intended victims.

But if the match was to be made with the woman sitting next to him, maybe it wouldn't be such a bad thing.

"Pen and paper, my lad," Ambrose said pointedly. "We'll give you such a list, genealogists worldwide will be green with envy."

Thomas rose with a sigh and dutifully retrieved what was requested. He sat back down and grabbed a book to use as a makeshift desk.

"Ready." He looked at Iolanthe. "What happened to your dad? Good end? Bad end?"

"You're determined to know, aren't you?" she asked, but she didn't look overly upset by it. "He's rotting in the Fergusson's dungeon, or so I hear. Good riddance to him." She looked at Ambrose. "And who else haunts the place with him? He can't be the only one starved to death in that pit."

"Ach, nay," Ambrose said pleasantly. "Many fine enemies, and a few allies as well, find themselves lingering there. And don't you know that Roger Fergusson still holds the key, even after all these centuries." He laughed. "Saints, but if that isn't a place to set a man's hair on end."

Thomas listened in fascination as they discussed the men of Iolanthe's day, allies and foes alike, as if they'd just seen them yesterday. And while he listened, when he could keep from staring at the woman sitting next to him who looked happier than he'd ever seen her, he made a list of whatever names they discussed. Ambrose was right. It was a genealogist's dream come true.

The conversation continued for quite some time as Ambrose and Iolanthe happily considered the nasty end of several people they apparently hadn't liked very much. They worked their way back past Iolanthe's father and then began to argue about who had been the first to discover the secret of her keep.

And then they apparently realized they weren't alone, because almost as one, they shut their mouths. Ambrose began to hum a cheerful tune, and Iolanthe looked around the room as if she strove to memorize every stick of furniture on the floor and every knickknack adorning every shelf.

So. There really was a secret to her keep.

Well, Thomas was no fool. There were several mountains he had climbed where the best route to the top was definitely not up the front face. He could sneak around the back just as skillfully as the next man.

"I think we forgot to list a few people," he said easily. "Iolanthe, you have siblings?"

She shot Ambrose a quick look, then turned to Thomas. She looked pathetically grateful to be talking about something else.

"Aye," she said, nodding enthusiastically. "And half-siblings."

"And their names?"

"Well, there was my next younger half-brother, Angus. A whoring, drinking, witless fool if there ever was one."

Thomas wrote Angus down, along with all the appropriate adjectives. "Any others?"

"My elder true brother, Alexandir," she said, less easily this time. "He died childless. He was murdered by our enemies, and Angus took his place."

Time to move on from there. Thomas didn't dawdle. "And your father's name was Malcolm, wasn't it?"

"Aye."

"And your grandfather?"

"William. A wonderful man. His father was Jesse." She hesitated and shot Ambrose a look before she carefully continued. "Jesse's father was James."

"How interesting," Thomas said, his nose twitching in appreciation of something definitely being up. So it had to do with James. But just what kind of secret could a Scottish keep have? He looked at them with a pleasant smile. "How about birth dates?" He would keep them talking, and sooner or later they would let something slip. He was betting on it.

"Mayhap close enough to serve you," Iolanthe said. She gave him several dates, which he dutifully wrote down.

"And death dates?" he asked. "Just for curiosity's sake."

He looked up to find Iolanthe and Ambrose looking at each other with what he couldn't quite term consternation, but it was definitely collusion.

"Ah," Ambrose said, "aye, we have those as well." He rattled off several dates, and Thomas wrote them down as well.

And then he realized they'd left one out.

"James?" he asked, looking up. "What about him?"

"Let us leave James in peace," Ambrose said smoothly. "Now, his son Jesse—"

"What's wrong with James?" Thomas asked.

The two were conspicuously silent.

"If you don't know when he died," Thomas said, "then just say you don't know."

Ambrose looked at Iolanthe, then at Thomas.

"We don't know when he died," Ambrose said firmly.

"You don't?"

"We've no idea."

Iolanthe snorted. "Nor will we for some time to come, I'll warrant."

Ambrose reached out and tugged sharply on her hair, then smiled pleasantly at Thomas.

"Any other questions, lad?"

Thomas looked at them both for several moments in silence. "I sense something very mysterious here."

"Too mysterious for tonight," Ambrose said. "You'd be better off to investigate the McKinnon side of your family first, my lad. Full of interesting characters."

There was obviously no more information forthcoming at present. Thomas looked at Iolanthe to find her industriously studying the fire. No help there.

"All right," Thomas said, "I'll give in. For the moment."

Ambrose rubbed his hands together. "Anyone for a tale or two of proper haunting?"

Not subtle, but effective just the same. Thomas considered the matter for a moment or two. There was no logical reason for them to be so reticent about when one of their ancestors had died. Even if he was a ghost, he would have had a death date.

Unless he hadn't died.

Well, that was just too ridiculous to even contemplate. Ghosts were one thing. A man who had never died was another. It couldn't happen. Men died, and that was that. He leaned back in his chair and turned his attentions to Ambrose, willing to be distracted.

He tried to listen, but he found that he couldn't keep his gaze from straying to the woman who sat next to him. After a while, he just gave up trying and stared at her unabashedly. He could hardly believe she'd agreed to come with him, that he had an entire evening to do nothing more than sit and stare at her in peace.

Even stranger still, that he couldn't imagine anything he would have rather been doing.

She glanced his way, then frowned. "What?" she demanded.

He only smiled. "Nothing."

"Cease."

"I can't."

"You won't."

He shrugged. "Same thing."

"It isn't."

He shook his head with another smile. "Iolanthe, you are a very beautiful woman, and I can't think of anything I'd rather be doing right now than staring at you."

"You . . . you . . ." She spluttered out a few more sounds, then shut her mouth with a snap.

"You don't have to watch me do it."

She looked at Ambrose. "Make him stop. Use your sword."

"The boy is an excellent judge of beauty," Ambrose said placidly. "Am I to run him through for that?"

She started to get up, but Thomas held out his hand. "Please don't go. I'll stop if you want."

She resumed her seat with a frown. "Do something more useful with your time."

Look up portrait painters in the Yellow Pages was his first thought. He wondered if she would sit long enough for a painter to do his work, or if she'd even consent to show herself for the same. But if she would, and if he could find the proper setting, he just couldn't imagine anything better to do with his money. He'd do something about it first thing in the morning. It would have probably been simpler to have had her photographed, but he suspected film wouldn't capture her likeness.

That led him to wonder why it was that he seemed to be able to see her, even when she didn't want him to. Maybe his mother would know. He would have to ask her.

Sometime when his father wasn't at home, obviously.

He could just hear his father's roar of aggravation when he learned that his son was . . . Well, what was he doing with Iolanthe? *Dating* seemed completely inappropriate—and rather impossible. *Wooing* was just as ridiculous.

He drew his hand over his eyes and wondered if the lateness of the hour was getting to him. It was crazy to think that anything—

"Thomas," Ambrose said sharply, "I'm for the pub. Step outside with me for a moment, won't you?"

Thomas rose in surprise, excused himself, and followed the older man out the door. Ambrose turned the moment the door was shut behind them.

"Mind your thoughts, my lad," he said quietly. "You're thinking them so hard, they're coming over as shouts, and I'm not the only one in the chamber who can hear them."

Thomas felt his mouth slide open. There he was, doing it again. Gaping was starting to become a very bad habit. "You're kidding."

"I am not. Now," Ambrose said, holding up his hand, "I'm

not saying that our young lass in there eavesdrops. For all I know, she didn't hear a thing you were thinking. But I know I did, and my hearing isn't as keen as it once was."

"Wonderful," Thomas said, wincing. "I never thought—"

"Up late, are we?"

Could things get any dicier? Mrs. Pruitt came trotting down the passageway and into the foyer. She joined the two of them and looked at Ambrose with undisguised admiration.

"You're looking well, my lord," she said, batting her eyelashes.

That was possibly one of the most unnerving things Thomas had ever seen. He looked quickly at Ambrose to find him darting furtive glances around as if he looked for an escape route—any escape route.

"A pleasure, good woman," he said, plucking a cap out of thin air and plopping it on his head. "I've things to see to, you know."

And with that, he turned and fairly bolted through the door. Mrs. Pruitt watched him go with a scowl.

"Damn man," she groused. "He's always running off 'afores I can have speech with him."

"Um," Thomas said, without a clue what to say, "maybe he has some haunting to do. Somewhere else."

"Hrmph," Mrs. Pruitt said. She turned on her heel, stuck her nose up in the air, and marched off back to her room.

Well, that was that. Actually, Thomas felt no compulsion to worry about either Ambrose or Mrs. Pruitt or any kind of relationship they might have together. Ambrose was the matchmaker. He could make his own matches. Thomas was in enough trouble as it was. He faced the sitting-room door and wondered if he dared go inside. Had Iolanthe heard any of his thoughts screeching her way? He wasn't sure if he was mortified or terrified. He wasn't used to either feeling, so maybe it didn't matter. He was damned uncomfortable, for whatever reason. Good grief, what was he supposed to do now? Stop thinking?

He blew out his breath, opened the door, and went inside. He went and sat back down in his chair. Well, no time like the present to get things out in the open.

"Can you read my thoughts?" he asked.

She blinked in surprise. "Aye, I suppose I could."

"Haven't you been?" he asked in surprise.

"I haven't done it in"—she paused and scrunched up her face—"well, in years at least. Not since after the '45."

"1745."

"Aye, that." She shook her head. "Too many women crying for their slain men. 'Twas too difficult to listen to them and watch their dreams. I trained myself not to listen."

He felt an intense sense of relief he sincerely hoped did not show on his face.

"Should I start listening to your thoughts?" she asked, looking at him with something he could almost call a glint in her eye.

"You shouldn't."

"Ah," she said, nodding. "I understand."

"Do you?"

"I've no illusion about my visage," she said stiffly. "If you wish to think on its ugliness and all my other undesirable traits, then you're welcome to and damn you for it."

He was going to make a concentrated effort not to gape anymore—maybe tomorrow when he'd recovered from today.

"Iolanthe, how can you possibly think that's how I see you? I think you're stunning."

She looked unconvinced.

"Should I start telling you what I think more often?"

She shrugged, but he suspected she wasn't as unconcerned as she seemed.

"Then again," he said slowly, "maybe you'd be better off not knowing everything I think—"

"Why not?" she asked suspiciously.

"Well, because I was thinking, well, you know, um, about . . . us," he finished as lamely as he ever had.

She blinked. "Us?"

"Us. You and me."

She looked immediately and horribly offended. "Why, ye wee lecher," she exclaimed. "How can ye consider such—"

It was amazing how her accent grew thicker the more irritated she became.

"I wasn't thinking lecherous thoughts," he said, though

now that she brought it up, he had to accept that having any kind of physical relationship with her was completely impossible and, well, it just didn't bear thinking about.

He slapped his hands on his thighs and rose. "I think it's time for bed."

She gasped. "As if I would share yours!"

This was not going very well.

"I'll go to my bed," he said, "and I'll show you the way to yours. That's all."

She rose with a sniff.

He scratched his head. It wasn't something he did very often, and he wasn't sure he was all that comfortable with having to do it. Did she *want* him to take her to bed? Did she just want him to *want* to take her to bed? Was she offended that he hadn't offered?

"I'm confused," he admitted.

"You're a man," she said haughtily.

And that, he supposed, said it all. He took a small measure of comfort in realizing, as with a great deal of bafflement he led her up the stairs and down the hall to her room, that she was, despite her ghostly status, a woman, and as such was completely out of his league when it came to truly comprehending the depths of her thought processes.

He paused in front of her door, turned, and looked at her. And then just the sight of her turned his stomach upside down and he promptly forgot everything he'd been thinking except that she was the most exceptional woman he'd ever laid eyes on and that he was very glad he'd brought her to his temporary home.

"I hope you'll be comfortable," he said quietly.

She nodded.

"I'm glad you came."

She seemed to relax a bit. "Thank you," she said. "I am, too."

Before he knew what he was doing, he thrust out his hand. Hell, sixteen all over again and surely a bigger idiot now than he'd ever been then. But what was done was done, and there was no taking it back.

Iolanthe looked at his hand for a moment, then slowly reached out and put her hand in his.

He stared down at it, and for a moment, his entire world shuddered. It was as if he'd done this a thousand times before. He met her eyes and saw there the echo of what he'd just experienced.

He felt no touch, though, and for some reason that was possibly the most devastating thing he'd ever felt.

She pulled her hand away quickly and tucked both hands under her arms.

"Thank you most kindly for the evening," she said formally. " 'Twas a pleasure."

"You'll stay the night?" The words were out before he could stop them. He simply couldn't bear the thought of her going back up to the castle and, well, just being there out in the cold and dark.

"Perhaps."

"Please, Iolanthe. Please stay."

She looked down. He would have given anything to have been able to put his hand under her chin and lift her face up.

"I'll go back with you in the morning," he promised.

She hesitated, then nodded. Thomas took that as a good sign. He opened the door, waited until she was inside, then shut the door behind her.

Then he rubbed his hands over his face and walked to his room before he did anything else stupid.

Like fall in love with a woman he could never have.

Chapter 14

Iolanthe woke and blinked at the sight of sunlight streaming in through a window. The sight was so unusual that she sat bolt upright in bed and looked about her in a panic. It took her several moments to realize where she was.

At the Boar's Head Inn.

As Thomas McKinnon's guest.

She flopped back onto the bed and stared up at the canopy above her. That she should have a chamber at an inn was unusual enough. Not once during her lifetime had she enjoyed the like. That a man should be providing the same for her was nothing short of miraculous. That Thomas McKinnon should be that man was indeed the most improbable of all.

She wondered if this counted as the rescue she'd always longed for.

Nay, there was no sense in speculation about that, for naught would come of it but more to think on, and she had enough of that already. She rose and forced herself to look over her surroundings, just in case she didn't return. For whatever reason.

The chamber was luxurious, to be sure. It was odd, but she'd never been inside any of the inn's bedchambers. She remembered vaguely when the inn had been built, but she hadn't come to look. Ambrose had, after his own demise, come to pay his respects when he'd come south for a wee holiday. He'd apparently found the inn to his liking, for he'd stayed for the subsequent centuries. She'd been inside the kitchen, of course, but never further.

She didn't want to think about what that said about her importance.

She dragged her hand through her hair. Perhaps 'twas best

that she not give that any more thought. She fashioned a comb from illusion, then rose to look for a mirror. She found the private bathing chamber with a white bathing tub and what seemed to be the modern equivalent of a garderobe. She looked to her left and saw a mirror above a basin. It was adequate, but the light was poor. She looked up at the lightbulbs and Thomas's discourse on electricity and its ilk came back to her. She looked about her for the switch Thomas had claimed would bring them to life.

It was by the door, and she stared at it for several moments before she mustered up the courage to try to work it. Moving things from the physical world was always excessively difficult. She had heard tell of those ghosties who could move things with naught but their wills, but she suspected that was a great deal of wishful thinking on the part of the talebearers. She did the best she could with what strength she had, which meant it took almost all that strength to push the lever up.

And, miraculously, the lights kindled themselves as they were supposed to.

The light fell down softly on her, providing a far brighter light than any poor candle she'd ever put flame to. She looked at her reflection in wonder. Her hair was pleasing enough, and she had a goodly quantity of it. Her visage was something she couldn't judge with objectivity, so she contented herself with deciding that perhaps she wasn't as ugly as her half-siblings had always said she was.

Weariness came upon her almost immediately. It was what she deserved, she supposed, from having the vanity to wish to see herself by the light of those wee bulbs. She sat down on the edge of the bathing tub to catch her breath. Last night was the first time in decades she'd actually slept—and how pleasant it had been—and she suspected she would be sleeping again very soon.

A knock would have startled her to her feet had she not been so exhausted.

"Aye?" she called weakly.

"It's Thomas."

She couldn't move. Thomas knocked several more times, then the door opened a crack.

"Iolanthe?"

The sound of her name spoken by that man, she feared, might be her undoing. "In here," she managed.

He came into the chamber, saw her, and rushed with a flattering amount of speed to her side. He knelt down.

"You're pale," he said. "What happened to you?"

She pointed up. "I lit the lights."

He blinked at her for a moment, then frowned. "I don't understand."

"Things from your physical world," she said with a weary smile, "are for the most part beyond my strength."

"Then I should be impressed."

"Aye, you should."

She realized that Thomas was kneeling in front of her, looking at her in that searching way he had, and she was suddenly very nervous. She was quite sure she had never been this close to a man in her life—at least a man who had something besides ridicule on his mind where she was concerned. But what did he have on his mind? She thought back on his question of the night before. He seemed powerfully concerned that she not be able to read his thoughts.

The temptation was almost overwhelming.

Then again, perhaps they would be unkind thoughts, and for some reason, believing that they might be such was almost too much for her to bear. There had been men aplenty, when she was alive, who had had naught but heartless words for her. Either that, or they'd been full of naught but unflattering offers to share their beds. She'd been too old, too tall, and too full of her own mind for any man to want her to wife.

"Iolanthe?"

"What?"

"You were very far away."

"Do you men," she asked tartly, "have any redeeming thoughts at all about any of the women you meet?"

He seemed to consider his answer, which to her mind was admission enough of his guilt.

"I think," he said slowly, "that you are without a doubt the most beautiful woman I've ever met, and I would like nothing better than to spend the day talking to you while I work on our castle. I'd like to have you tell me of your home in the Highlands. I'd like to hear about the past several hundred years that you've spent here on the border."

"Hrmph," she began, but he apparently wasn't finished.

"And while I'm listening, I'll be thinking about how lovely you are, and how your hands move when you're talking about something exciting, how your eyes turn a stormy gray when you're particularly irritated. I'll also be looking around for a suitable place for the painter I've hired to put his easel."

She opened her mouth to tell him he was full of foolishness; then his last words sank in.

"A painter?"

"I'd like to have your portrait painted."

She would have been certain she was hearing things, but she'd seen his lips move as well. "Me?" she asked in a small voice.

"You."

"But 'tis very expensive," she managed. "Those bloody artists will beggar you, if you let them."

"I'll worry about the money. You worry about what to wear."

She found herself rendered completely silent. That a man would throw away his hard-earned gold on such a silly . . . well, a more ridiculous idea she couldn't have come up with on her best day of thinking.

A portrait.

Of her.

"The only thing is," Thomas began slowly, "do you think he'll be able to see you?"

"If he has two good eyes in his head he can," she said. "I can make myself quite visible."

He smiled. "I'm sure there are many who could attest to that fact, though I don't know that they would be quite so calm about it."

She pursed her lips but said nothing more. It was probably better that he not know how many men she had truly frightened to death.

"Tell me about the lightbulbs again," she said, trying to distract him.

"If you want," he said, settling in for what looked to be a very thorough explanation.

She sat on the edge of the bathing tub and listened as he explained yet again the whole process of electricity. He told her about the lightbulb and its inventor, Thomas Edison; then he went on to tell her how many Scots had invented a great number of things.

After a time, he looked at her sheepishly. "Sorry. I tend to get carried away by these kinds of conversations. Will you come downstairs with me? I'm sure our preservationists have finished by now and are already up at the castle ready to tell me how much they hate my plans."

Iolanthe nodded and rose. She looked longingly at the chamber as they passed through it to the passageway.

"You know," he said, stopping her at the door, "the room is yours for as long as you want it. If you have anything you want to leave here, you can."

"Things?"

"Personal things."

"What personal things could I possibly need?" she asked.

He paused, then nodded briefly. "You're right. I think maybe I'm better off today just keeping my mouth shut and working."

She looked down at the comb she still held in her hand. 'Twas naught but illusion, of course, but it would last a very long time if she willed it. She'd kept her garden up for years at a time if she created it carefully enough. Why not a comb and a few trinkets lying about here to give her comfort?

She crossed the chamber, laid the comb on the little table under the window, then crossed back over to Thomas. He smiled at her, then opened the door for her. She left the chamber first, then followed him down the stairs and to the dining chamber.

There was no one breaking their fast at the table, but the moment Thomas pulled out a chair for her and then sat down himself, the innkeeper bustled in with food for him. She looked at Iolanthe.

"Will you . . . um . . ."

"I thank ye kindly, good woman," Iolanthe said, "but nay."

The woman would have looked relieved if her eyes hadn't

been bulging so far from her head. Thomas only chuckled into his eggs as the door closed behind the innkeeper.

"Do you find something amusing?" Iolanthe asked archly.

He shook his head. "It's just Mrs. Pruitt is probably dying to ask you a thousand questions—mostly about Ambrose—you're sitting there looking as regal as a queen, and she just doesn't dare."

"Perhaps she isn't comfortable with a ghost at her table."

"You haven't seen the way she looks at Ambrose."

She sighed. "She'll have little satisfaction from me, I fear. I can tell her far less about him than she'd like."

"Well, don't tell her that. I think she thinks she's just found the perfect source for details."

"Then she should choose a less ignorant woman."

He sat back in his chair and looked at her solemnly. "Why do you think you're ignorant?"

"Because I know nothing."

"What have you been doing the past six hundred years, Iolanthe?"

"Truthfully?"

"Yes."

She couldn't look at him, so she stared at the opposite wall. It was heavily paneled in the style so popular during Elizabeth I's day. That much of history she knew, for she'd been watching events if not with interest, at least with dismay.

"The first two hundred years, I mostly sat about and raged silently over the injustice of it all." She looked at him briefly. "It was passing unfair, you know."

"Yes. I know."

"The next two hundred years, I watched the events unfold around me. I saw men come and go through my gates, listened to their talk at the table, saw the armies going north. Frightening the worst of them seemed within my power, and I did it ruthlessly."

"To save your kin."

"Aye." She sighed deeply. "But after Culloden and the slaughter there, I couldn't watch anymore. I couldn't listen anymore. So I made certain than no man stayed more than a few hours inside my gates. The castle became part of a lord's estate, but I never cared to find out who. It fell into disrepair, and that suited me perfectly."

"But," he began quietly, "what did you do? What did you do each day from the time the sun rose until it set? What did you do each night as you watched the moon cross the sky?"

She did look at him then, because she could do nothing else.

"I waited," she said.

"For what?"

She paused. "Change."

He said nothing in return; he simply stared at her. Then he spoke.

"And has it come?"

There it was again. She breathed deeply, felt the tang of autumn's chill in the late-summer air. Autumn had always been her favorite season. Free from the long, endless flatness of summer. New colors on the mountains, crisp breezes filling the air, her mind full of thoughts of long winter evenings passed by the fire.

And dreams of a man to share it all with.

She looked at Thomas McKinnon, with his dark hair falling into pale blue eyes, with his beautiful face smiling just the slightest bit, with his strong hands resting on the arms of his chair, and she knew that change had come. It had come in the form of a man who wanted to build her a place of her own, who had thought her important enough to care for, who considered her shrewd enough to share the great secrets of modern marvels with.

With her. Iolanthe MacLeod. Eldest daughter of a man who didn't think enough of her to remember her name.

"Aye," she said finally. "It has."

"And is this a good thing?"

She managed a nod. "Aye. It is."

"I understand the feeling." He smiled at her. "Are you ready to go?"

She nodded and rose with him. They left the inn and walked back to the castle. Iolanthe hesitated at the gates. It almost felt as if she no longer belonged. She didn't think she'd spent a single night away from this place in over six hundred years.

But lest she look the fool for finding that odd, she put one foot in front of the other and continued on her way.

Over the course of the rest of the day, she learned a great deal about the man she was watching. First was that he wasn't afraid to work. It had to have been cold. A fine rain started up midday and didn't relent until evening, yet still he worked. His helpers had begged off for the day, yet still he didn't shrink from what he had to do.

And while he worked, he told her stories of his past. She didn't understand half of what he said, but she was loath to admit as much. And she tried not to feel shame when he looked searchingly at her a time or two, then repeated his tales with such simple details that even a child of few wits could have understood him.

He had received his university laurels for a study of history. He'd studied the law. Then he'd built an enterprise by himself and sold it at great profit. Of course, he didn't miss the opportunity to tell her of the impossibly high mountains he'd climbed. Even though she had seen the photographs, she couldn't even fathom it, so she merely nodded and humored him.

All of it made her feel that her own life had been very small and insignificant, yet somehow as the day wore on, he pried her own tales out of her.

And he made her feel that her own life had been very important indeed.

He was full of questions about how she'd lived, how her days had been passed. His admiration for what poor things she did know made her feel as if perhaps her days hadn't been completely wasted. After all, she did know much about physicking the ill, birthing babies, and tending livestock. She could spin, weave wool, and dye cloth with the herbs she gathered in the fields. She could feed many on little, knew how to count to one hundred, and could sing any number of lays and ballads while remaining almost completely on key.

By the time the sun had set, she wondered how it was she had passed the days before Thomas had come.

And she began to wonder how she would do the like when he left.

One thing she wasn't was a fool, and she knew that there

would be little to hold him at the castle once 'twas finished. The man was ambitious—that she recognized well enough. He would grow restive, then fractious, then he would pack up his belongings and be gone.

"Are you ready to go?"

She looked away from her contemplation of the courtyard. Thomas stood before her, quite filthy but smiling. Iolanthe took a deep breath.

"I think perhaps I will remain."

"Were you unhappy last evening?"

She shook her head, but she couldn't speak.

"Change is in the air, Iolanthe," he said gravely.

It frightens me, was what she wanted to say. Instead, she said, "I've a great deal to do here, what with the men and all."

"The men will keep."

"My garden—"

"That will keep, too."

"I—"

"Iolanthe," he said with a half smile, "come with me."

"But—"

"Just come."

"Why?" she asked him, pained. "What does it matter?"

"It matters. It matters very much."

She suspected that if he could have dragged her along by the hand, he would have. She sighed, rose, and walked with him down the road and back to the inn.

And she prayed she wasn't flinging herself into a battle for her heart that would end only one way.

Badly for her.

But as he drew her into the inn after him, smiling in welcome, she found that, foolish or not, her heart was eased. Perhaps it would go badly for her in the end, but for now she was content.

She steadfastly refused to think about the future.

Chapter 15

Thomas stood the next morning in Thorpewold's inner bailey and looked down at his blistered hands. He didn't need to flex his arms to know they were sore enough to fall off. It was a very romantic theory to rebuild the keep with hand tools. In reality, it was a really stupid idea. Though he'd already laid one floor and was well on his way to finishing the second, he knew he couldn't keep this up any longer.

He looked at his helpers. "Lads, this isn't working."

They looked so relieved, Thomas almost laughed. He handed them a day's wages.

"I've got to find a generator and some power tools. Any ideas on where?"

"Edinburgh," Burt replied promptly.

"Only place to go," said Charlie just as promptly.

And then they both promptly turned and fled out the front gates. Thomas supposed he couldn't blame them, even though Iolanthe's men had been on their best behavior. Except Connor, but Thomas suspected that there was a man who couldn't be controlled at any price. Poor Burt had borne the brunt of Connor's irritation because the laird had snarled at the boy every time he'd passed near him. From all appearances, Burt hadn't heard anything, but not even a simpleton could have missed the waves of ill will that flowed like the Force from the MacDougal.

Thomas turned to find Iolanthe in one of her usual places, sitting on a rock, watching him work. He shoved his hands in his pockets, then immediately regretted it and pulled them out. He walked across the bailey and sat down on a rock next to her.

"I think I'm going to have to get a generator."

"A generator?"

"It's portable power," he said. "I have a few tools that will make the building go much faster, but they need juice to run them." He looked down at his hands. "I could do it myself with what I have, but it doesn't get the tower finished very soon."

"Have you that much haste?"

He looked at her, surprised by the question. He wanted very much to believe that she didn't want him to finish because she liked having him around working, but he wasn't sure he could go that far. So he smiled gamely and went with the best thing he could think of short of asking her if she was afraid he would finish and go.

Because then she'd tell him she couldn't care less if and/or when he went, and he didn't want to hear that.

"The sooner the tower is finished, the sooner we have shelter for the winter."

"The weather doesn't plague me."

"But it plagues me to think about you standing out in it. I'd like to have your room finished so you have a comfortable place to be when you're at the castle. But," he added quickly, "you can stay at the inn as long as you like."

"Mrs. Pruitt is making herself daft trying to dust my things," she said with a glint in her eye.

Thomas laughed. "I don't think you should be enjoying it that much."

"She's trying to appease me so I will tell her tales of Ambrose."

"She wants him."

"Fiercely," Iolanthe agreed.

"I'd be scared if I were him."

Her smile faded abruptly. "Because she is mortal and he is a ghost?"

"Of course not," he said quickly. Perhaps he should have stopped to consider why she'd asked that, but he didn't dare. "If I were Ambrose, I would be terrified because she's Mrs. Pruitt, and once she gets her hands on him, his life will never be the same."

"Ah," Iolanthe said with a nod. "I see."

"Do you?"

"She is a rather formidable woman," Iolanthe said.

"She would have made a good field general," he agreed. He leaned back and enjoyed the weak sunlight, hoping that Iolanthe wouldn't notice his rather tangible relief over a land mine successfully negotiated. What had she meant by all that? That a relationship between a ghost and a mortal wasn't a bad thing? Was she concerned he might think it was? Was she actually considering the like between them?

Had he completely lost his mind?

"Let's go to Edinburgh," he said, rising abruptly and gingerly dusting off his jeans. He should have stopped sooner. His hands were fried. "I imagine it's the only place I'll find a generator, and it's not too far a drive."

She shook her head. "Thank you, but nay."

"Come on, Iolanthe," he said with a smile, "I promise not to run into anything."

"Thank you kindly, Thomas, but I've things to do here."

How was it that the sound of your very own name from a woman's lips could leave you wanting to go down on bended knee and promise eternal devotion?

Losing it?

No, he'd lost it.

Right then.

"What's the real reason?" he managed. "We may as well be honest with each other."

She glared at him. Silently.

"Are you embarrassed to be seen with me?" he asked.

"Of course not."

"Have you ever been to Edinburgh?"

"Nay."

"I hear it's a great city."

She looked at him in consternation, then panic, then she turned and vanished.

Damn it, he was going to gape again. He shut his mouth with a snap before his jaw got completely away from him. He looked around the bailey, but Iolanthe was nowhere to be seen, not even with his clear vision.

"All right," he said, finally. "I don't get it."

There was no answer.

"Are you sure you won't come?" he called.

The Victorian Fop, as Thomas had termed him, appeared before him, dressed to the nines.

"She said," he said curtly, "that she didn't want to go with you. So begone, and may you meet with a sad accident on your way and not return."

Thomas studied the other man and ran through his mind a list of uncomplimentary names he could call him. He didn't swear all that much, preferring to use an icy blue stare and a cutting remark to make his point. Because when it came right down to it, a carefully chosen insult just couldn't go wrong.

He looked down at the Fop's knees. "Your tights are baggy," he said.

The other man looked down and gasped in horror. "Bloody hell, will you look at that!"

"I am. Unfortunately."

The other drew his sabre with a flourish. "You'll pay for that insult." He brandished his sword and promptly dropped it point-down into his shoe.

"I'd learn how to use that before I started promising to do damage with it," Thomas said with a sad shake of his head. "To anyone but yourself, of course."

A chuckle caught his attention and he looked up to see Iolanthe's cousin, Duncan, standing nearby.

"He has it aright, Roderick," Duncan said, walking over and shoving the other man out of the way. "Be off with ye, ya frilly bugger, and leave us to our manly business."

Roderick spluttered and cursed, but when Duncan put his hand on his sword hilt, the other man vanished to parts unknown. Thomas looked at the older man with frank admiration.

"I'd like to learn to do that."

"Intimidate?"

"Wield a sword," Thomas said dryly. "The other I think I can manage on my own."

"Men of your ilk, perhaps," Duncan conceded. "Scots who're accustomed to battle? I think not."

"All right, so we'll start swordplay sooner than I planned," Thomas said.

"It will take time," Duncan said.

Thomas didn't miss the searching look.

"I'm not going anywhere."

"Until the keep is finished."

Thomas found that he had no good answer for that. His plans hadn't included living in England for the rest of his life.

Then again, his plans hadn't prepared him for Iolanthe.

"I have a great deal to think about," Thomas said with a sigh.

"Have a care with her heart."

Thomas looked at the older man, and an idea occurred to him suddenly. "Would you like to come to Edinburgh with me?"

"Weel, aye," Duncan said brightly, his eyes alight. " 'Twould be a pleasure. Last time I was there, they were walling people up in the closes on account of the plague."

"Closes?"

"Little streets of sorts," Duncan said. "You'll see." He rubbed his hands together. "Ah, who knows who I'll see thereabouts?"

"Don't tell me Edinburgh's haunted as well."

"Are ye daft, man?" Duncan asked, blinking.

"Um . . ."

"A city of that size? With that kind of bloody business done in the streets?" He looked at Thomas as if he'd just lost his mind. "Of course 'tis haunted!"

"Of course," Thomas agreed, wondering what he'd just gotten himself into. Did he really want to know what went on beyond most men's veil of sight in Edinburgh? A ghost walk was one thing, where you knew they were just telling you stories to give you goose bumps. Actually going on a ghost walk that was, well, a *ghost* walk with Duncan MacLeod as his guide—now, that was really something.

Well, his hand was already on the plough. No point in turning back now.

"While we're gone," Thomas said, "I'd like to ask you some questions if you don't—"

"The Tolbooth," Duncan was muttering to himself. "Aye, there's a fine place to start. The castle, to be sure, but later, after we've been to St. Giles . . ."

He walked off toward the barbican, still making his list. Thomas looked around hopefully for some kind of aid, but there was none to be seen. Iolanthe was nowhere in sight. He found himself torn between waiting for her to reappear and a desire to get on with his business so he would have a place for her to run to—a place he could find, that was.

Perhaps Duncan would know what had set her off. Maybe he had moved too fast for her. After all, he'd just managed to get her down to the inn a couple of days before. Maybe she'd never been in a car. Maybe she'd never been to a big city before.

He waited for another few minutes, but he had no sense of her being in the vicinity. With another look around the bailey, he gave up and walked toward the barbican. He wouldn't be gone long. With any luck, he wouldn't find himself thrown into jail for causing a public disturbance by bringing a ghost to town.

He caught up with Duncan on the paved road back to the inn.

"And that house of ill repute. Aye, there's the place for a goodly bit of speech with old mates!"

Heaven help them.

It was three days before Thomas managed to pry Duncan away from his buddies and get him back in the car to go back to the inn. He supposed he could have left the older man behind, but it seemed only polite to get him back before he forgot where he was supposed to live. Thomas found the proper road with only a minor amount of side-seat driving from Duncan, which consisted mainly of disparaging remarks about the constricting properties of roads versus the head-across-whatever-field-pleases-you freedom of a horse, and started toward home.

The trip had been worthwhile, even apart from Duncan's successes. Thomas had found everything he needed to finish the construction. He'd found a computer system he could live with, furniture for an office and a living room, and things for Iolanthe's room.

It was the last he'd been most concerned about, and he'd

spent a fair amount of time dragging Duncan to antique stores in various parts of town. He'd found much of what he wanted, but the rest he'd been forced to settle for in a department store. He hoped it would please her.

He hadn't pried as much information out of Duncan as he would have liked. The man was very skilled at talking at great length around the subject you were interested in. Pointed questions about Iolanthe's background had been met with blank stares. So Thomas had settled for hearing stories about her half-brothers and half-sister and used them to reconstruct what he thought her life might have been like.

What he had learned, though, was that her mother and brother had been wounded in a skirmish with a neighboring clan. The brother had died, and her mother had languished for some time before succumbing herself. Apparently, though, Iolanthe's father had been hard at work siring other children on a mistress during the last few years of Iolanthe's mother's life. Iolanthe's subsequent existence had seemed very Cinderella-ish with that crop of half-brothers and a half-sister who, after the death of Iolanthe's mother, had seemed to think she was put there just to see to their comfort.

But the circumstances surrounding Iolanthe's death were ones that Duncan absolutely refused to divulge. Not even a hint as to the details. Thomas had tried a half dozen different approaches, but all had left him still languishing at the bottom of the mountain, as it were. Duncan simply wouldn't budge. Thomas supposed if he ever learned the whole story, it would be from Iolanthe herself.

He wondered, however, if he would have the choice. Duncan had no idea, or so he professed, why she wouldn't have wanted to come to Edinburgh. Thomas wondered if it had to do with the car. Duncan had taken to it after a couple of involuntary whoops of some strong emotion as they hit the first major road. There was no predicting what Iolanthe would have done in the same place.

But if it wasn't the traveling that bothered her, then what?

Well, he'd get back to the inn and see if she'd been there. He'd show her what he'd bought her and describe the wonders of the city. With any luck, the next time he went, she would go with him.

And do what was the question, but it didn't deserve an answer. He could take her to the theater or the ballet. They could tramp over historic ruins. They could walk in the moonlight.

Everything else was superfluous.

Wasn't it?

Chapter 16

Iolanthe stood at the inn's back kitchen door and found herself suddenly quite unable to go any farther. She was, surprisingly enough, desperate for some kind of company besides that which she found herself surrounded by at the keep. But why she had come to the inn was a bit of a mystery, even to her. Never mind that she had a chamber there with things of her own lying about. She'd been up at the keep for three days now, ever since Thomas had gone to the city. She hadn't had the stomach to come back to the inn without him.

Which left her wondering what was possessing her that eve. Companionship, that was it. But what companions would she find at the inn? She'd seen Fulbert de Piaget and Hugh McKinnon walking down the road to the pub, arguing companionably about which was better, Scotch whiskey or British lager. Ambrose she'd already seen wandering off as well to parts unknown. That left no one at the inn she particularly wanted to see.

Unless Thomas had returned.

Which she knew by the lack of his automobile in the front he hadn't.

But that wasn't to say he wouldn't.

And that would leave her explaining her cowardice in the face of his invitation, which if she'd had any sense should have sent her back up to the keep to hide in her garden. But her cowardly ways she had put behind her once and for all. How better to show it than to go inside and mingle with those of his ilk, such as Mrs. Pruitt? It would keep her occupied until Thomas returned.

Iolanthe took a deep breath, then walked through the door. The woman in question was cleaning her stove with a fierceness that even Iolanthe had to admire. She pitied any speck of dirt that tried to hide from Mrs. Pruitt's seeking cloth. Indeed, the woman's concentration looked to be such that Iolanthe couldn't bring herself to interrupt her, so she made herself at home on the boot bench near the door and waited.

She tried not to think about the reasons she hadn't gone with Thomas, which included a fear of automobiles and an even greater fear that he'd get her to a large city and she would embarrass him in some way.

By being a ghost, for instance.

"Eeeek!"

Iolanthe blinked, then realized that Mrs. Pruitt was staring at her, her hand clutched to her throat.

Iolanthe tried to smile in a friendly fashion. "Good e'en to you."

"Ah . . ." Mrs. Pruitt began, then she got hold of herself. "Ah, well, the same to ye, miss."

"I've no mind to disturb your work," Iolanthe said, lest the woman think she had an untoward purpose in mind.

Mrs. Pruitt felt for a chair and sank down into it with apparent gratitude. "Not a'tall," she said weakly. "I was merely startled. I'm finished with me business here."

Iolanthe nodded and smiled companionably. "You've a fine kitchen here, Mrs. Pruitt."

"Thank ye, miss."

"Your guests are put to bed for the night?"

"Aye," Mrs. Pruitt managed. "All but young Thomas. I expected him to arrive in time to eat me stew, but 'twasn't to be."

"Will he return tomorrow?" Iolanthe asked, trying to sound as if she couldn't have cared less.

"I should think so."

"Hmmm," Iolanthe said.

A silence fell.

Iolanthe leaned back against the wall and folded her hands in her lap. She had no doubt Mrs. Pruitt was bursting with questions.

"Did you come to see your grandsire?" Mrs. Pruitt asked at length.

"Laird Ambrose?" Iolanthe asked.

"Aye," Mrs. Pruitt said reverently.

It was almost out of her mouth that the man was her nephew a time or two removed and not her grandsire, but that would have entailed explaining several things she wasn't sure Mrs. Pruitt could stomach, so she merely shook her head and let the misinterpretation stand.

"I think he's out for the evening," Iolanthe said. "Actually, I was just hungering for a little talk, and I thought perhaps you might be amenable."

Mrs. Pruitt looked as if St. George himself had come down and asked her to come with him on a quest. Iolanthe had a hard time not feeling ridiculously pleased over Mrs. Pruitt's obvious delight.

And then she had a hard time keeping up with the woman's conversation.

Mrs. Pruitt talked the way she cleaned: vigorously and with a thoroughness that left nothing to chance. Iolanthe nodded and agreed and mostly listened while the woman rattled on as if she hadn't had a good talk in years. By the time Iolanthe found herself peppered with questions about Ambrose, she was too overwhelmed to deny Mrs. Pruitt any answers.

"I think the laird Ambrose's marriage was arranged," Iolanthe managed when an answer to that was required. "I think the girl bore him a son or two, then passed on. I daresay it wasn't a love match."

"What a pity," Mrs. Pruitt said, sounding as if it wasn't. At all. "And he never wed again?"

"I daresay he was consumed with leading our clan. 'Tis a heavy responsibility, you know."

"Oh, aye," Mrs. Pruitt said, nodding vigorously. "I can just imagine. Poor man. I daresay he could do with a bit of pampering, wouldn't ye say?"

"Oh, aye," Iolanthe agreed, doing her best to hide her smile. "He's had a lonely afterlife."

Mrs. Pruitt was on her feet and bustling about so quickly, it almost made Iolanthe dizzy.

"That can be seen to," Mrs. Pruitt said firmly.

The dining chamber door swung open, and Iolanthe wondered if the reckoning of her enjoyment at Ambrose's expense would come sooner than she expected. But it wasn't Ambrose.

It was Thomas.

"Mrs. Pruitt," he said politely. Then he looked to his left. And he smiled.

Iolanthe thought she might perish from the sweetness of his look.

"My lady," he said.

She could only swallow in reply.

"Miss MacLeod has been telling me of the laird," Mrs. Pruitt said, her excitement barely contained. "You'll have to fend for yourself. I'm off to tidy up me hair for when he comes back, the poor, lonely man."

And with that, she was off.

Thomas came across the kitchen and sat down next to Iolanthe on the bench.

"You've been making trouble," he noted.

"Trouble?" she asked innocently. "I would never make trouble."

"He won't appreciate it."

" 'Twill be good for him. He's always making matches for others. Perhaps 'tis time someone made a match for him."

Thomas leaned back against the wall. "And what matches has he been making of late?"

"I daren't ask."

"Hmmm," he said. "Yes, maybe it's better not to know." He pulled a book from under his arm and laid it on his lap. "I brought you something."

She looked at it and frowned. "What is it?"

"A book on costumes. Different kinds of dresses worn by different women through the ages. I thought it might help you decide what to wear for your portrait. I'll turn the pages for you, if you like."

"I can do it," she said, feeling ashamed all of a sudden. She could do it, aye, but 'twould cost her dearly.

"But if I do it," Thomas said, "then I get to sit with you for as long as it takes to look at all the dresses. Believe me when I tell you it will be my pleasure."

And what was she to say to that? She tore her gaze from

the book, which did indeed look powerfully interesting, and met his eyes.

She cast about for something to distract him. "How did you find Edinburgh? Was it to your liking?"

"Yes," he said. "I hope you'll come next time. You would enjoy it."

"Did you obtain your tools?" she asked, desperate to avoid any prying questions.

"I did. I'll get to work first thing in the morning. Want to look at your book now?"

She was on her feet before she knew what she was doing and blurting out the first thing that came to mind.

"I'm for bed," she said.

"Are you staying here?"

"Aye," she said, then she left the kitchen at a dead run.

She ran all the way to the chamber she hadn't slept in for three days, stood just inside the door, and shook. So there went all her fine resolves to be brave.

"Coward," she whispered. Aye, that she was indeed. 'Twas nothing but a simple book. Looking at it would give her time to spend with a man she thought she might come to love.

Come to love?

She sank down on the floor, put her hands over her eyes, and wished she could weep.

I_t was rather late the next morning when she rose. She ignored Thomas's knock. Once she was fairly sure he had left the inn, she left her chamber, avoided those breaking their fasts at the dining table, and refused to answer any of Ambrose's questions about why she looked so poorly. She left him in the competent care of Mrs. Pruitt and escaped the inn. The last thing she wanted was to talk to anyone about why she was doing what she was doing.

She truly had little idea herself.

She toyed with the idea of taking herself off to some far-flung corner of the island, but where would she go? And why would she go anywhere else when her heart was inside her castle gates? In Thomas McKinnon's keeping?

She surrendered and turned toward the castle. She walked

up the way and into the courtyard. Thomas and his two village lads were huddled together, having speech. The garrison was clustered around them. Iolanthe parted the gaggle of men and looked into the circle.

Well, there obviously was the beast Thomas had brought to give life to his tools. 'Twas a handsome shade of red, she would give it that, but it had little else to recommend it.

"You know how the compressor works, don't you?" Thomas asked Burt and Charlie. "You turn on the generator to get the juice going . . ."

He turned on a black machine, then gave his attentions over to his red one. The noise that made was irritating but not unbearable.

"And then every now and again, the compressor will kick on and keep our tools going. Right?"

Burt and Charlie nodded sagely, as if they'd seen it all before. Iolanthe looked at her men all standing in a cluster about Thomas and wondered if they understood as well. They were all nodding just as wisely.

And then the red beast gave forth a mighty howl.

The shrieks of the men and the hisses of swords being yanked from their scabbards was deafening. Burt and Charlie apparently had their eyes quite suddenly opened, for they looked about them and began screaming themselves.

And then they bolted for the gates.

And Thomas said a very foul word.

"Weel, ye never said the wee demon would scream thusly!" Connor MacDougal said defensively. "We were taken unawares!"

"And now I've lost my work crew!" Thomas exclaimed.

The beast subsided into blessed silence. Iolanthe watched Thomas and the garrison study each other with varying degrees of disgust and distrust.

"Beg pardon, Thomas," said one of the men humbly.

"Shut up, Robert," Connor snarled. He resheathed his sword with a mighty thrust, then folded his arms over his chest. "What'll ye do now?"

"Look for other workers, I suppose," Thomas said with a heavy sigh. "Maybe from farther away."

"Mayhap this has taught ye a lesson," Connor continued archly. "Mayhap—"

"Mayhap when I finish the tower, I might start on the great hall and give you somewhere dry to put your feet up," Thomas said shortly. "What do you think about that, Laird MacDougal?"

The thought obviously was one Connor hadn't considered, if the look of surprise on his face was any indication. Iolanthe watched him turn the idea over in his head, then come to a decision.

"I accept your offer," Connor said, bowing formally. "Be about your work, man. I hate standing in the rain."

Thomas looked at Duncan. "Any ideas?"

He considered. "The lads could roam about for a bit. A few weeks. Just until you were finished."

"What a thought," Thomas muttered. "A visit to the seaside, maybe. A long one."

"London," said one of the men.

"France!" cried another.

"Oh, why stop there?" Thomas asked. "Make it Rome. Great place. I've been there several times. Lots to see. Lots of ruins. Lots of really fine looking Italian women."

"Dead?" Connor asked doubtfully.

"I'm just sure of it."

"Ach, weel, then," Connor said, adjusting his plaid. "Come along, lads, and leave the man to his work." He looked at Thomas. "Have me hall finished when I return."

Thomas grumbled at him, then turned back to his red beast.

Iolanthe watched as her entire garrison tromped out through the gates—with the unsurprising exception of both Duncan and Roderick, who remained behind. Thomas leaned over to pat his machine, then straightened and looked at the two men.

"Staying to help?"

"Oh, aye," Duncan said, nodding.

"To keep watch," Roderick said ominously.

Thomas frowned at him, then looked at Iolanthe and smiled. "An interesting morning so far, as you can see."

"Aye, I noticed."

"I'd better go down to the village and see if there's anyone left who hasn't heard their stories."

"Fetch the priest to come up," Duncan said wisely. "It'll make the lads feel better with a man of the cloth to protect them."

"No doubt." Thomas looked at Iolanthe. "Want to come?"

She chewed on her answer, trying to make a nay into an aye.

"Or you could meet me at the inn for dinner."

"Hrmph," Roderick said, sounding thoroughly offended.

"You can come, too," Thomas said smoothly. "And Duncan, of course. Ambrose would enjoy talking to you, I'm sure."

"We'll be there," Roderick said immediately. "Dressed properly, of course," he added with a pointed look at Thomas. "See if you can manage the same, old man, won't you?"

Iolanthe wondered if Thomas knew what he was letting himself in for. The saints only knew what sort of mischief Roderick would combine with a proper table set in front of him and silver at his disposal. She half pitied the guests at the inn.

"My lady?"

She looked at Thomas and nodded at his expectant expression. "I'll come. To dinner," she added.

"That's all that matters."

Roderick began to snort and huff about, but she ignored him. She ignored Duncan's hearty clearing of his throat. She was a fool, and she knew it, but she couldn't seem to help herself. She watched Thomas leave, then made her way to her garden before she had to listen to any words from either of her keepers.

She puttered amongst her flowers, but somehow, it didn't bring her the pleasure it usually did. She was used to longing for silence, for time apart from everyone in the keep. Her garden had been a haven of peace.

Now, it just seemed empty.

*I*t was several hours later that she found herself retiring to her chamber at the inn. Dinner had been less terrifying than she'd imagined, though Mrs. Pruitt had been run ragged seeing to Roderick's demands for this and that, not that he'd been able to ingest any of it. But the proper tableware had been a must for him, and Mrs. Pruitt had been bowled over enough by his manner to fetch it for him.

After dinner, Iolanthe had begged to be excused before she could find herself alone with Thomas. She hadn't made it through the door before he'd called after her that he would put her book in the sitting chamber. She'd left without acknowledging that she'd heard him.

It ate at her, that book. Knowing that it was downstairs. Knowing that he'd bought it to please her. It was all she could do to ignore it as long as she did.

It was very late when she finally made her way downstairs and walked into the sitting room.

Thomas was asleep in a chair.

The book was on the table, open to one of the pages.

Iolanthe moved quietly around a chair and knelt down in front of the table where she could look at the pictures. The colors themselves were a marvel, as was the detail in the photographs, visible even by firelight. The idea of photographs had ceased to startle her after having looked at Thomas's photographs of his mountains. Now, she rather liked them, for 'twas easy to see details that no scratching of charred wood on paper would ever provide.

She put her hand on the page, then took a deep breath and used all her strength to push the page over. It went, only after enormous effort on her part. She knelt back on her heels and panted as she looked at the next picture. It was equally as lovely, but not what she wanted. She marshaled all her strength for another flip of the page when suddenly she found a long arm in her way.

"Let me."

She didn't turn to look at him. She didn't dare. But neither did she protest when he continued to turn the pages for her. And then he turned the final page and she saw the dress.

The dress.

"Oh," she whispered.

Then she wondered if her choice of gowns might be better kept secret. She looked at Thomas.

"I'll decide later."

"Whatever you want."

"Thank you for the book."

"It seems like a very small thing," he said with a shrug. "But if you like it, then I'm happy."

She found that she couldn't look away from him. For the first time in either life or death, she was looking at a man who gazed at her with something a less reasonable woman would have mistaken for affection.

Strong affection.

She swallowed—with surprising difficulty, in light of her physical status.

"I should," she managed, "be off to bed."

"Is it late?"

"Very."

"Do you care?" he asked with a smile.

"I suppose I should."

He pulled a chair close to his and sat back. "Come and sit, Iolanthe. Tell me what you did the past few days."

She was going to refuse, but she made the mistake of looking into his eyes. And somehow, he worked his fey spell upon her yet again, and she found herself rising and sitting in the chair next to him.

Or mayhap it wasn't a spell. Mayhap 'twas that she wanted already in her heart to do what he'd merely asked her to do. Mayhap 'twas that she wanted with all her poor heart to do nothing but sit and have speech with a man whose beauty stole her breath, whose kindness brought tears to her eyes, and whose tenderness broke her heart.

So she sat and she told him all he wanted to hear. And when he told her of Edinburgh's marvels, and his eyes began to close, she sat and watched him dream.

And then she was truly lost.

Chapter 17

Thomas slowly opened the door of his room and peered out into the hallway. The coast was clear, so he quickly exited his room, locked it behind him, and hurried down the steps. Iolanthe could fend for herself, as far as he was concerned. Never mind the handful of tender moments they had shared over the past week since his return from Edinburgh. He was worried about getting breakfast before it was sabotaged.

He had seriously underestimated the deviousness and tenacity of the preservationists. In fact, he'd almost forgotten about them during his trip to Edinburgh. When he'd returned, he'd been concentrating so hard on Iolanthe that he hadn't really given them much thought.

But then they'd become hard to ignore.

They might have looked like proper, dignified citizens of a respectable age, but they played as dirty as junior high girls fighting over a boy. The attacks had started the day after he'd returned from Edinburgh. Once the generator had gone on, apparently all bets had been off.

First had come the continual litany of dire threats and warnings about restoring relics better left ruined, delivered via a megaphone. The alliterations and adages they had engaged in had made him slightly queasy after a few hours, but unfortunately he'd been without a garrison to drive them off. He'd had to settle for praying for rain.

Which had produced nothing but a week of sunshine.

He'd forgotten about Fulbert and Hugh, though. It would seem the two had taken enough time off from their continual feuding to get fed up with the warbling rendition of rousing patriotic melodies, because the megaphone had mysteriously disappeared.

But the protestors and protests had not.

The trio had apparently hired a flock of sheep to lounge lackadaisically on the road up to the keep. Once the sheep lounged to their satisfaction, they'd ambled up to cluster at the gates. Thomas had wondered what Mrs. Pruitt could whip up with mutton as the main ingredient, then thought better of it. It would be just his luck to find the sheep rented and himself facing a lawsuit for doing one of them in.

The next day had brought a group of schoolchildren weeping at the gates over the wanton destruction of a national treasure. Thomas had almost been moved by that when one of the more vocal of the boys had piped up and demanded to know when "we's off for the fish 'n chips ye promised us!"

He'd finished the roof that day with a clear conscience.

And then they'd pulled out the big guns.

The following morning, he'd eaten his breakfast as usual, made polite conversation with Iolanthe and the men, then headed up to find an amazing lack of protest at his gates. It had almost been unsettling, the quiet, until he'd headed out into the forest to relieve himself. This much he could say with certainty: blue urine was not what a man wanted to see pooling a discreet distance from his toes.

All right, so the last was really nothing but a harmless prank. Who knew what it would be next? Laxative brownies? Plastic wrap on the toilet seat? Plastic wrap on the toilet seat after a batch of laxative brownies?

The potential for truly staggering mischief boggled the mind.

All of which had given him the impetus to get downstairs as soon as possible before any other unwholesome substances were added to his breakfast behind Mrs. Pruitt's back.

He arrived in the dining room to find no one there. There was cereal on the sideboard as well as a pitcher of milk and some juice. He lifted the milk up and sniffed, then realized he probably wouldn't know if something had been added even if it reached up and tweaked him on the nose. He was momentarily tempted by the juice, then remembered that Mrs. Pruitt herself had slipped him sleeping pills in an innocent-looking glass of orange juice. Was there nowhere to turn?

He was just beginning to investigate the depths of the cereal box when Mrs. Pruitt came into the room bearing a plate heaped with scrambled eggs, sausages, fried tomatoes and mushrooms, and a bit of ham. Ah, breakfast. He looked hopefully in her other hand for some warm toast, but saw none.

"Toast?" he asked.

"Cooling in the kitchen," she informed him briskly.

Of course. He looked over his plate. "The traditional English breakfast," he noted.

She set the plate down at his place. "Aye."

"Has the traditional English breakfast left your sight at any time during its preparation?"

She looked at him as if he'd lost his mind. "How was that?"

"Did anyone ask you to place anything suspicious in the traditional English breakfast?"

Mrs. Pruitt just stared at him blankly.

He was starting to feel like airport security. But he had to face the fact that he didn't have a bag scanner. He supposed that he trusted Mrs. Pruitt, the orange juice scandal aside, so he sat down and dug in.

"Have ye gone daft, lad?"

"Just checking," he managed through a mouthful of egg. "This is delicious. Thank you."

"Eat hearty," she suggested. "You'll need it."

"Why?"

"You've another protest going on up the way, I shouldn't wonder," she said, bustling out the door.

Great. The furnishings for the tower were supposed to be delivered that morning. He could hardly wait to see what he would find in the middle of the road this time to prevent the same.

He finished his meal, sighed, and pushed away from the table. He took a brief moment to enjoy the peace and quiet before he left the inn and walked up the road. It didn't take him long to get to the castle. He knew it was nearby.

He could smell it.

Now, this was going too far. He stopped just down the

way from the walls and stared at the steaming pile of manure that blocked the way to the barbican. As he stood there, he realized that calling what he saw a mere pile was misrepresenting it. It wasn't a pile; it was a mountain. It was going to be impossible to get a truck backed in close enough to the barbican to unload his stuff. It was going to be equally as impossible to carry the furniture around the hill.

His ghostly acquaintances and kin stood to one side, surveying the disaster. Iolanthe looked at him as he came to a stop next to her.

"A gift for you," she noted.

"I'm at a loss for what to say," he said.

"Merde?" she offered.

He laughed in spite of himself.

" 'Tis one of the few French words I know," she said.

"It's appropriate." He looked at Ambrose. "You couldn't stop them?"

"What would you have suggested?"

He had a point. Thomas sighed. "You're right."

"They're passing determined," Ambrose noted. "I doubted a mere bit of haunting would stop them."

Thomas heard the roar of a truck in the distance. He sighed with a shake of his head. Just how was he going to solve this one? He watched as another truck pulled onto the gravel road. The only light in the gloom was that this other truck was delivering a contingent of his very-well-paid workers from a neighboring village. He paused to consider. This might make a difference.

Thomas walked to one side of the hill and looked at the contingent of preservationists who stood there gloating.

The leader of his workers came to a stop at his side. "Blimey, mate," he said in awe. "Never seen such a mighty pile o' sh—"

"Me neither," Thomas interrupted. "I imagine there are a few shovels back at the inn, don't you think?"

The man looked a little sick at the idea.

"Send someone to fetch as many as possible."

"But it'll take all day to move that," the man complained.

"I'm less concerned about how much we move than to where we move it."

The man blinked at him for a moment or two in silence, then realization slowly dawned. He grinned, then began to whistle as he walked off with a bounce to his step.

Thomas returned to stand next to Iolanthe and waited. It didn't take long before men with shovels had returned and set to work.

Almost immediately came a screech from the other side of the manure mountain. That screech was followed by howls of irritation and downright outrage. Thomas walked around the manure and viewed the damage.

The three members of the National Trustees Concerned with Preserving Ruins were coated quite liberally in a substance Thomas didn't want to examine too closely—especially since he knew its origin.

"How dare you!" Constance screeched.

"Blue pee," Thomas countered. He looked at the two men standing next to her, spluttering. "Missing tools. Hassles from morning until night."

They glared at him.

"I'm not spray-painting Buckingham Palace, for heaven's sake," he said in disgust. "Can't you just cut me some slack? I promise I won't touch the outer walls."

That at least stopped some of the gearing up for battle he could see going on in their heads. Nigel very carefully dabbed at his mouth with a handkerchief.

"Leave the hall alone as well," he said crisply.

"Can't," Thomas said. "Promised a ghost I'd give him somewhere dry to put his feet up."

Nigel looked skeptical.

"The MacDougal," Thomas clarified. "You'd recognize him if you saw him. You know the one carrying the six-foot broadsword?"

The three looked surprisingly pale under their newly acquired layer of muck.

"We can't give up," Constance said faintly.

"Pick on another ruin," Thomas suggested.

The three looked at each other. Gerard cleared his throat.

"The Queen is rumored to be installing a satellite dish on top of Big Ben. That could merit our attention."

"Her Majesty and MTV," Thomas said with a shudder. "Nasty thought."

Nigel shook himself off and put his shoulders back. "Our work here is done," he announced.

"But—" said Constance.

"We've done all we can."

"I agree," Gerard said, taking Constance gingerly by the arm. "We've left him something to remember us by until it decomposes. Let's be on our way."

Constance threw Thomas a look of promise. "We'll be back, young man. And if you've done anything untoward to the outside . . ."

Thomas waved them away and walked back over to where Iolanthe stood with her kin.

"Once we get this cleared, we'll get the furniture moved in." He smiled at her. "Do you want to wait in the garden and have it be a surprise?"

She looked powerfully embarrassed. "There's no need—"

"Come, granddaughter," Ambrose said, taking her by the arm. "Come show me your garden whilst young Thomas is about his work."

Thomas watched her walk off, then followed along behind to make sure everything was ready for when the lads had the road cleared.

The upside of his situation was no more preservation contingent and no cluster of Highlanders standing around ready to mock him for his wooing efforts. The downside was the mountain of manure in his driveway, but that he could live with. Maybe it wouldn't be so bad once he was ensconced in the tower.

It took the entire morning to remove enough compost to be able to get the truck close to the front gate. Once that was done, Thomas supervised the unloading and the setting up of his tower.

He'd bought furniture for the bottom floor, comfortable things that had reminded him of the sitting room at the inn. Lighting had been something of a problem, but he'd decided on camping lighting. Kerosene and candles weren't exactly convenient, but there wasn't much he could do about it.

The next floor was his office. He'd ordered a laptop with

a state-of-the-art solar-rechargeable battery system. Someone was coming later to install the solar panels on the roof and set him up with a little dish for a satellite Internet link.

And then came Iolanthe's room. He put a pair of chairs facing each other in front of the window. He set a desk along another wall with all kinds of obscure coffee-table books on it. He was fairly certain she couldn't read, so he'd found things he thought might interest her in pictures alone. He suspected that if she'd been as out of circulation as she'd said, even just the pictures would be mind-blowing enough.

He'd found a tapestry frame, and an armoire into which he'd put a portable stereo and a small collection of CDs. He hadn't had time to look for much else. He'd just have to convince her to go back to the city with him so she could pick out her own stuff.

He set everything up as well as he could, then paused for a moment and sat down in one of the chairs by the window. He stared out over the landscape in front of him with its rolling, sheep-dotted hills.

Could he look at this for the rest of his life?

He considered the things he might do with his nifty Internet hookup and his cell phone. He could carry on business, true. He could fly to New York every now and then just to keep things running in person. Or he could dump his company and think up something new to do. It wasn't as if he hadn't done that before. He didn't have to work if he didn't want to, but he knew he couldn't just sit around and atrophy for the rest of his life.

He turned over in his mind the idea of restoring the rest of the castle. After all, he'd bribed the MacDougal into leaving with a promise of a roof on the great hall. Heaven only knew what kind of hauntings would result from a failure to deliver on that. Maybe he could put a roof on the hall himself, but to restore anything else would take a stonemason. It could be done, but would it be worth it? He would need someplace of his own eventually. Much as he loved Megan's inn, he couldn't stay there indefinitely.

He considered the cost and the end result. If he really wanted to make the castle habitable, to make it a place he could live in, he would have to do something about power.

He supposed other castles in England had been modernized—
to the accompanying protests from the Preservation Three,
no doubt—but he imagined that the cost was staggering. And
if the cost didn't give him pause, the location did. He was a
good fifty miles from the coast on roads that made fifty miles
into two hours of travel, not one. Not that he minded camping, but he wasn't all that fond of being landlocked. He had
very happy memories of his house on the sea.

There was, however, a single thing that kept him where
he was. He glanced at the doorway and smiled at the very
person he'd been thinking about. Maybe thinking about his
future could be put off awhile longer.

Iolanthe had the same expression on her face she'd had
last night when she'd looked through the costume book.
Thomas could only hope that it was a look of happiness, not
distaste.

"Like it?" he asked.

She walked in, stood in the middle of the room, and turned
around, looking at everything as if she couldn't believe it.

"Whatever you don't like can be changed."

"Oh, nay," she managed. She sank down in the other chair
near the window and looked at him. "Thank you. 'Tis more
beautiful than I could have imagined."

Well, that was enough for him. He sat back in the chair
and watched her as she got up again and wandered around
the room, peering into corners and frowning over modern
contraptions that could be hidden behind armoire doors.

And while he watched her, he decided that perhaps this
was all he needed at the moment. There, in that room with
just the two of them, was enough.

"What are these?" she asked, pointing inside the armoire.

"CDs," he said. "Music locked onto little disks." He rose
and went to stand next to her. "Whatever kind of music you
like. Scottish pipes, symphony, choral, country."

She looked momentarily perplexed by the selection.
"Choose for me."

"Here's one with troubadour songs on it."

"That should be interesting."

He smiled. "Will you be critiquing the performance?"

"Doubtless," she said as she stood back. "Though I daresay

it can't be much worse than what I've heard over the years. Even Roderick tries his hand every now and again at some ballad or other."

"Frightening."

"Aye."

So he put on the CD, then sat with her by the window while she alternately sang along or shredded the performance. And he decided that there, in that little room, they could perhaps make their own corner of the world and have some peace, free from the opinions of anyone who might care to offer them.

"Ah, but they're very fine singers," Iolanthe said, when the CD was finished. "Put in another, won't you?"

Thomas rose to do as she asked, then found himself bowled over by the three old ghosts from the inn, plus Duncan and Roderick. The Fop immediately cast himself down in Thomas's place.

"I'll like it here," he said, picking a speck of imaginary dust off his immaculate velvet coat and settling quite comfortably into the chair.

Duncan drew his sword, and Roderick vacated the chair with a sigh. Thomas resumed his place, then found the room filled with conjured-up chairs supporting far-too-comfortable ghosts. Well, perhaps peace and privacy would come at a premium. But then he met Iolanthe's eyes, saw the twinkle there, and found himself thinking that they might survive after all.

And he studiously avoided thinking about the future.

The present would have to be enough for him.

Chapter 18

I**olanthe** sat in her newly fashioned chamber and looked about it in pleasure. She had several things to smile about, not the least of which was a door she could forbid anyone to pass through. Many over the past few days had stood outside knocking for what had seemed to her a shocking length of time. She had half suspected it was the comforts found within they sought and not her company that kept them so long at it.

She had, of course, been very choosy about whom she allowed inside her chamber.

There was one soul she knew came inside merely to be with her and 'twas to him she owed the comfort and peace of her chamber. Now that she had somewhere to go, she wondered how she'd survived so many centuries wandering about. She could sit in her chair and look out the window or demand that Roderick come turn the pages in her book of dresses for her, or listen to music that sounded as if an entire abbey full of monks were gathered in her chamber to sing for her ears alone. The marvels she had never known existed which she now called her own were overwhelming.

As were the feelings for Thomas she couldn't ignore. Never mind that he'd built a chamber especially for her. Never mind that he was the bravest, most pleasing-to-the-eye lad she'd ever seen. Never mind that he was kind, generous, and seemingly had no other desire than to pass the greater portion of his days in her company. It was the way he said her name. As if she were the most beautiful, the most desirable, the most wonderful person he knew.

As if he loved her.

She rested her chin on her fist and stared out the window with what she was sure was a foolish smile on her face.

Perhaps it had taken all those centuries of being alone to appreciate having someone to care for her. Not as Duncan cared, nor as Ambrose cared. But as a man who looked on her as a woman.

A knock sounded, interrupting her musings. She sighed and called out for the soul to enter.

Roderick walked through her door. He stopped in the middle of the chamber, looked at her, then pursed his lips.

"Mooning over *him*?" he asked shortly.

"And what if I am?"

He opened his mouth to speak, then shut it and shook his head. "I would ruin my reputation as a gentleman were I to give voice to my thoughts."

"The saints preserve us from that."

He looked at her darkly. "I predict disaster. Mortals and spirits were never meant to become entangled."

His words made her briefly uneasy, but she shrugged them off. If the mutterings of a bejeweled peacock could unsettle her, then she wasn't worthy of her name. She was a Mac-Leod. MacLeods took risks, did not bemoan their fate, and were firm in their purposes. If she had decided that having an . . . um . . . *association* with Thomas McKinnon was what she wanted, then have it she would, and the skeptics be damned.

"I understand the artist arrives on the morrow," Roderick said with a heavy sigh. "You'd best let me look at your gowns and give you my thoughts."

She studied him in silence for a moment or two.

"Dash it all, woman, I'll not lead you astray!" he exclaimed. "I have *excellent* taste. I would provide you with scores of testimonials, but I daresay we don't want to invite any of my fellows up here."

"Or your scores of former lovers?"

He pointedly ignored her remark. "You would find your lovely chamber overrun with card games, cigar smoke, and spilled drink. So, trust me on the merit of my word. I'll help you choose the appropriate gown."

Iolanthe weighed the alternatives. She could select her own gown, surely, but what if she chose amiss? Thomas was no doubt paying an enormous sum to have this all done. And

much as it galled her to admit it, she couldn't deny that
Roderick was always impeccably dressed. Even though his
personality left much to be desired, his attire did not.

She sighed and rose. She didn't need to look at the book
again to know what her choices were. She'd spent the past
three days studying the bloody thing.

One moment she was in her normal peasant dress, the next
she was wearing the illusion she'd created. The first gown
she made was Elizabethan in style, black in color. It was
covered with lace and encrusted with jewels. Iolanthe held
her hair up on top of her head and looked at Roderick.

"Well?" she asked.

He shook his head. "Not your color. Too many baubles.
The next?"

The next one was a simple dress, purple, and quite modern
in its style. It reached to the ground as a straight sheath of
material with all manner of sequins hanging from it. Thomas
had called it a flapper gown. Iolanthe looked at Roderick.

"Your thoughts?"

"It should be burned. Try something else."

She sighed and conjured up the final gown she'd found in
the book. She had thought it the loveliest of them all, and it
claimed to be from the proper period in time. How anyone
had decided what a medieval wedding gown looked like, she
wasn't sure, but given the fact that she hadn't attended all
that many medieval weddings, she supposed she wasn't in a
position to judge.

The gown was dark blue with a sort of stitching done on
the bodice in gold thread. The same thread outlined a subtle
pattern on the rest of the gown as well. She looked down at
her bare toes peeking from beneath the gown and decided
that perhaps she would have to think about shoes as well.
Then again, mayhap the painter wouldn't ask to see her feet,
and she would be all right as she was.

She took a deep breath to steel herself for Roderick's inevitable dislike, then looked at him.

He was watching her with the most sincerely unlecherous
expression she'd ever seen him wear. She held up part of her
gown.

"Well?" she asked.

"Perfect," he announced.

She held up a lock of her hair. "What should I do with this? Put it up?"

"Wear it down," he said shortly. He practically leaped to his feet, then stared at her with an expression she couldn't decipher. "Wear it down. You'll steal his breath."

"He'll need breath to paint," she said.

"I was speaking of *him,* not his bloody artist. You'll steal his breath away. And if he doesn't go down on his knees before you and beg you to be his, I'll stir myself to learn swordplay and then find a way to remove his empty head from his shoulders."

Iolanthe smiled before she could stop herself. "Then you like it."

"Since when did you care what I thought?" he demanded, sounding mightily irritated.

Since I found love, she started to say, then she realized just how true that was. She couldn't imagine anything more impossible, but it seemed as if everything about her was sweeter somehow. She treasured her friendships more. She suspected that she would even view the MacDougal with less animosity than she normally did. And it had everything to do with the softening of her own heart.

Because of him.

A knock sounded on the door, and she jumped in spite of herself.

"Change," Roderick said. "Don't let him see you in that gown until the artist arrives."

The blue dress vanished, and Iolanthe stood there in the dress she normally wore. And somehow, foolish though it was, she felt less.

"You know," Roderick said slowly, "you don't have to wear just that."

"Spoken by a preening peacock who changes his clothing upon the stroke of every passing hour," she said, stung.

"What else have I to do?" he asked as he walked to the door. He looked back at her. "What else have you to do?"

That said, he vanished.

Iolanthe stood there, gasping from the slap of his words. She was still trying to gather her wits about her when Thomas opened the door and peeked inside. 'Twas all she could do to dredge up a false smile.

"Good day to you, Thomas," she managed.

He stepped inside the chamber. "Are you okay?"

"I am well," she said, struggling to look as if she hadn't just had her pitiful existence rocked to the core.

What else did she have to do but change her clothes?

Love the man standing in front of her?

"Iolanthe, why don't you come downstairs with me?" he asked. "I've got the computer up and running."

"Ah . . ." she stalled.

"It'll be fun," he said, holding the door open for her. "I can show you hundreds of pictures of the ocean, both above it and below it."

Ocean you'll never see, ye silly twit, said a vicious voice in her head. *For you're too cowardly to go see it for yourself. Not that he'd want to take you anyway, uncouth and unlearned as ye are.*

"Iolanthe?"

She opened her mouth, but no sound came out. She felt rather than heard him cross the room to her. When he was standing not a handbreadth from her, she looked up into his beautiful face and found a bit of her own despair mirrored in his eyes.

"Don't think so much," he said quietly.

"But—"

"Life is what we make of it, Iolanthe."

She folded her arms over her chest. His words didn't help her any, but she supposed there wasn't really much he could say. Or do, for that matter. There, not a handbreadth from her, stood the most handsome man she'd ever known, one who apparently had at least a few fond feelings for her, yet there wasn't a bloody thing she could do about it.

"Come downstairs," he said, stepping back and smiling. "It'll be fun."

She wasn't sure *fun* was what she would have, given her recent insight into the uselessness of her own existence, but perhaps she wasn't served by thinking on it. Enjoying his company was far preferable to sitting in her chair, staring out the window, and bemoaning her fate.

A fate she could not change.

No matter how desperately she might have wished to.

"The sea, Iolanthe," Thomas said, luring her after him like a fey spirit. "Come with me and see it."

She followed him from the chamber only because she could do nothing else. In the end, perhaps he had it aright and looking at aught else would distract her. From the fact that she couldn't touch him. Or that she would never be held by him. Or bear him children.

She felt a sob catch in her throat before she could stop it. He spun on the step below her and looked at her in surprise.

"Iolanthe," he said in consternation.

She shook her head and motioned for him to go on. " 'Tis nothing. Idle thoughts."

"That didn't sound like an idle thought."

"It was."

He stared at her for several moments in silence, then smiled sadly. "Come with me, Iolanthe. Just come and look. It'll be okay."

"It isn't your machine I fear," she protested. "I had other reasons—"

"I know." He smiled briefly. "Believe me, I know."

She looked at him and realized that he likely had some idea of what troubled her. Perhaps he shared her thoughts.

Assuming, however, that he felt for her as she felt for him.

She put her shoulders back. Well, if this was all they would have together, then it behooved her to make the best of it. As Thomas seemed to be doing.

So she put a pleasant expression on her face and walked down the stairs behind him.

His chamber with its trappings of business was comfortable enough, she supposed. It was nothing compared with hers, surely, which led her to believe that he had certainly selected the innards of her chamber with more care than his own.

"Ready?" he asked.

"Is it necessary for me to be?" she asked, sitting down next to him.

He laughed. "Answer enough, I suppose. All right, I'll tell you what everything is, then we'll see what's on the Net."

She nodded, hoping she didn't look as bewildered as she already felt.

"This is my laptop," he said, pointing to a thin black box. "It's hooked up to this lovely monitor here, which is big enough that we both can look at it."

The monitor was a white box of sorts with a shiny front in which Iolanthe could see her reflection. When Thomas turned on his laptop, the front of the beast sprang to life in a riot of colors. Sound flooded the chamber, along with several annoying beeps and whistles.

"There are all kinds of programs loaded," he said. "Games, encyclopedias, learning tools. Math, spelling, reading. Whatever you could ever want, it's there."

Reading. She heard that and nothing else. Not that anything about reading would do her any good, given the fact that she couldn't even spell her own name. She supposed Duncan could. She had always been surprised by the depths of his knowledge. He knew a handful of tongues, could figure sums in his head, and yet wield a sword with great skill. She wondered why he hadn't married. He would have made a fine father.

Then again, he'd been father enough to her over the years, so perhaps his gift for it hadn't gone completely to waste.

"Okay," Thomas said, interrupting her thoughts. "Do you want to look at the ocean first, then what's in it, or the other way around?"

"What's in it?" she echoed.

"The fish. Whales, sharks, jellyfish." He grinned like a young boy let lose with his father's finest stallion. "You name it, I can get you a picture of it."

Iolanthe was surprised by how pleasing a thought it was to have Thomas at her disposal. Even more surprising was how genuinely keen she was on the idea of seeing the marvels Thomas promised her. Perhaps 'twould be a day of pleasure after all.

Night would come, of course, and with it too much time to think, but perhaps she would do well to follow his advice. *Don't think so much,* he had said.

She wouldn't.

Chapter 19

Two days later, Thomas stood at the base of his tower and contemplated the incongruities of his life. First was his own mortality and its accompanying trappings. He looked at the little portable toilet that stood sentry a discreet distance from the finished tower and decided that it was not a good addition to the landscape. It definitely would have to go.

In contrast to his own mortal frailties were the advantages of having a ghost for a girlfriend, and there seemed to be quite a few of those. All right, so *girlfriend* was probably pushing it. *Companion?* No, that wouldn't work either. *Friend who was a girl?* That was just as lame. No, he'd just have to call her his girlfriend. That's how he thought of her, and there was no use in trying to make it something it was too late to be. He was falling for her, hard, and there was no denying it.

Which led him back to his original thoughts of the advantages that came with a girlfriend who was neither mortal nor from the twentieth century. One of those was eating with a woman who didn't pick at her dinner while claiming she was just a light eater. Iolanthe just didn't eat anything at all, and it didn't seem to bother her that he ate like a starving lumberjack.

Secondly, she was free of all the twenty-first-century modus operandi that had guided the every move of the women he'd dated. He hated prissy women. He especially couldn't stand prissy women in linen suits who brushed seats off before they sat, were afraid of ballpark hot dogs loaded with condiments, and for whom anything less than a hired limousine was just unthinkable.

He never wanted to go to Tiffany's again under duress, never wanted to attend an exhibition of *important art* featuring strange substances plastered onto canvas in even stranger ways, and most especially never wanted to attend another glittering social gala where everyone air-kissed and made pointed references to the lengths of their yachts moored in the Mediterranean. Swords and plaids were starting to look good to him, and he actually couldn't imagine a better day than one spent lounging in the heather and perhaps stirring himself for a little haggis for dinner.

He was beginning to wonder if he'd spent too much time in the company of Highland males.

Which led him back to thoughts of the lady in question. She was a breath of very fresh air. The day before had been a revelation. He'd spent hours with her in front of the computer, finding her pleasure to be a tangible, contagious thing. How could he not be captivated by her? She laughed when she pleased, cursed when she pleased, and looked at him as if she were pleased. When she was angry, she said so. When she was sad, she cried.

And when she dressed up for her portrait, she was breathtaking.

He stood in the middle of the bailey and gaped at her as she walked across the dirt toward him.

Girlfriend, hell.

He wanted to make her his wife.

He wondered what kind of reaction that announcement would get. He suspected that now was not the time to make it. Maybe later, when he didn't mind her running away from him.

For the moment, he was content to stare at her and wonder if he would ever again catch his breath. He'd noticed the picture of that dress in the book, but he hadn't realized it would be her choice. The navy of the gown was stunning against her fair skin and the gold embroidery brought out highlights in her hair he'd never noticed before. She was nothing short of exquisite.

"You're beautiful," he managed.

She blushed and looked down at her dress. "Aye, the dress is lovely. Thank you for the idea."

"You could be wearing a burlap sack, and you'd be just as lovely. It isn't the dress."

"Oh," she said, smiling up at him. "Thank you."

"My pleasure." He started to hold out his hand, then realized he shouldn't, so he shoved his hands in the pockets of his coat as if he'd meant to do that from the start. "Ready?" he asked.

She looked up at the sky. "We'd best do this before it rains. I'm sure the painter wouldn't appreciate that."

"No doubt. Maybe we'll have him finish it at the inn. That'll be easier on him."

He walked with her to the garden, where the artist in question was blowing on his hands and looking anxious to get to work and probably get out of the cold. Thomas stood back and watched Iolanthe seat herself on the bench. He wondered if the painter with his trained eye could see things Thomas couldn't. Iolanthe looked perfectly normal. The only thing that was perhaps even a bit odd was the perfection of her dress and the way the breeze didn't touch her hair.

He looked at her sitting there with her gown about her and her hair spread out over her shoulders and an uncomfortable pain began in the middle of his chest. If he hadn't known better, he might have thought he was having a heart attack.

Was it longing he felt?

No, it was hell.

He thumped his chest and scowled. He'd once heard a definition of hell and it was *want to, but can't.* Want to go to heaven, but can't.

Want to have this woman for his, but can't.

Hell.

He wanted to look away from her, but he couldn't. All he could do was just stare at her with what he was certain was a look of pure, naked hunger. Never mind her body—though that would have been nice as well. He wanted her soul, wanted it as he'd wanted nothing before in his life.

She turned her head briefly to look at him.

He saw her mark the expression on his face, digest it, then watched the realization dawn in her eyes. He wouldn't have been surprised if she'd turned away either in dismay or disgust.

But she didn't.

He saw, for a brief moment, his own longing mirrored there, and the sight of it floored him.

And then, before he could move, speak, or breathe, the painter squawked.

"Don't move!" he said urgently. "Keep that exact look on your face. Don't change a thing!"

The man began to paint frantically. Thomas wondered if that was such a good idea, slapping that paint around so vigorously, but who was he to tell the man his business? Iolanthe wasn't moving, so neither did he. He found he couldn't look away from her. The longer he stared at her, the more she was all he could see, until he felt the oddest sensation. It was as if he'd left the trappings of his mortal frame behind, and he was looking at her, spirit to spirit. Time ceased to exist. If he could have made that moment go on forever, he would have been a happy man.

How long he stood there staring at her, he couldn't have said. It had to have been quite some time, because when the painter sat back and drew his hand over his eyes, Thomas realized he was so stiff he could hardly move. He shifted on his feet and heard his bones creak.

"Incredible!" the painter exclaimed.

Thomas went to stand behind the man and look at the portrait.

And he closed his eyes in self-defense.

"Bugger, but she's a stunner," the painter breathed.

He couldn't have agreed more.

"Thomas?"

Thomas opened his eyes and looked at Iolanthe, still sitting on the bench. "You should come look," he said. "I think."

"I've just begun," the painter warned. "I've still the back-ground to add."

Thomas couldn't have cared less about the background, but he supposed he shouldn't say as much.

"I daresay I'll want you back to capture more of the dress," the painter added.

Thomas watched Iolanthe come around to stand next to him. She looked at the painting, rough as it was, and caught her breath.

"By the saints," she whispered. "Is that how you see me?"

The woman on the canvas was not only breathtaking, she was haunting. Thomas wasn't sure how the man had done it, but in a few brush strokes he'd captured every bit of passion, poignance, and desire that seemed to vibrate in the air around his subject.

"Yes," Thomas said simply. He took a deep breath and spoke to the artist, to whom he planned to give a big, fat bonus. "You've done an amazing job. What else do you need from us?"

"Nothing more today," the man said, picking up his brush. "I'm going to just work on the background. I need time to recover."

"Don't we all," Thomas muttered.

"And what is that to mean?" Iolanthe asked sharply.

He smiled briefly at her. "Nothing. Let's go for a walk."

She looked at him closely but came with him just the same. Thomas found that words were simply beyond him, so he walked with his love out of the castle and down the road. And when they could have stopped at the inn, he continued to walk. Thoughts churned inside his head. He knew he had to get them out, but he had no idea where to begin.

"Are you planning to walk to London?" she asked.

He stopped, turned, and looked at her. "I love you."

She blinked. "What?"

"I love you."

She spluttered for a moment or two, then stammered out a reply. "You . . . you're daft."

"Why?" he asked.

"Because . . . because you cannot mean it."

"Of course I can. I do." And then an unpleasant thought occurred to him. "Are you trying to tell me that you don't care for me?" he asked. "That I didn't see in your face what I just saw five minutes ago?"

She started to speak several times, then simply shut her mouth and glared at him.

"Well?"

"If I did tell you I loved you, what would it matter?" she asked plaintively.

"It matters."

"It's hopeless!"

"That, Iolanthe, is where you're wrong," he said with all the conviction in his soul.

"I'm a ghost!"

"You're a woman."

She stomped around in a circle, then came back to face him. "You've lost what little wits you had left after listening to that compressor of yours."

"Actually, I think I've finally had the most coherent thoughts of my life in the past few minutes." He looked at her searchingly. "Can you love me?"

She took a step backward. "I don't want to speak of this."

"Can you love me?"

She took another step backward. "There is nothing to be gained by discussing this."

Thomas ground his teeth. "Running away will not solve anything!"

That at least stopped her.

"I wasn't running away."

"You were thinking about it."

"Ah, I see," she said. "Now 'tis my mind you know as well as your own."

He sighed and dragged his fingers through his hair. "Iolanthe, we need to talk about this."

"And I say we do not," she said stubbornly.

He turned and walked away, blew out his breath, and then returned. He stopped in front of her.

"We have to talk about how we're going to make this work," he said wearily.

"Make what work?"

"Don't be obtuse."

She blinked as if he'd slapped her. "You forget that I have no learning. I've no idea what that means."

He took a deep breath. "I'm sorry. A person is being obtuse when they refuse to look at what's right in front of them. I think we need to talk about how we're going to make this relationship work. I think you're ignoring the fact that we need to. That's being obtuse."

He watched her walk away and stare out over the fields. She wrapped her arms around herself and stood there for quite some time in silence. He would have given much to have been able to go to her, put his arms around her, and tell her that everything would work out.

He wished he could have been sure it would.

"Iolanthe," he began, taking a step or two toward her. "I'm sorry. Please—"

"Thomas! Oh, Thomas McKinnon!"

He looked to find Mrs. Pruitt bearing down on them, waving a piece of paper over her head. Well, so much for their precious privacy. Thomas sighed and waited until Mrs. Pruitt had come to a full stop in front of him.

"Your company," she said briskly, handing the paper to him. "It's going under. You'll have to catch the next flight to New York."

Thomas took the piece of paper and read what was written there: *Your company. It's going under. You'll have to catch the next flight to New York.* Perfect, he thought grimly. Out of all the words in the English language and all the different ways they could have been put together, those were certainly the only ones that would have brought him running, and his company president knew it.

He looked at Iolanthe, who still stood with her back to him. He folded the paper up and went to stand behind her.

"I have to go to New York," he said.

"So I heard."

"Come with me."

She turned to look at him then. A single tear rolled down her cheek. "You must be mad," she whispered.

Maybe he was. He considered all the arguments he might use to get her to come with him, but the simple fact was, he would be putting her out in public for public consumption. He couldn't be lucky enough for everyone they encountered not to notice that she was a ghost.

Passport. She didn't have a passport.

And then another thought occurred to him.

"Ambrose came to America," he said, "and I'm fairly sure he didn't fly in a plane."

"A plane?" she asked. "Are those the metal birds that fly so high in the sky?"

"Yes," he said gently. "Up there a little higher than Mount Everest, which you steadfastly refuse to believe is as tall as it is. If Ambrose can do it, can't he show you how? You could meet me in New York. We could go to the theater. Walk in the park. There are a million things to do in the city."

She took a step backward, never a good sign.

"I couldn't."

"Couldn't?" he asked. "Or won't?"

The moment the words left his mouth, he wished he hadn't said them. He held out his hands to stop her from leaving.

"That was a stupid thing to say," he said quickly. "I can't blame you for being hesitant. New York's a huge place. Even I get overwhelmed there now and then."

She looked primed to vanish.

Thomas tried a smile. "Come talk to me while I pack?"

She shook her head. "I shouldn't. I understand the garrison is coming back soon. I should be at the keep when they return."

"But—"

She smiled, but it was the falsest smile he'd ever seen. "Godspeed, Thomas," she said. Then she vanished.

Thomas stood there for several moments until he realized the heavy breathing he was listening to wasn't his, it was Mrs. Pruitt's. He turned and looked at her. She was watching him with something akin to pity.

"Change never comes without price," she said sagely.

Change.

Thomas shook his head, then rubbed his hand over his face. He took a deep breath and blew it out.

"You're right," he said. "It's never easy."

"Easier for some than others."

Well, much more advice like that, and he'd be jumping off the parapet himself. He nodded, then walked back to the inn with Mrs. Pruitt. It took him only a few minutes to throw clothes in a bag, book a flight, and be on his way out the door with sandwiches Mrs. Pruitt had packed for his journey.

He paused before he got into his car.

But the garden on the side of the house was empty. As was the driveway.

He was tempted to go up to the castle, but that wouldn't have served him. If Iolanthe didn't want to be found, she wouldn't be. And what good would it do to talk anymore, anyway? There was fantasy, then there was the brutal reality of their situation. He didn't believe she didn't have feelings for him. He might love her, and she might love him, but that didn't change the fact that he was mortal and she wasn't. Talking wouldn't change that.

But it might change how they dealt with it. Not that he was overly fond of endless rehashing of relationship details, but he couldn't deny that something had to be done. They couldn't go on as they were.

But later. He would fix the disaster in New York, then he would come home and they would work it out.

And hope to heaven they could find a solution.

Chapter 20

It was two days before Iolanthe had the courage to go back to the inn. She knew Thomas wasn't there. She knew this because the garrison had returned from their holiday, demanded to know where she'd hidden him, then gone to look for him themselves. They'd returned from the inn, disappointed and empty-handed. It had left them wandering restlessly about the keep. She told herself that she walked down the road simply to have some peace from their grumbles. But in truth, she wanted to be somewhere Thomas had been, somewhere they had passed time together in a pleasant manner.

She missed him.

She walked slowly along the way in the late evening, up the little road to the inn and around to the back gate. The kitchen light spilled out onto the garden path. Well, at least someone was still awake. She walked through the door without another thought and then came to a teetering halt when she realized that her kin were entertaining.

A woman sat in the kitchen between Ambrose and Hugh, chatting with them easily, as if she knew them well. Iolanthe looked at her and noted immediately that she was mortal. Perhaps she was a frequent guest at the inn. But to be so familiar with her kin? There had to be another answer.

"Do ye let him do his work, gel?" Fulbert was demanding. "Ye know I've much to say to ye on the subject."

"He works plenty," the woman assured him.

"Ye'll answer to me if he doesn't," Fulbert warned.

"Leave off, ye bloody Brit," Hugh growled. "She's *my* wee granddaughter, and I'll not have ye distressin' her."

Iolanthe stood there staring, openmouthed. This was someone of Hugh's kin?

Ambrose looked at Iolanthe. "Well met, daughter. Come sit with us, won't you?"

Iolanthe sank into the proffered chair, unable to take her eyes from the other woman. She wasn't unlovely, Iolanthe supposed. She had an abundance of red hair, and green eyes. Those were nice enough, but there was something that struck Iolanthe as very familiar. She stared at her for several moments in silence.

Then the woman smiled and Iolanthe knew her identity before anyone spoke.

"Megan MacLeod McKinnon de Piaget," Ambrose said, pointing toward the woman. He smiled at Iolanthe. "Might I introduce you?"

Iolanthe could only nod weakly. Thomas's sister. What, by the very saints of heaven, was she doing at the inn?

"Megan, this is Iolanthe MacLeod. She's kin of mine up the way. Iolanthe, Megan owns the inn. She's just come north for a little holiday and to make certain we haven't overrun the place."

Megan laughed at him. "You know I just came to visit my two favorite grandfathers." She looked at Fulbert and winked. "And my favorite great-uncle."

Fulbert scowled at her but said nothing.

Megan turned to Iolanthe. "It's nice to meet you," she said with an easy smile. "I suppose all this makes us related as well."

The sight of Megan's smile made Iolanthe miss Thomas all the more. She wondered how she would stand looking at the woman much longer if this was the reaction she would inspire.

"Aye," Iolanthe managed. "We're kin through your mother."

"She's your aunt," Fulbert said.

"Half-aunt," Ambrose corrected.

" 'Tis all the same when it comes to ye foul Highlanders," Fulbert grumbled. "Breedin' and carryin' on till the rest of us find ye hemmin' us in on all sides."

Megan only laughed. "Aren't you married to laird Ambrose's sister, Fulbert?"

Fulbert looked primed to say something nasty, but he buried whatever it was in his mug.

Iolanthe watched Megan banter with all three men and wondered how often she had come to the inn and Iolanthe had never been the wiser. She had missed out on much by remaining at the keep all those years.

"Laird Ambrose tells me you know my brother?"

Iolanthe blinked when she realized that Megan was talking to her. She managed what she hoped looked like a smile. "Aye, I've met him."

Fulbert snorted heartily.

Megan shot him a look, then returned her gaze to Iolanthe. "How is his work going on the castle?"

"He's finished one of the towers," Iolanthe said, finding herself growing increasingly uncomfortable. "He's in New York now."

"It figures, doesn't it?" Megan asked with another smile. "I come to make sure he's surviving, and he's off on another quest."

"Does he do that often?" Iolanthe asked.

"Only when he's compelled," Megan said with a wry smile. "Generally, he climbs mountains. He works now and then when he has to. Quests only happen when his chivalry gets the better of him."

"I see," Iolanthe said, not sure that she did or that she really wanted to. Was she a quest, then? Would he tire of her and return to his mountains and his labors?

To how many women did he say the words "I love you"?

She considered that for far too long. When she forced herself to concentrate on what was going on around her, she found that Megan was making her exit to bed. Iolanthe was on her feet immediately, grateful for the excuse to bolt.

"Daughter, you have a chamber here," Ambrose said.

"Things to do up at the keep," Iolanthe said. She smiled at Megan, then fled through the door before anyone could stop her. She couldn't stay any longer. If she had to see Thomas's smile on his sister's face one more time, she would scream.

She ensconced herself in her tower chamber, stared out the window into the darkness, and wondered what Thomas was doing. Did he think of her? Did he miss her company?

She closed her eyes and let the tears trickle out unimpeded.

S_{he} realized she had fallen asleep only because the soft knocking on her door finally woke her. The sun was streaming into her chamber, and its brightness made her blink several times in discomfort. The knocking continued. She sat up straighter in her chair and dragged a hand through her hair.

"Aye?" she asked hoarsely.

The door opened. Thomas's sister poked her head in just a bit. She smiled.

"Hi. I met some of your kinsmen downstairs, and they said this was your room. Can I come in?"

Iolanthe wished suddenly that she was as enamored of fine clothing as was Roderick. She felt positively rumpled in the same gown she always wore, with her hair in disarray, and her eyes still heavy with sleep. But there was naught to be done about it now. She sat up straighter still and tried to look as if such disorder was her custom.

"Aye," she said in her most regal tone. "Please come in."

Megan did, shutting the door behind her. She looked around her and smiled in pleasure. "Why, this is beautiful. What a peaceful place. You must love it here."

"I do," Iolanthe said, feeling unaccountably shy. " 'Tis the most glorious chamber I've ever seen."

"Thomas has excellent taste," Megan said, wandering about the chamber and touching things here and there. She opened the armoire door and peered at the CDs. She looked over her shoulder at Iolanthe. "Would you like me to put something in? Country? Opera? I can see Thomas's musical choices running rampant in here."

Iolanthe hardly knew what to say. There was a part of her that wanted to question Megan mercilessly, to see Thomas through another woman's eyes, to understand the parts of him he showed to his family. The other part of her was terrified to reveal that she had feelings for him. What would Megan think? Would she think her brother had lost his mind?

"Iolanthe?"

Iolanthe blinked. To hear her name coming so easily from

someone who was nearly a stranger was powerfully unsettling.

But it was perhaps the thing that made her realize that she was not so different from any other woman.

"Um," Iolanthe said, trying to think clearly through the swirl of emotions. "I like that Rach . . . um . . ."

"Rachmaninoff?" Megan asked, pulling out the CD. "The second piano concerto." She looked at Iolanthe. "Thomas's favorite."

"He's the one who bought it."

The music soon filled the chamber, but Iolanthe found herself less soothed than she usually was by it. The first time she had listened to it, the complicated notes cascading over one another had almost frightened her. Now, she found the passion of it glorious.

Even today, she became caught up in it, despite the fact that Thomas McKinnon's sister was still pacing about her chamber like a restless spirit. Megan finally turned the music down, then sat down in the chair facing Iolanthe. She smiled.

"Are you ready to talk?" she asked.

If Iolanthe had had any breath to lose, she would have lost it. Instead, she could only wheeze and stammer out a few incomprehensible words.

Megan waited patiently. Iolanthe seriously considered simply vanishing and leaving the woman to her own devices. But that would have made her seem an unforgivable coward, so she waved her hand toward the stereo, as if she couldn't bear to talk over the music, which unfortunately finished all too soon for her taste.

Iolanthe looked at the woman facing her and realized they were likely of an age. Perhaps Megan was a pair of years older than she, but the difference was not great. How would it have been to have had a woman to talk to during her lifetime? One of her age, who could have understood her trials?

How would it be to have such a friend now?

"You don't have to tell me anything, if you don't want to," Megan said kindly, "but I think sometimes it helps to have someone to talk to. A woman friend. Men, great as they are, sometimes just don't get it."

"Get it?"

"Truly understand a woman's heart," Megan clarified. "Not that they don't try, but they're men, after all. Now, I didn't used to be much for girl talk. I have sisters, of course, but I didn't talk to them when I was growing up. Too busy fighting, I guess."

"Aye, I can understand that," Iolanthe agreed.

"You have sisters?"

"One. A half-sister."

"Brothers?"

"One elder, who died when I was ten. Six half-brothers, who followed after me."

"Well, I only had Thomas, but he made enough trouble for several more of himself," Megan said. "Did you get along with your sister?"

"She sent me to my death," Iolanthe said. She had always suspected that Grudach had had a hand in the whole scheme, but at first she'd never thought her half-sister had orchestrated the thing. Duncan had told her as much a goodly time after the fact, but only when she'd forced him to. She should have seen it herself. Angus didn't have the wits to imagine up the idea of ridding himself of her by selling her to the English-man. Only Grudach could have been devious enough to see to those details.

"Well," Megan said, sounding as if she wished she hadn't brought it up. "Well," she said again, miserably.

Iolanthe shook her head. " 'Tis in the past. I shouldn't have said anything about it." She smiled weakly. "It doesn't pain me anymore. Not since T—" She closed her mouth abruptly, realizing what she was about to say.

But she saw the look in Megan's eye just the same. There would be no deceiving this one.

"Thomas?" Megan asked. "All right, Iolanthe, you have your listening ear. And I'm incredibly discreet."

" 'Tis nothing, truly—"

"Nothing?" Megan snorted. "I have one gift and one gift alone, and that is smelling out a romance. Now, tell me all the details, and don't leave anything out."

Iolanthe looked at her and for a moment was struck by the similarity between Megan McKinnon and her great-grandmother, Megan MacLeod. Though her great-grandmother had been ancient by the time Iolanthe had truly understood her, Megan MacLeod had still had a gleam in her eye when she talked about love. Wasn't she the reason Iolanthe had never gone to the shore?

Share it with your man, her great-grandmother had advised.

"Tell me how you first met him," Megan asked. "Was he charming, or did he make an ass of himself?"

There was no point in avoiding this conversation. Besides, she might learn something useful about the man she loved— such as his being utterly without redeeming qualities.

"Charming?" Iolanthe laughed a little uneasily. "He was senseless and snoring. The garrison had caught him unawares, I think, and he'd dashed his head against a rock."

Megan's eyes twinkled. "When I knew he was coming over here, I wondered what he'd be able to see. My husband couldn't see Ambrose or the others for quite some time. Even now, he still walks through ancestors without noticing them until they complain. So, what happened next? Did Thomas wake up, see you, then pledge undying devotion?"

"Nay, he came back up to the keep and insulted me."

"True to form."

"But then he apologized."

"Well," Megan said modestly, "we did our best to raise him right. Now, when did you fall in love?"

Iolanthe found she had lost all powers of speech. She cast about her for something to say, but all she could do was struggle for words and fail. How, by the saints, was she supposed to answer that? And to the man's sister no less!

"As I was saying before," Megan said conversationally, "having a woman friend is a wonderful thing. Whether it's your sister or someone you met during your life, it's a comfort." She looked at Iolanthe with a smile. "I know we don't know each other yet, but I'd like to be your friend. It seems to me that you need someone to talk to who isn't packing a sword or a hammer."

Iolanthe wanted desperately to believe she was serious. To have someone to pour her heart out to? Someone who might understand her fears of loving a man she could not hold? Of giving her heart where it might be cast aside in a year?

It would be a comfort indeed.

Iolanthe looked at Thomas's sister and found that she was merely waiting patiently, as if she had all the time in the world and nothing better to do with it than wait for Iolanthe to come to a decision.

She took a deep breath.

"I loved him," she began, "almost from the moment I laid eyes on him."

"Did you?" Megan asked gently.

"'Tis worse than that," Iolanthe admitted. "You see, I *knew* him."

Megan blinked. "You did? How? He's never been here before."

"It wasn't as if I'd seen him before. But in my youth, when I was trapped on my father's land with no hope of escape, I dreamed of a man who would come to rescue me. I lived each day with a hope that *this* would be the day he would come. That my life would begin in earnest when he freed me from that wolf's den I called home." She looked at Megan. "I know it sounds impossible, but it was of Thomas I dreamed."

Megan's eyes widened, but she looked only interested, not disbelieving. "So you saw him, recognized him, and then what?"

Iolanthe took a deep breath and recounted the events from there. She left out no detail, however slight. And all through the telling of the tale, Megan listened with a rapt expression. Iolanthe finished by telling her of the morning with the painter and how badly it had ended by her fleeing and Thomas leaving for New York.

"The painter is still at the inn," Megan said. "He's almost finished with your portrait. I didn't realize he was in the conservatory off the back of the house, though I suppose that's only logical because of the light there. I think if he hadn't been so close to being done, he would have thrown something at me for interrupting. As it was, he was just sitting there looking at you, falling in love."

"With me?" Iolanthe asked with a half laugh.

"You should see the painting."

"Then he has embellished."

"He hasn't. Not a stroke." Megan looked at her calculatingly. "What were you looking at when you were sitting for him—or should I ask whom?"

"What do you think?"

Megan laughed. "Well, it shows. Thomas will be ecstatic when he sees it."

"If he returns." Iolanthe looked out the window and sighed. "I couldn't blame him if he chooses to stay in his city. There isn't anything for him here."

"What about you? Aren't you here?"

"And what have I to offer him? Children? Warmth in his bed at night? Growing old together?" Iolanthe was on her feet pacing before the idea to do so entered her mind. "What kind of life is this? Trapped in this castle for the rest of his days?"

"You can still give him love," Megan protested. "You could travel with him. There is a world full of things you could share if you thought about it creatively. You could spend half a lifetime reading together, and that would be enough."

Iolanthe stopped in the middle of the chamber and bowed her head. "I am ignorant and unlearned," she said quietly. "Mark my words, sister. He will grow weary of me and leave."

"It sounds to me as if you've given up already."

"And just what else am I to do?"

"Fight for him!" Megan sat up and looked at her earnestly. "If you want him, if you want a life together, then fight for it. I'll tell you something about not giving up. Before I came to England, my life stank. I got fired from every job I'd ever had. My boyfriends were all creeps and dumped me regularly. Thomas had asked me to come over to look at your castle, and I knew that was just a pity job to keep me busy. I almost didn't come. I was ready to give up."

"And then?"

"And then I decided I would try one more time. I came over, met Gideon, and fell in love. And none of that would have happened if I hadn't given life one more chance to be good. And I also let Thomas do something for me I didn't have the means to do for myself. If I hadn't told him yes, where would I be?"

Iolanthe cast herself down into her chair.

"So am I to hope that Thomas will solve all the ills in my life?" she asked wearily.

"You could give him the chance."

"To what end?"

Megan smiled gravely. "So that you're both happy."

"But will we be?"

"Only you can answer that. But," she added, "I don't think you should decide that for Thomas."

"He deserves more."

"Let him be the judge."

"Could you love a ghost?"

Megan looked at her in silence for a moment or two. "I can't answer that. But I am not my brother either." She smiled. "I can't tell you what he wants; only he can. But I can tell you that what he tells you is the truth. He doesn't lie."

"So he said."

"Then believe him. And do your part. What Thomas can't fix, you can."

Iolanthe chewed on that for a time. Then she looked at Megan. "I suppose it would serve me to learn a little about the present day."

Megan smiled dryly. "It might. I imagine that locked door downstairs is hiding Thomas's business gear. He's got a computer, hasn't he?"

"Aye."

"Then use it. Use it to learn what you think you don't know. You'll have something to talk to him about when he gets home."

"I hardly know where to start."

"You start by getting out of this beautiful hiding place Thomas has built you. Let's walk down to the village and shop. I know there's not much there, but we'll make do." She bounced up out of her chair. "It'll be fun."

Iolanthe rose more slowly. "But what will the villagers think?"

"They'll think you're gorgeous unless you walk through a

door and scare the hell out of them. Just be casual."

Iolanthe looked down at her dress. "But my clothes—"

"Change."

There was that word again. She wondered if she would ever hear it without it fair knocking her to her knees with its many layers of meaning. Change her clothes. Change her hair.

Change her life.

Megan took off her coat. "Look at how I'm dressed. Jeans. Sweater. Sneakers on your feet. We'll look like twins, but you'll be the one they'll be staring at." She smiled encouragingly. "Go ahead, Iolanthe. Give it a try."

Well, she couldn't deny that she'd had practice in creating clothing from a picture. How much harder could it be to create them from someone standing in front of her? She looked carefully at Megan's clothes, front and back, then imagined them up on herself.

Megan blinked, then grinned. "Wow, I wish I could do that. See, that wasn't so hard, was it?"

Iolanthe looked down at herself, surprised at how strange it was to see herself in something besides her usual garb. Stranger still to see herself in blue trews. She felt almost indecent in clothing that showed the shape of her legs so clearly.

"I don't know . . ." Iolanthe said hesitantly.

"It's what everyone wears," Megan assured her. "You won't stand out."

"The garrison might have something to say about that," Iolanthe muttered. She looked at Megan and smiled weakly. "I suppose I'm ready."

"Then let's go. Today, the village. Tomorrow, Edinburgh. That's a *really* great place to shop."

"Well—"

Megan walked to the door. "Don't think about it, Iolanthe. We're worrying about today and today alone. Tomorrow will take care of itself."

Megan was already out the door before her last words were spoken, leaving Iolanthe no choice but to follow her. Iolanthe looked down at herself and wondered if she was making a horrible mistake.

Megan poked her head back in the door. "Coming?" she asked.

She looked so encouraging that Iolanthe found it impossible to beg off, which she would have done with any other person. So she put one foot in front of the other and followed Megan down the stairs to the dirt courtyard. She ignored the slack-mouthed stares of her garrison and Duncan's eyebrows, which were raised so far they disappeared under his hair.

"See?" Megan said with a wink as they walked through the gates. "Hardly a ripple in the water."

Even the MacDougal was speechless as they passed. Iolanthe supposed that perhaps new clothing now and then was a boon if that was the result.

She followed Megan from the castle, feeling as commandeered as she had the first time Thomas had pried her from her prison. Was this the way of things with all his family? Were they all so cunning? Or was she so weak she couldn't stand up to any of them?

"Isn't this fun?" Megan asked brightly as they walked down the path to the road. "You need to get out more, Iolanthe. It's good for you."

As was Megan de Piaget, apparently. Iolanthe smiled weakly and followed along, docile as a lamb.

The saints preserve her.

Chapter 21

A week later, Thomas sat in a glass-walled boardroom and stared out over the Manhattan skyline. He'd stopped listening an hour ago to the threats and counter-threats being swatted from one side of the table to the other like tennis balls. It wasn't that he didn't stand to make a great deal of money in the takeover. As chairman of the board, he would take home a very comfortable severance package. And it wasn't as if he was worried about his employees either. He'd already offered them the services of a professional headhunter to find them other comparable work if they so chose—at his expense. It wasn't even that someone had been sly enough to arrange things so selling was more attractive than being driven out of business by another larger firm.

It was that the firm doing the driving belonged to Arthur Davidson.

Tiffany's father.

Thomas pulled his gaze away from the afternoon sunlight glinting off buildings and looked at his erstwhile future father-in-law. The man was a shark and apparently had no compunction about backing Thomas into a corner because of his daughter's whim. Thomas had no doubt Tiffany was behind it. She'd already left a dozen messages at his hotel over the last week. He didn't suppose she was physically stalking him yet, but that couldn't be far behind.

Thomas began to look for an excuse to get out of there. What he needed was to call the inn and see how Iolanthe was doing. Maybe she was just hanging out in the sitting room and Mrs. Pruitt could hold the phone for her so they could talk. He'd known he would miss her, but he hadn't expected it to be this gut-wrenching.

The other surprising thing was how he now felt about the city. He'd always loved Manhattan. He'd loved the smell of the place, the sights, the sounds. But now it was just noise and dirt. He had a surprising longing for driving on the wrong side of the road, toast that was cold for breakfast, and drinks that didn't freeze your throat on the way down.

And he longed for Iolanthe. He wanted to tell her of the bloody siege going on in the boardroom, of the fools who fought on either side, of their stratagem that made his head ache. He wanted to sit in her room with her and listen to something on the stereo, sit in her garden and watch her flowers bloom, sit with her in the sitting room of the inn and enjoy the fire.

He looked at his attorney and wondered if making a break for the john would fly. It wasn't as if Jake couldn't handle the negotiations on his own. Thomas prized his attorney for his smooth-as-silk exterior, which hid a ruthlessness that had left Thomas awestruck the first time Jake had displayed it. Duncan MacLeod would have found the man very much to his liking.

Davidson's henchman excused himself, and Thomas saw his chance. He followed the man out, ready to tail him to the bathroom and then maybe down to the street for a snack.

Apparently, a trip to the can was a ruse. Thomas followed the man right into his office. Well, now he was there, there was no sense in not using the phone. The man walked around his desk and sat down, then looked up in surprise.

"Hey," he said crossly, "I came in here for some peace and quiet."

Thomas looked at the man's nameplate. He'd been thinking of him as "the snake" from the beginning; maybe it was time to start using his proper name. "Well, Mr. Anthony DiSalvio, you'll have it just as soon as I use your phone."

"Why?" DiSalvio asked with a smirk. "Calling in reinforcements?"

Thomas had developed a healthy dislike for the man over three days of meetings, and that comment only strengthened it.

"Calling home," Thomas said shortly.

"Sure you are."

"To Scotland. And don't bother billing me for it."

"We'll get it out of you one way or another." DiSalvio leaned back in his chair and shook his head. "What is it with that place, anyway? I know more people who've migrated there."

"Less stress."

"More sheep, more like," DiSalvio muttered as he shuffled papers on his desk. He looked up suddenly. "Know any MacLeods?"

Thomas paused in mid-dial. "What?"

"One of my old partners lives in England, but he's always going up to hang out in Scotland with a bunch of MacLeods. His sister married one."

"Did she?"

"The guy's name is James, I think." DiSalvio shook his head. "Crazy bunch. They all fool around with swords like some medieval fairy group. You know, those light-steps that dress up in skirts."

"Plaids."

"Whatever."

Thomas put the phone down. "James, did you say?"

"That's the guy."

"How interesting."

"Naw, it's nuts. I keep trying to get Alex—he's the guy who used to work for me, and what a barracuda! He makes your guy look like a fifth-grade girl. Anyway, I keep trying to get Alex to come back and work for me, but he says he can't handle the city anymore." DiSalvio sighed heavily. "A waste of a good mind, but I can't do anything about it. I even took him out for dinner last night, him and that Amazon he's married to. You wouldn't believe the money I offered him—or the money I spent on dinner!"

Thomas was just sure he'd heard the man wrong. "You had dinner with him last night? He's here in New York?"

"Yeah," DiSalvio said, taking a toothpick to his teeth. Apparently he was still looking for stray bits of last night's meal. "He comes over once a year just to torture me."

"I'm sure that's his main reason," Thomas said dryly.

"You don't know Alex. And you wouldn't want to know his wife." He looked almost unsettled. "She's a looker, but

I wouldn't want to meet her in a dark alley. She pulled a knife on me at dinner. She's another one of those reenactment wackos, though I'd sure like to see her in a pair of tights."

Thomas had the overwhelming desire to sit down. "They couldn't still be here."

"Oh, sure. They're over at the Plaza." He smiled proudly. "Alex can afford that and plenty more. He made a crapload of money while he was here—off saps like you, of course."

"Of course," Thomas said, wishing he had his own knife to brandish. "You couldn't get me the number, could you?"

DiSalvio picked up the phone. "Marj, get me Smith's number for the dead fish in here. Yeah, I'm doing him a favor, what's it to you?" He slammed down the phone. "Damned uppity Brooklyn women. Thinks she needs to run my life."

Marj, a very ancient and far-from-uppity-looking woman, entered the room shortly thereafter and shoved the number at DiSalvio.

"Don't be late for dinner," she snapped.

DiSalvio looked at Thomas sheepishly. "My ma. She's the only secretary I can seem to hold on to."

"Astonishing."

"Yeah, I think so, too." He shoved the paper at Thomas. "Here you go. Guess you sheep-lovers need to stick together."

Thomas's desire to grind Tony DiSalvio into the dust was tempered somewhat by the phone number he had in his hand. He had the same feeling of destiny he'd had when he'd first learned of his castle coming up on the auction block.

Alex Smith knew James MacLeod. James MacLeod's hobby apparently was fighting with swords.

Was that James MacLeod the same one Iolanthe couldn't seem to come up with a death date for?

Well, there was only one way to find out.

Thomas walked back to the conference room and leaned down to talk to his attorney.

"Get us out of this with as little damage as possible," he whispered.

Jake's jaw went slack. "But I thought you wanted them crushed."

Thomas considered, then nodded. "You're right. Stick it to them. But still get us out as quickly as possible." DiSalvio had bought himself that much leniency.

"You're the boss," Jake said doubtfully.

"Yeah."

"You're also crazy."

"You're right. Gotta go. Got things to do."

"More important than this?"

"Much."

The understatement of the year. Thomas straightened and tried not to leave the room at a dead run.

T_{wo} hours later, he was sitting in a very expensive sitting room of a suite at the Plaza, looking at two people he was almost certain possessed the key to his future.

Alexander Smith was your typically good-looking *GQ* poster boy, but the picture was spoiled by his dry wit and easygoing manner. Thomas would have thought Tony Di-Salvio had been talking about the wrong lawyer if it hadn't been for the shrewdness in Alex's eyes. His wife, Margaret, was every bit as good-looking as Tony had advertised, but Thomas was hard-pressed to believe she would pull a knife on anyone. She was poised, lovely, and gracious.

And then she opened her mouth to speak.

Her accent was English, but she sounded like she'd learned English from Chaucer. Not that Thomas was an expert or anything, but he'd been bored one semester in school, and he'd taken a poetry class to try to channel some of his energy into something creative. It had turned out to be not poetry writing, but poetry reading, and three-quarters of the semester had been spent bouncing between *Beowulf* and *The Canterbury Tales*. He'd excelled, given the gift for languages he certainly hadn't acquired except through his gene pool, and could still read the text in its original language and keep most of the words straight in his head.

He wondered how Margaret Smith would have done at the same task.

Interesting.

"You said it was urgent," Alex said with a disarming smile. "So, spill it."

"My mother is a MacLeod," Thomas said, hoping to win a few brownie points.

"The saints preserve us, we're surrounded by them," Margaret muttered.

Alex smiled at her, then turned back to Thomas. "Then you're family. What do you need?"

"You won't believe this—"

"Ah, but we likely will," Margaret said.

Alex laughed. "She's right. We'll believe just about anything."

Thomas took a deep breath. "All right, this is the deal. A couple of years ago, I bought a castle."

"In Scotland?" Alex asked.

"On the border. But that's not the thing about it. I finally went over about a month ago to check it out." He paused and hoped they wouldn't think he'd lost his mind. Just how was it one went about telling complete strangers that one owned a castle full of ghosts? Well, maybe the direct approach was the best. He smiled weakly. "It's haunted."

Margaret sighed. "I'm unsurprised."

"The thing is," Thomas said, "it's not so much the fact that it's haunted. It's who it's haunted by."

"All right," Alex said, "I'm biting. Who's it haunted by?"

"By a woman who is the great-granddaughter of Jesse MacLeod, who had a father named James, who doesn't have a death date." He paused for effect. "Ring any bells?"

There was absolute silence in the room for several moments. Alex opened his mouth to speak, then apparently swallowed the wrong way because he began to choke. Margaret slapped him forcefully on the back until he held up his hand for her to stop.

"Great story," Alex wheezed. "Couldn't be more interested. Really."

"I understand your brother-in-law is named James MacLeod."

Alex seemed to be beyond the point of coherent speech. That alone was enough to convince Thomas he'd struck gold. He moved in for the killing blow.

"Is he a ghost?"

Alex seemed to have great difficulty swallowing. Margaret had practically beaten him to a pulp before he managed to tell her to stop between coughs. Margaret looked at Thomas.

"Jamie's no ghost," she said, sounding very sure about it.

"No," Alex managed. "He's definitely very alive."

Well, that was a dead end. So much for the theory of James being a ghost. Not that his being a ghost would have helped much anyway, but Thomas had held out a hope that somehow beyond reason and logic, James would have had some kind of help to offer him.

"If your brother-in-law's not a ghost," Thomas said slowly, "then what's the secret of his castle? Everyone at my place who knows anything says there's a secret associated with the keep."

Oddly enough, both Alex and Margaret had gone completely still.

Well, that was something.

"The secret isn't that he's a ghost?"

Alex and Margaret looked like two people who didn't dare look at each other for fear of what they would give away.

"I *am* family," Thomas reminded them.

They did exchange a glance at that. Then Alex looked at him.

"Why do you want to know?" he asked carefully.

"Do you know the secret?"

"I know lots of secrets," Alex said easily. "Why don't you tell me your problem, and I'll see if I have a secret to fix it."

"Fair enough," Thomas agreed. "This is the problem. I met the woman who haunts my keep, and we fell in love. I was thinking that maybe the secret of her ancestral keep—which, by the way, she won't tell me—might be something that would help us, well, survive." He came to an abrupt halt and realized how utterly stupid he sounded. What kind of secret was going to fix what needed to be fixed? He was mortal; she was not.

There was no fixing that.

"Forget it," he said, shaking his head. "I don't know why I even asked."

He sat there and looked out their window with its fabulous view and felt more discouraged than he had in his entire life. That feeling wouldn't last, of course. He would get back to England and get Iolanthe somewhere she couldn't escape, then they would talk. It would all work out.

But for now he was incredibly bummed, and he had every intention of wallowing in it.

"You know what would be handy," Thomas said.

"What?" Margaret asked gently.

"If I could stop it. Stop her death."

There was silence in the room for quite some time. Thomas watched the sun's reflection disappear from skyscraper windows. Dusk fell. Stars no doubt came out, but he couldn't see them from where he sat.

Alex cleared his throat. "It just so happens," he said slowly, "that we might be able to help you with that."

Thomas blinked. "You might? How?"

"It just so happens," Alex said, "that the secret of the keep is . . . time travel."

Thomas looked at him, blinked several times in silence, then laughed. He threw back his head and laughed long and hard. He looked at Margaret and Alex, expecting them to share the sickest joke he'd ever heard.

But they weren't laughing.

"You aren't kidding," Thomas said, his smile fading abruptly.

Margaret rubbed her hands together briskly. "Let us be about this business. No time to waste." She pinned Thomas to the spot with a piercing glance. "Do you know when she died?"

He tried to nod but found suddenly that his neck wasn't working very well.

She looked at Alex triumphantly. "He could go back *before.*"

Alex shook his head. "If Jamie's theory of time-traveling is to be believed, her time in her century would have to be over. She'd have to be near death. As wonderful as I'm sure she would still be at the end of her life, I doubt Thomas would want to pull her forward when she was sixty-something."

"She was murdered," Thomas managed. "She was only twenty-four at the time."

"Perfect!" Margaret exclaimed. "He can go back *before* she was murdered and rescue her."

Alex paused, then shook his head. "Even if he could—and I'm not saying that it would work, because you know how fickle those gates are—even *if* he could, who's to say he'd arrive at the right time? He could get there three years before her death, or twenty minutes afterwards."

Margaret frowned thoughtfully. "I suppose you have it aright, husband." She looked at Thomas. "Forgive me, my friend. I hadn't thought the problem through."

Thomas swallowed with difficulty. "Are you serious? About this time travel business?"

Alex sighed. "I'm going to trust you and hope that my trust isn't misplaced."

"It won't be."

Alex took a deep breath. "Well, this is the thing. It's a long story, but my sister wound up in fourteenth-century Scotland and in time married the current laird of the day, James MacLeod."

Thomas blinked but said nothing. All right, so he had a castle full of ghosts. If that was possible, maybe there were other things possible that he hadn't banked on before.

"They came forward, back to the twentieth century, thanks to a time gate in the forest next to the keep."

"Really," Thomas said evenly.

Alex smiled briefly. "Hard to swallow, I know. And believe me, I wouldn't believe it either, but you see, I've used the gate in the forest. And I've used the other gates scattered all over his land."

"The one to medieval England, for instance," Margaret added.

Thomas looked at her with wide eyes. "Then you're—"

"Margaret of Falconberg," she said.

Thomas could only gape at her.

"I was born in the Year of Our Lord's Grace 1165," she added with a smile.

Thomas didn't want to believe it, but he had a single, compelling reason to.

Iolanthe.

What if he could travel back in time before her death? And stop it?

Thomas sat back in his chair and simply considered for several moments.

And as he considered, he remembered vividly the way he'd felt as he'd climbed the stairs to that cursed guard tower—as if he'd been there before. But he'd known he hadn't.

Yet, what if he had?

"Think on this, husband," Margaret was saying. "Even if all goes well, and Thomas reaches the proper time, how will his lady recognize him? She knows him from now, not then."

Thomas stared at her in horror. "I never thought of that."

"A pity you couldn't go back in time and have some kind of predetermined sign," Margaret mused. "So that she'd remember you."

Alex laughed suddenly, leaned over, and kissed Margaret full on the mouth.

"You're brilliant!" he exclaimed.

She looked momentarily startled, then smiled sweetly. "Am I?"

"I read an article on memory once," Alex said enthusiastically. He focused that enthusiasm on Thomas. "The theory was, our brains are only using a fraction of what we're capable of using."

"I wonder, husband, if you're using less of yours than usual," Margaret said.

"I'm not. This piece said that there's no reason we can't remember the future." He shrugged happily. "Who knows, maybe that whole déjà vu thing is the future we've already done and we're just remembering it."

"Well . . ." Thomas said slowly.

"Drivel," Margaret said crisply.

"And you have a better idea?" Alex asked her.

"Why raise the poor lad's hopes when 'tis an impossible task?"

"Why not raise them? Where's your faith?" Alex asked with a smile.

"I have faith in my blade——"

"So," Thomas interrupted, "you're saying that if I go back in time and stop her murder, that there's no reason that she couldn't remember me?"

"No reason that she could either," Margaret put in grimly.

"Do you remember where you read the article?" Thomas asked Alex.

He shook his head. "Sorry. But it seems logical enough, when you think about how the universe is going forward and backward in time concurrently."

Thomas looked at Margaret. "What do you think?"

"I think that if you love the girl, perhaps you have no choice. But 'tis a very great risk you take. What if you take all the pains to rescue her, and she'll have nothing to do with you?"

Thomas didn't want to think about that.

"And can you wield a sword?" she continued. "You cannot go back without that skill. You'd last the space of ten heart-beats, then find yourself dead or in someone's dungeon."

"She has a point there," Alex agreed.

Thomas gave that some thought, then looked at them. "Will you teach me?"

Alex shook his head. "You don't want us——"

"He certainly might want me," Margaret interrupted haughtily.

"He wants Jamie, my love," Alex said. "Who better to teach him to fight like a Scot?"

"I suppose," Margaret conceded reluctantly. "I must admit that I've no complaints about his skill."

"See," Alex said, looking at Thomas with a grin. "My wife's glowing recommendation of my sister's husband. Now, if you were to ask Jamie, he would tell you that he's unequaled, in any century."

"And is he right?" Thomas asked.

"It's a toss-up," Alex said. "Margaret is without peer as well."

"Wise man," Margaret said, smiling sweetly at him. "You'll live to fight another day."

Alex looked at his watch. "They're five hours ahead of us, which makes it after midnight. I'll call Jamie tomorrow morning and talk to him." He looked at Thomas. "If you like?"

"Please do."

Alex smiled. "It'll all work out. It always seems to."

Thomas had nothing to say to that. The thought of actually being able to do something about his situation was so astonishing, he could hardly take it in.

"I think," he said, standing slowly, "that I should go back to my hotel and try to recover."

"Leave us your number."

"Do you think I'd do otherwise?"

Alex laughed and got to his feet. He extended his hand and shook Thomas's. "I'll call you after I've talked to Jamie. I'm sure he can help."

Thomas nodded, said his good-byes to both Alex and Margaret, then stumbled from their room. He made his way back to his hotel in a daze, his thoughts nothing but a jumble in his head. Just what was he going to say to Jamie when he finally met him?

Hello, cousin. I'd like to time-travel through one of the gates on your land. Do you mind?

If he hadn't been so desperate, the idea would have been too silly to contemplate.

He sat on the end of his bed, stared at nothing, and thought back on what he'd heard that afternoon. He could try to go back in time and rescue Iolanthe before she was murdered, and maybe it *was* possible to remember the future.

But if he changed the past, would she have a future? What good would all these machinations do him if Iolanthe couldn't remember him?

What if that little fridge over there was really stocked with booze and not just pop?

He sat there and tried to catch the breath he'd suddenly lost. He felt as if he'd just run a marathon. His legs were shaking, his heart was pounding in his chest, and sweat was pouring down his face.

So he might be able to get to her before she died.

But if he saved her, she likely wouldn't know him.

Damn.

Chapter 22

I olanthe stood in the space Thomas had appropriated as his office and felt better than she had in centuries. She'd spent almost a week with Megan MacLeod McKinnon de Piaget and found her to be a marvelous companion. They had shopped in the village. Iolanthe had even ventured inside Megan's automobile and managed to keep from screaming as they traveled to a nearby village for different scenery. She hadn't braved Edinburgh, but Megan had assured her that perhaps it was better she go there for the first time with Thomas.

But even little ventures to a handful of little villages had widened Iolanthe's horizons. She'd learned to be unobtrusive in shops, to mask her ghostly condition, to avoid walking into and through things that would have bruised a mortal sorely.

She'd also discovered the pleasure of a nice change of clothes. No wonder Roderick found it so much to his liking. She and Megan had bought marvelous things called fashion magazines. They'd spent hours poring over clothes and shoes and ways to wear one's hair. Iolanthe had been scandalized by the pictures of women in scanty underclothing, but Megan had assured her it was nothing out of the ordinary. Iolanthe had remained unconvinced. She'd turned her attentions to the clothing she thought suitable and now found herself with dozens of ideas to try. Today she was wearing a long, patterned skirt with a dark blue sweater. It was lovely. It made her feel lovely.

Of course, clothes weren't the extent of the changes. Megan had been full of ideas on how to make Iolanthe's life more interesting. Books, music, art, travel. It was nothing Iolanthe had any experience with. She had been ashamed to

tell Megan the extent of her ignorance, but Megan hadn't
stood for any reticence. She'd grilled Iolanthe mercilessly,
leaving no embarrassment undiscovered. But she had done it
so gently and so relentlessly that Iolanthe hadn't been able
to resist her. And when the true depth of her lack of knowledge had been plumbed, Megan had turned her lack into what
seemed like an opportunity for great learning.

Had Iolanthe not loved her before, she would have then.

Which left her standing where she was at present, wearing
clothes from the twenty-first century and using one of its
handiest tools. She cleared her throat and gestured expan-
sively behind her to what sat on Thomas's desk.

"This," Iolanthe said to the assembled, ragtag group of
men clustered in front of her in the tower chamber, "is a
computer."

There were several murmurs of appreciation and wise nods
that answered that announcement.

" 'Tis shiny," one of the men said reverently.

"Handsome," another agreed.

"Fit fer tha rubbish bin," said Connor MacDougal with his
usual disdain for anything he hadn't intimidated with his
sword.

Iolanthe glared at him, then turned her attentions back to
the more appreciative members of her audience.

"Today, I am going to learn to read," she announced. "And
you are going to help me."

"I ken hoo ta scratch ma name," Connor said stiffly, "and
'tis enough fer me."

"Well," Iolanthe said, "it isn't enough for me."

Truer words had never been spoken, to her mind. Now,
were she to be completely honest, she hadn't been all that
excited about Thomas's machine when she'd first seen it either. Beeps and strange-sounding voices coming from the
little box, and a window filled with indecipherable scribblings? Never mind the astonishing pictures he'd shown her.
On the whole, she'd found it less than impressive. She'd
firmly decided it was beneath her to even investigate it further.

Then three things had changed her mind.

Thomas had gone to New York.

Megan had come to visit.

And she'd had the misfortune of eavesdropping on a handful of tourists from the Colonies.

She'd heard in glorious detail of the wonders New York had to offer. She surmised after listening for quite some time that 'twas a city definitely larger than the York that found itself in England, and much more interesting. Plays, music, and strange and exotic creatures called cabbies.

"And the women," one man had said with a rapturous sigh, which had earned him a sharp poke in the ribs from his lady wife. The poke hadn't deterred him or his male companions later when the women had gone off to examine the foliage in the forest. Iolanthe had listened with growing horror to the descriptions of the women. Intelligent, beautiful, rich, bedecked with jewels, and the equal of their men in every manner that counted.

And there she was, Iolanthe MacLeod, uneducated, unenlightened, and unalive.

Well, the last was nothing she could change. But the other things, aye, those she could do something about. That Thomas might not find her lacking.

It had unnerved her greatly when Megan had announced she needed to get back home to London. Iolanthe had come close to begging her to stay, but Megan had headed off that bit of groveling by promising to return often and see how things were going. She also introduced Iolanthe to the wonders of the modern telephone. Not that she would have been able to lift it on her own, but perhaps she might find someone to help her now and then. Megan had promised she would call Iolanthe often, then left the inn with tears in her eyes. Iolanthe had wept openly, then retreated to her chamber to mourn the loss of the first woman friend she'd ever had.

Her melancholy hadn't lasted long, though. She wasn't sure when Thomas would return, but she was certain it had to be soon. She wanted to be ready.

She had pressed Mrs. Pruitt into service by having her help with the computer. Megan had left Mrs. Pruitt with detailed instructions on how to get and keep the computer working. Megan had also shown Mrs. Pruitt how to work the magical connection that would feed the computer information from all parts of the globe.

Now, that was something Iolanthe wasn't sure she believed—the world being round, that was. Then again, she wouldn't have believed that little things set out into the sunlight would gather enough of what they needed to power a machine either. So she took the globe business on faith.

And now the reading. Mrs. Pruitt had agreed to give Iolanthe whatever aid she required—for a price. And that price was for Iolanthe to keep Ambrose captive in the sitting chamber long enough for Mrs. Pruitt to talk to him.

Iolanthe supposed a human's aid would be worth whatever it cost her, though Ambrose might have a different opinion. She'd found him soon after Mrs. Pruitt had set forth her terms. He'd balked at first, then relented when Iolanthe had told him what she stood to lose if he refused. He'd agreed with extreme reluctance to a meeting three days hence.

Mrs. Pruitt had told Iolanthe what to do, then departed for her chamber, where she said she planned to prepare her toilette for the upcoming tryst.

Which left Iolanthe in Thomas's office chamber, standing before the computer and commanding the attention of her garrison.

"You, Ian," Iolanthe said, beckoning to one of her men. "Mrs. Pruitt says to push this place here." She pointed to the button Mrs. Pruitt had shown her on the keyboard. "Push this to start my lessons."

Ian pushed manfully and the computer sprang to life.

And Ian fell over in a dead faint.

Iolanthe swore in irritation. "Weak-stomached fool. Move him out of the way, and someone else come to take his place. We'll have many of these things to push today, so the rest of you gather your courage and be about my business with me. Mayhap we'll all learn something."

"Aye, learn what fools we are," Connor grumbled.

Iolanthe looked at him. "Wouldn't you like to know something besides how to scribble out your own name?"

Connor merely scrunched up his face and was silent.

"There's more to life than swordplay."

"Now ye go too far, woman."

"You might read something to improve yours," she shot back.

"My what?" he demanded.

"Your swordplay!"

Connor stomped from the small tower chamber, his curses lingering in the air behind him. Iolanthe looked over her crew.

"Anyone else want to leave?"

Not a soul moved.

Duncan cleared his throat and came closer. "Come on, lads. She has it aright."

"I wish you luck," said the lace-bedecked ghost sprawled in a chair next to the computer's table.

Iolanthe looked at Roderick. "You could help."

"Aye, ye frilly bugger," Duncan said. "Or are ye too good to stir yerself for the likes of us?"

"And what do you care?" Roderick returned lazily. "You already know how to read."

Iolanthe looked at her cousin in surprise. "You do?"

Duncan looked almost embarrassed. "Aye. But that doesn't excuse that Victorian fool from his task here."

Roderick sighed, stretched, and came to stand next to Iolanthe. "I can see my skill is needed. The style of writing on this contraption is horrendous, but I suppose I can make out a word or two. Let's have it begin its lessons, and I'll do what I can."

Iolanthe looked back at the computer's window. "Stephen, push that button there. That's what Mrs. Pruitt said to do."

Her guardsman pushed mightily and the computer continued its work.

"Welcome to Smiley's Adult Reading Course," said the computer, leaving the chamber ringing with various gasps and curses of surprise. "We'll begin with the alphabet."

"Sensible enough," Roderick agreed.

Iolanthe glared him to silence, then turned back with only a minor bit of trepidation to the screen.

"This is the letter *A.*"

"Aaaaee," dutifully echoed all the souls in the chamber.

"That's right," said the computer. "*A.* Uppercase *A.* Lowercase *a.*"

"Well," Iolanthe said. "Two of them."

There was stunned silence.

"Nothing to be done about it," Iolanthe said, putting her shoulders back. "We'll just press on and do the best we can."

But she couldn't deny that she had begun to wonder quite seriously about the advisability of the scheme she had put her hand to.

Fortunately for her, 'twas too late to turn back now. She couldn't shame herself in front of the men. If that pampered puss Roderick could learn to read, then by the saints, so could she.

Because when Thomas came home, she intended to be reading several very difficult things that she might impress him. And then perhaps he wouldn't find the women he'd seen in New York quite so fascinating.

Assuming she could wrest the computer's will to carry out her own desires and master its lessons.

"The letter *B*," the computer said calmly.

Heaven help her.

Chapter 23

T *homas* drove up the lane and turned into the inn's driveway. He'd never been gladder for a sight in his life than that of the little Tudor-beamed inn nestled so securely against the hill. He pulled to a stop, turned off the key, and slouched down in his seat for a few minutes of uninterrupted quiet.

Well, the trip across the Atlantic had been better this time. Business class had definitely made things easier, as had hopping a shuttle up from London to Edinburgh. Driving an hour from the airport to get home was certainly preferable to eight. Of course, getting out of Manhattan and to the airport had been a sticky business, but it wasn't every day that he found himself tailed by a very familiar woman dressed in a trench coat, Vuarnet sunglasses, and a brown fedora covering an enormous red wig.

Tiffany Amber Davidson.

Undercover.

He hadn't noticed her at first. He'd been distracted by his talk with Alexander and Margaret Smith. Alex had called him the following morning to say Jamie was willing to do whatever he could to help; all Thomas had to do was call him when he was ready to act. Thomas had taken down Jamie's number dutifully, though he suspected he could have pried the same out of Ambrose without much difficulty.

Not that he would have had to. He could have called it to mind at any time, given that it was indelibly burned into his mind.

He'd spent a final pair of days at his office, closing up shop. It wasn't as if he hadn't done it a time or two before. And it wasn't as if he wasn't doing it with the satisfaction of knowing that Jake had gouged Arthur Davidson thoroughly. Jake had been unapologetically good-humored about his actions, presented Thomas with a bill for his exorbitant fee, then offered to tag along just in case Thomas found himself in other legal difficulties in the near future. Thomas had been tempted, just in case getting himself back to medieval Scotland would include getting himself free of an enemy's dungeon. He suspected that Jake could get them out of even that.

His long-time partner in crime had settled for several months in the south of France, invited Thomas to take him back on board for the next business venture, then skipped out of the office with the carefree expression of a man who had just made a good deal of money and enjoyed doing so.

Not that Thomas hadn't felt the same way. Tiffany had cost her father a bundle, and Thomas couldn't help but feel somewhat repaid for that alone.

After finishing up what needed to be done, he'd headed toward the airport. Along with his gear, he'd carried an envelope with a magazine article in it that Alexander Smith had left for him at the front desk of his hotel.

An article on remembering the future.

He'd been riveted to it the moment he'd begun reading. He'd read it in the cab on the way to the airport and reread it as he'd made his way to check-in. He'd thought about calling Iolanthe on his cell phone to tell her what he'd learned, then thought better of it. With as quickly as he planned to be home, there was no sense in possibly letting his plans slip before he had her in the same room to tell her about them. He'd found everything he needed to solve their untenable situation. Thinking about it had been all-consuming.

Which was why, likely enough, he hadn't noticed Samantha Spade following him at an indiscreet distance until he'd been standing in the British Air ticket line.

It was then that he realized he'd seen her several times before. New York was full of interesting characters. He'd just assumed she was another one of them.

Losing her in the airport had seemed improbable, so he'd merely pretended he hadn't seen her. He'd picked up his ticket, boarded the plane, then hung out near the cabin doors to see if she got on. He'd been almost sure she wouldn't, mostly because of her lack of luggage. So she would know he'd gone to London. England was a very big place, and it would take her a long time to track him down. Hopefully, by then he would have done his bit of time-traveling, rescued Iolanthe, and settled down happily in some century or other. Tiffany was nothing but an annoyance that would hopefully remain on yonder beckoning shores.

He heaved himself from the car, retrieved his suitcase, and entered the inn. Mrs. Pruitt gave him a cursory glance.

"You're home," she noted.

"Finally."

"Hrmph," Mrs. P. said. "Business go well?"

"Had to sell my company. But it cost them."

"Well done, then," she said approvingly. "Best be about your business here. You'll note there've been some changes made."

He could hardly wait to find out what those were. Had Connor MacDougal taken over the keep? Had Iolanthe departed for locations unknown?

He threw his gear into his room, dragged a hand through his hair, and left at what others might have called a dead run. He called it a quick trot. He was out of shape, anyway. Too much time in a boardroom was hazardous to one's bum. A little healthy jog up to the castle was just the ticket for him.

He slowed once he was within sight of Thorpewold, then he came to a halt in front of the barbican. At least there were no protestors.

Nor were there any ghosts.

He wandered inside the gates. The bailey was empty, and he wondered, with a brief flash of panic, if he might have imagined the past couple of months. Ghosts and all.

Then he heard a chorus of manly laughter and a few hearty curses coming from the tower, and the tension dropped off him like scales. Who needed New York with its hearty deli sandwiches, its world-class entertainment, and its mouthy cabbies? He had a keep full of ghosts who'd taught him to curse in Gaelic while he pounded nails into floorboards.

Life was good.

He walked across the bailey and up the steps. A pair of Highlanders guarded the door to his office, which stood ajar. They looked ready to alert the occupants of the room, but he shook his head quickly.

"Let me just look," he whispered.

"As ye will, my laird," whispered one of the men. The other one nodded with a wide smile.

Well, perhaps *my laird* was pushing things, but Thomas couldn't help but feel somewhat flattered by the title. He was tempted to let it go to his head, but he suspected Iolanthe would soon disabuse him of any delusions of grandeur he might have had.

He went to the doorway and listened. He could hear Iolanthe talking but couldn't make out what she was saying. So he leaned in the slightest bit and looked around the Highlanders who were standing at the door blocking his view.

He could hardly believe his eyes.

Iolanthe was sitting in his chair, reading aloud.

All right, if all he had seen was her with a book being held up in front of her by two struggling Scots, he would have been surprised. What he saw just floored him. Not only was she reading, she was wearing jeans and a sweatshirt that said "The Stone of Scone Rocks." Thomas opened his mouth to comment on that, then shut it and shook his head. Best to leave that one alone.

"Och, turn the page, ye silly twit," she snapped at one of her men. "Cannae ye see I'm finished with that one?"

"Sorry, lady," came the abashed reply of a bekilted soul who then apparently used most of his energy to heave a simple page over. He fell back on the floor, spent.

Iolanthe cleared her throat. "Here we are then. 'See the knight run. See him run after the dragon.'" She looked at her audience. "The dragon's snatched the wench, ye ken."

The men nodded obediently.

Iolanthe turned back to her book. "'See the dragon turn and spit fire.'" She cursed at another of her guardsmen. "I'm finished again, Robert. Follow along more closely next time."

"As ye will, lady," Robert said, struggling manfully to turn the page. "But I ken naught of this reading business."

"It's past time you learned," she said sternly. "Must we

turn Thomas's computer back on for another go at the alphabet?"

There was a hearty chorus of nays in answer.

"Well, then," she said. "Follow along and see if you can't
keep up." She looked over her shoulder at Roderick, who
lounged behind her. "Sit up, you fool. This is the difficult
part, and I may need help."

Thomas smiled and leaned against the doorframe where
he could look at her but be hidden behind several substantial
guardsmen. He listened in wonder as she plowed through the
simple book. So the book was easy. The fact that she'd
learned to read in the short time he'd been gone was nothing
short of amazing.

What surprised him even more was suspecting that she
hadn't done it just for herself. She'd had centuries in which
to learn to read. That she had chosen the past two weeks
while he'd been gone had to have some significance.

A half hour and twenty guardsmen later, Iolanthe had finished her book. The final pair of book holders collapsed with
groans, and the rest of the guardsmen, those who hadn't been
incapacitated by their labors, got to their feet and filed out
of the doorway. Thomas stood back to let them pass. Connor
MacDougal looked at him with a scowl.

" 'Tis drivel, that," he said curtly.

"Sounded like a good story to me."

The MacDougal looked down at him disdainfully. "No
doubt it would to a simpleton such as yerself."

So things hadn't changed that drastically if Connor
MacDougal was still being nasty. Thomas leaned against the
doorframe until the last man had passed, then looked inside.
There were several bodies still littering the floor. Roderick
sat next to Iolanthe, sprawled in some chair of his own imagining.

But it was Iolanthe who Thomas could not tear his gaze
from. She was looking over his desk, apparently selecting
her next tome for the enlightenment of the garrison. What
he wouldn't have given to have walked into the room, put his
arms around her, and spun her around to kiss her soundly.

Actually, he was willing to give quite a lot for the privi-
lege.

"What think you of *The Ogre and the Troll*?" Iolanthe asked absently.

"Oh, please no," Roderick begged. "I can't listen to that yet another time."

"Then I'll find someone else willing to aid me—"

"How about me?" Thomas asked, stepping into the room. Iolanthe spun around and gaped at him. "You're home."

You're home. Sweeter words had never caressed his ears. He smiled at her.

"Yes. I can see you've been busy."

She looked as if she couldn't decide if she was pleased or horrified. She smoothed her clothes self-consciously, then finally clasped her hands in front of her and looked at him in consternation.

"You look nice," he said.

"At your sister's feet lies the blame," she said with her chin up. "She lured me into all manner of shops in the village."

He felt his jaw go slack. "Megan was here?"

"For a se'nnight."

He wasn't sure what he was more surprised by: that his sister had been up without having let him know she was coming, or that she and Iolanthe had bonded enough to go shopping together. In fact, the more he looked at the woman he loved, the more he could see his sister's stamp on her wardrobe. Jeans, sweatshirt, Keds. Megan's standard uniform.

"She sent me the books as well," Megan said, gesturing behind her.

"I recognized her favorite titles," Thomas said. He looked at her and could hardly believe the change in her. It wasn't just her clothes that had changed. Something had happened to her over the past couple of weeks. He shuddered to think the things his sister had introduced her to.

But that wasn't what affected him the most. It was looking at her and realizing how much he'd missed her. He should have called her every day. He should have sent her gifts, filled her room with flowers, written her letters. He would make up for it. He wouldn't leave again.

Well, unless you counted the little trip he planned to make

to Jamie's castle to use that forest time machine.

He walked over and picked up one of the books. "I'll turn the pages for you, if you like."

"I've only just learned," she said defensively. "You would find these books quite beneath you."

"Would I?" he asked. "Why don't you let me be the judge?"

She pursed her lips. "Your sister said that often about you."

"Well," he said cheerfully, "of the lot of them, Megan knows me best." He reached around and picked up one of the books. "Let's go read."

She wasn't moving.

He smiled encouragingly at her. "Come on, Iolanthe. It'll be fun. Do you want to go back to the inn, or shall we stay here?"

She shrugged. "I don't care."

"It's your choice."

"Nay, you choose."

"*I'll* choose," Roderick said, standing up with a curse. "I cannot listen to the two of you any longer. Let us away to the inn and see what the good Mrs. Pruitt is cooking, then we can pass the evening in the sitting room listening to our lady read her delightful little tales."

There was one thing Thomas had no trouble deciding, and that was that he had no desire to spend the evening with Roderick as a third wheel.

"Ah, ye're back, lad," Duncan said, coming in behind him. "How was your battle on yonder fair shores? I'm for the inn where we might tell such tales with a fine supper under our noses."

Thomas looked around for any more interruptions. When none materialized, he tried to judge Iolanthe's preferences. She didn't seem any more excited about accompanying Roderick and Duncan to the inn than he felt. So he invited the pair to go on to the inn ahead of them. He looked down at the bodies still littering his floor, then at Iolanthe.

"How does a walk sound?" he asked.

"Pleasing enough," she said carefully.

"A walk to the village?" he suggested.

She nodded. "Lovely. 'Tis a lovely place."

"And such lovely company," he agreed. "It sounds like a perfect afternoon."

That she was willing to even venture to the village was noteworthy. Who knew what other adventures she'd be willing to go on?

Perhaps one to save her life?

"I met some people in New York," he said casually as they walked through the gates. "People you might be interested in."

"Who?"

"A man and a woman."

"Interesting," she said absently.

"They were, actually, and for a very specific reason. The man, Alexander Smith, has a sister who's married to a Highlander."

"A wise choice on her part," Iolanthe said, "but why would that interest me?"

"Because that Highlander is James MacLeod."

She, quite suddenly, choked.

"Yes," Thomas said, looking at her with one raised eyebrow. "That James MacLeod who is, I believe, your great-great-grandfather. You know, the one without a death date."

"Um," she managed.

"My thoughts exactly," he said. "Are you interested in all the other things I learned?"

"Ah . . ." she stalled.

"It would seem," he continued, "that there are little gates on his land through which a person can travel back in time." He stopped and looked at her. "Any of this beginning to sound familiar?"

She shifted uncomfortably. "Well, there are the rumors, of course."

"Ambrose didn't know?"

"I'm not one to be speaking for that one—"

"Iolanthe," he warned.

She sighed and relented. "Very well. Aye, Ambrose knows."

"And you know."

"Aye," she admitted. "I know as well."

"And you didn't tell me?"

"What was I to tell you?" she asked. "My grandfather told me there was a means of traveling through time, and that there was a place in the forest where it could be done. But I never tried it myself, so how was I to know 'twas more than fancy?"

"Because you were willing to die for the secret."

"Aye, well," she said, "there is that." She gave him a small smile. "I knew the secret, 'tis true. I also knew that there was a king's ransom in jewels and gold hidden in the fireplace, put there by my great-grandfather, who had extorted them from various smugglers who had come through that same forest gate. And I'd given my word that neither secret would pass my lips on pain of death." She paused. "Can you fault me for being a woman of my word?"

"Six hundred years after—did you say cache of cash in the fireplace?"

"Supposedly. But I had no proof of it. The time-traveling I believed even less." She shrugged. "I've never been back to the Highlands, so all I had were the rumors, and they seemed so fanciful, I couldn't credit them. Ambrose claimed 'twas true, but laird though he might be, he has a powerful weakness for idle tales."

"Well," Thomas said crossing his arms over his chest, "apparently the rumors are true."

"How would you know?"

"Alexander Smith married a woman from the twelfth century. I saw her with my own eyes and listened to the way she talked. And then there is your great-great-grandfather. You have to agree that Jamie is who he says he is. Ambrose's word has to be enough for you on that."

"Aye, I suppose it is." She looked down at the floor. "So," she asked reluctantly, "how is it done?"

"I don't know exactly how it works. What I do know is that in your great-great-grandfather's case, apparently Alex's sister stumbled back into fourteenth-century Scotland and met him then. They married—"

"They always do," she said darkly.

"—and used a time-travel gate in the forest near your home to come back to the twentieth century."

She frowned at him. "Why would you care? Do you have some great desire to see the poverty of Scotland in the past?"

No time like the present to spring his plan on her. "Actually," he said, "I have a very great desire to see just that."

"Why?"

This was the moment, the do-or-die moment that would shape the rest of his life. He hoped it would turn out the way he wanted.

He took a deep breath.

"Because," he said slowly, "because I want to go back to get you."

Chapter 24

Iolanthe stood at the door of the sitting chamber and looked at Thomas, who was talking on the phone to his parents. He was spouting an elaborate ruse about what he planned to do for the next pair of months. By the look on his face, she suspected that he wasn't all that skilled at lying. He hardly sounded convincing, even to her ears. Perhaps he was fortunate in that he was using the telephone instead of having to face his parents. One look would have told them all they needed to know.

"Dad, I know it's the end of September, but it isn't as if I haven't climbed in inclement weather before." Thomas smiled easily, as if willing his parents to believe him. "I'll be perfectly fine."

He held the phone away, which led Iolanthe to believe that his father wasn't very enthusiastic about Thomas's plans.

"I'll be back before Christmas. We'll have a great celebration here at the inn."

The phone was held abruptly away, then Thomas gingerly listened again.

"Mom? Mom, you know I'll be okay. I'm a very good climber."

A stillness came over him, and Iolanthe couldn't help but wonder if the moment of truth had come.

Thomas sighed. "No, no, and no. I've written Megan a letter and sent it to her. If I'm not home in two months, she'll open it, and you'll know what I've been up to." He paused. "What am I really doing?"

He looked across the room. Iolanthe found herself staring into bright blue eyes.

"I'm saving a life, Mom. A life that deserves saving."

Iolanthe felt her way into the chamber and sank into a

chair. It wasn't as if she were truly weary; not having a body
had certain advantages. But that didn't mean her spirit
couldn't feel itself go weak in the knees, and such was the
case at present. She leaned her head against the back of her
chair and waited for Thomas to finish. And while she did,
she listened to the easy banter he had with his mother and
heard the affection in his voice. It had been so long since
she'd had such tender communications with her mother.

Or with her love. She looked up as he sat down next to
her. They hadn't spoken much since the afternoon before,
when he'd told her of his scheme.

If she'd had hands, she would have clouted him strongly
aside the head to try to bring sense back to him. Trying to
shove him while shouting curses at him had been powerfully
unsatisfying. She'd eventually given up and glared at him as
he'd spouted more foolishness about having found a way for
them to be together.

She'd said the price was too high.

He'd said he loved her, and he thought it worth the risk.

She'd begged him not to go.

He'd said he wanted her in his life, in his arms, and in his
bed, and he was going to do everything in his power to get
her there.

After that, she hadn't been able to do anything but stay by
his side and breathe through the terror that swept over her.
Perhaps he could travel back through time, but to what end?

To find himself adorning the end of a sword?

And leave her alone, six hundred years in the future?

Thomas smiled suddenly. "I'm glad you came in. I left the
door open for you."

He'd left the door open for her. How true that was. He'd
left so many doors open for her, doors to a different life. He'd
come to her keep, bringing change and possibility and
hope.

A hope for life.

"I called Jamie this morning."

She looked at him in surprise. "Did you?"

"I'm going tomorrow." He looked at her. "Didn't you
come south in the fall?"

She swallowed with difficulty. "Aye," she managed.

"Then the sooner I start, the better, don't you think?"

What she thought was that he was mad. What she thought was that she might never see him again. What she thought was that he was the single most beautiful man she had ever known, and the rest of her existence would mean nothing if he were not there.

But she couldn't say any of that.

"Iolanthe."

She refused to look at him.

"I wish you'd come with me to Jamie's."

She had been expecting that and had already made her decision. "I cannot."

"I don't understand why."

She looked into the fire. "Perhaps 'tis that I have no faith."

"In me?"

She looked at him and wished with all her heart that she might feel some of the hope that he seemed to.

"I'm afraid to hope."

He sighed. "But—"

"Can you fault me for it?"

He studied her for several moments in silence, then shook his head slowly. "I suppose I can't. But that doesn't change what I plan to do."

She put her face in her hands. "If you survive the journey, how will you rescue me? And if you rescue me, how will I remember you?"

"There's no reason you can't remember the future."

"But I can't remember tomorrow!"

"You have to believe you can, Iolanthe."

"I can't believe something that's impossible!" She shivered. "Besides, if you save me before I'm murdered, I'll never have been a ghost and I'll never have met you anyway. There'll be nothing to remember."

"I don't believe time works that way," he insisted. "What's done is done, and I don't believe that if we stepped around time and made a change in the past that it will change events that have already happened."

"But it will change my future," she insisted.

"It might. But it won't change anyone else's," he said. "You'll still be known."

"It makes no sense!"

He sighed in exasperation. "Then write it down," he said. "Write down your memories of the past six hundred years. When I bring you forward, you'll still have that book. Even if you don't remember, you'll still have it written down."

"Foolishness," she said in despair. " 'Tis naught but foolishness and I cannot believe you're willing to take this risk."

"I love you," he said simply. "And that's worth taking any risk."

She found there was no point in arguing with that. For her, loving him meant she didn't want him to go. They were at cross purposes, and nothing would change that.

"You could help me," he said slowly, "by telling me of your family."

"So they don't slay you the moment you walk through the hall doors?" she asked darkly.

"Something like that."

"And if you manage to find me and rescue me, what will you do then?"

"What do you mean what will I do then? I'll grab you and we'll run like hell."

"Where to?" she asked. "When to?"

He seemed to have no ready answer for that. "I hadn't thought much about that, actually. Would you want to go back to your home?"

"Never." The word was out before she knew she intended to speak it.

"Well, that solves that." He looked at her. "How about a house on the sea?"

"Unfair. You tempt me with what my heart desires most."

"My house in Maine is on the shore."

"You didn't tell me that."

"You never asked."

She sighed and looked into the fire. "I don't know what I would want."

"You have your pick of any century. What would suit you best?"

"You cannot be in earnest."

"Why not?" he asked placidly. "We may not want fourteenth-century Scotland, but there's no reason we might not want some other time. Or pick your country. If you could live in Scotland in any century, when would it be?"

"There's not much choice," she said grimly. "Clan wars or wars with the English? And 'tis only recently that I've learned what happened after the outlawing of the plaid." She shook her head. "If I were to live there, it would be in your day. At least there are tourists to keep my people alive in the north."

"All right, then," he said. "We'll come back to the present. If you like, we'll live in Scotland. If you'd rather, we'll go live on the shore in Maine."

"In the Colonies?"

"Don't make it sound like it's just short of Hell. There's a lot to be said for America."

"Is there?"

He shot her an amused glance. "We'll live in both places; then you can decide for yourself."

She laced her hands together. "Doesn't it matter to you? Where your home is?"

"Home, Iolanthe," he said slowly, "is people, not a place. If you'll allow it, my home will be with you. Wherever. Whenever."

She met his gaze and felt her damnable tears start again. He blinked a time or two himself, then managed a roguish smile.

"Since I'm hoisting a sword in your defense, how would you like to give me the details I'll need?"

"You're assuming I don't want to be a ghost anymore."

He hesitated, but so slightly she would have missed it had she not been watching him so closely.

"Yes, I'm assuming that. Now, details, if you don't mind. It may mean both our lives this time around."

Well, if he wanted to delude himself with the possibility of actually rescuing her from a man who had murdered her six hundred years earlier, she supposed the least she could do was humor him. What would likely happen was he would spend a nasty night in the forest and find himself with a healthy case of the ague. He'd come back to the inn, and she would end up nursing him as best she could. At least then she could avail herself of the chance to tell him he'd been a fool.

Unless he actually succeeded.

And the hope that bloomed suddenly in her heart from that was almost too painful to be borne.

She waited until she could breathe normally again, then began to speak.

"I'll tell you of my family," she said quietly. "And believe me when I tell you that these are the things that only those who lived them would know."

"You and Duncan."

"Aye," she said. "Though he would likely tell the stories with more charity than I will."

He looked at her briefly. "I'm sorry to make you do this."

"Nay," she said with a wave of her hand. " 'Tis best you know the truth." She sat back, gathered her thoughts, then plunged in. "My father, Malcolm, married quite young. My mother bore him first a son, Alexandir, and then me a pair of years later."

"And then no more?"

She shook her head. "No bairns of my mother. My father's love, if he'd ever felt it, soured almost immediately. 'Tis nothing short of a miracle that I was ever conceived. My sire had a lover in the village and 'twas in her bed he sought his pleasure almost from the start."

"Great guy."

She smiled without humor. "Aye. Now the trouble began when I reached my tenth summer. My brother, ten-and-two, was a strong, strapping lad even then. He had accompanied my mother to see her kin when they were set upon by our enemies. Duncan had been out riding the borders and stumbled upon the deed as it was happening. My brother had already fallen from wounds that were grievous. My mother had been set upon, in the way a woman ofttimes finds herself, by that band of misbegotten curs. Duncan slew them all in a mighty anger, but 'twas too late to stop the harm done."

"Oh, Iolanthe," Thomas said with a sigh.

She shrugged. "It was long ago, and my mother has long since found her rest."

"I'm sorry."

"My brother died a handful of days after the skirmish. My mother never recovered. She wasted away, and half a year later, she followed Alexandir into the earth."

"Leaving your father to his mistress."

"And their children, aye." She took a deep breath. "I was, as you might imagine, an uncomfortable reminder of my brother's death. My father, I think, after a year or two, forgot about me. I lived in the hall, true, but he never spoke to me or acknowledged me."

"And your half-brothers and -sister?"

She smiled at him. "What do you think, Thomas?"

"I think I'll give them all a piece of my mind when I see them."

"How gallant you are."

"No," he said, looking at her. "Desperate."

The intensity of his glance made whatever she'd been planning to say die on her lips. By the saints, the madman was truly in earnest.

"You *are* going to do this," she whispered.

"You're convinced only now?"

She closed her eyes briefly, then looked at him again.

"You'll need their names," she said quietly. "If you're to survive."

"Thank you."

"Duncan you'll know, though I suppose he won't remember you. He was a very practical man though, even then, with no great love for my father."

"I can't blame him for that."

"Neither can I, actually. My half-brother, Angus, is the eldest of the brood my father sired on his whore. The next was Grudach, his younger sister. 'Twas they, those two, who beguiled me into leaving with the English-man."

"How?"

She smiled bitterly. "They told me his keep was on the sea. You see, my sire had sent Angus out into the world, partly because the fool impregnated too many village wenches when he was at home and partly because he had a gift—so my father supposed—for making alliances."

"And your father thought you needed them?" Thomas asked. "Isn't your home pretty far north?"

" 'You can never have too many allies,' " she said, "which is the wisest thing my father ever said. He had, of course, learned the saying from his father. He never could have invented it on his own. The mistake he made was thinking his firstborn of that whore was equal to the task."

"Would you have been better at it?"

She blinked. "Why do you ask?"

"It seems to rankle."

"A sheep would have been better suited," she said shortly. "And nay, it never occurred to me. I was a woman, and my tasks were at home."

"It was a different world then," he murmured.

"Aye, it was." She cleared her throat. "Now, Angus had been about his task of traveling, and scattering his seed from one end of Scotland to the other, no doubt, when he met an English-man in Edinburgh."

"And you heard this from . . . ?" he asked.

"Angus and my father."

"And you believed them?"

"What choice did I have? Angus said he'd met this man in Edinburgh, that the man was very wealthy, and that I was to be traded as the valuable prize to the man for making an alliance with us."

"And didn't it strike you as strange that a Brit would want to make an alliance with people three hundred miles away?"

"What choice did I have?" she asked again, sharply. "I had nowhere to go, no one to care for me, and no say in the matter. My father sold me. Angus told me the man's keep was on the sea. I knew I had no choice but to make of it what I could."

He was silent for a moment. "I'm sorry," he said finally.

"Aye," she said, "so was I. It was only after I died that I learned I had been sold to pay a debt Angus owed the man."

"Who told you?"

"Duncan did. He'd overheard the conversings between the English-man and my father. Angus had promised the man that I knew the secret of our keep and would give it to him when we returned to England. Then, once he wed me, as my husband, he would be able to return to Scotland now and again and avail himself of the untold riches that the secret would provide him."

"The secret of time travel, or the jewels in the chimney?"

"Angus would have known neither, but he knew there was something of value in our keep. He likely made up whatever tale suited him. It apparently suited the English-man, for he took me readily enough."

"Why didn't Angus know the truth?"

"My grandfather William knew, and he told me, but I know he never told my father, nor Angus."

"William didn't trust either of them?"

"Not with his most rotten bit of meat. I daresay none of my family knew the particulars, save it was a secret that must be kept close, and when they had proved themselves, my grandfather would tell them."

"Did he ever?"

She smiled briefly. "He died before he could."

He nodded thoughtfully. "So, you went with the man. Did you know his name?"

"I never stirred myself to ask. I didn't pay him any heed until I was woken that morning and put on a horse to go with him."

"And you went because you had no choice."

"Aye. I tried to escape, but that went badly for me."

Thomas sucked in his breath. "Did he . . . ?"

She wrinkled her nose. "He told me he wouldn't lower himself to bed a wench of Scots breeding. But he didn't mind hitting me, which he did quite frequently." She sighed. "We rode for what seemed a lifetime. He didn't bother with any refreshment once we reached his keep. He took me up and locked me in the tower chamber, saw to his men, then returned and demanded the secret of my home."

"And when you didn't give it to him?"

"He gave me the choice of the sword or starving to death."

Thomas was silent for several minutes. "You made a brave choice, then."

She couldn't help but laugh. "Nay, the coward's choice, surely. I'd seen men starved to death in my father's pit. A quick death, no matter how painful, seemed much more bearable."

"I'm sorry."

"Nay, you needn't be. I don't think on it much now. Though I used to," she said, turning her face away. "Every moment of every day for what seemed like centuries." She paused. "It likely was centuries."

"I'll stop it this time."

She looked at him. "I hope you can."

Silence fell. She found that she had nothing else to say. What else was there to say? He was determined, and there was nothing she could do to dissuade him.

And in the secret, innermost place in her heart, she didn't want to dissuade him. If he succeeded, it would be miraculous.

"Will you change your mind and come with me? To the Highlands?" he asked.

Of course, that didn't mean she could bear to watch it.

She shook her head. "I cannot."

It was a very long time before either of them spoke again.

Chapter 25

Thomas knocked on Iolanthe's door. There was no answer, but he hadn't exactly expected one. He wouldn't say the night before had ended badly. They'd spent most of the day in the sitting room talking about her family. The entire time he'd sat there, he'd been almost drowning in the realization that it was possibly the last time he might see her. The odds of success were, in reality, not really very good. He was going to an incredibly inhospitable place where dangers of the unanticipated kind might assault him at any turn.

Then again, didn't that describe Everest? If there was an unfriendly place on earth, that was it. Man wasn't made to linger at 29,000 feet. Yet he'd managed it. He'd survived the cold, the hunger, the weariness, and the altitude. If he could survive that, couldn't he survive the Middle Ages?

Then again, Everest hadn't been coming at him with a sword.

He sighed. There was no use in comparing the two. The only thing he knew for sure was that thinking about failure was a sure way to ensure the same. He shook aside his doubts, picked up his bag, and descended the steps. He reached the entry hall, then came to an abrupt halt.

Ambrose was in his usual place, leaning negligently against the sideboard. But next to him was a broadsword. A bright, shiny, new broadsword. Thomas looked at his ancestor.

"Nice," he said.

Ambrose snorted. "Nice? Lad, this is perfection. Best not practice with it, though. You're liable to nick Jamie, and then you'll find yourself in his lady's sights."

Thomas slung his bag over his shoulder, then walked across the floor to touch the hilt. He looked at Ambrose.

"You didn't have to do this."

Ambrose only smiled. "I know. But we wanted to, Hugh, Fulbert, and I. Duncan designed it. A man of many talents, that one."

"He certainly is. But who made the blade?"

"A smith in the Highlands." Ambrose smiled. "One quite used to unusual customers, I daresay. But he takes our gold and delivers to our door, so none of us has any complaints."

Thomas ran his finger over the finely tooled sheath. "I don't quite know what to say."

" 'Thank you' will do, my lad. Use it well."

"Thank you. And I'll do my best."

"You'll have to do better than that."

Thomas nodded in acknowledgment, then hesitated, unsure just how he should say good-bye. He looked at Ambrose, but saw nothing but encouragement in the older man's eyes.

"Watch your back," Ambrose said.

Well, maybe that was all that needed to be said. Thomas nodded confidently, then picked up his new sword and headed out the door. He tried not to think about the complete weirdness of the fact that in one hand he was carrying a duffel bag and in the other he was carrying what for all intents and purposes was a medieval broadsword.

He stowed his gear in the car, then jogged down the driveway and out onto the road. It wasn't so much that he was in a hurry as it was he supposed that after two months of not really working out, he'd better start. Who knew what sorts of tortures awaited him up in Scotland?

He slowed to a walk once he reached the road leading to the castle. This was a place that deserved a little more time taken with it. He looked at the surrounding countryside, memorizing the general layout. Six hundred years would have changed the foliage but not the bone structure. With any luck, he'd be slipping in and out of the place—in the past, of course—without any undue problems.

Like finding himself a helpless captive right alongside Iolanthe.

He shook off the negative thought. He'd managed impossible tasks before. He could do this one as well, especially when so much rode on his success.

The customary Highlanders decorated the outside of the castle walls. Thomas nodded to them and received respectful nods and not a few suggestions on what to do to Iolanthe's father, should he meet him. He filed those away for future reference. He wouldn't have thought the garrison would know what he was up to, but maybe word traveled faster than he supposed.

Thomas continued on into the bailey. The MacDougal was standing there with his arms folded across his chest. Thomas was prepared for another onslaught of nastiness.

"Ye willna succeed," the MacDougal said.

Thomas stopped. "You would think," he said slowly, "that you would be overjoyed if I did. If the lady isn't a ghost, the lady isn't here to be top dog. Then you are."

Connor MacDougal opened his mouth, then shut it suddenly. He gave Thomas a glare, then walked off, muttering to himself. Thomas shrugged. The only thing that would have surprised him would have been if the MacDougal had been pleasant. At least the status quo was still the same.

He shoved his hands in his pockets and continued on his way. He checked all the rooms in the tower but found them empty. The garden was nothing but dirt and dead weeds. Thomas turned back and had almost walked out the gates when he realized the one place he hadn't looked.

It was, perhaps, fitting that he look there last.

He walked into the great hall and saw her immediately. It was as if the first time he'd seen her was happening all over again. She stood in the center of the hall with the sun shining down on her, alone. She was wearing some long flowery skirt and a navy sweater—another outfit that looked like it had come straight out of Megan's closet—but that was the only difference. Her hair still hung down her back in long, heavy curls, and the sunlight still fell down on her like fine strands of silk. Thomas stopped just short of her.

"Iolanthe," he said quietly.

She looked up at him but said nothing.

"Are you sure you won't come?"

She shook her head.

Well, there was nothing else to be said then. Thomas smiled gamely.

"I'll see you soon," he said.

She wasn't smiling. "And if I don't remember you?"

"You will remember me. And if you don't, we'll start over again. How could you not help but like me?"

"How can you not help but fall by the sword before you see the inside of my hall?" she returned.

"Have faith."

A single tear slipped down her cheek. "Thomas, after everything we've said, I simply cannot believe that the risk you intend to take is worth it."

He lifted his hand to touch her cheek, then let his arm fall back to his side. "Iolanthe," he said, "it will work. You'll see."

More tears joined the first. He found himself jamming his hands in his pockets to keep from reaching out to her.

"Oh, Iolanthe," he whispered. "Please, don't."

She dragged her sleeve across her nose and sniffed mightily. "This is not," she said, putting her shoulders back, "how a woman sends her man off into battle."

"Then you have words of encouragement for me?"

"Aye. Duck often."

He laughed in spite of himself. "Thanks. I'll remember that." He paused. "You're sure you won't—"

"Aye, I'm certain."

He wasn't going to push her any more. She knew where her family home was, and if she'd forgotten, he was quite sure Ambrose could help her find the way. He shifted, unsure how one went about leaving behind the woman he loved when he couldn't pull her into his arms and kiss her senseless.

"Off with you," she said, stepping back. "I've books to read, you know. Mrs. Pruitt has generously offered to turn the pages for me whilst you're about your business."

Thomas spared a thought over what Mrs. P. had extorted from Iolanthe for that service, decided it definitely had something to do with Ambrose, then nodded. He could have stood there forever saying good-bye to her, but there was no use in it. If he was going to go, then he needed to go.

Before reason set in and he decided he had lost his mind for real this time.

"I'll see you soon," he said, trying to make it sound as if he was just going to the store. "If you need more books, tell Mrs. P. to use my charge card to pay for them. Spend whatever you like."

She only nodded.

He found he couldn't move.

"Go," she said, shooing him away.

"I'm trying."

"Turn around and walk," she suggested.

He looked at her for a final time, memorizing every detail, then turned and walked from the hall.

He didn't dare look over his shoulder but continued on through the gates, nodding briefly to the guardsmen there. Duncan fell into step with him.

"Laird Jamie will teach you what you must ken," Duncan said.

"I hope so."

"Learn the lessons well."

"My life will depend on it?"

Duncan shot him a look that made Thomas pause.

"Do you know something you're not telling me?" he asked.

"I ken many things," Duncan said simply. "If you'll have my advice, lad, then you'll heed your master and learn what he has to teach. Scotland in my day is a bloody place."

"Any other words of cheer?"

Duncan seemed to consider for a moment, then he spoke. "If you wish to convince me you're in earnest, then I'll tell you something only I know. Something known only to myself and Moira, Iolanthe's mother."

Thomas almost made an offhand remark, when the potential import of Duncan's words struck him. He felt his jaw slide down.

"You didn't."

Duncan looked around as if he was afraid someone might be listening, then glared at Thomas. "Tell no one."

Thomas frowned. "Maybe I'm not understanding what it is I'm not supposed to be telling."

"What I'm saying," Duncan said through clenched teeth, "is that I loved her ma."

"Then . . ."

"If you want to catch my attention, tell me that," Duncan said, "and I'll listen."

"If you don't slit my throat first. Are you telling me that you and . . . and Iolanthe's mother—"

"Must I give you the particulars?" Duncan asked, pained.

"Is Iolanthe yours?"

"Why else, lad, do you think I am here?" Duncan asked.

Thomas could hardly believe his ears. "If you're Iolanthe's father, then why haven't you told her?"

Duncan's face turned a dull shade of red. "Why would she want me?" he demanded. "Laird's daughter or the bastard daughter of a nameless cousin of her sire?"

"I think," Thomas said slowly, "that you undervalue yourself. I think she would very much want to know." He smiled at Duncan. "I think you should tell her. But I've got go now, so I can't stay and help you out with that. You're on your own."

Duncan looked horribly indecisive.

"Tell her," Thomas said, more gently. "I think she'd want to know. I'm thrilled. She's not my half-aunt anymore." He made Duncan a bow. "I'll see you soon."

And with that he left, before anyone else showed up to make any more revelations he wasn't sure he could take in. He forced himself not to look back at the castle as he made his way down to the main road. It was unsettling enough to think that the next time he'd be on that road, it would be several centuries in the past.

Assuming, of course, that everything worked the way it should. Jamie had said there were no guarantees—something Thomas hadn't wanted to share with Iolanthe.

Well, there was nothing he could do about it now. His foot was to the path; there was no turning back.

He made his way back to his car, took another look at his map, then got under way before he thought any more about anything.

It was safer that way.

* * *

He'd driven very fast on the long, unlovely stretch of road from Edinburgh to Inverness. It was something he thought he'd like to forget as soon as possible. He'd passed too many caravans and trucks that he'd had no business passing, but he'd done it anyway. *Haste* seemed to be the watchword of the day.

By the time he'd made it up into the Highlands and driven up the little winding roads that led through the forests and glens, he was exhausted. It was very dark before he managed to find his way—after several misturns and U-turns—to Jamie's keep. Maybe the most unsettling thing about it was the feeling that he'd been there before, but with a different landscape. By the time he actually pulled inside the gates and turned off the car, the feeling had become such a constant companion that he had almost accustomed himself to it.

He crawled from the car, stretched, then sighed. One step closer to his goal, and all he wanted to do was beg for a bed and use it.

He walked up the wide, broad steps leading up to James MacLeod's hall and shivered. It was just too familiar.

The door opened suddenly.

"Yeah, what do you want?"

Thomas stared at the young man standing there with a Ding-Dong in one hand and a carton of milk in the other. A huge swig was taken, a mouth wiped with a shirtsleeve, and a look of complete and utter boredom once again descended on the face. If the man hadn't looked so much like a younger version of Alexander Smith, Thomas might have suspected he'd come to the wrong place.

"Thomas McKinnon," Thomas said.

The young man looked him over from head to toe, then nodded a weary nod. "Of course you are. Come on in. I'm Zachary, the doorman."

Thomas walked in and found himself in the middle of an enormous argument over the origins of haggis.

" 'Tis not a Scottish dish!" one man was saying quite loudly.

" 'Tis!" another said, just as loudly.

"Ian, you're a daft dolt."

"William, you're an Englishman, and that says it all!"

Thomas blinked in surprise as the two men pulled out swords and started hacking at each other right there in the great hall. Chairs were kicked out of the way as the fight continued in earnest. Thomas noted that a handful of women were sitting by the fire, watching the scene with placid expressions. A handful of men sat with them, sprawled in their chairs, looking equally as unconcerned.

"Standard fare," Zachary said. "Come on. Jamie's been waiting for you." He led Thomas across the room. "That's Ian MacLeod," Zachary said, pointing at the combatant wearing a plaid. "He's Jamie's cousin. His wife is Jane. The other one fighting is William de Piaget; he's the Brit. That's his wife, Julianna. She was my sister's college roommate. That's my sister, Elizabeth, who married Jamie. That's him there, and that's his brother Patrick. And their minstrel Joshua." He looked over his shoulder at Thomas. "You getting all this?"

"Sure," Thomas said, though in reality, his mind was spinning. He could hardly keep from gaping at the two men who were, by their swearing and bearing, quite obviously not from the twentieth century, swordfighting in the middle of a great hall, with their very twentieth-century looking wives watching without any trace of panic on their faces.

Until a toddler started toward the combatants. Elizabeth leaped to her feet and bellowed for them to stop.

"That's enough, the both of you! Haggis *was* a British dish that the Scots took over for their own in the early eighteenth century and, as far as I'm concerned, I wish the Brits had kept it. Now, can we finally have supper before you kill one of the children?"

Thomas watched in admiration as the two men meekly put up their swords and returned to their seats. He followed Zachary over to the group in front of the fire and felt distinctly like he was being sized up. And then James MacLeod stood.

And Thomas wondered if he was out of his mind.

Not that he wasn't tall himself, and in good shape. And it wasn't as if he wasn't rugged. He spent a lot of time out-of-doors, and that tended to put a rough edge on his boardroom persona. But what he wasn't was a medieval clansman who'd cut his teeth on hardship and bloodshed.

Like the medieval clansman before him, for instance.

Jamie was big, he was broad, and he had a pirate's grin that made Thomas suspect he was in for one hell of a month of training.

"Thomas," Jamie said, extending one great paw for a handshake. "You found us easily enough, I see."

"No problem," Thomas said, returning the very firm grip.

"Sit for a moment," Jamie said, indicating a chair in front of the fire. "We'll eat very soon, for I've no doubt you haven't yet."

"I didn't want to take the time."

Ian, one of the ones who had been fighting, laughed. "Ah, well, that's the last time you'll say that. When we've started in on you, you'll be begging for meals simply to rest."

The way they all grinned left Thomas feeling decidedly queasy—if he ever felt queasy, which he didn't, because he was a manly man and unafraid.

"You look like your sister," Elizabeth said kindly. "I imagine even more so when you smile."

Thomas managed a smile just to prove her point. Then he realized what Elizabeth had said. "When was Megan here?"

"Stopped in on her honeymoon," Elizabeth said with a smile of her own. "Isn't it great to have family?"

"It is," Thomas said.

Jamie clapped his hands on his knees, then rose. "Dinner first, then speech. We've a great deal to accomplish tonight."

Dinner was, for better or worse, not haggis, though the conversation revolved around it for some time.

And once they had finished, Jamie pushed away his plate. "Thomas, I know most of your tale, but the others do not. As you will likely need all our aid to have success, perhaps it would not be amiss to recount it again."

Jamie couldn't have known that much, because Thomas had listened to Alex give him the short version. He was obviously skilled at filling in the blanks.

And so Thomas began. He told it from his point of view and left little out. His mention of Everest had Jamie peppering him with questions.

"Jamie," Elizabeth warned. "Do *not* even entertain the thought."

"But to go back in time and climb it before Hillary managed it," Jamie said. "What a feat!"

"No," she said firmly. "No, no, and no." She looked at Thomas. "Go on. And hurry, before he really starts thinking about it seriously."

So Thomas took up his tale again, told of the castle and how he'd seen it in his dreams before he'd gotten Megan's pictures. He told of his journey to England, his thoughts on restoring the castle, and the purpose of his year in England. He told them of meeting Iolanthe.

And of learning who, and what, she was.

There was a good stretch of silence then, but no vapors and no uncomfortable shifting.

"And what did she think of you?" Jamie asked.

"I'm sure she thought I was a pompous ass."

Elizabeth laughed. "And so runs the course of true love. What did you think of her?"

"I wanted to fall to her feet and pledge undying love."

"Sounds familiar," Jamie said, with a sigh. "Go on."

Thomas told them of his trip to New York, and of meeting Alex. And he gave them his thoughts on what he wanted to do. Then he turned to Iolanthe's story and told it as faithfully as he could.

"All of which led me to calling you," he said, "and here I am."

Jamie nodded. "You've quite a task before you. I think you'll find the proper time easily enough. But passing yourself off as any kind of medieval man will be difficult." He looked at Thomas. "You could go as a McKinnon. We were allies enough at the time. But 'twill mean a goodly amount of training."

"I assumed as much. For how long?"

Jamie smiled briefly. "You could train a year and still not be ready."

"Fortunately for you," his cousin Ian said with a wolfish grin, "we've a dire-straits course that will take just over a month. Gaelic, swordplay, and the swagger, all for a modest fee."

Jamie snorted. "Ian's given up cattle raiding for teaching

swordplay. He brings poor, hapless souls up to his land and tortures them for weeks at a time."

"And they pay me for it," Ian agreed. "Hollywood types, rich men with more money than wits, lads with more energy than maturity. Aye, I wreak havoc upon them all."

"I'll pay you whatever you ask," Thomas said promptly. "It'll be worth it."

"Fee waived," Ian said with another smile. "I do what I can for the course of true love."

Elizabeth ruffled his hair affectionately. "You always were a romantic."

"I don't mind that about him," his wife Jane agreed happily. "But then again, I benefit from it."

Jamie waved toward William de Piaget. "Here is our lone English-man. We allow him to stay now and then because of his knowledge of England. You'll need his skills as well."

"Aye," William said, "but I pay for my heritage each day."

"Ha," Ian said with a snort. "Who pays? You're now running those bloody medieval reenactment tours and making a fortune! I'm the one who's sweating from dawn to dusk."

Julianna smiled at Thomas. "We're just here for a visit. We just bought a large estate in England, actually, near the castle where William grew up."

"That would be Artane," William supplied with a nod. "And it would please me to aid you as I can." He looked at Thomas unflinchingly. " 'Tis a bloody dangerous time, that. You'll need your wits about you."

Jamie put his hands on the table and rose. "Which means to bed now. You'll want an early start on the morrow, Thomas. We'll all help you as we can."

Thomas looked around the table. "I don't know how to thank you. I really don't. It's more than I could have hoped for."

Jamie's brother Patrick laughed. "We'll speak of this again in a se'nnight and see if you're still grateful then. I know what it's like to fight with Jamie and Ian each day, and I can't say as I'm grateful for it."

"Lazy whelp," Jamie threw at his brother.

Patrick only shrugged with a smile. " 'Tis the duty of the second son to take things as lightly as possible."

Jamie opened his mouth to retort, but Elizabeth got to her feet before he could.

"Why don't you two leave that discussion for tomorrow?" she suggested, juggling a sleeping toddler in her arms. "It's late, and Thomas looks beat. You can tell him all your gory tales when you have at him outside." She placed her son in Jamie's arms, then smiled at Thomas. "Come on, and I'll show you your room."

"If it's no trouble," he said. "I really could go stay at a B and B—"

"An inn?" Jamie asked, looking appalled. "You're family. You'll stay here."

And that, Thomas supposed, was that. He said his good nights, then followed Elizabeth from the kitchen and across the great hall. He looked to his left, and a chill went over him. Elizabeth looked at him with a puzzled expression.

"What?" she asked.

"What's through that doorway?"

"A storeroom now, for swords and things like that."

He halted in midstep. "The dungeon used to be there."

She looked at him in shock. "Yes, it did. How did you know?"

He met her gaze. "I just knew."

"Well," she said, taking his arm and pulling him along, "as one who has spent a night in Jamie's pit, his medieval pit, mind you, I'm here to tell you that you don't want to become familiar with that place."

Thomas couldn't have agreed more.

Chapter 26

A se'nnight later, Iolanthe stood behind a fat, obnoxious couple from the Colonies who were dressed in shirts adorned with orange, yellow, and pink flowers, sporting some sort of woven straw hats, and arguing loudly over whether or not the castle they were tromping through had any historical importance. The man yelled at the woman, the woman began to cry, and Iolanthe found herself acting without thinking. She placed herself in front of the man, made herself unmistakably visible, and scowled her most formidable scowl.

"This castle has importance in that it's haunted," she said pointedly.

And then she took off her head and tucked it under her arm.

The woman screamed and fell over in a dead faint.

The man, apparently overcome, wet himself, then fell over in a manner like his wife.

Iolanthe dispensed with her headless illusion. The men in the garrison applauded, then went on their way after offering various and sundry congratulations on a haunting well done. Even the MacDougal unbent enough to grunt at her in a less-gruff-than-usual manner. All of it should have left her feeling rather pleased with herself.

"Now, daughter," Ambrose said, clucking his tongue as he came to stand beside her, "did you have to do that?"

Iolanthe glared at the older man. Older was, of course, misleading. Would that he'd been a toddler she could have turned over her knee.

"I am in a foul mood," she said pointedly.

"Aye, I can see that. What ails you? Thoughts of turning me over your knee?"

"Actually, aye. 'Tis a powerfully tempting thought."

He only smiled. "You wouldn't of course, even had I been your child. You've too kind a heart and will make a wonderful mother."

"In what existence do you speak of?" she asked bitterly. "Certainly not this one."

"The one Thomas will provide for you," Ambrose said. "He'll succeed."

Iolanthe had decided over the course of a se'nnight that she couldn't care less if Thomas succeeded or failed. The man had had a perfectly acceptable existence with her, but apparently it hadn't been enough.

"He can go to the devil for all I care," she said.

"Hmmm," Ambrose said. "Well, as he intends to seek to restore you to life at great personal sacrifice, perhaps you should begin to care."

She glared at him. "I am finished having speech with you."

"I've no doubt you are, as I'm quite sure anything I have to say to you, you won't wish to hear."

"No doubt."

Ambrose reached out and put his hand on her shoulder. "You should go home. Have speech with your laird. Ask him if there is aught you can do to aid the man who loves you so much."

Ach, but she could bear no more of this, for every word was a like a knife in her heart. She knew she should have gone with Thomas to the Highlands. That she hadn't only weighed her soul down with each day that passed. He risked his life to save hers. The least she could have done was watch him prepare to do it.

"My dear," Ambrose began.

She clapped her hands over her ears and vanished like the coward she truly was.

It took her another three weeks to resign herself to the fact that Ambrose was right, and she was wrong. She had spent those weeks counting each hour and damning herself the more as they passed. She hadn't even allowed herself the luxury of her private chamber. She'd lingered in the garden, but without the heart to even create anything.

It occurred to her, midway through that third se'nnight, that she had come full circle. When Thomas had come into her life, she'd been bitter and lonely, passing the hours in misery. And now that he was gone, she had come back to the same place, with the same lack of joy.

Which made that precious time between those points even more painful to think about.

Finally, when she could bear it no more, she sought Ambrose out. He was, as usual, holding court in the inn's kitchen with Hugh and Fulbert. Iolanthe ignored the other two.

"I'm ready," she said to Ambrose.

"For what, little one?"

"To go home."

"Well done," Ambrose said, clapping his hands. He beamed his approval on her. "We'll go on the morrow."

She had several questions to ask, but she surely wasn't going to admit her ignorance before the other two men. So she simply waited, unmoving and silent.

"Lads," Ambrose said, looking at her closely, "I think the lady and I have things to discuss. Seek your ease elsewhere."

The other two left soon enough, after farewells and other such rituals of parting and good night. Iolanthe just wished they'd hurry their bloody business up.

But once they were gone, she found that asking her questions was a much different matter than thinking about asking her questions. She sat slowly.

"On the morrow," Ambrose began without preamble, "we'll just pop ourselves up to the Highlands—"

"Pop?"

He smiled modestly. "You think about where you want to go, then quite suddenly you find yourself there. 'Tis a bit unsettling at first, but I think you'll find it to your liking in the end."

"And then?"

"And then we'll have ourselves a look about and see how young Thomas fares. Once we've sorted that out, we'll talk to James."

She sighed. "And then?"

"And then we'll wait."

She'd done far too much of that, but perhaps she had no choice.

"Will you stay here?" Ambrose asked kindly. "Mrs. Pruitt has your chamber put to rights, no doubt. Or perhaps you would care to come to the sitting room and we'll have speech about nothing in particular."

It may be for the last time.

He hadn't said the words, but she had heard them just the same. So she nodded and followed him into the other chamber.

They left shortly after sunrise the next morning. It took less than the space of a breath to move herself from Thorpewold to her ancestral home. She came to a teetering halt next to Ambrose, the breath and her wits completely stolen from her.

"Ah," Ambrose said, stretching like a satisfied cat, "that was a proper journey. Would that I could have traveled that stretch in such good time when I was alive."

Iolanthe was too shaken for words, so she merely looked around her and marveled at the things that had changed. And the things that had not.

There was still a forest surrounding her home, though she was certain the trees couldn't be the ones she had walked under in life. The pond was still behind her and the entrance to the garden still before her. And the keep still rose up to the sky in much the same way it had before.

"He's made a few additions," Ambrose said with a nod. "But nothing that you'd notice from the outside. You'll see the inside soon enough." He beckoned for her to follow him as he walked around to the front gates. He entered without hesitation.

Iolanthe followed more slowly. The keep had sported no such wall in her day. The village provided whatever poor buffer they'd had against the outside world. This wall before her was intimidating, to be sure. She followed Ambrose in past the iron gates and through the courtyard to the training yard. The sounds of a mighty battle came from there. That was nothing unusual, for her kin had always trained with much enthusiasm.

But now Thomas was in their midst.

Iolanthe stood in the shadow of the hall and took in the scene before her. None of the men were ones she knew, save Thomas, though she immediately identified the Scots. They fought in strange short trews, but she could tell by their bold and clever fighting that they were kin of hers, for if there was one thing a MacLeod could do, 'twas fight with his wits and his blade alike. Another man wore armor like the English had many centuries before, so she assumed that was his origin.

Then there was their leader. She couldn't call him anything else. He was taller, broader, and more fierce than any of the others. His curses blistered her ears—and the sweetness of hearing Gaelic from a mortal mouth was a joy she hadn't expected—and he laughed as he wielded his great sword.

"The laird, James," Ambrose said.

"Aye, I supposed it was," she murmured.

"But see your man," Ambrose said with a nod. "He doesn't shame himself overmuch, does he?"

She looked at Ambrose narrowly. "Have you been here recently?"

He only smiled pleasantly, but she had no trouble divining the answer to her question.

"Busybody."

"Thomas is my grandson, several times removed. Kin looks after kin, as he strives to look after you, though I doubt he does it for that reason. He seeks to give you another chance at life, and for that you should be grateful. Look you how hard he's trained."

She looked at Thomas critically. She couldn't have in all honesty said that he was Jamie's equal by anyone's measure, but then again, neither was anyone else in that yard. Iolanthe had to admit that, all things considered, Thomas was holding his own rather respectably. She listened in frank amazement as he spewed forth his own selection of curses in her native tongue. She'd listened to him learn a few things from her garrison at Thorpewold, but those curses had been nothing like this. She had to admit that he was not only inventive but thorough.

And, she admitted reluctantly to herself, he was beautiful. And determined.

The intensity on his face was plain to the eye. Whatever he seemingly fought for, he fought to win.

"He has worked hard," Ambrose repeated. "For you."

The enormity of his sacrifice truly struck her for the first time. 'Twas one thing to speculate about his sincerity, fight with him over the stupidity of the idea, and watch him leave and suppose perhaps that he went on holiday to warm his toes at her ancestral fire.

'Twas another thing entirely to see him with his muscles straining, sweat pouring down his face, his eyes blazing with the light of battle.

She turned and walked away while she still could. She walked out the gates and paused, trying to decide which way to go. The meadow stretched for a goodly distance both north and south of the keep, but it was south she went. Though she had often trudged up the hill behind the keep in life, she had just as often walked down the meadow and sat in the long grass where she didn't have to look at her home.

She sat herself down, and for the first time allowed herself to imagine how it might be to actually sit again thusly and have a body to enjoy the sitting. To smell the heather, to feel the wind in her hair and the sun on her shoulders.

To have a man who loved her hold her in his arms.

My house in Maine is on the shore.

His words came back to her. She could hardly credit him with guile, for she'd never told him of her heart's desire. For all she knew, 'twas something he loved as well.

She sat there the whole of the day, noting the movement of the sun overhead but feeling none of its warmth. She watched the wind move the grasses. She heard the birds in the trees.

And then she realized someone was behind her.

She didn't move as he cast himself down on the earth next to her. He sported a plaid, a finely wrought saffron shirt, and a mighty blade. His hair was dripping wet, as if he'd just bathed to become presentable. She looked at him, and her eyes burned with tears she couldn't bring herself to shed.

"Iolanthe."

She closed her eyes in self-defense, but said nothing.

"I'm glad you came."

She managed a nod.

"I'm leaving tomorrow morning."

She opened her eyes at that. "So soon?"

He shrugged and smiled easily. "I could spend a year here and not learn everything I need to know."

"But—"

"I'll manage. I've been talking to Duncan—"

"Duncan was here as well?" she interrupted incredulously.

"Yes."

"My whole bloody family is thick in this plot!"

He looked at her for several minutes in silence. "A wiser man might begin to believe that you are truly opposed to this."

She turned her face away. What was she to say, that she feared for his life? That the chance he took was more than she could stomach? That she would rather have a part of him than none of him?

Ah, but there was danger in that as well. There was little she could offer him. He would grow weary of their life together, then leave. Then not only would she be left with her miserable existence, she'd have a broken heart as well.

"Or are you worried about me?"

"Of course I'm worried, you fool!" she said, whirling on him. "You might die!"

"Oh," he said, looking enormously pleased. "You *are* worried."

She jumped to her feet, but he leaped to his just as quickly.

"Please, Iolanthe, don't," he said, holding up his hands in surrender. "I won't tease you. Please sit with me a little longer."

She sat back down grudgingly.

"I'll be okay," he said, sitting down next to her. "I promise."

"You have no idea what you face."

"I'll manage."

She shook her head. "You'll be in my father's pit before you know it. 'Tis an unwholesome place."

"I'll manage."

She sighed. "At least if he kills you, we'll both be ghosts."

"Well," Thomas said thoughtfully, "there is that."

"How can you jest about this?" she asked, pained.

He looked at her with such tenderness that she found she could scarce see him for her tears.

"Iolanthe, I love you," he said quietly, "and there isn't anything I wouldn't do for you. Or give up for you."

"But not your life," she protested.

"Well," he said with half a smile, "I won't answer that. You know, I think sometimes it's just as hard to live for someone than it is to die for them. And believe me when I tell you that I intend to live a very long time. With you."

"Ach, Thomas—"

"It's going to be all right, you'll see."

She paused. "How did you know I was here? Did Ambrose tell you?"

"Of course not," he said with a smile. "I felt you the moment you set foot on Jamie's land."

"You are a fey man," she managed. "Fey and daft."

"But you love me."

She couldn't even manage a decent response to put him off the scent. All she could do was stare at him and make certain that she didn't weep.

"Thank you for coming," he said with a small smile. "It means a lot."

She nodded, waving him away.

"You could come back to the keep with me," he offered.

She shook her head. "I can't." She looked away. "I just can't, Thomas."

"Well, then," he said, "that's that." He stood. "I'll see you soon."

She looked at him miserably. "But I won't know you."

"But you'll remember me," he said confidently.

She shook her head, but he held up his hand.

"It may take a little while," he conceded, "but you'll remember. Something will click. You'll wonder why I know your name, or how I know so much about your clan."

"I'll think you're a spy from an enemy and stick a knife between your ribs," she said darkly.

He laughed uneasily. "Let's hope not." He smiled at her. "It'll all work. Trust me."

"I have no choice," she said simply.

He hesitated. "Do you mean that? Do you really not want me to try?"

"How can I answer that?" she managed. "You're offering me another chance at life. A chance to be loved and love in return. How can I forbid you to make that possible? Nay," she said, shaking her head, "I am the one who is selfish, for you do this all for me—and at the dearest risk to yourself. Rather I should be telling you to save yourself."

"I am," he said with another smile. "Trust me, I am."

She sighed. "Very well, then. Be off with you, and take your rest. I'm certain you'll need it. My kin are a troublesome lot, and you'll need all your wits about you."

"I'll see you soon."

She nodded, but she couldn't speak. She did watch him walk back up to the keep and saw him hold up his sword in farewell before he went inside the gates.

And she wondered if that might be the last time she saw him.

She hid herself far in the forest the next morning, that she might not witness whatever happened. It was evening before she dared venture back to the keep. Ambrose was nowhere to be found. She went inside the hall and looked about her. It was empty save for the fire banked in the hearth. She walked up the stairs, feeling an eerie sense of having been in this exact place before, though 'twas a certainty the inside of the keep had been changed greatly. It was far larger than it had been in her day.

But as she walked down the passageway to the laird's solar, she shivered.

She had done this before, and not during her lifetime.

The door was ajar. She went inside to find that her great-great-grandfather sat at his table, scratching away with his pen. There was a chair there next to the desk. She made her way to it and sat down slowly.

She saw Jamie stiffen, then watched him look up. When he saw her, he took a deep breath.

"Ah," he managed, then closed his mouth. He took a deep breath. "Good e'en to you, lady."

"And to you, my laird."

He leaned back in his chair carefully. "Thomas left this morning."

"Aye, I know."

He considered for several moments, then spoke again. "I asked him your name, but he said he wasn't at liberty to give it to me."

I'll be discreet, Thomas had said.

And so he had been. And that was perhaps the only thing, or mayhap 'twas the final thing, that made her burden more than she could bear. She bowed her head and wept.

She wondered absently if she'd ever wept as she did then.

When she had regained some bit of control, she found that Jamie was making little sounds of distress and wringing his hands as if he wasn't quite sure what he should be doing.

It was somehow comforting to see that men were still men, no matter the century.

"There, there, my girl," he said, looking as cornered as if she'd had him pinned in the stables with three dozen blades at her disposal.

She would have laughed, but her heart hurt too much for laughter. So she dried her tears as best she could and sniffed a time or two.

"I'm Iolanthe, my laird," she said, finally.

"Iolanthe," he repeated. "I'm James."

"My grandfather's grandfather," she agreed.

He shook his head with a wry smile. "Aye, that as well." He looked at her with a goodly bit of relief she could only credit to the cessation of her tears. "How can I serve you?"

She considered, for she wished not to ask amiss. Then she gathered her courage.

"I imagine I will be here as long as he doesn't succeed in his task. If he succeeds, I . . . well, I suppose I will be pulled backward. Through time." She looked at Jamie. "Think you?"

"Aye," Jamie agreed. "I do."

"Then," she began slowly, "will you sit with me whilst I wait?"

"Gladly," Jamie said without hesitation. "What else?"

She took a deep breath. "Will you," she asked, "write down my tale? My memories?"

"Ach," he said softly.

"That I might not forget?" She paused. "In case I do forget."

"Of course," he said quietly.

He stood and rummaged about in the collection that resided in a handsome wooden bookcase. He pulled forth a leather volume, then sat back down and opened to the first page. Iolanthe looked over to find that the page was blank.

"Empty?" she asked in surprise.

"Waiting for your words," he said. He looked down at the pen in his hand, then at her. "Will you begin it?"

Well, she could read, but she certainly hadn't had much practice writing except with pen and paper she had fashioned from her own imagination.

But she took the pen just the same and with great effort scrawled the words *I, Iolanthe MacLeod*, and then she dropped the pen on the desk and sat back in her chair.

"I can do no more," she said wearily.

" 'Tis enough, my girl. I'll do the rest." He took the pen and looked at her. "Where shall we begin?"

"At the beginning, I suppose." She gathered her thoughts, then spoke. "I, Iolanthe MacLeod, was born in the year of Our Lord 1358 to Malcolm MacLeod and Moira MacDonnell at our keep in the shadow of the Benmore Forest . . ."

Chapter 27

Well, the first place Thomas hadn't counted on visiting after his arrival in the past was Malcolm MacLeod's pit. Elizabeth had been right. It was not a place anyone with any brains at all would want to linger. The only good thing to come of the past hour was that he was sitting upright. He could vividly remember being tossed unceremoniously into the hole without much consideration for how he might meet the floor he was landing onto.

Or, rather, into.

He couldn't see much, but there was enough light coming through the grated trapdoor that he could tell that the floor under him was moving. A lesser man might have gotten the willies. Fortunately for him, he'd been in all kinds of slimy places and eaten all manner of very scary things over the course of his travels and climbs, so this was nothing but a minor annoyance.

It was getting himself the hell out of there that was beginning to worry him.

He leaned against the wall and winced as a tender spot on the back of his head made contact with the stone. It was yet another blow to his head that had rendered him dazed enough for half a dozen men to have overpowered him and carried him off to the pit. Well, at least he'd avoided another pride-reducing tumble into unconsciousness. It was the only success he could count as his since arriving in the MacLeod keep.

Things were not exactly going as he'd planned.

Long conversations with Jamie over the past month had given him the knowledge of how to use the forest gate and a fairly accurate idea of what to expect when he reached his destination. They had discussed strategy, potential problems, and how to get himself in the front door without getting himself killed first. He'd had all the right gear, the right accent, and what he'd hoped would be the right swagger.

The trip through the forest gate had gone off without a hitch. He'd focused his energies on where he wanted to go, opened his eyes, and found himself leaving the forest to stare at a very familiar yet different keep. It had been midmorning. He hadn't protested when MacLeod scouts had ushered him up the meadow and into the keep with their bared swords at his back. He'd claimed to have business with Malcolm and that had at least kept him alive long enough to get inside the door.

He'd found the hall in an uproar. It had taken him a few minutes to tune his ear to the sounds, and when he had, he'd realized he was looking at Malcolm screaming at his son, Angus, for being foolish enough to indebt himself to an English-man. Thomas had looked in astonishment at Iolanthe's half-brother, but he wasn't sure if it was surprise that he was actually looking at the man in the flesh or that such a pimply faced boy would actually be sent by his father on errands of diplomacy. Maybe Iolanthe was right, and her father sent him away to get rid of him. Thomas wasn't sure he wouldn't have done the same thing in the man's place.

Of course, he hadn't had the chance to say as much. What he had gotten out when presented to the furious laird was something along the lines of "I'm Thomas McKinnon, and there are things you need to know about that English-man before you send your daughter away with him."

Apparently direct and to the point didn't fly with Malcolm MacLeod. Thomas would let Jamie know that if he ever saw him again.

The sound of voices drew nearer, accompanied by heavy footsteps. Perhaps he would have a chance to try another approach sooner than he'd hoped. The trapdoor was flung back. Thomas was almost blinded by the light of the torch as it was shoved into the pit. It was pulled back and a ladder shoved down.

"Up, McKinnon dog," a man snarled.

Well, that didn't sound good. Yet another thing to tell Jamie when he got home.

But the offer to leave the pit was a good one, so Thomas took it. He crawled up the ladder and tried to look unthreatening. Even so, he was pushed and shoved out into the great hall where Malcolm was apparently holding court. Thomas looked around quickly, trying to identify the players.

Angus was there, shadowed closely by an older woman who resembled him so strongly, Thomas had to assume she was his mother. It was readily apparent where Angus got his unwholesome looks. There were too many other men and boys loitering there for him to put faces to any of Iolanthe's additional descriptions.

All except Duncan.

Thomas gaped at Iolanthe's true father, feeling as if he'd just seen a ghost. But there Duncan was in the flesh. Thomas almost said something to him, then realized he was being addressed.

"State your business," Malcolm snarled, "and be quick about it. I've business of my own to see accomplished this day."

The odds of him getting out more than a few words were slim, so he dove right in.

"Don't trust the English-man," he said quickly. "He's beguiled your son and seeks to destroy all of you." All right, so the last wasn't technically true, but it was close enough. If the man had his way, the MacLeods would have been beggared or destroyed soon enough.

"Lord Charles is an honorable man," Malcolm said stiffly. He gestured to his right, and a sea of men parted to reveal Lord Charles himself sitting there, looking honorable.

Wonderful.

Thomas turned back to Malcolm. "I'll pay Angus's debts. And I want your daughter in return."

"Grudach?" Malcolm asked in surprise.

"No, the other one. Your elder daughter."

"That girl?" Malcolm asked, sounding even more surprised. Then his eyes narrowed. "Where is your gold?"

"Where it can be reached. Give me the girl first."

"Cheeky bastard!" Angus exclaimed. "Father, put him to the sword."

"Silence, whelp," Malcolm growled. He looked at Thomas.

"Show me the gold, and I'll consider it."

"Show me the girl, and I'll tell you where the gold is."

Malcolm waved to one of his men, who headed toward the stairs. Thomas suppressed the urge to reach inside his plaid and touch the bag of gold hiding there. He had consulted long and hard with Jamie as to a price Malcolm wouldn't be able to refuse, and how best to pay that price. He'd settled for struck coins that, even though they weren't authentic, were close enough to resemble things Malcolm would be familiar with.

Thomas waited until he heard the vociferous complaints of a woman being dragged down the stairs before he pulled out the bag he'd attached to his belly with duct tape.

And then he realized his mistake.

"Father, what is this madness?"

That wasn't Iolanthe. Damn Malcolm MacLeod to hell, that was Grudach! Thomas glared at the man and received a smirk in return before half a dozen clansmen fell on him and ripped the bag out of his hands. He fought off the blows that followed, but even with as buff as his time in Jamie's boot camp had left him, he had to admit he wasn't a match for that many men.

"Toss him back in the pit," Malcolm said with a negligent wave of his hand. He hefted the bag of gold as he turned to the English-man. "Now, Lord Charles, let us speak of our business. You want my eldest?"

"Your son assures me she is the most desirable."

Thomas started to protest, then found a fist in his mouth. He tried to avoid the hands that clutched at him. The only thing the unholy ruckus he raised earned him was another round of debilitating blows. One thing he knew, though, was that he couldn't find himself thrown back in that pit. There was still time to somehow get Iolanthe and get the hell out of there.

And then he saw Duncan.

The man was looking at him like he'd just seen a ghost.

"Duncan," Thomas croaked. "You've got to help me."

Duncan looked startled. "How do ye know me?" he asked, crossing himself.

"I—" Thomas gasped at the fist in his belly. He found

himself completely without wind, or his feet underneath him.
But as he was dragged off, he looked at Duncan and wheezed
out the two things he was sure would get the man's attention.

"Greek," he gasped. "Violet."

Duncan blinked, and his hand fell to his side. He continued
to stare at Thomas until Thomas couldn't see him any longer.

His next trip down into the pit was accomplished with
even less ceremony than the first. He tried to land on his feet
but wound up doing the better part of a belly flop into the
muck. It winded him so thoroughly, he wondered if he'd ever
again regain his breath.

It occurred to him, as he felt consciousness begin to fade,
that he really should have spent more time brawling in bars.
It would have been much better preparation for medieval
Scotland even than Jamie's crash course in swordplay.

Hrmph. A helluva lot of good his sword did him upstairs.

Maybe they'd cut off his head and end his misery with his
own blade.

Damn it anyway.

He woke to the sound of a footfall above him. He shook
his head and heaved himself up to his knees. His world spun
violently, and he wondered if he was going to puke. He probably would have, if he'd had anything to eat in recent memory.

He breathed as silently as he could and listened for the
sound that had woken him. There were the snores of the
guardsmen above him and the irritating drip, drip, drip of
something draining into the pit.

No, there it was again.

The sound of a footstep.

Thomas squinted against the faint torchlight coming from
above, then felt his nerves stretch uncomfortably taut as the
trapdoor was opened very slowly. A ladder was let down
into the pit.

A hand was extended as well.

Thomas needed no further invitation. He clambered up,
took the hand, and found himself soundlessly aided onto the
solid floor, which was a vast improvement from the shifting

vermin he'd been loitering in for who knew how long. A day? Two days? An eternity? He looked at his rescuer and couldn't stop his smile.

"Thank you," he mouthed.

Duncan handed Thomas his sword, pulled the ladder back up, and shut the trapdoor, all with a silence that was absolute.

"The guards are drunk," Duncan whispered, as if he were either unsurprised at their laxity or as if he'd engineered the whole thing himself. "Follow me."

Thomas stopped him with a hand on his arm. "Is she still here?"

Duncan looked at him again as if he just couldn't quite believe what he was either seeing or hearing, then shook his head.

"Left this afternoon. We've a hard ride before us. Make haste."

"Gladly."

It was touch and go in the hall, but apparently the men who were awake were properly intimidated by Duncan's sharp hisses and meaningful hand motions. Thomas followed the older man from the keep and through the village. There were two horses being held by a man Thomas didn't know. Along with a horse came fresh clothes.

"Well done, Stephen," Duncan whispered. He looked at Thomas. "One of the lady's cousins."

Thomas pulled the clean clothing on, then looked at Stephen and nodded briefly. "You're doing the right thing."

"She was beguiled and betrayed," the young man said. "I'll throw the laird off the scent while ye go after her."

Duncan shook his head. "Don't endanger yourself, lad. Malcolm will know I'm behind this. Put the blame onto my shoulders and let that be enough."

Stephen nodded, then looked at Thomas. "I dinna ken who ye are, but ye canna be worse than the English."

Thomas wanted to thank him for the vote of confidence, but instead he merely nodded and considered that enough.

"I fear he'll kill her," Stephen continued. "He'll want what she will not give."

"I won't let anything happen to her," Thomas promised.

Stephen then handed over the reins. "May God keep ye."

Thomas strapped his sword to his saddle the way Jamie had taught him. Duncan looked at him carefully as he did so, but said nothing. When they were mounted, Duncan led the way. Thomas followed him, not bothering to ask where they were going or if he'd still have his life by sunrise. It was enough to be free of MacLeod's pit and riding in what he hoped was the right direction. He couldn't see a thing in the dark, and though Iolanthe had given him some landmarks she thought she remembered, he was equally aware that she'd told him not to count on her memory.

She had promised him, however, that Duncan was unparalleled in his tracking skills. Thomas had no choice but to trust the man.

And hope that he didn't unwittingly lead them both into an ambush.

It was daybreak before they stopped to water the horses. Duncan drank deeply from the stream as well, then looked at Thomas.

"Ye've told me a name known only to myself and two other people," Duncan said without preamble. "Either ye're a demon or ye're possessing Sight more powerful than I've ever seen."

Thomas took a deep breath. "Would you believe me if I told you neither?"

"Yer Gaelic is poor."

"My French is better."

"French it is," Duncan said smoothly. In flawless French.

Thomas stared at him in surprise. Well, this was news. He wondered how many other things Duncan hadn't told him.

"I'll have the tale," Duncan said, folding his arms over his chest. "The entire tale, if you please."

"Um," Thomas stalled.

"But first, I'll know how you know the lady's name."

In for a penny, in for a pound, Thomas supposed.

"You and Moira gave it to her," he said. "A minstrel had come through, one who knew many languages and gave you a word for the color of Moira's eyes, which would be the color of her daughter's eyes. Moira asked you what the girl should be named." He took a deep breath. "And you, as her father, named her."

Duncan stuck his jaw out and considered. "And how, lad," he asked carefully, "would you be knowing any of that?"

"You told me yourself."

"I did not."

"You did, in the year 2001."

Duncan didn't move or give any indication that he thought Thomas's story was madness. He merely nodded slowly, then spoke.

"The entire tale. All of it."

"I'm not a demon," Thomas assured him.

"I'll judge that."

"I love her. I've come to save her."

Duncan folded his arms over his chest. "The tale. Briefly. We need to catch them first, then find a proper place to try to take them. We're two against a dozen, and those are poor odds in any battle."

"I can wield a sword."

"A body can hope. Now, the tale."

Thomas sent a prayer flying heavenward before he plunged in. "Okay," he said, "this is the future—or what will be the future if we don't go soon. The English-man will take Iolanthe to his castle, try to force the secret of the MacLeod keep from her, she'll refuse, and she'll be murdered. I'll come along six hundred years later, buy the castle, and fall in love with her. I'll discover the secret of your keep, travel back in time to try to stop the murder from happening, find myself thrown in Malcolm's pit, you'll rescue me, and we'll end up standing here with me telling you a story that sounds unbelievable."

Duncan stared at him so long in such silence that Thomas wondered if he'd been too blunt. Much too blunt. He found himself easing up on the balls of his feet and wondering if he could get his sword from off his horse before Duncan reached for his.

And then Duncan stirred.

"Her name," he began, then he cleared his throat. "Did she give it to you? In this Future of yours?

"I guessed it," Thomas admitted. "Then she gave me permission to use it."

Duncan considered. "And I told you these things about Moira?"

"Before I left, yes," Thomas said. "You said it would get your attention."

"It did." He paced a ways off, then came back to stand in front of Thomas. "Does Iolanthe know I'm her sire?"

Thomas shook his head. "You never told her. Neither did I. I figured it was your knowledge to share or not, as you would."

"And I knew you then," Duncan said, sounding rather stunned. "But I don't know you now."

"It's complicated."

"How do you expect that the lass will know you?"

"I'm hoping she'll remember the future."

"That, my lad, is daft."

Thomas smiled grimly. "People believe different things about how time passes."

"Slowly or quickly," Duncan said dryly, "depending on the skill of the bard telling the tale."

"Right," Thomas said, acknowledging the barb with a smile. "Anyway, this is what I know. Some people think time goes along in a straight line, like on a string. Some people believe that it has a single starting point, then it goes backward and forward at the same time. Other people say it's like a ring, with no beginning and no end, which leaves it open to all kinds of speculation."

Duncan looked at him with faint consternation.

"It's entirely possible that she will remember me."

Duncan grunted.

"All right," Thomas conceded. "Maybe she won't at first. But it's possible that if I can get to her before she's killed and take her away to the future, that she'll remember the life she lived as a ghost."

"How do I die?"

Thomas blinked, completely blindsided by the question. "Um," he said, not sure how to answer.

"The truth."

"That is one question I never asked you, and believe me when I tell you that I asked you a lot of questions."

Duncan rubbed his hand suddenly over his face and sighed

deeply. "Such thoughts are too complicated for my old head. Let us be about our business. That you know her name will startle her enough that she'll listen to you at least. I can't guarantee what she'll do after that." He looked at Thomas critically. "You're a braw lad. She could do worse."

"Thank you," Thomas said dryly.

"I'm here with you. What more display of faith do you want?"

Thomas smiled. "None. Shall we go?"

"Aye."

"Can you find her?"

"Aye."

They mounted again and set off. Thomas closed his eyes briefly in gratitude that he'd escaped Malcolm's pit, that he had his sword near his side, and that he had an ally in Duncan MacLeod. He was sure, as time passed and he became quite lost, that if he succeeded at all, it would be because of Duncan.

He didn't want to think about what would have happened otherwise.

Chapter 28

I, Iolanthe MacLeod, do make this record, not by my own hand, but by the hand of my laird, James MacLeod. I make it in the year of Our Lord's Grace 2001, in the autumn of that year. I have returned to my home after six hundred years of self-imposed exile in a keep on the border between England and Scotland.

I make this record because mayhap I will be restored to the life I lost in 1382. And should that happen, 'tis also possible I might lose my memories.

And I want to remember.

My laird tells me that the book before him has many pages and that my six centuries of haunting should be written down. I will do so more fully later. Now, I can only bear to speak briefly of that which has passed.

My earliest memory is of my mother. She was beautiful and good, and I loved her for the ten years I had her. I believe she loved me as well, for she gave me a beautiful name, as well as her gentle hands tending my hurts and sorrows, and her smiles at the expectation of my company, even when she was ailing.

I had a brother as well, Alexandir, who died in battle. Other brothers I had, as well as a sister, though they were sired on a different woman. Angus was the eldest of these; I have nothing to say about him for he betrayed me to my death. He also scattered his seed carelessly so that I daresay there was a mighty battle for the chieftainship on his death. My sister Grudach deserves no kind word either, for she betrayed me along with my brother. Of my other half-siblings, I can say naught but that they weren't overly unkind. What I can say is that when I was forced to leave my home, I was not unhappy about never having to see them again.

I was sold to an English-man who believed there was

a secret held in my father's keep that would bring him vast riches. When he demanded the secret from me, I would not give it to him. I knew of what he spoke, for my grandfather had trusted me with the knowledge, but I had never given the like to another soul, not even my sire. Why would I tell a stranger?

I was murdered at sunset. I did not cry out, for I am a MacLeod. And at the time I had nothing left but my virtue and my pride.

Nay, I did not cry out.

It seemed as if I dreamed for a goodly while, for when I awoke to myself, it was to find that I was not mortal, yet not a pure spirit either. There was enough substance to me that others could see me if I willed it, yet I felt no pain.

Nor joy.

Nor the sun on my back nor the breeze on my face.

I was angry for a goodly while. The English-man who took my life died in the great hall as a sniveling, terrified rabbit, surrounded by men he had bid protect him. He was the only one who could see me, and I took my revenge on him in full measure, though it did nothing to relieve my pain.

At first I paid attention to life as it went on around me. When I could aid my countrymen against the English, I did so. Many ghostly Highlanders found their way to my keep, and they joined me in my efforts.

But then the tide turned for my country. The slaughter became greater, and I saw my people, both friends and enemies, begin to despair. After the battle at Culloden, I closed my eyes and my ears. I know now that my people were swept off their land to make way for more profitable crops such as sheep, rather than noble men and women living and working their small fields.

Few mortals came over the years to the keep I called mine. The ones who came didn't stay long. The hall soon fell into disrepair. The years stretched out before and behind me like a long, featureless road. There were no seasons that I could mark, no change in the unlife that had been forced upon me. I knew the sun rose each morn and set each evening. I watched the moon travel her path each night. I had tasks I set myself in the garden, and I had kin about me and nearby that provided a goodly bit of speech now and then. But it was all the same. I had no hope, no faith, no surety that something would come and change my existence.

And then change came.

He walked into my hall, that Thomas McKinnon, and insulted me. For the first time in centuries I wept, but they were tears of fury. I would have gladly pushed him off the nearest wall had I had the strength, yet something kept me from doing it.

The memory of an autumn breeze against my cheek, I suppose.

Or that I knew him.

'Twas those memories that assaulted me whenever I was near him. I knew we had never met, yet I knew his face as intimately as if I'd gazed on it every day for the whole of my life.

For I had dreamed of a man who would come to rescue me.

And, beyond all reason, that man was Thomas McKinnon.

He is fey, of that there is no doubt. He knew things before he was told, saw spirits who should have remained hidden, read the innermost secrets of my heart as if they'd been written on a page before him. He knew my name before I had given it to him.

It was the first time I'd heard it from mortal or unmortal lips since my mother died.

And such was my undoing.

I passed time with him, finding that 'twas sweet indeed to have a man look at me as if he found me beautiful. That it was pleasurable to have him listen as if what I said mattered to him. And that the thought of him possibly losing his life to give me back mine was the most terrible thing of all.

He had a mad thought, a thought that he could actually go back in time and save me before I was murdered. I told him nay, that 'twas foolish. I ignored him when he spoke of it. I favored him fully with my anger when nothing else seemed to deter him.

Yet still he persisted. Either 'tis love in truth that he feels for me, or he's simply a mad fool on a foolish errand. Yet what man gives up his life willingly, if not for something or someone he loves?

He left Thorpewold and came north, to my ancestral home near the feet of the Benmore Forest. My great-great-grandfather, who had been the one to discover the time gates, trained him in swordplay and other necessities. But how much can a man learn of a way of life in merely a pair of fortnights?

I came home the day before he left. He found me in the meadow. He told me he loved me. He told me that there was no reason I couldn't remember the future. That should he be successful and I not lose my life, there was still no reason I couldn't remember my life as a ghost. My laird James tells me 'tis possible, but I wonder if the two have spent too many nights slipping into their cups and they are both daft. James speaks of alternate realities, but it makes little sense to me. All I know is that I might be restored to my life.

Yet I will lose the life I have had.

So I have written these few words. My laird still bids me give more of the tale. He has it aright, but I wonder how much time I have left. Thomas has been gone a pair of days. If he succeeds, will I simply cease to exist here? Or will I be pulled backward in time, with my centuries of memories intact? Or will it be as if those centuries had never happened and I will remember nothing of my kin, my enemies, my friends?

My love?

He is a braw lad, though, so perhaps if I cannot remember him, I'll see my way clear to love him again.

For I loved Thomas McKinnon as a ghost. I never said as much to him, and for that I have my regrets. But I did love him, and I would have passed the rest of his life happily with him, sharing whatever small things we could have shared.

I'll make an end here. If time is allotted to me, I'll go through the centuries in another part of this book. But as for this much, I've said enough.

I, Iolanthe MacLeod, write this by the hand of my laird, James MacLeod, and I make it in the year of Our Lord's Grace 2001, in the autumn of that year.

Chapter 29

Thomas wondered, as he stood near a group of trees in the middle of some guy's field and fought for his life, if Jamie's training really had been adequate. He stood back to back with Duncan, wielded his sword for all he was worth, and decided as he had to jerk aside to avoid being skewered that perhaps he was just a little bit out of his league. It was one thing to pretend to fight off men you were fairly sure wouldn't maim you if push came to shove. It was another thing entirely to fight off ragged, unkempt soldiers who seemed to find the idea of two Scots surrounded by a half a dozen English-men to be good entertainment for the afternoon.

He'd never killed before. In fact, he'd always made it a point to leave as little trace of his passing as possible when he climbed mountains. All right, so maybe he'd done in numerous rabbits over the course of his long and illustrious career out in the wild; that was dinner, and the bones were probably biodegradable after a few centuries. The thing about this was, he had no intentions of eating the grim-looking characters he faced at present.

The only upside he could see at present was that Lord Charles had left behind the majority of his troops. If he and Duncan could do these guys in, they would be home free. Thomas was certain that the entire party, including Iolanthe, hadn't been made up of more than ten. That he and Duncan merited such a large force was a compliment.

On the whole, though, he would have preferred to have been insulted.

He heard Duncan grunt behind him, which in and of itself wasn't noteworthy. But it was a sound that was somehow unsettling. Thomas didn't dare turn to find out how he was, or even to ask him, so he merely concentrated on keeping his own head resting comfortably on his shoulders and all his limbs intact.

His chance to finish his side of the battle came sooner than he'd hoped. He stabbed the man in front of him with a clean stroke through the gut, grabbed the man's knife from his belt as he fell, then turned to face the other two. They came at him both at once, and he found himself reacting out of the instinct Jamie and Ian had instilled in him. He thrust one way, ducked and came up under the sword of the other man, plunging his knife into the other's belly.

He stepped back from the dying men, then turned and looked at Duncan. Duncan finished his last man with a vicious swipe across his neck that made Thomas very glad he wasn't standing next in the enemy line.

"Well done," Thomas said with a grin, dragging his arm across his forehead. "Let's get out of here."

And then Duncan turned.

And Thomas saw that his tunic was drenched with blood. Thomas would have believed that it was someone else's but for the way Duncan held his hand to the wound. Thomas met the older man's eyes and found himself so stunned, he couldn't form articulate sounds.

Duncan grimaced, then stepped across a fallen foe to put his hand on Thomas's shoulder. "Go," he wheezed. "Quickly."

"I can't leave," Thomas said, but he knew he would have to.

"Your task is to see to my girl," Duncan said, straightening with an effort. "Else my death is in vain."

"Oh, Duncan," Thomas said, sheathing his sword and putting both of his hands on the other man's shoulders. "I'm so sorry." He blinked back tears he hadn't known were near. "It wasn't supposed to happen this way. You never told me—"

"I was always known for keeping my secrets close," Duncan said with a hint of a smile. "I suppose even as a ghost I did the same."

"But," Thomas said, feeling set adrift, "how am I—"

"You've a plan," Duncan said sharply. "Follow it. Follow

her and save her before she loses her life as well." He sank
to his knees. "I suppose I'll know if you succeed. You'd best
succeed, or you'll find me haunting you for the rest of your
days."

Thomas squatted down in front of him. "What can I do to
make you more comfortable?"

Duncan looked around, then pointed to a nearby tree.
"Help me over there, then go. There's naught you can do."

Thomas helped him hobble over to the tree, quietly appalled by the amount of blood that seemed to be seeping into
Duncan's clothes. He wouldn't last long with that kind of
blood loss.

"Duncan . . ."

"Get on that horse, Thomas lad, and let me see you ridin'
off to rescue my girl." Duncan pulled a knife free of his belt
and handed it to Thomas. "Take this. Iolanthe will recognize
it as mine. You never know but that such a thing might serve
you."

Thomas took the knife and rose slowly to his feet. "There
aren't words to thank you for this," he said, gesturing behind
him. "I never would have managed it on my own."

"Well, you haven't managed the rest of it yet, have you,
so cease with your boasting. Be off with you."

Thomas hesitated. "Should I tell her? The truth?"

"Tell her I died aiding you to rescue her."

"That's a great gift."

Duncan looked up at him and smiled faintly. "Ach, but
what else is a father to do?"

Thomas would have replied, but there was nothing else to
be said. He retrieved his horse, and Duncan's, too, then came
back for a final farewell. He realized then that he just didn't
have it in him to leave Duncan. Iolanthe had died alone. He
couldn't leave Duncan to do that.

He knelt down next to the older man and grasped his hand.

"Shall I tell you of the future?" Thomas asked softly.

"Aye," Duncan breathed. "A . . . comfort . . ."

"Well, in the future that's already passed, you find Iolanthe
at the castle which is called Thorpewold. By the time I arrive,
you've been there six hundred years with her. She said that
when you first came, you went down on your knee and

pledged fealty to her, as you would have to your laird. I suppose you can imagine what that meant to her, but I can tell you that she only spoke of it once, and it was with tears in her eyes."

Duncan smiled.

"You were a father to her for centuries. She loved you as such. You gave her the gift of unconditional love and unwavering support. You couldn't have given her more."

He took a breath to continue, then realized there was no point.

He closed Duncan's eyes, took a final look at the man's faint smile, then bowed his head and sighed. There wasn't even time for a decent burial. Every minute he lagged behind was another minute Lord Charles had on him. Duncan would have heartily agreed with the sentiment.

He did, however, spare a moment or two to grieve for the short time he'd had to spend in Duncan's company. He suspected that a lifetime wouldn't have been long enough to discover all the man's secrets. He would have been a wonderful father-in-law and a marvelous grandfather.

Which he still could be, in a sense, but only if Thomas managed to succeed in rescuing Iolanthe. So he unbuckled the brooch that held Duncan's plaid to his shoulder, pulled that material over his face, then pinned it in place. He laid Duncan's sword by his side, then turned and looked around him. It occurred to him that if he and Iolanthe did manage to escape anywhere near the border, they would need something appropriate to wear.

Without emotion, he stripped clothing off a pair of the slain men, clothing with the least amount of blood on it—and that was no mean feat. He bundled it up, stuck it behind his saddle, and mounted.

He left the scene of battle and hoped the small bit of tracking Duncan had been able to teach him would be enough.

It would have to be.

*T*wo days later, Thomas wondered if he would manage to rescue Iolanthe after all. Try as he might, he could never catch the English-man, though he seemed to pause to water his horse only moments behind the small party. He'd barely missed having his life taken more than once, and the only good thing to come of that was that he'd managed to knock off one more of Charles's guardsmen. That left Charles, another man, and Iolanthe.

The odds were getting better all the time.

Or they would have been, had Thomas been able to catch the trio.

He paused, the morning of the third day of travel by himself, to water his horse, Duncan's horse, and his own head. What he wanted desperately was sleep. He would have given anything for a caffeinated beverage of some sort. He'd gone through all his stores of food. He'd even taken to munching on bark, but all that had done was give him a nasty taste in his mouth. Didn't Charles ever sleep? The man was a machine.

A twig snapped behind him and Thomas rolled into the river and came up with his sword in his hands. He swung before he thought, belatedly grateful that he hadn't cut Iolanthe in two.

Charles's remaining guardsman clutched his belly to keep his insides inside, then looked at Thomas with wide eyes.

"Who *are* you?" he gasped.

There was no use in answering that. The man slid slowly to the earth, then fell onto his back. Thomas waited until his eyes stared lifelessly at nothing, then turned back to his horse and mounted. He could afford no more time to wait. He took up the trail again. Unfortunately, the terrain was beginning to look all too familiar. He was getting within a day's ride of Thorpewold. He'd planned to have Iolanthe safely spirited away long before now.

He kept on his southeasterly course, straining his eyes to see anything in front of him. Had he lost them? Had he taken five minutes too long to let his horse drink? Would he come too late?

And then he saw them, two tiny specks a great distance in front of him.

He kicked his poor horse into a gallop, apologizing out loud as he did so. The gelding gave his all, and Thomas found himself drawing nearer. For the first time, he really believed he might manage what he'd set out to do. In the distance, he could see Thorpewold rising up against the horizon. If he could only catch Charles and Iolanthe. He could take Charles. He couldn't let himself believe anything less. If he could just catch them, which couldn't take more than another half hour. He rode, willing his mount to keep up the grueling pace.

And then his mount stumbled and pulled up lame.

Thomas didn't think. He merely jumped down off his horse, grabbed the spare clothes, and switched to Duncan's. He kicked Duncan's horse into a gallop. The chestnut hadn't had the burden of a man for three days and leaped ahead as if he'd just come from a nice warm stall, fully rested and fed. Thomas pushed the horse as fast as he would go. He felt victory within his grasp and found himself feeling more hopeful than he had in days.

And then from nowhere came a whizzing by Thomas's ear that set his horse to rearing. It was all he could do to stay in the saddle. He heard another twang, felt his horse shudder, and looked down to see an arrow protruding from the beast's neck.

He barely had his sword from its sheath before another man was bearing down on him, swearing in something that sounded remarkably like English. Thomas ducked, then heaved himself off his horse before it went down in a tangle of legs and whinnies. The other man's horse tried to leap over the fallen horse, but it tripped and went down as well, crushing its rider underneath it as it fell. It struggled to its feet, then trotted off toward Thorpewold as if nothing had happened.

Thomas looked down at the fallen guardsman, saw him wearing Charles's colors, and considered his options. Then he noticed the compound fracture of the other man's leg. The kindest thing he could do would probably be to finish ahead of time what rampant infection probably would later.

He took a deep breath, then slit the man's throat. And that, somehow, was just too much for him. He turned aside and lost the remains of tree bark he'd been eating for the past forty-eight hours. He stood, dragged his sleeve across his mouth, then looked up and scanned the countryside around him for any more assaults coming his way.

He saw nothing.

Not even Charles or Iolanthe.

He sheathed his sword, grabbed his gear, and began to jog. Iolanthe said she'd been murdered at sunset. It was just past noon now. He still had time.

F_{our} hours later, he had the castle in his sights but no plan in mind. It wasn't as if he could just walk up and force his way inside. He found some cover, stripped off his plaid and put on a dead English-man's clothes. He bundled up another outfit and tied it around his waist. He stood, adjusted his sword, then put his shoulders back and faced the road that led to his castle. He stepped onto it without hesitation.

And the déjà vu almost knocked him over.

He had to hunch over with his hands on his thighs and simply gasp for a few moments until the dizzying assault receded. Once he thought he could walk without reeling, he started up the way to the keep as if he had the right to. He looked around him and saw nothing but land stripped of vegetation. Then he blinked.

And saw the way lined with people.

Knights and peasants. Men, women, and children. Old, young. There were probably fifty or sixty people there, lining the road, staring at him. Thomas froze in midstep. A year ago, he would have thought he had just lost his mind. Now he knew better.

He walked up to one of the peasants and tried to make his accent as Chaucer-like as possible.

"What business have you here?" Thomas asked politely.

The man looked at him in surprise. "Can ye see me?"

"Well, of course I can."

He soon found himself completely surrounded by souls that were apparently very surprised they could be seen. Thomas wondered absently if he was going to spend the rest of his life with this gift. One thing he could say for himself: He would never be bored.

One of the knights stepped forward. He spoke in French, which helped greatly.

"What business have *you* here?" the knight demanded.

Thomas looked at the keep. "Lord Charles has taken the woman I love and intends to murder her. I'm here to stop it."

"Is that so?"

"It is. And none of you will hinder me."

The knight snorted. "Hinder? Rather we should aid you. The bloody bastard slew me for givin' him a cross look."

"And me for spilling his porridge," said another.

"Me for no reason a'tall!"

Thomas found himself inundated with tales of murder and mayhem. Not a soul stood about him who hadn't been done in one way or another. The connecting thread through the stories was the identity of the man doing the slaying.

Too bad Charles didn't see very clearly. His life would have been hell otherwise.

"We'll aid ye," said another knight, stepping forward and drawing his sword.

Thomas considered. "Can you make yourselves visible?"

There was a resounding chorus of ayes. Well, there was something to be said for that. It was one thing to be a single man assaulting a medieval castle. It was quite another thing to arrive with an army.

Never mind that the army wasn't corporeal.

Thomas formulated a plan. He laid it out for his new contingent of ghostly helpers, then thanked them kindly and continued on his way.

The guards didn't even bother to shoot at him. They heckled him from atop the walls, and he only nodded in appreciation. The more helpless they thought him, the better. As long as they didn't pull up the drawbridge, he was in business.

He paused at the barbican and faced a guardsman with a drawn sword.

"State your business," the man said.

"I'm here to kill Lord Charles."

"Are you now?" the man asked with a laugh.

"I am," Thomas replied.

The man briefly looked as if he just might be for the idea, then apparently he thought better of it. He smiled pleasantly.

"Come in, then," the man said, waving him in. "We'll see to your comfort right away."

"I have some friends who want to come, too," Thomas admitted.

"Bring them as well," the guard said pleasantly. "We've space enough in the dungeon for many."

But space for ghosts waving swords and farm implements? Thomas smiled to himself as the guard soon found himself facing two score of armed knights and peasant men he hadn't seen the second before.

His eyes rolled back in his head, and he slumped to the ground.

"Too easy," said one of the knights grimly. "There'll be sterner tests than this before us."

"Yes, well, let's try to surmount them quietly," Thomas said. "I'd like the element of surprise to be on my side."

The knight waved him away. "Be about yer business, man, and leave us to ours. We'll see to the garrison."

Thomas left him to it. He himself dispatched three men on his way to the tower, but once he was on the steps, he found himself alone.

With his memories.

He struggled for air as he trudged up the same steps he had climbed only once before.

Or had it been more than once?

Had he been up these steps countless times? Was he stuck in some kind of cosmic vicious circle that only continued forever because he failed each time? Was someone trying to tell him that he wasn't going to succeed?

He pushed aside his thoughts and staggered up the few remaining steps. He stopped on the landing and heard . . . nothing.

He leaned against the door frame and panted, despair crashing down on him.

Had he come too late?

Chapter 30

J ames MacLeod considered himself a fairly learned man. After all, he'd been laird in his day, and he'd passed a goodly number of years in the Future with all its methods of learning just there for the taking. He'd also traveled a great deal in various centuries. Up until a se'nnight ago, he'd believed that he'd seen and done much that any man would be proud to call to mind.

And then he'd seen his great-great-granddaughter and found that she was a ghost.

And then he'd begun to write down her memories.

It was, he supposed, a bit like traveling through time. The painful thing about her memories, though, was the things she had missed. The sights, smells, tastes: all the things he had taken so for granted.

He set his pen down, realizing that Iolanthe had stopped speaking some time earlier. Jamie looked down at the book on his desk and realized that there were but two more pages. One was already covered with Iolanthe's delicate scrawl, and he quickly flipped past it. She'd obviously taken great pains to write something there and 'twas no affair of his what she said. The last page was still blank, and he found that he was loath to write anything else there. He looked at it and felt impressed to leave it as it was. Perhaps when she was restored to life, she herself would fill it with her own words written in her own hand.

That the rest of the book was finished at all was something of an accomplishment. He'd been at it for hours at a stretch, relieved by others in his family for hours at a time as well. He suspected there wasn't a soul in the keep who hadn't taken down at least a few pages of Iolanthe's tale.

"What do you think will happen?"

Jamie looked up, startled by the sound of her voice. "What?"

She fixed him with those pale, grayish violet eyes of hers, and he realized she was near to weeping.

"If he succeeds," she whispered, "what will happen?"

"Ah," Jamie said, scrambling mightily for something to say to stave off her tears, "I wish I knew, my girl."

"Will it be painful, do you think?" she asked, looking away.

"I couldn't say," Jamie managed. "Traveling through time has no pain. Perhaps it is like unto that."

She nodded thoughtfully. "Aye, my laird. Perhaps you have it aright." She sighed. "I can only hope 'tis done quickly."

"Some things are better done in haste," he agreed.

She looked at him and smiled. "Thank you for aiding me with my tale."

Jamie put his elbows on the desk and knocked his pen on the floor as a result. He leaned over to pick it up.

"It was my pleasure," he said, straightening. "Now about the . . . other . . . "

She was gone.

"Iolanthe?" he called.

There was no answer.

Jamie sat there in silence for several minutes. He took her book in his hand, flipping through the pages and looking at the various scripts there.

He hoped it had been without pain for her.

He took a ribbon and bound the book closed. He looked about his thinking chamber and considered where he might store it until she would be able to read it again for herself. If her memories had remained her own, she would enjoy rereading her tale.

But if she lost them, the book would be vital.

In the end, he slipped the book inside his desk drawer, shut it, and stood. There was nothing more he could do.

He turned off the light and went to bed.

Chapter 31

"Will you starve, or will you be put to the sword?"

Iolanthe MacLeod stood in the English-man's tower chamber and felt as if her heart might shake the very walls surrounding her with the force of its pounding. A slow death or a less slow one. Where was the choice in that? She'd seen men starve to death in her father's pit, and it wasn't pleasant. Perhaps there would be pain with the other, but it would be over much sooner. And it seemed a braver way to die, if one had to die.

The man facing her drew his sword. Perhaps he thought he offered her a merciful death. She felt herself tremble and she suddenly found her thoughts less on what she would never have and more on not shaming herself by falling to her knees or weeping. She was, after all, a MacLeod, and a MacLeod always died well if he could.

So she lifted her chin, stared her murderer full in the face, and let his sword do its foul work unhindered.

She expected agony.

What she felt, however, was merely the brush of cool steel against her ribs.

She looked down, saw that her dress was torn, but there was no blood gushing from a life-ending wound. She realized what had happened and felt the strong desire to curse. What kind of fool was this, that he couldn't end her life with a single stroke? She'd heard the sudden banging on the door as well, but she hadn't expected her executioner to be so inept that being startled would cause his thrust to go wide.

The banging continued, much louder, until the door burst asunder and a man stumbled into the chamber. Her erstwhile murderer turned to face him, blocking her view.

"*Merde,*" snarled the English-man.

Well, that word she knew. She could curse in three languages, and though 'twas a simple skill, it was one she was rather proud of. Then the two men began to speak in that despised peasant's English her grandsire had insisted she learn.

Ye never ken when it'll serve ye, my gel, he would say, with that damnedable glint in his eye.

"You don't need her," the other man said. "Release her."

Iolanthe felt her mouth hang open of its own accord. She was to be released?

The English-man laughed shortly. "And have her scurry home and bring her kin down upon me? Never."

His answer was unsurprising. What was surprising was that someone had come to rescue her. Iolanthe looked around her abductor to see who that someone might be. One of her brothers' friends? A cousin she'd never marked? One of her sire's enemies with foul designs upon her person?

But it wasn't. It wasn't any of them.

If she'd been a maid given to weakness, she might have felt her legs grow unsteady beneath her.

He was, despite how filthy and travel-stained he looked, the most handsome man she had ever clapped eyes on. Tall, aye, and broad. Dark-haired with eyes so vivid a blue she could see their color from where she stood across the chamber. His face was finely fashioned with the beginnings of a beard, though she suspected by its length that it wasn't his custom to wear one. But none of that was what was so startling.

It was that she recognized him.

That in itself was almost enough to make her wish for a sturdy chair beneath her backside, that she might contemplate the mystery in comfort.

She had spent the past ten-and-four years of her life wishing for a braw lad to come and rescue her from her sorry state. Almost from the moment she'd begun wishing for such a thing, the vision of a man's face had come to her with a clarity that was almost frightening.

This man's face.

And now he'd come.

His strong hands were empty, but she saw the hilt of a

sword peeking over his back. That made her frown. That was how her kin ofttimes wore their blades, when they needed their hands free for other business of death. Was the man a Scot? His clothing bespoke otherwise. He sported things she'd only seen English-men wear, but 'twas ill-fitting. It might not be his.

Who *was* he then?

"I know," the man said slowly, "the secret of the MacLeod keep."

Iolanthe gasped before she could stop herself.

The man hesitated, but he didn't look at her. He continued to look at her captor.

"Release her, and I'll give it to you."

The English-man scoffed. "I'll have the secret and then kill you both."

"Will you?" the man asked, amused. "I think not."

The English-man swung his sword, and Iolanthe clapped her hands over her eyes so that she might not see her rescuer be cut in half. But instead of a scream, she heard metal on metal.

And then the sound of a mighty battle.

She pressed herself back into the alcove and watched as the two men fought fiercely in a space that was much too small for such a contest. The English-man fought like a man who was sure that a score of men waited without, ready at his slightest command to burst in and destroy whatever troubled him.

Her rescuer, which was all she could call him, fought with less skill but more determination. She was tempted to wonder about the fact that he didn't look as if he'd grown to manhood with a sword in his hand, but the direness of her situation left her little time for that. Speculation could come later, if she was alive to indulge in any.

It was beginning to look as if her defender might need aid. She cast about for a solution. It might be possible to snatch the English-man's dagger from his belt and stab him with it whilst he was otherwise occupied.

She watched and waited, then leaped forward and ducked under the English-man's arm. She pulled his dagger free only to have him whirl on her and swipe viciously at her with his sword. Blessing all the miserable years spent ducking blows and like slashes from blunted swords wielded by her evil half-brothers, she dropped down and found herself still with her head atop her shoulders. Before the English-man could sweep backward with his blade, her rescuer had dealt the man a mighty blow to the head with the flat of his sword and sent him stumbling.

The English-man straightened, roaring like a stuck boar. Iolanthe didn't wait to see if her rescuer would be equal to fending off that attack. The moment the English whoreson's back was turned, she plunged her blade into his sword arm. He howled and dropped his weapon, but before he could turn on her, he found himself with a face full of sword hilt. Iolanthe watched her rescuer slam the hilt of his sword again into the English-man's nose. The crunch was a very satisfying sound.

The man slumped to the ground with a groan.

"Roll him over," said the man—in Gaelic, no less. "We'll tie him up and leave him."

"But—"

The man looked up at her, and Iolanthe found her protest dying on her lips. She stared down at him and felt as if her very soul had shuddered.

Despite her dreams, she was certain she had never seen the man before.

Yet for a frozen instant, she felt as if she had been in this place before, with this man kneeling at her feet, facing the question of life or death.

"Would you rather finish him?" he asked. "Could you do it?"

She should have been able to. It would have been a simple thing to pull the man's head back and slit his throat. She'd slaughtered sheep. What difference was there with a man who had intended to kill her?

Yet she found that somehow, she could not.

"His life will be hell if we let him live," the man promised. "Trust me on that."

Iolanthe pulled the English-man's dagger free of his arm and hastily cut strips from her dress. She held her rescuer's sword while he bound the man hand and foot. He stuffed cloth in the man's mouth and bound it as well.

The English-man began to stir, then he apparently realized what had happened to him, for he began to thrash. It was futile. Iolanthe looked down at him, then spat on him.

"May you die without honor or courage," she said.

Her rescuer grunted. "Rather we should hope he lives a long life to relive his cowardice." He looked down at the man. "I hope you live decades and find yourself haunted by the souls of those who you've slain in this very chamber." Then he leaned over and clouted the man on the head again.

The English-man slumped into senselessness.

Her rescuer looked at her, then held out his hand for his sword. Iolanthe handed it back to him, but kept the dagger she'd taken from the man lying before them.

"I brought clothes," he said, untying a bundle from his waist. "You'll need to wear them. I don't think we'll have trouble from the guards, but better we be viewed as two English-men just in case."

He turned away from her. Iolanthe held the clothes he had thrust at her and looked at his back.

"Who are you?" she asked.

He was silent for a moment. "It is a very long tale," he said finally.

That was another puzzle. He spoke Gaelic, but less well than he would have had he grown to manhood in the Highlands. She frowned. "Are you friend or enemy?"

"Friend, surely."

She considered. "What secret do you think you kn—"

He looked over his shoulder at her. "Hurry. We can talk later."

"We'll speak now," she insisted.

He turned his back on her. "Later. When we're not standing in the midst of the enemy's keep."

She couldn't argue with that, so she set the dagger down on the floor next to her, then stripped and dressed. She braided her hair and tucked it down the back of her stolen tunic. She left her dress on the floor. She looked down at her former captor, then stole his belt, slipping her filched dagger into it.

"I will have my answers," she said to her rescuer, putting her hand on the hilt of her dagger meaningfully.

He turned around, then looked at her hand. He met her eyes gravely. "You will," he assured her.

And then he smiled at her.

His smile was her undoing. It was as if he'd just found his heart's desire. The tenderness, nay, the undisguised joy in it was surely the most beautiful sight she'd ever beheld.

The man was obviously daft.

He held out his hand. She looked down at the poorly healed blisters, then met his eyes with a frown.

"Are you a monk that you have such blisters from unaccustomed swordplay?"

"Hardly," he said with a short laugh. "But what I will be is a dead man if we don't leave soon." He continued to hold out his damaged hand. "Come with me."

When her other choice was remaining with a soon-to-awaken-and-be-furious English-man, the madman before her seemed a most appealing alternative. Of course, there was the fact that she'd waited the whole of her life for him to come and get her. She took a deep breath, then slowly put her hand in his.

And then she saw a single tear roll down his cheek.

"What ails you?" she asked, looking him over for wounds.

He only smiled and shook his head. "I'll tell you later. Let's go now."

She took a deep breath and followed him from the chamber. He let go of her hand, took up his sword, and led the way down the stairs. That she was actually going back down those steps as anything but a corpse was noteworthy. That she was doing so with the man from her most secret dreams was surely a miracle.

They walked out into the freedom of the evening. Iolanthe took a deep breath, grateful for being able to do so. She looked around her, wondering what new tests of their mettle they would face before they escaped the castle.

Then she froze.

The sight in the bailey was something she was quite certain she would never forget. The sun had set, but the twilight gave enough illumination that she saw things quite clearly.

Every man in the bailey stood backed against the walls as if held there by some unseen rope. Some were weeping. Others were begging for mercy. Still others were in the throes of being heartily sick. Iolanthe looked at her rescuer and found him smiling in satisfaction.

Ach, by the saints, what had she done? Had she just traded death for something far worse? She looked at the man who had rescued her and crossed herself against him.

"You're a demon," she breathed.

He looked at her in surprise. "What?"

"You're the devil!" she said, backing away in horror. "Only the devil could make such a work—"

He took her by the arm before she could run. She struggled furiously. In the end, he had to drop his sword to hold her. She kicked him full in his privates. As he was doubled over, gasping for air as all her brothers had done when treated thusly, she snatched his sword. She waited until he had straightened before she looked him full in the face and pronounced his doom.

"You'll die—"

"I'm not the devil!" he said with a mighty bout of coughing.

"A demon, then," she shouted. "You've enspelled the entire keep!"

"Ghosts," he wheezed. "Can't you see the ghosts?"

She looked about her, but all she saw were terrified men. Whatever unseen bogles held them there, she couldn't have said. But she was damned sure that despite whatever the man wanted to name them, they were demons like he was.

"I don't believe in ghosties," she announced.

And that, for some reason, made him stop still. He stood there, hunched over with his hands on his thighs, and stared at her in complete astonishment. Then he bowed his head and laughed.

"Fool," she said, taking a swing at him.

Demon, devil, or madman, he was still quick on his feet. He ducked, then came up under the blade and wrapped his hands around hers that still held the hilt.

"I'm no demon," he said, his eyes alight with a combination of good humor and seriousness. "If I were, why would I need a sword?"

"You don't wield it very well."

"I didn't have much time to learn."

"See?" she said pointedly. "Handling things you aren't accustomed to. Demon's work, I'd say."

"I'm just a man. I came to rescue you. What does that tell you?"

She had no good answer for that. What it told her was that he had risked his life for hers, and she should be grateful. She started to say as much, then something else occurred to her.

"Ha," she said, wagging her finger at him. "How would you know I was here? Unless you were a demon who knows things he shouldn't?"

"I came with Duncan—"

"Duncan?" she asked. She released his sword. "Where is he?" By the saints, this was welcome news indeed. She looked about her for her kinsman, but she couldn't see him.

Then she realized the man wasn't answering her. And she felt something descend, a quiet that could betide only one thing. She looked back at the man. "Duncan?"

He nodded slowly. "I'm sorry—"

"You killed him?" she said, feeling rage sweep over her.

"I didn't," he said quickly. "We came down from Scotland together. He died helping me finish off half a dozen Englishmen so I could come get you."

"Oh," she said quietly. "I see." She looked about the keep again, then closed her eyes and shivered. "I fear to trust you."

"Just because I see things you apparently don't doesn't mean you can't trust me."

She opened her eyes and looked at him. "You're fey."

"I'm sure that won't be the last time you say that."

"Who *are* you?"

"Thomas McKinnon."

She stared at him for several moments, trying to judge what kind of man he was. He didn't look evil, when she actually looked at him calmly, and 'twas a certainty he had rescued her from a very bad end. Duncan had trusted him, else he wouldn't have come so far from the Highlands with him.

But why had this man come? How had he known to come? How had she known to dream his beautiful face?

"Come with me," he said, holding out his hand again. "We need to steal a pair of horses and get out of here before any of these lads realize they're being pinned to the wall by spirits and not flesh-and-blood men."

"You're fey. Fey and daft."

"Maybe, but I'm saving your life. Isn't that enough?"

"Why? Why are you doing that?"

"Because it's a life worth saving. Now, just trust me, and come."

Well, despite the fairness of his visage and the fact that he'd rescued her from certain death, she wasn't going to trust him. But she would go with him. 'Twas far easier to escape a single man in the open than it was a keep full of soldiers, so she followed him.

So Duncan had supposedly come with him. Was that true, or had he overtaken Duncan trying to rescue her, wrung the circumstances of her departure from him, then come on his own to try to wrest the secret of her keep from her? How had he come to her home in the first place? He looked powerfully filthy, and she had her suspicions, by the layer of crust on the back of his hair, that he'd spent a goodly portion of his time in her father's pit.

She followed him.

But warily.

Chapter 32

T wo days later, Thomas decided that he might have a tiny bit of a problem. It all stemmed from the fact that he had made the serious mistake of falling asleep sometime during the wee hours of the morning. It hadn't been for long, he was sure of that. But it had apparently been long enough for Iolanthe to have taken his sword and clobbered him on the temple with it. He remembered a blinding flash of light as his brain exploded, then a long, uninterrupted slide into unconsciousness.

Now it was dawn. He'd woken but a moment before and found himself trussed up, as his father would have said, snugger than a Christmas goose.

The cliché was annoying but unfortunately quite accurate. He had a sudden sympathy for any kind of bird destined for the supper table.

He tried to move, but it was futile. He spared a moment for admiration over the security of Iolanthe's knots, then turned his mind to his more immediate problem, namely pacifying the woman who was staring at him while flipping Duncan's knife up in the air, over and over again, and looking at him as if he really shouldn't have had such a thing in his possession.

He tried a smile, but he imagined it came out as more of a grimace than anything. His head was pounding like the drum section of a college halftime band, and his mouth tasted as if the aforementioned band had spent the night marching through it.

"Morning," he said hoarsely.

"Aye," she said shortly. " 'Tis. I suppose even a fiend such as yourself would recognize it as such."

This was just not going very well. He wished he'd done

more research on the whole time-traveling business before he'd attempted it. Or maybe just more research on the mindset of the incomprehensible medieval maiden. He certainly should have called his sister for advice on how to quickly gain the trust of a woman who quite obviously didn't know him from Adam.

The upside of the whole thing was, however, that he was facing a very real, very corporeal Iolanthe MacLeod.

Too bad she was mad as hell.

"You know," he said conversationally, "we could have ruffians leaping out of the bushes at any moment to rob us, and here I am all tied up and unable to help."

She pursed her lips. "Your swordplay leaves a bit to be desired."

"It rescued you," he said, the blisters on his hands setting up a renewed clamoring at the slander. All right, so he wasn't Jamie MacLeod—or any of his kinsmen for that matter—but he'd done his best. He'd gained calluses in places he didn't know a man could, and blisters on top of those calluses.

She only snorted and looked away.

Well, this wasn't getting them anywhere fast. He cleared his throat.

"My lady," he began carefully, deciding that using her name was a bad idea. Perhaps he'd try later, when he'd managed to get her back to the twentieth century and she hadn't killed everything in sight.

And speaking of killing, he suspected that even if she did think him a demon, she was harboring a soft spot for him in her heart. Just the night before, after two days of riding like the jaws of Hell themselves were gaping after them, they'd paused to water their horses and drink. Thomas had been leaning over, washing his face, when he'd heard Iolanthe gasp, then felt her push him over. He'd sat up in the middle of the stream and wiped the water from his eyes, prepared to snap at her for being so careless.

Then he'd seen a man lying not five feet from him staring up into the evening sky, pupils fixed and dilated, with a knife hilt buried in his chest.

And Iolanthe standing over him, shaking.

But that had been yesterday. Apparently, she'd had second

thoughts about his trustworthiness sometime during the previous night. Which was no doubt why he found himself in his current straits.

"My lady," he said again, "untie me and let us be on our way. Perhaps I am not the equal of your brothers in swordplay, nor any of your kin" —*and wasn't that the truth*, he thought with a rueful sigh— "but I can guard your back. And I can take you somewhere safe."

"Where?" she asked with a snort. "To your deserted hut where you will do with me what you will?"

"No. I would never do anything you hadn't agreed on."

Besides save your life and apparently wipe out all memories of me you ever had.

She sat down on a stump facing him and looked him over thoroughly. It was all he could do to take in the fact that she was actually there in the flesh. He had held her hand. It had been all he could do not to haul her in his arms and crush her against him.

Heaven only knows what kind of retribution that would have earned him.

"I don't believe in ghosties," she said finally.

"I know."

She studied him. "I think you're lying."

"Well, we could argue the point for quite a while," he said, "but the only way to prove it to you is for you to come with me."

"Where?"

"The future."

Her jaw slipped down. "The *what?*"

"The future," he said evenly, not taking his eyes from her. "You know, the place that gate in your forest can take a man—with enough luck and skill on his part."

He wondered, then, if he might have said too much. She had jumped to her feet, spluttering. She looked around, then grabbed his sword and turned to him, looking as if she meant business.

"Who told you?" she demanded. "Whom did you kill for that knowledge?"

Thomas tried to look as unmurderous as possible. "Your great-great-grandfather Jamie did, when I asked him. He's still very much alive several hundred years from now. I'll take you to him, if you'll let me."

Now she was looking at him as if he really had sprouted horns.

This was not good.

"Did you kill Duncan for the knowing?" she whispered.

"You know that Duncan didn't know about the gate," Thomas said, not making it a question. "I'm not lying. Jamie showed me how the gate worked. He trained me in sword-play. He and his kin taught me Gaelic."

"Why?" she asked suspiciously.

Tread carefully, McKinnon, Thomas thought to himself. "Because," he said, choosing his words with the same kind of care he would have used in choosing a foothold on a sheer rock face, "because I wanted to come rescue you."

The sword wavered, then dipped down. "You did?"

"Yes," he said gravely. "I did."

She sat down. "And what would there be in that future of yours for me?" she asked.

"More than is in your past," he said, thinking of Jamie and Elizabeth and the family Iolanthe would have if she'd accept them.

Oh, and him, too.

But it was probably better not to spring that one on her quite yet.

Why didn't someone tell him that getting a woman to fall for you twice was more than twice as difficult?

"I think I should just leave you here to rot," she grumbled. "I vow I can scarce stomach your tale." She shot him a look. "And 'tis difficult for me to divine if you're telling the truth or not."

"Let's look at it this way," he said conversationally. "Let's say you walk away and leave me here. You're a woman dressed in a dead man's clothes, his English clothes, and you're obviously a Scot. How are you going to make it all the way back to the Highlands by yourself?"

"I could."

"And if someone overtook you, or a handful of someones, what do you think would happen?"

"I would fight. As would you. Think you that you would fare any better than I?" she demanded.

He would have shrugged, but she'd been too thorough in tying him up. "It's the awful truth, but I'm a man. I'd probably find my throat slit quite readily, but I doubt I'd be raped."

She glared at him but said nothing.

And that being a look he was intensely familiar with, he relaxed a bit.

"Do you want to go back to the Highlands?" he asked. "To your family? If that's what you want, I'll get you there, and we'll forget the future."

"My family, nay. The Highlands . . ." She was silent for a moment. "Aye, I would miss them."

Well, this was getting them somewhere.

"The Highlands it is, then," he said. Then he paused. "Would you like to see for yourself?" he asked slowly. "If the secret of your keep is true or if it's merely a fable?"

She leaned the sword against her knee. "How would I learn the truth of it?"

"You could come with me. Come to the future with me. See what's left of your keep and who inhabits it. See if you like it. And if you don't, I swear I will bring you back here."

"And leave me to myself?" she asked grimly.

He paused for a moment or two. "This is the thing," he said finally. "As long as I have breath in my body, I will not let harm come to you."

She looked at him, and Thomas prayed that she wouldn't take him up on his offer. Unfortunely, he had meant it. If she wanted to come back to the fourteenth century, he would.

Heaven help him.

But when she looked at him with those eyes that from this distance looked as gray as storm clouds, he couldn't help but wish that whatever century she decided on, she would someday want him to share it with her.

"Cut me loose and let's go," he urged.

"Where—"

A shout in the distance had both of them gasping in surprise.

"Now!" he exclaimed.

She pulled out her dagger. Thomas had the briefest flash of fear that she intended to slit his throat and then take off. Instead, she merely cut his hands and ankles and hauled him to his feet. He groaned at the pain of blood rushing to his abused extremities.

"Here," she said shoving his sword at him.

He stumbled behind her to their horses. Fortunately they had no gear, which made breaking camp an exceptionally easy thing to do. Thomas flung himself onto his horse and watched Iolanthe do the same.

"There they are!" she said, pointing in front of him to his right. "It's the English-man!"

"Damn," Thomas said as he pulled his horse around and plunged it into the shadows of trees. "I didn't think he'd come after us!"

"Wounded pride," Iolanthe said. "Where go we?"

Away was the only direction he could think of, so he led them at an unsafe speed away from the shouts until the shouts were nothing but curses fading into the distance.

He followed a trail that led through the woods until it broke suddenly out onto a road. And the road stretched for what seemed like miles without any kind of cover on either side of it. He looked up at the sun, trying to judge their position. Based on his own calculations—which probably weren't that accurate, given the week he'd had so far—he thought they were south of the inn and probably fifty miles west of the eastern coast of Northumberland.

Very much in England.

Rather far away from anything useful.

Jamie had shown him a map of England with the gates they'd investigated so far. Thomas had memorized it and also memorized the gates that Jamie said he wasn't all that sure about. Those had seemed a risky proposition, but Thomas hadn't been willing to discount any possibilities.

The one gate Jamie was sure of was the one near Falconberg. It was a faery ring that Alex and Margaret had discovered, and it apparently led one immediately back to Jamie's land. Thomas considered it, then discarded it. Falconberg was a good hundred fifty miles south of their position and well inland.

More unpredictable were another pair of gates that Jamie had suspected might serve. He hadn't traveled through them personally, but apparently Alex and Margaret had had a few unexpected visitors come their way, and those were the locations they'd been given. Thomas could only hope that such gates might serve in getting him and Iolanthe back to the England of his time. They were closer, true, but the real reason was he just wasn't sure he wanted to go to Scotland with her yet. Too much baggage associated with her home. Foolish though it might have been, he wanted her to himself for a while before she found herself surrounded with family. She would need time to gain her footing.

To remember him, if she could.

To get to know him, if she wanted to.

"Are you asleep?" she hissed. "Make haste, you fool!"

All right, so maybe all she needed was time to decide he wasn't a complete jerk.

He made a decision and moved forward on the road. They would head south for a bit, then turn east and go to the coast once they'd outridden their pursuers.

"How fast can you ride?" he asked, looking at her.

She gave him a look of supreme condescension, then kicked her mount into a gallop. Thomas sighed and followed suit. He wished heartily that he'd had more than a month to learn to ride, wield a sword, and swear like a medieval clansman.

All of which would have served him well at the moment.

He followed her and considered their destination as best he could with dirt flying up into his eyes and his mouth. He promised himself a bit of proper enjoyment of the sight of Iolanthe racing ahead of him, barefoot, with her hair streaming down her back. What was it the painter had said?

Bugger, she's a stunner.

Thomas spared a moment to wonder if the painting would still exist and if he should show it to her before he managed to get her to the altar. Assuming she would condescend to come with him to the altar.

A rock clipped him smartly on the ear, and he shook his head free of his speculation. If he wasn't careful, her horse would kick up something that would kill him, and then where would they both be?

East, he decided suddenly. One of the gates was on the coast. It seemed like the most likely suspect. One, it would keep them well out of Lord Charles's way. Two, they might make use of an ally or two. He struggled to remember what William de Piaget had said about the surrounding countryside and who held sway where. Artane, he was sure he could find. Mrs. Pruitt had several travel brochures littering an entryway table, and Thomas had seen the one advertising the castle. It was massive and sat squat on a hill overlooking an impressive beach.

Iolanthe would love it.

But depending on how far south they came, they would have to cross a fair bit of country on their way back up. Thomas considered the castles he knew dotted the coast. Burwyck-on-the-Sea, Blackmour, and then Artane.

Well, however they got there, the important thing was to reach a safe harbor for awhile. Thomas wasn't opposed to laboring with his hands for their support, though he certainly would try to pass himself off as a nobleman if he could. Yes, that was the ticket. A nobleman and his wife who'd been robbed and barely escaped with their lives. They'd had everything stolen, including their clothes, and this was why they found themselves in this kind of shape.

The six-foot broadsword might be a problem, as well as the Gaelic curses Iolanthe tended to spew at him without warning, but he could come up with a story for that. His French was flawless, and he had a wonderful imagination. What more did he need?

He rode hard after his lady and in spite of the direness of their straits, he couldn't help grinning like a fool.

He'd done it.

Everything else was gravy.

Chapter 33

Iolanthe stood behind Thomas in the dark courtyard of the most enormous castle she'd ever laid eyes on. Not that she was really one to judge these kinds of matters, given how few castles she'd seen over the course of her life, but from what she could tell, the bloody place was immense. Dusk allowed but a miserly light, but 'twas enough to show her that she was standing in a grander place than she'd ever even imagined. Thomas had told her that 'twas called Artane, and that he knew a lad who'd grown to manhood here. He felt certain that the lord would offer them hospitality. He bid her look as if she'd just been robbed of all her jewels, and keep her thoughts to herself.

The last of which wasn't all that hard, given that she couldn't find any words to describe how overwhelmed she felt at the moment.

Or how low.

By the saints, she'd never considered herself to be completely without value, but when faced by the well-dressed, well-groomed folk holding their torches down so they could stare at her bare feet, all she wanted to do was go hide in the stables where she was certain she would feel more comfortable.

Thomas was spinning some tale or other, and apparently he was doing it quite well, for the lord of the keep, his lady, her ladies, and most of his guardsmen were clustered in the courtyard, listening with rapt attention.

When they weren't looking at her filthy feet, that is.

Without warning, the lord clapped his hands, and the assembled group moved in all different directions at once. But the lord remained where he was, then looked at Iolanthe and asked Thomas a question.

"He wants to know if you speak French," Thomas asked in her native tongue.

She had to admit that his Gaelic wasn't all that poor. Mayhap arguing with her over the past three days had improved it. 'Twas certain that riding like demons from Hell had improved his horsemanship. She wondered just what he had done in that unimaginable Future of his that had left him without these skills from childhood.

That she actually believed his tale was enough to set her to shaking her head.

He claimed to know her grandfather's grandfather. He claimed Jamie was alive and well six hundred years in the Future. He claimed to have met the man and eaten at his board.

Lies?

Somehow, beyond reason, she didn't think so. He hadn't lied to her about anything so far. He'd certainly withheld a bit of truth, but he hadn't lied. But she suspected that the truth he withheld would be that which interested her the most.

"My lady?" Thomas asked again. "The lord wishes to know if you speak French."

She looked at the lord of Artane and smiled weakly.

"Merde," she said.

It was, after all, one of the few words she knew.

The lord looked at her with wide eyes, then suddenly burst into hearty laughter. He clapped Thomas on the shoulder and pulled him up the stairs toward the great hall. Thomas took her hand and pulled her up the steps after him.

The hall was enormous, and it even smelled passable. She walked over the fairly fresh rushes and soon found herself seated at the high table with Thomas next to her. When the lord found himself engaged by a man of his house, Thomas leaned close to her.

"Roger," he said. "The lord Artane. I told him I was French, you were Bulgarian, and ours was a love match which displeased our parents. I gave him a few names he would recognize and be impressed by and asked him for hospitality until we recover from our traumatic journey."

Perhaps he was a better liar than she'd supposed.

"Did you," she whispered, "give him a reason for our journey?"

"Pilgrimage," he said. "I told him we'd heard tell of a new shrine in Edinburgh, made all the more desirable because of the dangers involved in getting there."

"Those barbaric Scots," she said darkly.

He grinned at her. "Something like that."

She nodded, then realized something he'd said. "Wed?" she said, choking on her wine. "We're wed?"

"Can you think of any other reason we'd be traveling alone together? Well, besides the fact that all our household was murdered and by that malcontent, Lord Charles."

"You didn't," she breathed.

"I had to tell him something—*Oui, seigneur*," he said, turning to face the lord of Artane.

And then he was off babbling in a tongue she couldn't understand. But what she did understand was that he had saved her from looking like a whore.

She found her hand suddenly captured in his and held up for Artane's inspection. Thomas pointed to her fingers and made motions that left even her realizing that her wedding ring had apparently been absconded with.

Ach, those bloody thieves.

She found that, for the first time in years, she was actually enjoying herself. Her only regret was that she couldn't understand Thomas. But his hand gestures, his bearing, his very voice wrung noises of sympathy and outrage from their host.

And it won them a meal.

Iolanthe was certain she hadn't eaten in days. She did her best not to fall upon the food like a savage, but that was a true test of her mettle. Thomas ate with just as much enthusiasm, so she didn't feel so clumsy.

It seemed hours before Lord Artane stood. Thomas rose as well. Iolanthe followed him, simply because she didn't know what else to do. Thomas listened intently, then bowed and gave a great and lengthy speech of thanks.

Merci, she knew as well.

He looked at Iolanthe.

"Baths, my lady," he said, looking as if the idea pleased him. "And new clothes, if we're fortunate."

"At this late hour?"

"He worries about our comfort."

A bath? Och, she'd swum in streams often enough, especially when escaping her more cowardly brothers who thought the waters cursed, but to willingly step into a cauldron of steaming water?

And she'd thought facing a sword had been difficult.

"No?" he asked.

"Oh, aye," she said, swallowing back her fear. "If they like."

So she found herself led off to a chamber she couldn't have found again had her life depended on it. She was stripped and put into a tub of steaming water. She tried not to flinch as she was soaped, rinsed, and dried off.

And then she was given clothing so fine that it almost made up for all the previous tortures.

The gown was, however, predictably too short, but that was remedied soon enough by a pair of industrious seamstresses who attached extra material to the hem and made it look as if such a thing had been planned. A tanner was then brought in. He measured her feet and stitched her a pair of soft leather shoes so quickly it seemed as if he'd produced them by some magical means.

Her feet were shod, her nether limbs covered, and her hair brushed until the women gave up trying to straighten it and let it be about its usual business of twisting and turning around her face and down her back.

She smiled and bowed her thanks and received smiles and bows in return. She opened the door, hoping against hope that one of the women would take pity on her and lead her back to something she recognized, such as a bed, so she could collapse with exhaustion.

Yet there someone she recognized stood, leaning against the far wall and looking so magnificently handsome that she caught her breath.

He straightened and stared at her with just as much surprise.

"You're beautiful," he said. Then he cleared his throat hastily. "Not that you weren't before."

"You're cleaner," she noted.

"I am," he agreed cheerfully.

"And braw enough, I suppose."

He put his hand over his heart and made her a little bow. "Milady's compliments leave me weak." He looked up from his bow and smiled at her.

Which made her feel distinctly weak in the knees.

"Off with ye, ye wee silly man," she said with as much bluster as she could manage. "Ye'll make yerself dizzy, bowin' and scrapin' thusly."

He held out his hand. "I have a surprise for you. If you're not too tired."

She looked at his hand and was surprised to find that her hand was putting itself in his, just as boldly as you pleased.

But once it was there, there was no sense in not leaving it there, or in not following him, since he seemed determined to lead her to the saints only knew where. The pathway led up, so perhaps 'twas safe to believe he wasn't leading her down to Hell.

"How do you know your way so well?" she asked. "Have you been here before?"

He hesitated, then smiled briefly over his shoulder at her. "Not exactly. I've heard it described, though."

She pursed her lips but didn't press him. Daft as a duck, poor man.

He continued to lead her up stairways and down passageways until he came to a final circle of steps.

"Up here," he said, "then close your eyes when I tell you to."

She followed him up, then, against her better judgment, she closed her eyes. But she kept one eye open a slit, just on the off chance he intended to do something untoward with her.

He opened a door and led her out into the open. Iolanthe watched her feet and saw they were on a walkway. She hugged the wall to her right. Better that she not slip off to the left, even if that was Thomas's plan.

But by the way he clutched her hand, then put his other arm around her shoulders, she suspected that pushing her off the parapet was not his intention.

He turned her into a breeze and held her steady.

"Open your eyes."

She did and gasped in surprise. She rubbed her eyes for good measure, but nothing had changed in the sight before her.

For there before her, in all its glory, was the sea. The moon shone in the sky, lighting the waves as if by a lantern. The sound, the smell, the sight was almost more than she could bear.

"Merciful saints above," she breathed as tears burned in her eyes. "Ach, by the saints, 'tis more beautiful than I imagined it could be."

"Isn't it?" he murmured.

She looked up to find he was regarding her with a smile. She found her wits long enough to scowl at him.

"The strand, you fool," she said pointedly. "I spoke of the strand."

"And I meant you," he said with a smile, "but it seems like a silly thing to argue about, doesn't it? You watch the water, I'll watch you, and we'll both be content."

She couldn't tear her eyes from his face. Perhaps she was a poor judge of men, but she believed that a score and some years of living in her hall amidst the intrigues and jealousies had given her a fair eye for a liar. The shifting eyes, the easy smile, the spewing tongue.

But there was no lie in his face.

"Who *are* you?" she asked, and she knew it would likely not be the last time she asked the question.

"Someone who loves you," he said simply.

"How?" she asked, pained. "You don't know me!"

"It's a very long story. I'll tell you tomorrow in the daylight. Right now, I think you should just enjoy your view of the ocean."

Mayhap he had it aright. She stared out over the wall and watched the water lap ceaselessly at the shore. She leaned her elbows on the wall before her and drank in the sight until she felt every bit of tension leave her.

For the first time in her life, she felt peace.

"We can stay as long as you like," he said quietly.

"Here on the wall?" she asked.

"No," he said gently, "here at Artane. Near the beach."

She found that quite suddenly her eyes were once again filled with tears. It was a terrible habit she was acquiring, this blubbering without provocation.

"Surely not," she said. "We don't know the lord—"

"I know his cousin, William," Thomas said. "Apparently that is enough to have us be considered family."

"Is it," she said, but it wasn't a question.

"I have decent skill with sums," Thomas said, but not boastfully. "I offered to check his accounts in return for our keep." He smiled easily. "He refused, of course, but I'll do it just the same. Me not being much of a swordsman, of course, and probably no help to his garrison."

She at least had the grace to feel a bit of shame. "You saved my life, and I disparaged your skill just the same." She chewed on her lip for a moment, then spat out an apology as quickly as possible, for it didn't come easily to her.

"Well," he said with a laugh, "if you hadn't stowed that dagger in his arm, we'd both be dead, so thanks have to go to you as well."

She nodded briefly in return, then looked back over the shore. "Thank you for this," she said quietly. " 'Tis a very great gift."

"It's my pleasure," he said. "Truly."

She stood next to him for what seemed like hours, letting the sound of the sea soothe her. When she finally gave in to her shivers, Thomas put his hands on her shoulders and turned her toward the tower door.

"It'll be there tomorrow," he said. "It's late, and we're exhausted. I think they have a chamber for us."

She dug her heels in. "For us? The two of us? But—"

"You're perfectly safe with me."

"But—"

"We'll put pillows between us on the bed. I'm fairly sure you'll be too tired to ravish me, so I'll sleep quite easily."

She whirled around. "Thomas!"

The look he gave her had the rest of her complaints dying on her lips.

"Say my name again," he said quietly.

"Daft man, I will not."

"That wasn't it. Another try, if you please."

She scowled at him. "I'm not set to ravish you, Thomas McKinnon, no matter the beauty of your face. I'll take the bed, and you'll have the floor."

"If you say my name a few more times, I will probably end up doing just that without complaint." He smiled and turned her around. "Let's go, violet eyes."

She stumbled, but he caught her and steadied her. She didn't dare turn around, and she wondered again if she had just consigned herself to a night in a chamber with a madman.

Why had he called her that?

She tried to give it thought, but the feeling of his warm hands on her shoulders was damnably distracting. And when he took her hand and led her downstairs, all she could do was follow like an obedient pup. And when she found herself all tucked up in the finest bed she had ever enjoyed in the whole of her life, she almost began to feel guilty about him sleeping rolled up on the floor in a blanket.

"Thomas . . ." she began.

"Don't worry, my lady," he said, sounding as if he smiled. "I've slept in worse. At least the floor isn't moving."

"Did you pass a night or two in my father's pit?"

"Yes," he said with a half laugh. "I take it Malcolm isn't known for his hospitality?"

"He isn't," she agreed, then found that sleep was overtaking her with a relentlessness she couldn't avoid. "Good night, Thomas."

"Good night, Iolanthe," he whispered.

She was almost asleep when she realized what he'd said. Her eyes flew open.

Damn the man, who *was* he?

Chapter 34

T homas leaned back on his elbows and looked at the beach in front of him. It seemed like a pretty normal afternoon, actually. He was sitting on a blanket that was covered with sand from being walked on too often. He had the remains of a picnic in a basket next to him along with a bottle of very fine drink that had turned out to be wine made from a berry he couldn't and didn't particularly care to identify. He was obviously being blessed for good behavior because, despite it being close to the middle of November, the sun was shining overhead, clouds billowed in a particularly cheerful manner, and he had just woken up from a peaceful nap.

To the sight of a medieval Highland woman cavorting in the water like an especially undignified eight-year-old.

Ah, such was life in the Middle Ages. He watched Iolanthe play on the shore and wondered if he could really get used to the lack of toilet paper, satellite dishes, and ice cubes.

Then again, there had been an appalling lack of ice cubes in twenty-first-century Britain as well, so maybe that last item wasn't anything to consider.

Not that they were living a particularly deprived life. Bathroom amenities aside, Artane was a pretty luxurious place. Three square meals a day, which were perfectly tasty as long as you didn't question the age of the meat. He was big on sauces anyway, so it didn't bother him.

The nightly entertainment was great, and he thought with enough practice he just might learn a few dance steps while he was there. His medieval French was coming along quite nicely, and he'd even ventured out in the lists each day and returned at noon with his pride and his body intact.

He and Iolanthe had been clothed in sumptuous fabrics

and bedecked with several baubles that probably each would have fed a handful of peasants for a handful of years. They had peace and quiet. They had time for loitering on the beach with the only question being what they would have for lunch. It had been blissful.

But as pleasant as all those things were, they weren't what made him seriously consider staying.

It was the woman collecting shells near the water.

Of course, the previous week hadn't been all smooth sailing. He'd gone to sleep that first night kicking himself for having used her name. He hadn't meant to. It had just slipped out. He'd been very surprised she hadn't leaped from the bed and demanded all her answers right then and there.

Of course, waking the next day to find her sitting comfortably on a stool not two feet from him, pointing the business end of Duncan's knife at him had certainly come as no surprise. He'd tried to deny having said what he'd said, then ended up promising her all the answers she could have wanted if she would just come walk on the beach with him. And while she was considering that, he'd asked her just what it was he was supposed to call her.

Her look of utter discomfort had been so familiar, he'd almost smiled. In the end, she had told him he was a very bad liar, expressed her amazement that he'd been able to concoct a story that had bought them food and shelter for as long as they wanted it, and then defiantly given him her name as if she couldn't spit it out fast enough for public consumption.

Given that he knew what it had cost her, he received it with what he'd hoped was an appropriate amount of reverence.

And he hadn't used it very much at first. Watching the woman he loved fondle a knife hilt while looking at him purposefully was more unsettling than he ever would have imagined it could be.

The beach had been, fortunately, a stroke of genius. Just walking along it had changed her somehow. She hadn't asked him any questions, and he hadn't given her any answers. He still suspected that she thought he was out of his mind, but after a week of spending her afternoons on the shore, she didn't throw that at him with any venom—and with less and less seriousness.

She laughed more.

He could hardly believe it was the same woman he'd known six hundred years in the future, yet he couldn't deny it.

He sat up as he realized she was running toward him. She was carrying heaven knew what in her skirts that she'd hiked up. Apparently, she didn't mind wandering around in her slip, and to be honest, neither did he. The first time he'd teased her about it, she'd looked at him archly and asked him if he'd never seen a woman's legs before. When he'd squirmed instead of answering, she'd merely tossed her head and wandered off to gather more things in her skirts.

She came to a teetering halt before him, knelt, and dumped out handfuls of shells.

"Look at them," she panted. "Bonny, aye?"

"Magnificent," he agreed.

"Ach, ye wee lecher, look at the shells," she chided.

"Oh," he said, sitting up and looking down. "Yes. They're nice, too."

She shoved them aside and sprawled out on the blanket. "By the saints, this agrees with me."

"I can see that," he said with a smile. "It's a good place."

She rolled over on her back and looked up at him. "We canna remain here forever, Thomas."

"Sure we can."

She shook her head and sat up. She took up a handful of shells and began to sort through them.

"Tell me the tale," she said simply. "Now."

"But—"

"And spare me nothing."

"Io—"

She looked at him and smiled easily. "I like that name you call me. Io. Seems simpler, aye?"

Would the woman never cease to leave him breathless? He managed a weak nod. "Yes, it does."

She looked down at her hands. "You've done a merry dance this past se'nnight with the truth."

"I didn't want to spoil the peace."

She stole a look at him. "And will the tale do that?"

"It might," he admitted. "Parts of it are pretty unbelievable."

"Today," she said, looking up at the sky, "today, I think I could believe anything." She looked at him and smiled again. "Even one of your tales, you poor, daft man."

"Are you sure you want it all?"

"Aye. All of it."

He took a deep breath and prayed he wasn't making the biggest mistake of his life.

"All right," he said, crawling to his feet. "Let's walk."

"The truth pricks at you so?"

"It'll be easier to catch you when you run if I'm already on my feet." He held out his hand for her and pulled her up. "Where do you want me to start?"

"At the beginning."

It figured. Thomas put his hands behind his back and started to walk down the beach with her. If she wanted the whole thing, perhaps she had a right to it. It was, after all, her story. He took a deep breath.

"Well, you see, I bought a castle."

"You must be very rich."

He was, but there was no sense in bringing that up right then. "Actually, it was a fairly old castle and it had fallen into disrepair."

"An old castle?" she asked, frowning. "Are there such things?"

"Where I come from, yes, there are. Now, I bought this castle without having seen it, though when I saw it, I . . . I wasn't surprised by how it looked."

He could feel her eyes on him, but he couldn't look at her. The whole thing was still too unsettling to think about. Who would have thought that a simple check made out to someone he didn't know would eventually have landed him in medieval England, walking next to the woman he had loved when she'd been a ghost, and who was now as corporeal as he?

"Why weren't you?" she asked. "Surprised, that is."

"Because I'd seen it before." He paused. "In my dreams."

She was, amazingly enough, silent.

Thomas looked at her. "Daft? Fey? Anything to call me?"

She only shook her head. "I've had dreams as well."

"Have you?"

She looked at him, and Thomas was surprised by the familiarity in her gaze. As if she had known him all her life.

As if she might have loved him at least that long.

And then the look was gone as quickly as it had come, so quickly that he wondered if he'd imagined it.

"Aye, I have," she said briskly. "Now, continue on, if you will."

He smiled, then shrugged. "Well, I came to take possession of my castle only to find that it wasn't empty. There was a garrison of Highlanders and a particularly unpleasant man named Connor MacDougal—"

She stopped so suddenly that he had to back up to look at her.

"MacDougal?" she asked, her forehead wrinkling.

"Yes. Know him?"

"Where was your castle?"

"In England," he said slowly, but he didn't dare tell her more than that. Yet.

"I see," she said, chewing on her lip.

"I was so startled by seeing all these men in kilts," he continued, "and by Laird MacDougal waving his sword at me, that I stumbled backward, tripped, and hit my head on a rock."

She laughed. "Ah, but your pride must have been wounded. Did they strip you and leave you out in the open for others to mock or merely toss you outside the gates and leave you to the wild beasties?"

"Neither," he said, scowling. "They argued plenty over what to do with me, but left me alone. In the end, I managed to get myself back to the inn down the way. It was a day or two before I came back to the castle, but I managed it eventually—"

"Without your pride," she interrupted.

"Yes," he said. "Which only added to my problems. The MacDougal said I didn't have any rights and that I'd find *that* out soon enough when I went inside and met with the real lord of the castle."

He paused.

"Only it wasn't a lord."

She looked at him and waited. "Aye?"

He started walking again. "It was a woman, and the keep was undeniably hers."

"I imagine she wasn't too happy about you taking it from her."

"That, my lady, is the understatement of the millennium," he said dryly. "No, she wasn't happy about it, and I was quite rude to her. We didn't exactly begin our relationship on the best of terms."

"And then?"

He shrugged. "I tried to rebuild the keep, with her permission of course, and we became friends. Then I fell in love with her."

"Oh," she said softly.

He stole a look at her. A more foolish man might have thought she seemed the slightest bit disappointed.

"Then you loved her very much?" she asked.

"With my whole soul," he said.

"Hmmm," she said, turning her face away from him and looking out to sea. "A remarkable tale."

Well, now this was something. Could she be jealous? The thought was almost startling enough to make him stop, but he thought he might be on a roll, so he pressed on.

"We had a problem, the lady and I," he continued, "and there was only one way to solve it. So I took myself on a very long journey."

"To my home," she put in absently.

"Yes. I studied swordplay and learned Gaelic. It's then that the story takes a different turn."

"No doubt."

He stopped and waited until she had reluctantly turned toward him. "This is the truth of it. I traveled through time, then found myself in your father's pit. Duncan rescued me. He and I followed your trail. We overtook Charles's men, only to find you not among them. We fought with them just the same. We slew them, but at the cost of Duncan's life."

"Why did Duncan come?" she asked, looking pained.

"Because he loved you. And he believed me when I told

him Lord Charles would kill you if left to himself."

She bowed her head. "Duncan protected me quite often at great cost to himself. He was a good man."

You don't know the half of it, Thomas thought to himself.

Then she looked up at him suddenly. "How did you know where the English-man was taking me? Not even my sire knew that."

Later, he thought. *Later, when you'll believe me.* "Duncan helped me," he said, which wasn't untrue. "After Duncan was slain, I took up the trail and followed you. I trailed you to the English-man's keep, got inside, and walked up the stairs to the tower room."

"How did you get past the guards?"

"The same way we got out of the castle. With the help of the ghosts. Charles had killed scores of people. Their ghosts were milling about outside the keep. They spoke to me and told me their tale. I asked for their help."

She looked at him skeptically but didn't stop him.

"So," he continued, "I got inside the tower chamber, distracted Charles, and the rest you know. Except," he added slowly, "for a couple of things that make the story make sense."

"Such as?"

"The secret of the MacLeod keep."

She was very still. "Aye?" she asked carefully.

"Well, the secret really *is* time travel," he said. "I wouldn't believe it if I hadn't experienced it myself."

She was watching him closely, but she wasn't calling him names or shaking her head. Those were good signs.

"And I really can see ghosts," he said. "My mother can, too. So can my sister."

"Your father?" she prompted.

"My father would"— he wanted to say *come unglued,* but that wasn't exactly medieval terminology— "he would roar endlessly if he knew I could, so believe me, he knows nothing of it. I didn't ask for this."

She nodded. " 'Tis understandable."

"He thinks we're all out of our minds."

"I think I would like him," she murmured.

"You probably would. And all I can say is it's lucky I can

see ghosts, or we wouldn't be standing here today."

"Why is that?"

Thomas wondered how the hell he was going to get out of this intact. He wished he'd had a comfortable pair of jeans with pockets just made for him to jam his hands into.

"Well, there are several reasons," he said, hoping he managed to get through all of them before she either walked away or decked him. Why hadn't he thought to offer to hold her knife for her? "First is that the year I bought the castle was 2001."

She only blinked.

"And the keep was Thorpewold."

At that, she flinched.

"And the Highlanders I saw, including Connor Mac-Dougal, were ghosts."

"Ah," she said; then she felt silent.

That silence became as tangible as a third person standing there. The sea still roared next to them, and the birds still wheeled in the sky above. But between the two of them, there was a stillness that half made him begin to wonder if they would remain frozen there forever.

Iolanthe took a deep breath. "And the woman?"

Thomas nodded slowly. "Yes. She was a ghost as well."

"And her name?"

He paused. "Iolanthe MacLeod."

She closed her eyes and swallowed. Hard. He could see her struggle with something, but whether it was disbelief or fear or revulsion, he couldn't tell. Then she opened her eyes and looked at him.

"I can scarce believe it," she said hoarsely.

"I know."

" 'Tis madness."

"I was hoping," he said slowly, "that you would remember."

"Remember what?" she asked with a humorless laugh. "My own death?"

"No, six hundred years of haunting," he said.

"And why," she asked with a break in her voice, "why, by the very saints of heaven, would I *want* to remember such a thing?" She wrapped her arms around herself. "Ach, but what a misery that must have been!"

He nodded slowly. "Yes, I think it was."

She took several paces away from him, then came back and stood in front of him. She looked up at him. "Did I . . ." She asked, "Did I love you?"

Now that was the question for the ages. He had no idea how he was supposed to answer it. He could lie, he supposed, but what good would that do? He took a deep breath. The truth it would be.

"Yes," he said quietly. "Yes, I think you did."

She stared at him for several moments, then looked down at her feet. "Let's walk," she said.

"Of course."

They walked in silence for a very long time. Then she stopped. Thomas stopped, turned, and looked down at her. She was studying him as if she'd never seen him before.

"You could have been killed," she said quietly.

He shrugged with half a smile. "Perhaps."

"If all this is true," she said, but she didn't sound as skeptical as she had before, "then you took a very great risk."

"That, too."

"Yet that did not deter you."

"You were here. I had to come."

She nodded slowly, then turned and walked toward the place where the sea met the sand. Thomas watched her go, watched her stand with her head bowed and her arms around herself, watched her tremble.

And he wondered if she would manage to digest it all without losing it or breaking down.

He wondered what would be worse.

Then she put her shoulders back. She turned and walked purposefully toward him.

The look on her face made him realize that he was definitely not out of the woods yet.

"Prove it to me," she said, sticking her chin out. "Take me to your time. Let me see it for myself."

He smiled faintly. "Are you sure?"

She wasn't smiling. "Aye. I am."

He felt his smile fade, and he looked at her gravely. "Very well. I can't guarantee that what you'll see won't upset you."

"I am a MacLeod," she said. "I'll survive it."

He ran his hand through his hair and sighed. "I imagine you will. All right, we'll go. When do you want to leave?"

"Tomorrow."

He blinked in surprise. "Really? So soon?"

"Aye, so soon." She looked about her for a moment. "Does this beach still exist in your time?"

"It does. And, oddly enough, my sister's father-in-law is lord of Artane," he said with a nod over his shoulder toward Artane.

"In truth?" she asked, sounding impressed. "He must be very wealthy."

"Not as wealthy as he'd like to be, no doubt, but I imagine he does well enough." Thomas smiled. "He lets tourists tromp through his house now and then—"

"Tourists," she said with a shudder. "Passing unpleasant . . . lot . . ." she finished uneasily. She looked up at him. "Tourists?"

"People who pay you so they can come gawk at your possessions," Thomas said, trying to hide his surprise.

She was silent for a moment. "But how would I know anything about them?"

"Well—"

She shivered. "Let us go back."

"Iolanthe, please don't let that ruin your day," he said. "I've probably rambled on about tourists over the last few days."

She nodded but looked very unconvinced. "Tomorrow, Thomas. I need to know."

He walked reluctantly back with her over the dunes and up the way to the castle. He found himself suddenly very unwilling to leave the peace of the shore. The farther they walked away from the water, the more he realized that he was losing the tentative truce they'd managed to forge over the past week.

He caught her hand as they neared the drawbridge. "Io," he began, then stopped short at the look in her eye. "Oh, Iolanthe," he whispered.

She reached up and touched his face briefly, then let her hand drop. "I have to know, Thomas. Before I can do anything else, I have to know the truth. I have to see it for myself."

He understood. She wasn't going to start anything with him until she'd unraveled the truth of her past. Her future. He drew his hand over his face and wondered briefly if scaling Artane's outer wall several times with nothing but his bare hands and feet would be enough to distract him from the truth of his present.

He had, he suspected, lost her.

He wondered just what it would take to have her back.

Chapter 35

I olanthe stood on the steps leading down from the great hall and looked at the packhorse that had been loaded with gifts that neither she nor Thomas had been able to refuse. She wore the clothing she'd been given upon her arrival, as well as a warm cloak around her that was finer than anything she'd ever seen in her life. That Artane's lord should bedeck himself in such finery didn't surprise her. That he should shower such luxuries on strangers was almost beyond belief. She could do nothing but marvel that there were actually folk in the world who lived their lives with generosity to others. It was certainly nothing she'd ever seen her father do. Yet how many examples she'd seen of it over the past se'nnight? Lord Roger and his gifts. His lady and her gifts.

Thomas and his greatest gift to her: the gift of her life.

She could scarce fathom it.

The door behind her opened, and she turned to watch as Thomas and Lord Roger descended the stairs. Thomas was dressed warmly as well, and she had to admit that the fine clothes suited him. The cloak sat well on his broad shoulders, and the cloth of his hose clung to his well-shaped legs. But it was his face that drew her. Despite her desperate desire to see his Future, to see for herself if the tale he told was true, all she truly wanted to do was go to him, rest her head against his chest, and never leave the peace of his embrace.

He looked down at her at precisely that moment. She suspected that her desire was unmistakably written on her face. He stared at her as if he could scarce believe what he was seeing.

Fool that she was, she could only smile weakly and quickly look away. Damnation, but this was her own fault.

She could have been going into his arms, safe and secure. She suspected that Thomas would have been amenable to whatever she suggested.

But she couldn't.

Not yet.

Not until she had seen the truth of his tale for herself.

"There came a man to my gates yesterday," Lord Roger was saying. "I didn't like the look of him."

She realized then that he was speaking the peasant's English. He wasn't looking at her, but she wondered if he were testing her.

"Oh?" asked Thomas, sounding only mildly interested. "What did he want?"

"He claimed he was searching for a woman who had been stolen from him, a woman he'd purchased as his bride." Lord Roger smiled pleasantly. "Said she was a Scot." He looked at Iolanthe. "I supposed she was an unwilling bride," he said.

In Gaelic.

That he could speak her language made her wonder quite quickly just what she had said to Thomas in whispers at the supper table. She felt herself coloring before she could stop it.

"Well, my lord," she managed, "I would say you deserve the truth."

Lord Roger shook his head with a smile. "Never fear, Lady Iolanthe. I sent him away unanswered and unsatisfied."

Thomas cleared his throat. "My lord, ours is a delicate situation."

"So I gathered, my friend."

"And he is a poor liar," Iolanthe said, nodding toward Thomas. "But this much I will say for him: He rescued me when that man would have slain me in cold blood. And for that I owe him my life"—she took a deep breath—"and my loyalty. So, I would ask you to look on him with compassion and know that what he has done, he has done for me."

"Ah, a romance," Lord Roger said, clapping Thomas on the shoulder. "Never fear, Thomas, I am not angry. I would have done the same in your shoes. And I did not tell this to you or your lady to shame you. I like to trot out my languages where I can. There are so few here to be impressed by my skill."

"I am impressed," Iolanthe said weakly. "Truly."

Lord Roger smiled at her, then sobered as he turned to Thomas. "Be aware, my friend, that Lord Charles is very angry. He will not rest until his pride is assuaged."

"He should be hanged," Thomas said. "He's murdered dozens."

Lord Roger nodded. "Aye, we know. But we've yet to catch him at it, and he covers his crimes all too well. Rest assured, I will watch him more closely." He looked at Iolanthe. "My only wish now is that we had the time for your entire tale. I feel certain 'tis something quite unlike anything I've ever heard before."

Iolanthe could only smile faintly. If the man only knew!

"Thank you again, my lord," Thomas said, "for your most generous hospitality and these gifts. Truly, it is more than we can ever repay."

Artane waved a dismissive hand. "You've given me an idea or two for my steward and provided me with hours of pleasant conversation. I consider myself well repaid. If you've a need for shelter in the future, know that my hall is always open to you."

Apparently Thomas wasn't above considering that as a possibility. Iolanthe wondered, judging by his willingness to accept that possible invitation, if he was all that confident in his ability to land them in the Future.

But that didn't stop her from following him out through Artane's massive gatehouse and up the road heading north. What else was she to do? Strike out on her own? And go where? Home, to her uncaring father and corrupt siblings? Without Thomas?

Thomas reined in his horse and looked at her. "Just a few miles north. We'll be there by noon."

Perhaps the true question was, even if she'd had a choice, would she have chosen to remain with this man?

It wasn't a question she could answer with any sort of detachment. He had saved her life, and for that she was grateful. He had given her the most peaceful week of her life at Artane. He was taking her back to his Future with him, to a time when she might meet those of her kin who were certainly more affable than her sire.

"Io?"

She nodded, hoping that she was answering aye to something she meant to, for she hadn't heard a thing he'd been saying.

Perhaps thinking too long on anything was ill-advised. What she wanted was to be at her journey's end, then sit and think.

She wanted to be home.

But not her home in 1382.

The sun climbed steadily in the crisp, autumn air. Iolanthe was uncomfortable taking such an exposed road, but Thomas seemed to think it was the fastest way and perhaps the safest. At least they would see an assault coming.

Maybe 'twas her blood that spoke to her and told her that the forests were a better path. How much easier to hide when one had the cover of trees.

"Thomas," she said, feeling as if she'd voiced her opinion on the matter more times than he cared to hear, "I do not like this road."

"Just a little farther, Iolanthe. I'm sure of it."

Now, had he had Duncan's ability to find a road through a briar patch, she would have refrained from further comment. She was almost positive he hadn't spent his life honing his tracking skills in her Scottish forests. He seemed to know mostly where he was going, but who couldn't find their way on a well-traveled road?

Then again, it wasn't as if he'd led them astray . . . yet. She simply didn't want to find herself on the end of the sword before they realized he'd led them in the wrong direction.

She took a deep breath for a final attempt.

"Lord Charles might see us," she said.

Thomas reined in his horse, opened his mouth to speak, then shut it. He pointed to the left.

"There," he said.

She looked, but saw nothing but a clutch of rocks. Was the man truly losing his wits?

"Jamie said it was three miles north of Artane, near the coast. A group of rocks that looked like a horse."

Iolanthe turned her head this way and that, trying to see the same. What she saw before her was a group of rocks that looked unremarkably like a group of rocks. There was no horselike shape there that she could see.

"Let's try it," he said, urging his horse forward. "What have we got to lose?"

"Our heads?" she muttered, but she followed him just the same. At least the rocks were close to a copse of trees. If something untoward happened, they would at least have a tiny bit of shelter. At the moment, she was willing to humor Thomas any way he pleased. Anything to be off that cursed road.

Thomas dismounted and led his horse and the packhorse toward the rocks. Iolanthe slowly slipped down from her horse. Thomas was looking about them, apparently searching for some kind of sign that this was the proper place.

"Well?" she asked.

He shrugged. "The gate in the forest near your house is just as unassuming. We'll just have to wait. I'll think about the Future, and you think about staying with me. That should do it."

He closed his eyes. Iolanthe assumed he was concentrating, not napping, so she did the same and willed herself to remain with Thomas.

It was, surprisingly, not an unpleasant thought.

They stood thusly for what seemed to her a goodly amount of time. Half an hour? Half the day? She couldn't have said.

She cleared her throat finally. "Thomas?"

"I know," he said grimly. "I know."

She looked around her. She felt thoroughly uneasy. "We should go."

He nodded. "We have two choices, then. We can go south to Falconberg and try the faery ring there, or we can go farther north."

"Did Jamie give you directions to these places?"

"He did. This was one of the ones he wasn't sure about. Falconberg he said would definitely work."

"And the spot farther north?"

"He had no personal experience with it. Just rumors."

"As with this place," she stated.

He nodded. Then he looked around. "Do you think Charles knows about these gates?"

She snorted. "How could he? Angus had no idea of them. The only way he would have learned about them was from me, and I can assure you I said nothing."

"I'm sure you didn't," Thomas agreed.

"Besides, the secret he's after isn't that one."

Thomas pursed his lips. "The jewels in the fireplace?"

"You know about that, too?" she said faintly.

"Yes." He looked around them uneasily. "Did your father know?"

"Nay, just me." She smiled briefly. "So perhaps Angus hadn't guessed amiss to send me with the English butcher."

"I suspect," Thomas said, "that no one found those things until Jamie did. His keep looks very good—and no wonder. He's probably had the money to hire people to do his re-modeling for him." He sighed. "Let's go. We'll try north."

"Where is Falconberg?"

"Lord Roger said it's almost two week's travel south. Even with all our supplies, I don't think that's what we want. Not if another hour can get us where we're going."

"I am losing my faith in your landmarks."

"We don't have a choice, Iolanthe. Either we try, or we stay here. To tell you the truth, I'd be perfectly happy to spend the rest of my days at Artane with you on the beach, but that doesn't answer many of your questions."

She had no choice but to agree with him. She swung up into her saddle. "North it is. Lead on, Thomas."

He mounted as well and kept hold of the packhorse. "This will work."

She nodded. One could hope.

They had gone only a pair of miles before Thomas was again leading them off the road to a clutch of rocks that looked very much unlike the new-breed animal he claimed they resembled. But she'd promised herself that she would have faith in him, so she did her best.

Then she heard the shouts from the way they'd come. She

looked back along the road and saw the dust being kicked up.

"Ruffians," she said, jerking her horse's head up.

"*Wait,*" Thomas said, grabbing her reins. "Just wait."

Iolanthe could scarce believe that he'd brought her all this way and at such peril to die in such a foolish manner.

He reached over his horse and grabbed her hand. "Concentrate on me," he commanded urgently. "Believe, Iolanthe."

She stared into his eyes and wished with all her heart that she might live long enough to have faith in him. She stared into his pale blue eyes, felt the warmth of his hand around hers, strong and sure, and did her very best to believe that he could do what he said.

After all, hadn't he saved her from certain death?

He blinked, then hesitantly looked over his shoulder.

And then he smiled.

Iolanthe looked back the way they had come. She had to blink several times just to make certain she wasn't imagining what she was seeing. Or wasn't, actually.

The ruffians were gone.

And then a sound so horrendous and terrifying surrounded her the moment before it exploded and receded into the distance. If she'd had any wits left, she would have screamed in terror, much as the horses were. As it was, she could only manage to keep herself in the saddle and watch as Thomas did his best with his two beasts.

She looked at him and wondered if he was just as terrified.

But the fool was grinning madly.

"Military jets," he said.

"Military jets?"

"It means we're in the right time, give or take ten years. It's close enough."

She looked around her. "Where are we?"

"About fifteen yards from the A1," he said, pointing to the road nearby.

It was only then that Iolanthe noticed that although the horrendous noise had abated, there were other kinds of noises nearby—noises that were reminiscent of a sword slicing through the air near your ear or a bolt buzzing past your face. Only these were scores of times more powerful.

"Cars," Thomas said.

Iolanthe followed his arm and marveled that it didn't shake. Her hands were shaking so badly as she held the reins, 'twas a wonder her horse didn't bolt.

"Cars?" she managed.

"The things with wheels," he said.

He pointed to shiny boxes that flew past with a speed she had never in her life imagined.

She was powerfully tempted to get off her horse and lie down until the nightmare passed.

"Iolanthe?"

She looked at him and tried to smile. She failed.

"It'll be okay," he said.

Well, he at least looked vastly relieved. And if this was his time, then surely he could see to their needs.

So she took a deep breath and nodded. "Where do we go?"

"Back to the inn," he said, looking around him with a frown. "Now how to get there."

"You don't know?" Maybe she'd been too hasty in crediting him with being able to see to them.

"In a car? Sure. On horseback? Well, that'll take some doing."

She couldn't understand the trouble, but perhaps there were several things she wouldn't understand at first.

Such as what she was going to do with the rest of her life now that she had it to worry about.

By the saints, she hoped Thomas hadn't made a mistake in rescuing her.

Chapter 36

Thomas decided, as he rode up to the inn and dismounted, that he would never again complain about the miracles of modern travel. He'd done probably three hundred miles on horseback over the past month, most of it at a gallop, and all he wanted was to sit on something that didn't move. Sitting for a week at Artane hadn't counted. He wanted to sit in an overstuffed chair in Mrs. Pruitt's sitting room and vegetate until he was sure his backside had recovered from its abuse.

The good news was, he was now positive he'd made it back to the right century. Mrs. Pruitt's little car was tucked snugly against the house.

The bad news was, he just wasn't sure what was going on inside Iolanthe's head. He looked up at her still sitting astride her horse. He could hardly believe that she was real. All things considered, getting her home had been a very easy thing.

Too easy.

He wondered if this was how men felt walking innocently into a field and subsequently finding out it was full of mines.

One false move and he was toast.

"Shall we go in?" he asked.

She nodded, then started to dismount.

"Wait—" he began, but she had slid down off her horse before he could help her.

"I am able," she said.

He shook his head. "I was just trying to help."

"But you've done so much already."

"It wasn't that much."

She looked up at him but said nothing.

He could see the misery in her eyes, and the indecision.

And in that instant, he understood the predicament he'd put her in. He'd considered it before, briefly, but it hadn't been enough to stop his plans. But now he couldn't ignore it.

There she was, in an alien world with no one to help her but a man who claimed that he loved her and that she had loved him in a different time. A time she had no memory of. Obligated to a man she didn't know.

Hell, what was he supposed to do now?

Solve it later. Yes, that's what he'd do. For the moment, though, what he wanted was a hot shower, dinner, and a good night's rest. Preferably in that order.

"How about a bath, then dinner?" he asked gently.

She looked so desperately out of her element that he found himself acting without thinking. He reached out and gently tucked an errant strand of hair behind her ear, then smiled gamely.

"Rough day?"

"I fear such will be my lot in this Future of yours," she said with a wince.

"Let's get something to eat and some rest. You'll feel better in the morning."

She only hesitated a moment before she nodded. "Who will see to our animals?"

"Good point," he said, looking around hopefully for a stableboy to materialize. Maybe there was something to be said for fourteenth-century living. Finding no servants lingering about for his pleasure, he tethered their horses to a handy Mercedes side-view mirror, then led Iolanthe into the house.

And who should he see leaning against the sideboard but that proud laird, Ambrose MacLeod.

Thomas smiled broadly. "How are you, my lord?"

Ambrose's smile was just as broad. "I could not feel more myself, lad. And look who you have with you. Our lady, in the flesh."

Thomas looked at Iolanthe to find her staring at him as if he'd lost his mind.

"Who," she managed in a strangled voice, "are you speaking to?"

Thomas blinked. "You can't see him?"

"See who?"

Thomas looked at Ambrose to find the laird frowning thoughtfully.

"No one," Thomas said, turning back to Iolanthe. He smiled. "No one at all. Let's go find Mrs. Pruitt. She's the innkeeper. She'll get you settled."

Iolanthe looked at him skeptically. "More ghosts?"

"Do you really want the answer to that?"

She looked slightly queasy, so he didn't press the issue. He put his hand under her elbow and started toward the reception desk. As if on cue, Mrs. Pruitt appeared. And when she saw Iolanthe, she nodded in her usual fashion, then looked at Thomas.

"A costume, lad? Rather a fine one, I'd say, but a bit travel-stained. Mayhap ye should get yerself clean before ye dirty up me entryway."

"I have three horses," Thomas began. "I'm not sure—"

"Horses, now?" she said, frowning in displeasure. "Yer gear was no trouble, to be sure, for it went in the shed, but horses?"

"Back garden?" Thomas suggested.

Mrs. Pruitt drew herself up. "Trampling me rosebushes?"

"Fertilizing them," Thomas countered.

Mrs. Pruitt considered, then nodded shortly. "Very well. For the moment, mind ye. I'll ring hereabouts and see if I can find ye a stable for the morrow."

"I'd appreciate it. Now, if it wouldn't be too much trouble, would you mind seeing to Miss MacLeod?"

Mrs. Pruitt waved her away. "Up the stairs, me girl. You know where it is."

Iolanthe looked at her archly. "My good woman, I do *not* know where anything is in your inn. How would I?"

Mrs. Pruitt blinked, then peered closely at Iolanthe. She approached, looked at her even more closely, then reached out and poked her in the arm with her finger.

Iolanthe gasped.

Mrs. Pruitt gasped.

And then that stout-hearted woman fainted.

Ambrose sighed. Thomas was ignoring him and could only

try to rouse Mrs. Pruitt without any aid or comment from Mrs. Pruitt's would-be beau.

"What ails her?" Iolanthe asked.

"Weak constitution," Thomas muttered. He managed to haul Mrs. Pruitt up into a sitting position, then patted her cheeks gently until she came to with a splutter. She looked at Iolanthe with wide eyes.

"Why . . . ye're . . . um . . ."

Iolanthe grunted. "Aye, most likely."

"Laird Ambrose said . . . but I never expected . . ." She looked at Thomas with wide eyes. "Ye were successful, then."

"Yes."

"Ye'll be wantin' a bath," Mrs. Pruitt said, sounding stronger already. She accepted Thomas's help to her feet, then shook her head. "What a disappointment I've been. Falling apart at me post—"

"Don't give it another thought," Thomas said. "This has been a hard day for everyone. You know, what we'd really like is a bath, then maybe some dinner if that wouldn't be too much trouble."

"Not at all," Mrs. Pruitt said. She looked at Iolanthe and took a deep breath. "Might I help ye with a bath, miss?"

"You might," Iolanthe said, rubbing the shoulder where she'd been poked quite enthusiastically. "Though I imagine I can manage to get myself clean enough if water can be fetched."

Mrs. Pruitt seemed to gather her wits about her. "No need to fetch water, miss," she said. "It comes straight into the bath."

"How?"

"Come up, and I'll show ye." She looked Iolanthe over quickly. "No bags? Well, we'll find something for ye. Lady Blythwood is surely yer size. I feel confident she's left things behind that will suit."

Thomas watched Mrs. Pruitt hustle Iolanthe off up the stairs, receiving only a quick look of panic from Iolanthe and an equally brief look of command from Mrs. Pruitt.

"Poor girl," Ambrose said. "You were successful, I see."

"For all the good it will do me. She didn't remember me."

"It was a slim hope that she would, my lad."

"Yet you remember her, don't you?"

"I do indeed."

"Then how do you remember her, if she was never a ghost?"

Ambrose stroked his chin thoughtfully. "I daresay, Thomas my lad, that our grasp of time is very flawed. To my mind, she was a ghost for several hundred years. Just because I now see her in the flesh doesn't change the past."

"But I changed the future."

"Did you?"

Thomas rubbed his hands over his face. "This gives me a headache."

"You created a new future," Ambrose pressed on. "But that doesn't negate the old one. 'Tis only Iolanthe who cannot find herself in two places at once. But she has already walked the path of a ghost. Walking now as a mortal woman doesn't change that."

"Then why can't she remember it?"

Ambrose smiled kindly. "A mortal frame draws something of a veil over the spirit's mind, Thomas. I daresay, were you free of its confines, you would find yourself remembering a number of things you wouldn't believe you'd forgotten. Perhaps when that time comes that she finally and in truth passes over to the other side, she will remember all that has transpired before. In both her lifetimes."

"She probably won't like me any better then than she does now," Thomas said. "Which isn't much, apparently."

"Truly?" Ambrose asked, sounding surprised. "She didn't seem opposed to you."

"She isn't falling into my arms either."

"By the saints," Ambrose said with a laugh, "you complain of another chance to win your lady? It was done once. You can now do it again with fewer mistakes."

"I didn't make *that* many mistakes the first time."

Ambrose pushed away from the buffet he'd been leaning against. "Give her time, lad. And after she goes to bed, come to me in the sitting chamber. I'll be interested to hear how your adventure went."

Thomas nodded, then looked at Ambrose. "Why do I feel like the hard part is in front of me?"

"Because you lost something you loved," Ambrose said gently, "and the thought of losing it forever grieves you."

"Wouldn't it you?"

"Och, aye," Ambrose said, with feeling. "But at least in your case, there will likely come a day when you'll hold your love in your arms in truth. Wasn't that why you took this risk?"

"Yes."

"Then off with ye, my lad, and soak your head. Perhaps that and a bit of fine supper will restore your wits to you."

Thomas was tempted to ask Ambrose how his own love life was going, but he thought better of it. Whatever was going on between the laird and Mrs. Pruitt was probably better left private.

Thomas wasted no time showering and dressing in things he'd left behind in his room. After two months of kilts, threadbare stolen goods, and fine lordly clothes, he was more than ready for a nice, broken-in pair of 501s.

He left his room only to find Mrs. Pruitt softly closing Iolanthe's door. Thomas looked at her and lifted one eyebrow in question.

"Asleep, the poor lamb," Mrs. Pruitt said, clucking her tongue. "Worn out, and no mistake."

"I can't say that I blame her."

"Dinner's in an hour, me lad," Mrs. Pruitt said, smoothing down her starched apron. "Hie yerself up to the castle if ye like. No doubt thems who're up the way will be wanting to see ye."

Thomas considered. Maybe a quick walk would clear his head. Besides, he wanted to see the place as a ruin. It would put his nightmares to rest.

It took him only a few minutes to jog there. He came to a teetering halt at the sight of a very familiar trio adorning his outer gates.

"What are you guys doing here?" he asked, astonished.

"Visiting the sight of former glories," Constance said, patting her hair into place.

"The society gave us the sack," Nigel said, looking defeated. "We annoyed the Queen."

Gerard only scribbled despondently into his notebook.

"Oh," Thomas said, feeling unaccountably sorry for them. "Well, surely there's some wreck around here that could use some rescuing."

"No business titles," Constance said glumly.

"No business cards," Nigel agreed.

"No business funds," Gerard said succinctly.

Thomas opened his mouth to tell them it was too bad when an idea of simply diabolic proportions popped into his mind. He jammed his hands into his pockets and gave it some more thought, finding that as he turned the idea over in his mind, he simply couldn't find a single fault with it.

Arthur Davidson had in his portfolio a construction division. Thomas distinctly remembered hearing Jake say that Davidson was getting ready to demolish one of the Lower East Side's least appreciated historical landmarks to build himself a trendy little office complex.

A pity all that history should go down into the Dumpster, unprotested, unheckled, unheralded.

"I'll fund you," Thomas said. "If you'll go to the States for a rescue project I have in mind."

The three threw off their gloom and doom like a ratty raincoat.

"Why don't you head back to the inn until we can figure out the particulars," Thomas said pleasantly. "My treat."

"Good show!"

"Well done!"

"Quick, before he changes his mind."

Thomas watched them trot off back down the road and smiled pleasantly to himself. Perhaps there was such a thing as just deserts.

He walked up the way to the castle, but slowed as he did so. The realization of just what had transpired there not two weeks ago was sobering. And miraculous. There were so many things that could have gone wrong. He could have come too late. Indeed, he'd thought he'd come too late. He could have gotten lost. He could have died any number of times.

He approached the gates and found Duncan waiting for him.

"Duncan," he said with a smile, reaching out to clasp his hand. And then it came back to him with full force just what had happened the last time he'd seen Duncan. He let his hand slip down to his side.

"Do you remember?" he asked quietly.

"Och, aye, lad," Duncan said with a small smile.

"But did it . . . I mean, did you die . . ."

"I remember one death."

Thomas blinked. "Then when you first saw me . . ."

Duncan smiled again. "Aye, I knew."

"And you didn't want to run me through with your sword?"

"It wasn't your fault, Tommy lad."

Thomas suppressed the urge to scratch his head. "I just don't get it. How could you have known me? Before I ever went back through Jamie's gate?"

"Because, Thomas, me lad, that was the past, and this is the future. And somewhere in between, you were born to the task you took on."

Thomas had the intense desire to sit down. "Do you know," he said conversationally, "that I really thought I understood how things worked."

"I think," Duncan said slowly, "that there are certain truths in the world. And out of the world," he added. "And then, lad, there is such a vast amount we don't understand, that if we knew just how much it was, we would go to bed and never arise again."

Thomas looked at him. "You're a very wise man, Duncan."

"I've had a long time to think."

"Thank you," Thomas said simply. "For my life."

Duncan shrugged. " 'Twas a life worth savin', surely. She'll come to feel that way about her own in time."

"How do you know she doesn't already?"

Duncan smiled dryly. "I've known her for centuries, Thomas. She was no different as a ghost than she was a woman. And just because you saved her from being murdered doesn't change the lass and who she is."

"Maybe you're the one I need courting advice from."

"Me?" Duncan asked with a laugh. He held up his hands in surrender. "Nay, lad, I'm hardly the one to tell you how to woo a lady."

"She's your daughter."

"Aye, and that likely makes me the last person you should ask."

Thomas paused. "But I should be asking you if I can marry her."

Duncan laughed. "Ah, Tommy lad, wouldn't she laugh at the thought of me saying you yea or nay?" He chuckled a time or two more, then shook his head. " 'Tis the lass's heart you'll have to win."

Thomas sighed. "I think I've said too much for that to be done easily."

"What foolish thing did you do?"

"I told her I loved her. And that she'd been a ghost for six hundred years."

"And?"

"And that she'd loved me, too."

Duncan clucked his tongue. "Now, laddie, that was perhaps goin' a bit too far, don't ye think? Never," he said, wagging his finger at Thomas, "*never* tell a woman how she's supposed to feel. There is no surer way to set them off."

"Thank you," Thomas said with a scowl. "I realize that now."

"Shoulda realized it then."

"It's too late, thank you very much," Thomas said, through gritted teeth. "Do you have any useful advice?"

"Watch your back."

"Huh?" Thomas said, then turned and ducked just before Connor MacDougal's sword sliced through the air where Thomas's neck had recently been. He straightened and glared at the taller man. "Laird MacDougal."

"I'd hoped we'd be rid of ye fer guid," the laird growled.

"Not yet."

"Then there's still time fer me ta use ye to decorate me gates." He raised his sword and grinned a wicked grin that sent chills down Thomas's spine. "Don't move, little rabbit."

Thomas pursed his lips. "I'm unimpressed, MacDougal." He paused and a thought struck him. "You're a Highlander. I have a Highland girl to woo and win. Have you got any ideas on how I might go about that?"

The MacDougal stopped in midswing and blinked in surprise. He lowered his sword. "Weel," he said, looking almost pleased, "weel, laddie, now there's a matter I've quite a bit of experience with."

"Do you?"

"Aye, but I do." He made patting motions over Thomas's shoulder. "I'll give it some thought and give ye a list at me earliest opportunity."

"You do that," Thomas said faintly. He waited until the other man was gone before he turned back to Duncan. "I'm stunned."

"Wait until he gives you his list," Duncan said with a shudder. "Poor wenches who had to endure him."

"Maybe I should be scared."

"I would be, were I you."

"Well, let's get back to something less terrifying. What's your advice?" Thomas asked.

"My advice," Duncan said slowly. "Aye, well, here it is."

Thomas waited. And he waited some more. "Well?"

Duncan looked at him gravely. "Let her go."

"What!"

"Let her go," Duncan said. "Take her back home, and let her go."

"You're crazy."

"She knows where you live."

Thomas folded his arms over his chest. "No."

"What else will you do, Tommy, me lad?" Duncan asked. "Hold her here against her will? I thought that was why you went back to save her, to free her from this place."

"Yes, but . . ." He almost said, *Yes, but not to free her from me.*

He stood still for a moment and considered the ramifications of that. He'd known that last day at Artane that he was losing whatever tenuous grasp he'd ever imagined he'd held on her. Nothing had changed. Was he to hold on to her so tightly that she couldn't escape simply to keep her near him?

If he wanted to take her freedom, then he was no better than Charles, who had taken her life from her.

"She knows where you live," Duncan repeated. "And if you're unwilling to let her go so far away, get you to Scotland with her."

"Scotland?"

"Aye. Go up and stay with young Ian. He has room enough for you. He's only a stone's throw from the laird's keep."

Thomas sighed. "All right," he conceded. "I'll go back to the inn and do what Iolanthe wants to do." He looked at Duncan. "Want to come?"

Duncan smiled. "There's naught for me here any longer, laddie. Aye, I'll come with you."

Thomas looked around him at the castle and realized that for him, too, there was nothing there. If Iolanthe wanted to come look at the place, he'd bring her. If she wanted to keep it, he'd give it to her. If not, he'd give the place to someone who would be a match for Connor MacDougal.

His sister, Victoria, for instance.

The thought of that was so astonishingly perfect that he laughed.

"Lad?"

Thomas smiled at Duncan. "Just idle thoughts. Tell me, is Connor married?"

"Wed?" Duncan asked, sounding shocked. "Ach, aye, but she left him and a pair of wee babes behind as she took up with a minstrel and fled to France."

"I'm unsurprised."

"Don't know that he wasn't a pleasant sort before his lady left him," Duncan continued. "As pleasant as you can be with a rowdy lot like his clan to look after. Why do you ask?"

"I was thinking I'd give the castle to one of my sisters. She'd whip the MacDougal into shape."

"He's old."

"So is she," Thomas said dryly. His sister was thirty-two going on a hundred when it came to being jaded. Perhaps that had something to do with too much time spent with actors. "Besides, he can't be more than mid-thirties."

"But foul enough to be pitched into the cesspit," Duncan said, "no matter his age."

Thomas shook his head with a smile. "Never mind. They were just idle thoughts."

"Aye, and idle thoughts get Laird Ambrose into peril, so I'd avoid them, were I you."

Thomas nodded, then looked at Duncan and smiled. "It's good to see you, Duncan."

"Aye, lad. That it is." He hesitated, then cleared his throat. "Did you tell her?"

Thomas smiled, "That you're her father? No, I thought you should."

"Can she see me?"

"Not yet. I'm hoping that will change eventually. In the meantime you can figure out what to say."

"Whose lot is worse?" Duncan asked grimly. "Yours, that you should have to win her, or mine, that I should try not to lose her?"

"Duncan, my friend, we're in the same boat, believe me."

They made their way back along the road to the inn. Thomas could smell dinner from the road, and for some reason that was an enormous comfort. He took a deep breath and continued up the driveway. Duncan was right. He'd give Iolanthe a couple of days to settle in, then he'd drive her up to the Highlands and take his chances with her home.

And pray that he wasn't making a colossal mistake.

Chapter 37

*I*olanthe sank down into the chair before the polished looking glass and wondered if she was truly equal to the task of surviving the Future. Perhaps Thomas had done her a disservice by saving her life. Surely all those years of being a ghost couldn't have been as taxing on her as less than a day and a night full of wonders she'd never imagined.

Not that she remembered much of the day before. By the time she'd finished with her bath and found herself dressed in a shift of some marvelous fabric that reportedly belonged to Thomas's sister, she hadn't had the energy to do much besides fall into bed.

Apparently, sleeping on her hair while it was wet wasn't a good idea. Had her head looked so misshapen her whole life and she'd never been the wiser? There was, she decided as she took a very elegant brush to her untamed locks, much to be said for having no idea what you looked like.

Her visage, however, wasn't in such a sorry state. She leaned forward and studied her face. Try as she might, she honestly couldn't see what her brothers and sister had found so objectionable about her appearance. Her teeth were well shaped, and none were missing. Her nose was straight, and her eyes weren't crossed. In fact, had she been forced to be completely honest with herself, she couldn't help but admit that she found herself if not pleasing to the eye, at least not worthy of the flinches Angus and Grudach had ever favored her with. Mayhap it would have served her to have had a polished glass at her disposal much earlier. It might have helped her sort the truth from the lies.

And thinking on those lies made her wonder what else they had told her that wasn't true.

Was she too tall, too old, and too homely for any man to

want her? The mirror had contradicted the last. Perhaps her height was not a bad thing. And perhaps there were men who wouldn't care how old she was.

Men such as Thomas.

She closed her eyes and leaned her head down on the table before her. So many conflicting emotions raged within her, she scarce knew where to begin in sorting them out. She was grateful to him, aye, for rescuing her. She was very grateful to him for the se'nnight of luxury at Artane. And she suspected that in time she might even be grateful to him for bringing her to a time of such wonders.

But gratitude alone did not a happy marriage make.

Did I love you?

I think you did.

Her conversation with him on the shore came back to her in a poignant fragment. He said he loved her, that he'd loved her as a ghost, and that he loved her still. Had she loved him?

It was more than she could bear to think about. She had no idea what she was supposed to do with herself now, but 'twas a certainty that whatever she decided, 'twould be better done while dressed. She put the brush down and rose. Mrs. Pruitt had laid out clothing for her on a chair.

She fingered the things there, then frowned. Had the good woman lost her wits? There were hose there, fashioned from a heavy blue material, but certainly nothing appropriate for a woman! She looked about for the things she'd worn to the inn, but a thorough search of every nook and cranny in the chamber produced nothing but a pain between her eyes.

In frustration, she ripped the top blanket off the bed, wrapped it around herself, and went in search of the innkeeper. Surely Mrs. Pruitt could find something more suitable than what she'd provided thus far. What of the gear on the packhorse? There had been a pair of very lovely dresses there. If nothing else, Iolanthe would have happily received her old clothing in return.

She descended the steps in a fine temper. The entryway was full of people, and that likely should have given her pause, but she was too irritated to pay them any heed. She found Mrs. Pruitt standing behind a little wooden table with all manner of shiny things adorning its top. Promising herself a good look later when she was suitably attired, she fixed Mrs. Pruitt with a scalding look.

"Good woman," she said crisply, "what have you done with my clothing?"

There was a brief chorus of groans behind her. Iolanthe looked behind her and saw that the trio of souls she'd dismissed had fallen to the floor in various stages of incapacitation. Iolanthe turned back to the errant innkeeper.

"My things from the horse," Iolanthe said. "Where have you hidden them?"

"Young Thomas has them," Mrs. Pruitt replied, sounding rather less apologetic than Iolanthe would have liked. "He afeared to wake ye last eve, so he put them in his room. He also said that if ye didn't find anything to suit, you were welcome to go through more of his sister's things."

"He has a sister?"

"Aye, miss. Megan, Lady Blythwood."

"Megan," Iolanthe said, finding the name surprisingly familiar on her tongue. Immediately an image came to mind of a red-haired girl with a smile that greatly resembled—

"Anything wrong?"

Iolanthe turned to her right and saw that smile on the face of the man coming down the stairs. He stopped at the bottom and put his hand over his mouth—no doubt to hide another smile.

"My clothes," Iolanthe demanded. "Where are they?"

The words were scarce from her mouth before she realized how ungrateful she sounded. By the saints, she'd never experienced such finery in the whole of her life and there she was demanding its return? She felt her shoulders begin to sag.

"Forgive me," she said quietly. "I've no right to demand—"

"You have every right," Thomas said. "Come on, and I'll show you where the stuff is. I just didn't want to wake you up last night by emptying saddlebags into your room. Didn't you like what Mrs. Pruitt brought you of Megan's clothes?"

"They were scandalous," she said promptly.

He laughed. "Do you think? I don't imagine anyone's ever said that about Megan's wardrobe. She'll love it."

Iolanthe sighed. In what other way would she show herself ignorant and poorly spoken that morn? "I meant no offense—"

"Io," he said gently, tugging on her elbow to get her to move, "don't apologize. Say what you want, when you want, and to whom you want." He smiled. "I can take it. I'm a MacLeod, too. We're made of stern stock."

"You're a *what*?" she gasped.

"My mother was a MacLeod. But trust me, you and I are very, *very* distant cousins. So distant that the McKinnon blood more than makes up for anything that isn't exceptionally distant."

She wasn't sure what was more shocking, that he was possibly kin, or that he was falling all over himself to convince her that he wasn't possibly kin.

What she did know was that he was pulling her up the stairs by her elbow, and it was all she could do to keep her bedclothes draped over herself with any kind of modesty. She waited in the passageway whilst Thomas fetched her gear and put it in her chamber. He stood aside to let her pass inside, then paused by the doorway.

"You know, you could go look in Megan's closet, if you'd rather. She has more than just jeans in there, I'm sure."

"Jeans?"

He tugged on his long-legged trews. "These."

Iolanthe looked at the clothing he'd set on the bed, then back at him. "What I have doesn't suit?"

"What you have suits perfectly," he said firmly. "Don't change a thing. Why don't I wait for you downstairs? We can have breakfast. Then I thought you might like to go for a walk."

"To the castle?"

He nodded. "If you like."

"I likely should."

"Probably."

She clutched the bedclothes to her throat. "I'll dress now."

He smiled and turned to leave the chamber. Iolanthe pursed her lips. She couldn't say much for his trews, but she also couldn't deny that there was something powerfully fetching about the view from—

She stomped across the room and shut the door. The very last thing she needed to be doing was dwelling on Thomas McKinnon's backside, no matter how fetching it might find itself to be. She turned back to the bed and dug through the saddlebag there. She dressed in one of the extra gowns the lady of Artane had seen made for her, put on her soft leather shoes, then had a final look at her hair in the mirror. Short of getting it wet again, there was nothing to be done. She braided it quickly, tied it with a ribbon to match her dress, then left the chamber.

Thomas was indeed waiting for her at the bottom of the stairs, apparently talking to himself again.

"Thomas, if you don't cease that kind of babbling," she said patiently, "people will think you're daft. I'm not unconvinced, myself."

He only turned away from looking at one of the side tables, smiled placidly, then led her into the dining chamber.

The meal was unremarkable. She was far too busy watching the other souls at the table who were watching her. She felt exceptionally self-conscious as she chewed, but she wasn't going to allow a few foolish stares to ruin the chance to fill her belly.

It wasn't long before Thomas had excused them and was leading her from the inn. She went, feeling a tingle go through her as she passed through the doorway. She'd done that before. Beyond reason, she knew that she'd passed through that portal—and more than just the night before.

But that was impossible. How could she have? She'd never been so far south in her life.

Unless Thomas's tale was the truth.

The thought of that was almost enough to send her back to bed. She shook her head. It just wasn't possible that she'd lived so many centuries as a ghost.

Was it?

Nay, she could not accept it. Not yet. But she was also no coward, so she walked with Thomas down to the road. He walked beside her easily, with his hands tucked in the pockets of his jeans. The day was gloomy, the sky flat as a trencher, and she suspected they would see rain before long. But despite that, the walk was pleasant, and she couldn't deny that the company was fine. It was a perfectly lovely way to pass a morning.

Except that she was going back to the place where she'd almost died.

Without warning, a finely packed road veered off to the right. Iolanthe came to a halt. She found, strangely enough, that she could not move. She knew where the road led. Putting her foot to that path was unthinkable.

"Iolanthe?"

She looked up at Thomas. "I cannot," she said helplessly. "I cannot move."

There was profound sympathy in his eyes. "To be honest, I had the same feeling the first time I came here." He shivered. "It was as if I'd been here before, only I never had."

She took a deep breath. "I know 'tis mad, but—"

"It's like walking over your own grave." He smiled briefly. "I understand, believe me."

And then he paused.

"Are you sorry?" he asked.

"About what?"

"That I . . . that I interrupted your . . ."

"Death?" she finished. She struggled for several moments with an answer. There was no good one, and that she had none to give him shamed her. "I am ungrateful," she said finally.

He stood there for several moments in silence. Then he cleared his throat.

"I wish I could say that I regretted doing it," he said. "But I can't. I couldn't let it happen when there was a chance to stop it."

She nodded, then looked at him and tried to smile. She found it almost impossible.

"I fear I'm . . ."

"Overwhelmed?"

"Aye."

"We don't have to go up there today. Or any day. We can—"

"Nay," she said. "Waiting will not make it any easier. Besides," she said, nodding to herself, "I should do this. It will prove to me that I really have come to your Future."

"Mrs. Pruitt's traditional English breakfast didn't do it for you?" he asked with a smile. Then he sobered. "All right. Let's go."

But still she found she couldn't make herself put a foot onto that cursed path. She found herself groping for something and when she found it, she clung tightly to it.

Thomas's hand.

She didn't dare look at him. She merely clutched his hand and forced herself to put one foot in front of the other. Thomas's hand was warm and secure around hers, and from it she drew strength.

She watched the ground until she realized she had no choice but to look up at the castle or find herself crashing into it. It was almost more than she could do to look up.

Thomas waited with seemingly endless patience.

Iolanthe took a deep breath, then looked up.

"Well," she managed finally. "Crumbling outer walls."

"I haven't gotten around to them yet," Thomas agreed. "It is odd, though, isn't it? To have seen this place in perfect condition two weeks ago and now to see it falling down?"

Odd wasn't the word for it. Iolanthe looked at the outer walls, feeling Thomas rub his thumb over the back of her hand until it was almost distracting.

Then without warning, he gasped and ducked, pulling her down with him.

"Knock it off, MacDougal," he snapped, straightening and glaring at nothing. "She doesn't need this."

Iolanthe straightened as well, wondering if too much time-traveling had left him truly witless. Then she remembered that he could see things she couldn't.

"A ghostie?" she asked.

"Connor MacDougal," Thomas said, tossing a very displeased look to his left.

"You spoke of him at Artane."

"Yeah, and those few days without him were bliss. Let's keep going."

Iolanthe pulled her hand from his, not because she wanted to, but because she found herself suddenly self-conscious. If there were those about watching them, they might find her clutching of Thomas's hand like a child quite silly. Thomas didn't seem to notice her discomfort. Either that, or he pretended not to notice.

Iolanthe walked under the barbican gate and paused in the courtyard. She remembered vividly the last time she'd been in the place. Lord Charles's men had been pinned against the walls by unseen foes; their screams still assaulted her ears.

But now the courtyard was empty except for a pair of tourists.

"Tourists?" she said aloud.

"I can't seem to keep them out," Thomas said with a sigh. "Besides, it gives the gar—" He looked startled, then shut his mouth immediately.

"The what?"

"Nothing," he said promptly. "I'm just babbling."

"It gives the what?" she prodded. "Tell me what you were going to say."

"It gives the garrison something to do," he said quickly. "They like to entertain people from time to time, I think. I didn't want to spoil their fun."

Iolanthe looked around the inner bailey, but could see nothing but the couple standing by the great hall. No ghosties. No bogles. No garrisons of spirits.

She pursed her lips, said *hrmph*, then studied her surroundings. To her left was the guard tower where she'd been taken. At the far corner of that wall was another, larger tower. The great hall sat in the middle of the bailey. She looked to her right and saw another wall with an arch cut in it. The gates were open, and she could see into a barren field. The lists, no doubt. For a moment she saw the place filled with flowers, but she shook aside the vision. Too many eggs for breakfast, no doubt.

It was the far tower that drew her. She made her way across the bailey, feeling Thomas a step or two behind her. She walked up the flights of steps on the outside of the tower, wooden steps that looked as if they'd just been recently built. She ignored the lower two floors. 'Twas the uppermost that drew her, though she couldn't have said why. She was certain Lord Charles had never shown her this part of his prison.

She put her hand on the door latch. She found that she couldn't move. Soon Thomas's hand swam into view. It was only then that she realized she had tears streaming down her face. She watched his hand fit a key into a lock and turn it. She opened the door herself, then looked into a solar of such beauty, she could only stand there and gape at it.

Thomas was silent.

She looked at him briefly before she stepped inside the chamber. She touched the armoire, the desk, the tapestry frame. She sat down in a chair near the window and felt as if she'd done the same thing hundreds of times. There were bound manuscripts sitting on a small stool in front of her. She picked them up and almost managed a smile at the drawings on the covers. She opened her mouth to ask whom the books belonged to, then realized she had no need.

They were hers.

She looked at Thomas, who still stood just inside the doorway.

"I . . . I . . ."

He pushed off the door frame and came to sit down across from her. The familiarity of the scene struck her with such force, she could scarce breathe. Thomas said nothing. He merely waited, looking at her with concern that was plain even to her unschooled eye.

"The chamber is beautiful," she managed finally.

"I'm glad you like it."

"Did you make it for . . ."

"Yes."

Why couldn't she say her own name? She looked about the chamber again and saw the loving details that had been put there for a woman's comfort. Her comfort—though she suspected that if she had in truth been a spirit, she likely hadn't had much use for a tapestry needle. It was a place of peace, though, and obviously built with love. Iolanthe looked at Thomas and found that she could manage at least a small smile.

"Thank you," she said quietly. " 'Tis very peaceful."

He nodded. "That was the intention."

She looked out the window. Her surroundings should have soothed her. Instead, they unsettled her. She knew that the truth of an existence she couldn't remember was all around her, but she could hardly bear to look at it.

"May we go?" she asked, rising suddenly.

She didn't wait for him to answer. She fled from the chamber and down the stairs. She gained the front gate before the tears were falling so fast that she could no longer see. She stood there and sobbed.

But she didn't weep alone for very long. She felt Thomas's hands on her shoulders, then found herself turned around and drawn into his arms.

"Oh, Iolanthe," he whispered. "I'm so sorry."

She flung her arms around him and wept as if her heart was breaking. She wasn't sure that it wasn't. There behind her in that accursed keep was undeniable proof that Thomas had built a chamber for a woman who bore her name, a woman he had loved and who had likely loved him in return.

A woman she didn't know.

But one she was beginning to remember.

She pulled back, sniffed, then scrubbed away her tears with her sleeve.

"Forgive me," she said.

He released her, though she sensed that it was reluctantly done. She knew it was the wisest course for her, though, so she didn't say aught.

"Perhaps we should go home," he said.

"Home?" she asked. "My home? In Scotland?"

He hesitated—but only slightly. "Yes," he said firmly.

She wanted it. She wanted to go home with every fiber of her being, though she knew that her keep would be different. Her family, such as it was, wouldn't be there. But to walk on her land again, to feel the sun on her face and smell the meadow flowers—aye, perhaps home was the place for her. At least she would feel more herself there. She would recognize where she was walking only because she'd once put a mortal foot there. This business of almost remembering things she couldn't possibly have seen before was more than she could bear.

She looked up at Thomas, trying to judge his willingness to do such a thing. He had traveled so far already on her behalf. Could she truly ask him to take her so much farther?

And if he was unwilling to take her back, what was she to do? She couldn't force him.

"The inn," she said, before she could make a fool of herself by begging. "I only meant home to the inn."

He looked at her skeptically, but said nothing.

Iolanthe scarce remembered the journey back. She managed to get herself through the doorway before she pleaded a headache and escaped to her chamber. Mrs. Pruitt came some time later with a tray of foodstuffs for her. Iolanthe ate heartily, then spent the rest of the afternoon and a goodly portion of the evening staring out her window at nothing.

It was very late before she stirred. She wandered around her chamber like a restless spirit, then realized what she was doing. She had no need to haunt such a small space. She left the chamber, then descended the steps.

She turned into the sitting chamber. She didn't know how she knew where it was, but she did. The thought was dismaying, but she ignored it.

She sat down before the fire. She saw something out of the corner of her eye and whirled around to look.

There was nothing there.

But she couldn't deny the feeling that she was no longer alone. She knew that if she could have looked hard enough, stretched herself enough, she would have been able to see what her mortal eyes could not.

She leaned back in her chair with a sigh. "I cannae see ye," she grumbled. "Leave off yammerin' at me."

Silence descended. Iolanthe closed her eyes. Her first day at Thomas's inn. She couldn't say it had been a success.

She could only hope the rest of her days wouldn't be passed in like manner.

Chapter 38

Thomas looked at Iolanthe standing in the front doorway, gazing with longing at her stolen horse that grazed in Mrs. Pruitt's front yard, and wondered about the advisability of what he currently contemplated. It wasn't that he didn't have things to keep him busy. He could have spent another day going through all the treasures Lord Roger had forced on them. He could have gone up to the castle and found something to swing a hammer against. He could have looked for a hill and climbed it a dozen times. On his hands.

Instead, he was planning a trip to the city. Not Edinburgh. Heaven only knew what Iolanthe would think of that. No, he was taking a little jaunt to Jedburgh, the closest metropolis with reputedly enough shopping to keep anyone happy for awhile.

Shopping, yes, that was the ticket. He'd never met a woman who couldn't be soothed, placated, or distracted by shopping. He'd learned the principle at his father's knee while watching his father soothe, placate, and distract a wife and three daughters. Surely Iolanthe could be soothed, placated, and distracted the same way.

Then again Iolanthe was neither his sister nor his mother, nor like any other woman he'd ever met.

And she wasn't overly eager to get in his car.

Which left him wondering again about the wisdom of his plan.

Then there was the other complication. He'd called his parents the night before just to let them know he was back safely from his little jaunt to his falsified destination. They hadn't been at home. As unsettling as that was, a call to his sister Megan had revealed that his parents were staying at *her* house in London and were currently out at the theater.

This was not good news. The very last thing he needed was his dad complicating the mix. Well, there was nothing to be done except hope his mom and dad would stay put until Iolanthe had gotten used to her surroundings.

But given the way she was sizing up his rental car, he suspected that getting used to her surroundings wouldn't happen any time soon.

Thomas opened the car door and smiled encouragingly. His car was still at Jamie's castle, and taking Mrs. Pruitt's tiny Mini hadn't been an option. Neither he nor Iolanthe would have fit, and he suspected that she would feel claustrophobic enough as it was.

"To the city?" she asked doubtfully.

"It's a little city. Queen Mary stayed there with the flu once, I think. It's a great place."

"Queen Mary?"

"Um," he said, wondering if he could actually go two hours in a row without putting his foot into his mouth, "Queen Mary came along a few years after Robert the Bruce. I'll tell you about her sometime."

"Hmmm."

"You need clothes," he said, hoping a change of topic would get him out of trouble.

"Then call in a seamstress."

"And shoes," he continued. "And other girl things. The city's not very far."

"So you say."

"I think there's an abbey there, too," he added. "You'll love it."

She looked completely unconvinced, and he had no idea how to motivate her. He supposed he could have gone shopping by himself, but he wasn't ready to let her out of his sight yet. He suspected that if he left his keys out and his back turned, she'd be in the car and on her way home before he knew it. Either that or she'd take her horse and be on her way. He knew he'd have to take her home soon, but he also knew that when he did so, he wouldn't have her alone for a good long time. Best he have her to himself while he could.

"We could go to Artane tomorrow," he offered. "If the driving today sits well with you."

She chewed on that for a minute or two.

"Jedburgh today," she agreed grudgingly. "But do not make the car go too fast."

"I'll try not to."

He got her into the car, got her buckled up, and down the driveway without her losing it. The road to the village was touch and go. She was closing her eyes and praying out loud.

And he wasn't even doing twenty.

"A little faster now," he said, turning onto a bigger road.

"The saints preserve me."

"Well, that's always a good sentiment," he said as he reminded himself that it would behoove him to drive on the left. Things were definitely easier with a horse and no dividing lines.

An hour and several prayers later, they had reached their destination. Jedburgh was as cute as Mrs. Pruitt had advertised and boasted shops enough for his purposes. He parked, sat back, and sighed deeply. He turned to Iolanthe.

"Made it."

"The saints be praised," she said, peeling her fingers from the armrest. "I hope this is worth that torture."

"So do I," he said with a smile, then crawled out of the car and came around to get her.

He pointed her toward a likely clothing shop and turned her loose inside it. She wandered around for a few minutes, touching things with what he thought might have been reverence—or complete disgust.

Then she turned to look at him.

"These?" she hissed, tugging on a pair of jeans. "I'm to wear these?"

Okay, strike one.

"I wear them," he offered.

"You're a man."

She had a point. He shrugged with a smile. "You don't have to. They have dresses, too. See, over there?"

She approached the dresses with all the enthusiasm of a woman contemplating picking up a dead rat. It took her a moment or two to figure out how to get the hanger off the rack, but once she had, she held the dress up to her and gasped at the length.

"This?" she said, looking scandalized. "So short?"

It hit her well below the knees. Thomas decided that perhaps he would do well never to show her a miniskirt. Maybe it was time to take a break from shopping.

"How about lunch?" he asked.

"We just broke our fast not two hours ago."

"All the more reason to get something else to eat. I saw a little tea shop down the street. It's close."

She hung the dress back up with a look of distaste, then stomped out of the store beside him, her face set in lines of extreme disapproval.

He decided that perhaps silence was the better part of valor at the moment.

He took her to the tea shop, saw her seated, then sat down across from her. He'd chosen a table near the window, and he pulled back the curtain for good measure. He watched her watch the passersby, then watched the wheels begin to turn in her head. Thomas looked up as the waitress came to give them menus.

Iolanthe was regarding the woman with openmouthed astonishment. Thomas looked at their waitress. All right, so it was the middle of November and definitely too cold outside for a sleeveless shirt and short skirt. Maybe it was hot in the kitchen.

"What would you like, Io?" he asked.

"Whatever they have," she said, not taking her eyes from the girl waiting for their order.

Thomas ordered tea and scones, then watched Iolanthe watch the girl walk away. She shut her mouth, then looked at him.

"Do they all dress thusly?" she demanded.

"Some do. Some don't. I think it's a little cold for that outfit, but maybe she's been cooking."

Iolanthe nodded uncertainly, then stared back out the window. Thomas sat back in his chair and took the opportunity to look at her. She was dressed in a gown she'd been given at Artane, her hair was hanging down around her face, and she'd thrown her cloak back over her shoulders. She looked as if she'd just stepped out of the pages of history, but that wasn't what made him smile. She was just so beautiful and so *real*. He couldn't get over the fact that if she'd allowed it, he could have reached over and held her hand. He could have kissed her.

He could have married her.

"Should I cut my hair, do you think?" she asked, twirling the end of it around her finger.

He blinked. "What?"

She looked over the other patrons. "Many women seem to have short hair. Should I cut mine?"

"No," he said immediately.

"I see you have an opinion on it."

How could he tell her that the first time he'd ever seen her, she'd been standing in the middle of her great hall and the sun had been shining down on that riot of hair and it had been all he could do not to go over and gather great handfuls of it? That he had spent hours staring at the way it fell over her shoulders? That she never would have had to bribe him to brush it?

"Please don't cut it," was all he said.

"It is fashionable as it is?"

"Do you care?"

She blinked in surprise. "I thought . . . I mean, I assumed that—"

"I think you would look stunning in a horse blanket."

He watched her digest that, then found himself wishing he hadn't said anything. Damn. She was furious.

"Then why did you bring me here," she exclaimed, "if not for me to look like these other women?"

"Ah," he said, searching for the perfect answer, "that certainly wasn't my intention."

"Wasn't it?"

"No," he said with feeling. "My mom and sisters love to shop. I thought you might like it, too."

She looked at him narrowly. "And that is all?"

"That's all. Definitely."

She drummed her fingers on the table as she looked around the café. "And do you like how these women look?"

"I hadn't really noticed."

"Then look."

He sighed and looked around. There was a collection of different women there for his perusal. He had a look, then shrugged. Nothing out of the ordinary. He turned back to Iolanthe to find her studying him closely.

"I looked," he said.

"And?"

"I'd rather look at you."

"That isn't my question."

He blew out his breath and wondered how he was going to get himself out of this one. Just when a guy thought he was doing the right thing . . .

"It's what I'm accustomed to seeing," he said. "The way they dress. To be honest, I think many wear their trousers too tight, their shoes too weird, and their hair too short."

"I see."

"Dress how you like. Like I said, I'd rather look at you than anyone else, and I don't care what you wear. I just wanted to buy you what you liked and hope that you had a good time while we were at it."

She merely looked at him.

"You'll need warmer things," he said. "And boots probably. It snows at your keep, doesn't it?"

That caught her attention. "My keep?"

He could hardly believe he was going to say what he was going to say, but it was out of his mouth before he could stop it.

"I thought you might want to go home soon."

"Oh," she said softly. Then she smiled at him, a smile of such radiance that he almost flinched. "Aye, I would like that."

He felt like he'd just signed his own death warrant.

"Boots," he said, finding that was just about all he could get out. "You'll need them for winter."

He suspected he would have felt better if she hadn't looked so damned relieved. In reality, he supposed he couldn't blame her. Maybe she just needed to go somewhere where she wasn't walking over her own grave. He could understand that. He didn't like it, but he could understand it.

He drank tea that tasted like poison and ate a scone that tasted like dust. He would have to let her go and hope she would remember him when she got used to her life. Maybe Ian wouldn't mind a boarder for the winter.

He could only assume it wouldn't bother Iolanthe to have him stay so close.

He'd obviously have to come up with a damned good excuse for mooching off her uncle several times removed. Maybe he could concoct some story about always having wanted to climb the mountains in her backyard. Maybe swordplay had been his burning desire, and now was the time to really hone his skill. Maybe he was going to start a new company with Ian as president. He was just certain that, given enough time, he could come up with a convincing story.

He spent the greater part of the afternoon working on that while at the same time convincing Iolanthe to buy more than just a pair of boots, which she so earnestly promised to repay him for that it broke his heart. She tried on the other things he asked her to, but he could see her mentally totaling up how much she would owe him.

"Iolanthe," he said with a sigh as he watched her reject half a dozen things she was definitely going to need up north, "will you please stop counting the cost?"

She looked at him miserably. "But I've no coin."

"I have plenty for the both of us. Please, *please* just let me buy you a few things."

"I'd listen to him, lovey," the saleswoman said with a knowing nod. "Be grateful for a man who's willing to treat you to a few pretty things."

Iolanthe relented, reluctantly, but at least Thomas had something to put in the trunk. He wished, absently, that Megan had been around to show Iolanthe the ropes.

He especially wished it when he realized he would probably have to hit the intimate apparel store with her.

He stood on the sidewalk and pointed toward the door.

"I draw the line here," he said.

"Afeared, are you?"

"Damn right," he said, leaning firmly and immovably against the window. "I'll be right here. I'm sure someone inside will help." He pulled out his wallet and handed her a hundred pounds. "That ought to cover it."

She put her shoulders back, took a deep breath, and marched inside. Thomas resolutely refused to speculate on the potential for odd conversations inside or about the directions those conversations might take. He concentrated instead on the rain that was starting to fall in a typically misty way and the way his hands were so comfortable inside the pockets of his leather jacket. He wondered if it might be possible to find such a coat for Iolanthe.

He looked across the street and saw just the kind of shop he was looking for. He leaned his head into the lingerie shop and looked around for a salesperson. He saw one, told her where he was going and to tell Iolanthe the same, then ducked across the street. He found her a coat and bought it in record time, but still he wasn't fast enough. He stepped out onto the sidewalk and saw her across the street, looking as if she'd just lost her last link to civilization.

He walked across the street, keeping his eyes on her, just in case she decided to bolt. She saw him the moment he put his foot on her sidewalk.

The relief on her face almost brought him to his knees.

"Oh," she said, flinging herself into his arms. "I thought ye'd left!"

He wrapped his arms around her and enjoyed for an eternity the feel of her clinging to him. He knew it couldn't last for long.

"Oh, Iolanthe," he whispered, "where would I go?"

And for a brief, heart-shattering moment, she stayed in his arms as if she wanted to be there.

Then she stepped back, and smiled up at him with watery eyes.

"I'm a fool," she said with half a laugh. "They told me you had gone, but didn't tell me where. I should have trusted that you'd come back."

He wanted to say, *I always will,* but he didn't want to ruin whatever kind feelings she was having for him at the moment, so he kept his mouth shut, took her arm, and steered her toward the car.

The drive back to the inn took far less time than he would have liked. Iolanthe was silent. She wasn't even praying as she stared out the window. Thomas kept to his plan and didn't disturb the peace.

They had almost reached the inn when she spoke.

"Thomas?"

"Yes."

"When can we go?"

He didn't have to ask where. "Whenever you'd like."

"Tomorrow?"

"Tomorrow it is, then."

Let her go, came Duncan's advice in his mind. Ambrose's suggestion of *Give her time* came hard on its heels. Thomas didn't like either one, but he realized he didn't have much choice.

Besides, what was a month or two in the grander scheme of things?

Or a year. Or two.

After all, Iolanthe had waited six hundred.

What was a couple of years when compared to that?

Chapter 39

I *olanthe* stared at the clothing she had laid out on her bed.
On the right was her own poor dress, having been cleaned
and mended by Artane's skilled seamstresses. Alongside it
was the finery she'd been gifted. She shuddered to think what
the material alone had cost. Mayhap Lord Roger was so rich
that a pair of gowns to a stranger troubled him not.

But if those things had come so dear, what was she to say
about what she saw to her left? Jeans, tunics, sweaters, things
to go under the lot, as well as shoes. Dresses too, of course,
but hopefully more modest ones than she'd seen sported by
the wench who'd served them tea. Iolanthe reached out and
touched the coat Thomas had bought her. The leather was
black and so fine, she was sure she'd never seen its like.

She closed her eyes and swallowed with difficulty. She
could never repay him for any of it, not if she worked a
lifetime. That he should give her so much when she had so
little to give him in return was truly shameful. The least she
could have done was return his love.

Yet how was she to give herself to a man she didn't know?
Never mind her dreams of him. Never mind the times she
looked at him and felt as if she had truly passed half a lifetime with him. The stirrings of her heart were overwhelmed
by the churnings of her mind. How could she give her heart,
when she was so unsure of it? Would she be loving him for
what he'd given her, or for what he was?

She wrapped her arms around herself. There was only one
way to find out. She reached over and began to fold up the
things she'd brought from the past. Once she had carefully
tucked them into her satchel, she turned toward the clothing
of the Future. Her past was behind her, and there was no
turning back now—not that she would have wanted to. There

was nothing in 1382 for her. She would have to make herself a place in 2001.

And hope that Thomas could be patient whilst she did so.

She dressed herself in underclothing as the women had shown her, then took a deep breath and put on the jeans.

"Scandalous," she muttered as she tugged on the zipper.

A blue sweater pleased her eye. She looked at the shoes, then decided that perhaps since the floors of the inn were laid with tapestries, there was no need for anything on her feet. She dragged her hands through her hair, considered using a brush, then decided 'twas futile. She turned toward her chamber door. Dinner awaited her. Dinner with souls from the Future. Mayhap with new clothing, the other diners wouldn't gape at her so fiercely.

She had scarce descended the steps when the front door blew open and several people tumbled in. The wind gusted enough that it took the two men there to heave the door to.

"Damn it, Helen," the elder of the men grumbled, "why is it always raining here?"

"It's England, dear. I like the rain. Don't you, Gideon?"

The younger man smiled, and Iolanthe couldn't help but admit that he was very handsome. "Aye, Mum," he said, giving the older of the two women a peck on the cheek. "It makes things quite green. Don't you agree, darling?"

Iolanthe looked at the younger of the two women and found that she had quite suddenly lost her breath. It didn't matter that the woman looked as much like Thomas as a woman could and still be beautiful. Her red hair had been much abused by the wind and stood out in all directions. Her cheeks were just as red, and her green eyes were damp, apparently from enduring the inclement weather.

But it was her smile that Iolanthe couldn't look away from. When she looked at that smile, she saw Thomas.

And for some reason, that made something inside her shift, like her heart settling into place.

Home.

"Iolanthe!"

Iolanthe found herself immediately embraced by that same red-haired woman, who was laughing and crying at the same time. She was jumping up and down as she hugged Iolanthe hard enough to render her breathless. Iolanthe closed her eyes and heard the faintest voice of a memory come back to her.

Megan.

When the woman realized that Iolanthe wasn't hopping up and down as well, she pulled back with a puzzled expression on her face.

"Iolanthe?"

Iolanthe closed her eyes briefly, then looked at Thomas's sister. "Megan," she croaked.

Megan burst into another smile. "You *remembered!* You remembered me! When Thomas called yesterday and told me what he'd done, I just couldn't wait to come see you. I'm so happy for you!"

Her man, perhaps he was her husband, put his hand on her shoulder and smiled. "How do you do?" he said with the crisp tones she'd come to associate with most of the people in the inn. "I'm Megan's husband, Gideon, though I don't suppose she talked about me all that much the last time she was here."

Iolanthe looked at Megan. "You were here?"

Megan smiled. "About a month ago. But that was before . . ." She looked up behind Iolanthe, and her smile returned. "Thomas, she remembered me!"

Iolanthe turned to see Thomas standing halfway down the stairs, looking as stunned as she felt.

"What," he managed in a strangled voice, "are you guys doing here?"

"Megan made us come," the older man grumbled. "We're scouting out the place for Christmas. Can't understand why we'd want to, but there it is."

Iolanthe surmised that this was Thomas's father. He looked a bit like him, and when Thomas crossed the entryway to embrace the older man, she knew she was right. Thomas embraced his mother, shook Gideon's hand, then swept Megan off her feet in a crushing hug. Iolanthe found herself feeling immediately and thoroughly out of place.

Until, that is, Megan slung her arm around her shoulders and kept her from fleeing.

"Mom, Dad, this is Iolanthe. She's a friend of mine."

"And mine," Thomas put in pointedly.

Megan waved him away. "Yeah, yeah, and who went shopping with her for the first time? We bonded over Keds. What have you done for her?"

Iolanthe opened her mouth to protest, then realized Megan was teasing her brother. She decided that perhaps it would behoove her to keep silent and see how things played out. She would have gladly escaped back upstairs, but Megan seemed determined to keep her nearby.

She suffered through discreetly speculative looks from Thomas's parents, then found herself taken in hand by both Thomas's mother and his sister while the men dealt with the gear.

It was a miserable evening. She couldn't believe that Thomas's parents weren't burning with questions they didn't dare ask. Judging by the looks Megan was giving her, Megan had already had many of her questions answered and Iolanthe had to wonder by whom.

Perhaps by her own self?

A month ago?

The thought of trying to work that out gave her pains in the head. Apparently she had known Megan before—or was that after? If Megan's words were true, Thomas had called her the day before and told her of his successful journey. But none of that soothed Iolanthe. To be faced so inescapably by her past that was in reality perhaps her future was almost more than she could take. By the time dinner was over, and the family had retreated to the sitting chamber, she thought she would weep if she didn't have some air.

Thomas grabbed her hand before she entered.

"Be back in a minute," he said to the occupants, then shut the door. He looked down at Iolanthe. "I had no idea they were coming."

She squirmed miserably. "Thomas—"

"I only called Megan to tell her I was back."

" 'Tis fine—"

"I couldn't not tell her that you were okay."

"Thomas, 'tis nothing. She didn't grieve me."

"But my parents and their intense desire to pry into your life probably did." He smiled down at her, but it was a pained smile. "How about a walk in the garden to clear our heads? I'll go grab our coats and your shoes."

She nodded, grateful for the reprieve. Thomas returned, helped her into her coat, put her shoes on her feet like a servant, then walked with her through the dining chamber, through the kitchen, and out into the back garden. He didn't touch her, didn't speak, didn't force her down any path. He merely walked where she did with his head bowed.

"Thomas," she said quietly, "I cannot repay you for the clothes. Or for anything else."

"I wish," he said wearily, "that you would stop trying." He looked at her, and there was no smile on his face. "Iolanthe, I did what I did because I loved you. I knew the risks. You didn't want me to go back in time, but I did it anyway, and that's my price to pay. I'm not asking you to love me, and I think I'm sorry I ever suggested that you once did." He paused, looking as if he'd already said too much. Then he sighed. "I want you to be happy."

She nodded, feeling altogether wretched.

"We'll leave tomorrow morning, just as we planned."

She didn't argue.

He looked as if he planned to say something else, then shook his head.

"It's late," he said quietly. "We'll make an early start."

"Aye."

She wanted to go into his arms, bury herself in his embrace, and never leave it. She also wanted to cease feeling indebted to him for all he'd done for her. There was surely no means for her to repay him. Perhaps he had it aright and she should cease trying.

Home. It called her like a beacon. She felt almost certain that 'twas there she would find her answers.

She took a deep breath. "Thank you, Thomas."

"It's my pleasure, Iolanthe."

It took two days to reach her home. Thomas had driven like a man who wasn't in a hurry. She hadn't protested, for the speed of the automobile was still unsettling to her.

The other reason she hadn't urged him to greater haste

was that the slow travel gave her ample time to study the
man beside her. She looked at his legs encased in those well-
worn jeans and wondered how many miles he'd walked and
ridden to chase after her and the English-man who would
have murdered her. His arms were hidden by a shirt the same
color as his jeans, but she'd watched those arms strain under
poor cloth and seen the muscles there. She had to admit to
having watched him in Artane's lists a time or two. He was
not the most skilled, but he was far from the least. Had he
learned swordplay simply for her? She suspected that if he'd
had enough time, he could have been the equal of any one
of her kin.

She looked next at his hands that rested on the wheel of
the car. They were strong hands, scarred here and there from
she knew not what. How did he earn his bread in this Future
of his? What did he do for pleasure? He'd told her that 'twas
a goodly part of his own labor that had rebuilt the tower of
Thorpewold. Was he a mason, then? How would those hands
look tending a child?

Which made her realize, with a start, that she didn't know
if he had a wife or not.

Then it occurred to her that he would hardly have been
rushing off to rescue her if he'd been wed.

It was his face, though, that she spent most of her time
studying. It had been, over the past two days, a rather serious
face. To distract him, she had asked him, far into the morning
of their first day of travel north, to tell her of his life.

It had eased the tension in his shoulders. And his tales of
enterprise had been interesting, as were his boasts of mountains climbed. It was those stories she had liked the best, for
she had seen the passion in his face and heard it in his voice.

Somewhere long past Edinburgh, long past Inverness, she
had begun to realize how it was a woman could easily fall
in love with the man.

And then she had realized, to her astonishment, that for
her, such a thing might have begun long before that moment.

"We're close," he said, interrupting her musings.

She blinked, then looked around, realizing that he spoke
the truth. Though she knew the countryside around her home,
she could see how things had changed. Trees had grown up

and others had obviously been hewn down. A road cut through land that had seen nothing but cattle and horses in her time.

She wiped her hands on her jeans, finding herself unaccountably nervous.

"Will I be disturbing them, do you think?" she asked.

He looked at her with such frank astonishment that she almost smiled.

"Well, no," he said. "They're expecting us. I called them last night to let them know we're coming." He smiled faintly. "They're excited to see you, Iolanthe."

She nodded and scrubbed her hands some more on her legs. She looked out the window, but that didn't soothe her. The closer she came to her destination, the more nervous she became.

"Thomas," she managed. "I don't know . . . what if—"

"Io, it's your family. They love you."

"They don't know me!"

He was silent. She supposed it could have been because he was pulling through the gates to her family home. Perhaps he'd suddenly found himself without a voice. And then it occurred to her just why he might be avoiding her question.

"Did I . . . was I here?"

He turned off the car, put both hands on the wheel, then looked at her.

"I think," he said slowly, "that you shouldn't worry about the past. Let things unfold as they will. Jamie is your grandfather's grandfather. If anyone should understand the shock of a different century, it's him. He'll be a great help to you. As for the other, I'm not going to say any more. Ask Jamie if you really want the answer." He smiled, and that took away the sting of his words. "He'll be able to tell you things I can't."

She nodded, then watched him get out of the car. She fumbled at her side, then found that the door was opened for her. Thomas stood back and waited for her to get out.

"Our things?" she asked, gesturing toward the trunk.

"I'll get them later," he said. "Come on, Io. Your family's waiting."

She had no choice but to follow him.

She stood at the door as he knocked, finding herself slipping her hands into the pockets of her coat as Thomas often did. No wonder he found it so comforting.

After an eternity of waiting, the front door opened.

"Hey, Zach," Thomas said easily. "How's tricks?"

The young man facing him gaped, a forgotten snack dangling from his hand. He stared at Iolanthe, then at Thomas, then back at her until she wondered if she'd failed to dress herself properly.

"Iolanthe, this is Zachary. He's Elizabeth's youngest brother. Elizabeth is Jamie's wife." Thomas pushed Zachary aside and led her into the hall. "Zach, close the door. Io, come with me, and I'll make the introductions."

Iolanthe followed him, then found herself shadowed by Zachary, who continued to stare at her as if he couldn't believe what he was seeing. Thomas reached over and gave him a companionable shove.

"You're drooling," Thomas said pleasantly.

Zachary shut his mouth with a snap, but the look of complete idiocy didn't leave his face.

"Is he daft, then?" Iolanthe whispered to Thomas.

"Just awestruck," Thomas said dryly. "Don't worry, he'll get over it."

Iolanthe nodded, then looked around her, noting the familiar things and the changes. The lack of rushes was a vast improvement, but the hearths looked the same. There were new doors off the great hall, but the same stairs leading up to a pair of other chambers that had been built adjacent to the great hall in Jamie's day. She wondered absently if that part of the keep had been added to. With the way Jamie seemed to accept strangers and family alike, he would need a goodly amount of room to house them all.

"My laird."

Iolanthe stiffened when she heard Thomas's voice laced with affection and respect. She turned to look at the recipient of such consideration and found herself rendered immobile. Why, the man couldn't have looked more like her grandsire if he'd been his twin. He stood and came over to her.

"Granddaughter," he said.

"My laird," she whispered.

Then she burst into tears.

Jamie gathered her into his arms and patted her back soothingly. "Ach, there, there, lass. No need for tears."

She wept as if she'd never wept before in her life. It was unseemly and untidy, but she couldn't seem to stop herself.

"By the saints, Thomas," Jamie said, his voice rumbling in his chest, "what have you done to the girl?"

Iolanthe shook her head and pulled away. Thomas shoved a cloth into her hand, and she dried her eyes and blew her nose. She looked at Jamie and managed a smile.

"He saved my life, my laird," she said. "A braver rescue I couldn't have asked for."

"Well, then," Jamie said, beaming his approval on Thomas, "give us the tale, man. Here, sit with your lady and tell us how 'twas done. We've worried mightily over you both."

His lady. Iolanthe sat next to Thomas and found, surprisingly, that being addressed as such was not only tolerable, it was highly desirable. She did her best to remember names as introductions were made, then promptly forgot everything as she listened to Thomas give his report. It took most of the late afternoon, through dinner and through more talk before the fire. She couldn't remember the last time she'd passed such a pleasant evening.

Well, outside of all the evenings she'd passed in Thomas's company since his rescue of her.

Iolanthe felt her eyelids begin to grow heavy and wondered if anyone would notice if she simply went to sleep.

Peacefully.

Without fear.

She realized she had actually fallen asleep only when she heard Thomas calling her name softly. She opened her eyes and found him standing in front of her. She smiled up at him.

"Aye?"

"I've brought your things in," he said gently. "Elizabeth has a room all ready for you. I put your gear in there."

"Thank you." She looked at him, then frowned. "You've your coat still on. Have you more things to fetch?"

He shook his head. "I'm not staying."

She sat bolt upright. "You're *what*?"

"I'm not staying."

"But . . . but . . ." she spluttered. "But you can't go back to Thorpewold."

"I'm not. I'm just going to . . . um . . . Ian's for a few days," he said, gesturing vaguely. "He lives close by. We have some . . . um, business together. Yes, business."

She snorted. "You're a poor liar, Thomas McKinnon."

He blew out his breath and squatted down in front of her. "All right, I'm going to Ian's to give you time. I want you to have peace here to decide if you want me or not. Is that truthful enough for you?"

"Well," she said, taken aback, "you've no need for a temper."

"Ha," he said, rising. He looked at her crossly. "Ha." Then he seemed to consider, discard, then consider again.

The next thing she knew, he had hauled her up to her feet by her arms, pulled her into his arms, and clutched her to him with his face not a finger's breadth from hers.

"Make up your mind, Io," he said. "Please."

And just when she thought he might just kiss her, he seemed to think better of it. He released her with less reluctance than she would have liked, but she couldn't blame him. She had led him on a merry dance the past few days. 'Twas little wonder he had no patience left for her.

He turned and left the great hall. Iolanthe watched him go. The door shut, and she found herself very much alone. She sank back down into her chair and looked over her shoulder at the door for several moments, expecting Thomas to come back in and say he'd been jesting with her, that he had no intention of leaving.

But the door remained closed.

At length, she turned to look at the fire, feeling the silence descend.

And with that silence came perhaps what she had needed from the beginning.

Peace for thinking.

She closed her eyes. Mayhap Thomas had things aright, and that was the best thing for her. She would make herself a place in his world, then find Thomas and thank him.

And hope she hadn't waited too long to give him the answer he wanted.

Chapter 40

Thomas stood in Ian MacLeod's kitchen and looked at what was supposed to serve as dinner. What had he been thinking to pit his pitiful cooking skills against an AGA stove? Who cooked on that thing anyway with any success? Since when did a wood fire replace a good, old-fashioned gas oven? He wanted to turn a dial and have the right temperature. He didn't want to coax a fire, feed a fire, and subsequently have that fire incinerate his supper.

It was shaping up to be a helluva Thanksgiving.

"I've seen worse," Ian MacLeod said, folding his arms across his chest and regarding the well-done bird. "Much worse."

Thomas didn't doubt it. After all, it was Ian's stove. Thomas just couldn't believe that Ian hadn't burned his share of things initially as well.

"You know," Thomas said, "you could have warned me about this thing."

Ian grinned in a way that left Thomas with no doubts that he'd raised more hell than was good for him in a former lifetime.

"You needed aught to occupy your mind," Ian said pleasantly. "What better to do than to try and best my cooker?"

"I can think of lots of things," Thomas said with a scowl.

"Don't worry. There's a bit to be saved here," Ian said, poking the chicken with a knife. "And we've other things as well. See here, my fine, golden browned rolls." He sniffed appreciatively. "Truly, I have missed my calling in life."

Thomas had a great deal of experience with both Ian's cooking and his swordplay, and, nice as the food was, Ian's swordplay was what was stellar.

"Nah," Thomas said, taking a roll and testing it, "you'd be bored with just food."

"Perhaps," Ian agreed. "Though I must say the convenience of a modern kitchen has definitely improved the contents of my suppers." He looked at Thomas. "I daresay you've had experience with that, having spent your own amount of time in medieval Scotland."

"I ate pretty well once we got to Artane," Thomas said. "But before then, yes, it was pretty much touch and go." He finished his roll, then stretched. "I still say you're a better swordmaster than a cook. Besides, where's the joy in life if you can't do something every day to keep up the blisters on your hands?"

Ian clapped him on the back. "I don't have blisters on my hands," he said with a grin.

"Thanks for reminding me," Thomas grumbled.

Ian laughed. "You've done very well for yourself, and should you continue on this path you've chosen, your blisters will disappear as well. The MacLeod blood runs true in you, Tommy lad."

"For all the good it does me."

"It provides me with sport enough," Ian said, filching a roll. "What say you we finish this fine feast, then indulge ourselves in a bit of the same?"

"It's snowing outside, Ian."

Ian looked puzzled. "Aye."

Thomas wondered, and it hadn't been for the first time in the past week, just what he'd been thinking to want to come stay with this maniac.

"Maybe tomorrow," Thomas said. "There's probably football on your satellite dish. We should watch it. It's tradition."

"Ah, well," Ian said, patting his disgustingly steel-like belly, "I suppose a day of leisure now and then wouldn't harm me."

"It'll give the rest of us a chance to catch up," Thomas assured him. "Let's get this served."

"I'll fetch my lady."

Thomas put everything on the table and waited for Ian and his family to return. Just the sight of the three of them so happily settled was enough to make him think perhaps a little swordplay wasn't such a bad idea. It would certainly take his mind off his own problems.

Such as a week with no sign of Iolanthe.

If he hadn't known better, he would have suspected he had dreamed her.

"Lovely dinner, Thomas," Jane said, settling her son in his chair and sitting down next to her husband. "Crunchy chicken. I like it."

"That's a good thing," Thomas said dryly, "since that's all that's available."

"Trust me," she said with feeling, "we've had worse."

Ian put his hand over his heart. "You wound me. I thought you had forgotten those days when I strove to master the beast."

Jane leaned over and kissed his cheek. "You're a great cook. Now," she added with a smile.

Thomas smiled into his potatoes as he listened to them banter affectionately. It reminded him sharply of his own parents.

Dinner was alternately scary and delicious, depending on who had cooked what. The chicken, its crunchy outside aside, was a good substitute for turkey, and everything else was certainly something Thomas would have found on his own table.

But it was the company that left him filled. Ian and Jane were a wonderful couple, and they seemed to have no trouble drawing him into their circle.

Ah, that such a family could be his.

When there were little more than scraps left on the table, Ian leaned back and pushed his plate away. He stretched, then settled himself more comfortably in his chair.

"I heard your tale at Jamie's, Thomas," he said, "but your lady was sitting there next to you, and I wondered how freely you spoke. I would have an entire retelling now, if you've a mind for it."

Thomas almost said he didn't think he could get through it again, then it occurred to him whom he was talking to. Just like Jamie, Ian had also come from medieval Scotland. Who better to tell his story to than a medieval Scot and his very twentieth-century wife? If anyone could help him understand where Iolanthe was coming from, it would be these two. Of course, neither of them had been a ghost for six hundred years, but maybe that was muddying the waters where they didn't need to be.

So he launched into a retelling of his story, and he left nothing out. That wasn't to say that he laid bare his heart. He suspected, though, that enough of it came out just the same, because Jane looked at him sympathetically, and Ian cleared his throat roughly more than once.

He found himself lingering over his week with Iolanthe at Artane, realizing as he did so that it was without a doubt the most precious time he'd had with her. At the moment, he suspected there was little he wouldn't give to have returned to that time and the simplicity of their relationship.

He described their first failed attempt at time-traveling, then their success. Ian had been enormously amused by Iolanthe's reaction to cars buzzing by on the freeway.

"Poor lass," he said with a chuckle. "I doubt I would have found it so startling, but then again, I am accustomed to the sounds of fierce battle."

Jane looked at him with one eyebrow raised. "We won't talk about your first ride in a taxi. Or about all the times you almost electrocuted yourself by trying to investigate various appliances—or the television insides—with your sword."

Ian looked just the slightest bit sheepish. "Finish your tale, Thomas," he said. "And make haste before my lady embarrasses me further."

"There isn't much more to tell," Thomas said. "It took us a day and a half to get from the rocks to the inn. We camped in someone's field overnight, and I guess I can just be grateful we didn't get thrown in jail for trespassing."

"That could have been ugly," Jane agreed.

"We took a day to settle in, went up to the castle, which was a disaster, then took a day to go shopping."

"Did that please her?" Ian asked. "You took her in a car, I assume."

"She didn't care all that much for that. The shopping even less. But the worst was to come. Once we were home, my family showed up."

"And?" Ian asked.

"Iolanthe ran into them on her own. I came down the stairs to find my sister strangling her, she was so happy to see her."

"And this is a bad thing?" Ian asked.

"She'd known Iolanthe before."

Before. With a capital *B*. He couldn't say the word that he didn't think of it that way.

"And Iolanthe? How did she react?" Jane asked.

"I think she felt suffocated. For various reasons."

"Your family couldn't have grieved her," Ian said with a frown. "Did they startle her?"

Thomas shook his head. "I don't think so. I think the problem was that Iolanthe recognized Megan. She seems to have these flashes of memory every now and then."

"That has to be unsettling," Jane said gently.

"I'm sure it is," Thomas agreed. He drained his glass, then sat back. "So there you have it. After enduring my family for an evening, she begged me to bring her home, and so I did. So there she is over there, and here I am over here. And I haven't got a clue what to do to close the distance."

"Maybe she just needs time," Jane offered. "She's been through a lot."

"I wish that time didn't have to exclude me," he said. "And I wish she wouldn't feel so indebted to me. Why can't she just let me do what I want to for her?"

"How would you feel were the places reversed?" Ian asked with a brief smile. "You saved her life, you've fed and clothed her, and you've delivered her to her home. Would you be so willing to accept such from a woman?"

"Were you?" Thomas asked frankly.

Ian smiled as he shook his head. "Of course not, though at first I had no choice."

Thomas looked briefly at Jane. "I don't want to pry into your finances—"

"We're an open book," Jane said. "I had enough money to get us to Scotland, and Ian's done everything since."

"How . . . ?"

"Some of Jamie's wealth was mine," Ian said. "So Jane didn't have to fund us for long."

"Which was good, because I was broke," Jane said.

"Then I began my training school," Ian continued. "That

has added considerably to my funds. At the very least, it pays for nappies for the wee one."

"Tell the truth," Jane chided. "You could be living on your inheritance for decades."

"The old cache in the fireplace story?" Thomas asked, just as dryly.

"Do you know of it?" Ian asked, surprised.

"Iolanthe told me. Her grandfather had told her. Apparently it was quite a hoard."

"Was and still is," Ian said. "There is surely enough there for Iolanthe to have a share."

"She doesn't need a share," Thomas said. "I have more money than I'll ever spend in a lifetime."

"But that isn't the point," Jane argued. "She needs her own money."

"Why?" Thomas asked. "I have plenty."

Ian shook his head in warning. "Don't start her on this. There is no good reason for it, but Jane insists. She makes her own funds by weaving, so she'll have her own coin to spend." He looked at Thomas earnestly. "Spare yourself, brother, and do not argue with them on this."

"Some women need their own checking accounts," Jane insisted. "It has nothing to do with love or money. It has to do with independence."

"From what?" Thomas asked, ignoring Ian's frantic motions to stop. "From their husbands?"

"In part."

"I don't understand."

"You're a man," Ian interjected. "Save yourself and leave it at that."

Jane frowned at her husband, then looked at Thomas. "I imagine Iolanthe doesn't want to feel completely obligated to you."

"But I don't mind!"

"Well, I imagine she does. Think about it, Thomas," she said. "You saved her life, gave her the clothes on her back, and now you've brought her halfway across the island to her home. I imagine she wants to love you just because she loves you, not because she feels obligated to."

"And you think she thinks having her own money will make this happen?"

"I do."

Thomas looked at Ian. "I'm baffled."

"Aye," Ian agreed. " 'Tis the way of things."

"Some women don't care," Jane continued, "some women do. It's your job to figure out how your woman feels about it and respect that."

"I think," Thomas said slowly, "that things were a lot simpler back in the Middle Ages. The man carried a sword, and the woman didn't."

Ian laughed heartily. "Aye, you're a lucky lad to have had a wee taste of life as it truly was. In truth, though, I knew many a woman as skilled with a knife as I." He shook his head. "We're all the same, no matter the century. But I daresay my Jane has it aright. Jamie should give your lady an inheritance."

"I could give him—"

Ian shook his head.

"Then he could give her—"

"Nay, Thomas. Jamie wouldn't accept your money; it would insult him."

"But no one worries about insulting me," Thomas pointed out.

Ian shrugged with a grin. "You'll have bairns enough to drain your coffers. Now, as I was saying, let Jamie give her an inheritance so she feels as if she could make her own way if necessary. Then are you both on the same footing."

"And then I can put money into her checking account?"

"Bingo," Jane said with a smile.

"I think I just don't get it."

"Don't try," Ian advised. " 'Twill do nothing but give you pains in your head."

"I think it's very simple," Jane said.

"And I think that maybe a little sword work in the snow is making more sense to me all the time." He looked at Ian. "Interested?"

Ian leaned over and kissed Jane. "I'll return for the dishes, love."

"You cooked, I'll clean," she said cheerfully. "I don't mind."

"You haven't seen Thomas's cooking pot."

"Oh, I'll leave that for him," she said with a grin.

"I imagined you would," Thomas said. "Thanks for the edible half of dinner, Ian."

"You'll improve your skills," Ian offered. "Either that or you won't. There's no middle ground with my cooker."

Thomas was beginning to wonder if there was any middle ground with anything in his life at present.

What he did know was that a few hours of swinging a sword would distract him. He couldn't ask for much more than that at present, so he headed up to his room to fetch his coat.

The house was quiet when he finally put his feet up on a stool near Ian's fire-engine red AGA stove with a cup of cider in his hands. He gave thought to Ian's idea of an inheritance for Iolanthe and surrendered to a greater wisdom than his. Maybe Ian was right, and a passel of kids would drain his bank account soon enough. Maybe he wouldn't be opposed to Iolanthe having her own money. And maybe all Iolanthe needed was to feel like she didn't owe him for so much. He didn't want her to feel obligated. He just wanted her to be happy.

He wondered how things were playing out over at Jamie's. Did she think about him? Or was she wishing he would just pack up his things and go home?

At least working out for hours every day with Ian was taking his mind off things. They were using blunted training swords, but even then, the flat of a blade on his ribs stung like a handful of hornets. He played a game with himself, that it really was life or death and that his skill would be all that saved the day. It was when he treated his training that seriously that Ian began to grin. Jamie had once remarked that when Ian grinned, the true sport began, but that few challenged him enough to bring on that feral smile. Thomas certainly didn't want to credit himself with more skill than he possessed, but it certainly bolstered his pride when his swordmaster smiled.

The kitchen door burst open, followed by a gust of wind. Thomas was on his feet, grasping for his nonexistent sword, which he remembered with a curse was propped up against his bed, when he realized that the body stamping off the snow and blowing on his hands really had no need to do either.

"Chilly out," Ambrose said. He smiled at Thomas. "Well met, grandson."

"Well met yourself, my laird," Thomas said, closing the door and sitting back down with a thump.

Fulbert blew in directly behind Ambrose, followed immediately by Hugh. Apparently, the little party wasn't complete, because Duncan came in just as enthusiastically. The four ghosts drew up chairs, conjured up tankards of ale, and began to warm their toes against the stove as well. Thomas looked at Duncan with pursed lips.

"Are you taking up matchmaking as well?"

Duncan shrugged with a smile. "Seems a goodly work, doesn't it?"

Thomas snorted. "I'm not the one to ask."

"Ah, Thomas lad," Ambrose said with a smile, "give your lass time. As I said before, you've another chance to win her. Who wouldn't want that?"

Thomas supposed there was something to that, but then again, wooing one's lady was much more productive when one had one's lady in the same general vicinity.

Well, she would either send for him, or she wouldn't. There was nothing he could do about that besides wait. In the meantime, there were glorious tales of battle and some damned funny hauntings to listen to. He looked around at the half circle of men and realized they had come to keep him company. He counted himself blessed to be able to see them.

And then a thought struck him.

He looked at Ambrose. "Am I one of your matches?" he asked, interrupting the man.

"Well, aye, lad. Of course."

Thomas frowned. "What's your success rate?"

Ambrose grinned. "I'll let you know later, laddie. I'll let you know later."

Thomas buried his sigh in his mug. Apparently, some questions were just better left unasked.

He sipped and listened and laughed, and the longer he did so, the more he realized that he couldn't just sit and wait any longer. Training with Ian was good for his body, but he wasn't sure it was so good for his soul. What he needed was to be climbing. Maybe at the top of a mountain, he would find the peace he was so desperately in need of.

Or at least a damn good diversion until Iolanthe made her decision.

Yes, out in the wild was the place for him. He felt better already knowing that he would get up in the morning and start looking for a place to pit his skills against, skills that were his, skills that were honed and perfected.

A climb.

It might make all the difference for him.

Chapter 41

I olanthe stuck her pitchfork under a pile of straw and swung it into the wheelbarrow. She repeated the motion half a dozen times until she'd finished filling the stall, then sat down on a bale of hay to catch her breath. Jamie had a stableboy for this kind of thing, but she hadn't cared. It was good, mind-numbing work. She'd certainly done it often enough in her past. Most of her half-brothers had been willing to go to great lengths to avoid any kind of useful labor, so mucking out the stables had always been a good way for her to avoid having to see them.

She leaned back against the wall and closed her eyes. She was tired, aye, so tired she suspected she could sleep for a se'nnight and wake only to seek out the bathroom. The trouble with sleeping, though, was that then she would dream.

And she was powerfully unsettled by her dreams.

One thing she could say for a se'nnight at Jamie's hall was that she was certainly more used to the ways of the Future. She'd grown accustomed to jeans, boots, and sweaters—so much so that she wondered how she'd managed without them.

She'd also made a friend of Elizabeth. She had come to realize that having another woman to talk to was a pleasure. It felt very familiar and easy, which made her wonder if she hadn't done something like unto it in another lifetime.

A ghostly lifetime, perhaps.

She turned away from that thought. True or not, she had no stomach for thinking on it. What she thought she might be able to stomach was more of that double-fudge ripple from the freezer. Along with all of Elizabeth's other fine qualities was the uncanny ability to choose a very fine ice cream.

"Iolanthe?"

She opened her eyes in surprise, then smiled at the sight of Jamie standing there. "Aye, my laird?"

Jamie looked at her gravely. "I have something that perhaps you should see."

It was a moment that she was sure she would look back on fifty years in the future and remember with perfect clarity. She would remember the smell of hay, dung, and horse. She would hear the whickers of beasts, the shifting of hooves, and the patter of rain against the roof. She would see Jamie with the light of a modern lamp falling over him just so, and she would feel her hands suddenly flex of their own accord.

Thomas would have called it déjà vu.

She had no name for it but destiny.

"Of course, my laird."

She rose and followed him into the house and all the way up to his thinking chamber. He gestured for her to sit down in the chair next to his desk. She started to, then froze. For an instant, she felt as if she'd done the like before. Of course, she *had* done the like before, as she had spent a goodly amount of time talking to Jamie over the past se'nnight. She'd sat in that chair numerous times.

But not with this eerie sense of memory hovering over her.

But she was no coward, so she sat and clasped her hands in her lap—so fiercely that her knuckles turned white.

Jamie reached into the drawer of his desk and pulled out a book.

She closed her eyes before she truly had a good look at it, but that didn't matter. She knew it, knew it intimately, knew what the pages contained, knew that it had been an empty book that Jamie had pulled out of his case of books at some point in the past.

Past. Future. She couldn't tell the difference anymore.

But there was a difference with the book.

This time she could hold it.

She opened her eyes and held out her hands. Jamie handed her the book. She felt the smooth, cool leather beneath her fingers. She smelled the tanned calfskin. She ran her fingers over the black ribbon that kept the book closed.

She put the book down on her lap and folded her hands over it. And then she spoke.

"I, Iolanthe MacLeod, do make this record, not by my own hand, but by the hand of my laird, James MacLeod," she whispered. She looked at Jamie. "In the year of Our Lord's Grace 2001. In the autumn of that year."

His mouth had slipped open. "Do you remember it?"

She shivered. "Nay. 'Tis but a dream in my head. When I think on it too long, it fades from me."

"Well," Jamie said, then fell silent. "These are tidings indeed."

"I know not what they mean."

"Open your book, granddaughter, and see if your tale aids you."

"I cannot read, my laird."

"You could, Iolanthe. You could before."

"You mean after."

"Aye, that as well, I suppose."

" 'Tis a perplexing snarl, isn't it?"

"I'm still sorting it out," he agreed. "I will someday, then perhaps I'll find a few more destinations for my traveling."

She had to smile. "Your lady will have aught to say about that."

"Aye, my girl, she always does."

Iolanthe looked down and untied the book before the unease caught her up again. She opened to the first page and looked down at the writing there. It looked as mysterious as all writing looked to her. She shook her head.

"I cannot read this."

"Lessons, then," Jamie said, rubbing his hands together. "As quick as may be."

"Will you not read it to me?" she asked.

He smiled briefly. "Lass, 'tis far better that you read it yourself."

"But you wrote it."

"I wrote down your words, aye. As did everyone else in my household."

She blinked. "They did? In truth?"

"In truth? Aye. Six hundred years of tale takes a bit of

doing to set down. We wrote at all hours till your tale was done."

"I can't believe 'tis mine."

"That's your hand there," he said, pointing to the first bit of scribbling. "It cost you, I'm afraid, for apparently 'tis very difficult for a . . . um . . ."

"Spirit," she supplied.

"Aye," he agreed quickly, "for a spirit to handle things from our mortal world. But you did it, signed your name and all. Then we finished it for you. All but the last page. You wrote a bit more there, but I never read it."

"Then," she said slowly, " 'tis left to me to see to this."

"I would say so."

She looked at him. "Can you teach me to read these scribblings?"

He looked powerfully pleased. "Aye, I can. We'll start now."

And with those simple words, her lessons began.

It was slow going at first, but at some point during the third day of trying to make sense of the letters and how they fit together, she realized that she was relearning something she already knew something about. From then on, things went much more quickly, and by the end of the week, she had begun to read something that Jamie had claimed she'd dictated.

But had she in truth? Had she spoken those words and had others write them down?

She decided to test it, because she couldn't bear not to.

She had waited until things were quiet one afternoon, snuck up to Jamie's study, then pulled out a pen and paper. The pen fit easily in her hand now, after all the practice she'd had, but writing the words that would either free her or condemn her was one of the most difficult things she'd ever done.

Iolanthe MacLeod, do make this record . . .

She pulled the book out of Jamie's desk and held it closed for several moments while she decided if this was really something she needed to do.

The temptation to look was too strong. She opened the book and laid it flat on the desk, next to what she'd just written.

She compared the two.

They were, unsurprisingly, a perfect match.

She closed her eyes and tried to take normal breaths. To her amazement, it wasn't difficult to accept what she'd just proved to herself. Mayhap 'twas that she'd had well over a month to think on the possibility that Thomas was telling the truth. At first, the very notion that she might have lived centuries as a ghost was abhorrent. She'd been unable to fathom such an existence.

But since the afternoon on the shore near Artane when Thomas had told her his truth, she'd found that she'd known things she shouldn't have. She remembered experiences she'd never lived through. She recognized places she'd never seen before.

The Sight?

She didn't think so. Thomas McKinnon was blessed with it in abundance. She, on the other hand, could scarce see her hand before her face, much less anything of a less corporeal nature. Nay, she had no gift for that.

All of which led her to only one conclusion: Thomas had been telling the truth.

She looked down at the book before her. Perhaps 'twas past time she read her own account. She couldn't deny that she had written those first words before her. It could only mean that she'd dictated what was to follow. Jamie would never lie about such a thing.

She put the pen away, folded up the sheaf of paper, and stuck it in the back of the book. Then she made herself comfortable and started to read. There would perhaps be words she wouldn't understand, but Elizabeth was nearby and could aid her. The differing hands might also pose a challenge, but that could be surmounted.

She would read her own tale, then hie herself over to Ian's afterward and find Thomas.

And then she would do what she needed to do.

* * *

> *I loved Thomas McKinnon as a ghost. I never said as much to him, and for that I have my regrets. But I did love him, and I would have passed the rest of his life happily with him, sharing whatever small things we could have shared.*

Iolanthe put down the book. She was sitting in Jamie's study just after breakfast, as had become her habit over the past few days. She leaned her head back against the comfortable leather chair and sighed. The words she'd read were at the beginning of her book and at the end. Apparently she'd considered them important enough to repeat.

What a thorough ghost she'd been.

She flipped the page and blinked in surprise. There in her own hand were another few lines. She wondered, given what she'd learned of her other existence, what it had cost her to write what she had.

> *Don't be a fool, Iolanthe MacLeod. You dreamed him first. You loved him next. You can love him now.*

Well, she supposed that said it all. She flipped to the last page, which was empty, and stared at it. If she were to add anything, what would she add? She took a pencil off Jamie's desk, then absently began to draw. She wasn't much of an artist, but after a time, a scene began to take shape. Jamie had asked her to think on what she would have if she could have anything, who she would share her life with if she could share it with anyone in this century or hers. He suggested she write it down where she might have it to look at later. She supposed drawing it was equally as acceptable.

She drew the sea as it rolled ceaselessly against the shore. A house began to appear on the beach, and as she drew it, she realized she'd dreamed it. It looked nothing like her keep, nothing like Thorpewold, nothing like Mrs. Pruitt's inn. The more she drew, though, the more at peace she felt. Ah, that such a place might be hers in truth.

And that she might have a man to share it with.

That man being, of course, Thomas McKinnon.

She shut the book, then debated whether she should take

it with her to show him or leave it behind and show him later. She opened Jamie's desk drawer and put the volume inside it. She would probably need two hands to wrap around Thomas. Best she not have anything to distract her from that embrace.

Assuming, of course, that he was amenable.

She went to her room to fetch her coat, then looked at Duncan's knife sitting on her night table. In her time, she'd never left the keep without a knife, once Duncan had taught her to wield it. Perhaps 'twas right that she should take it with her even now. Mayhap she would need to brandish it at Thomas to convince him she was in earnest about having recognized the feelings of her heart for what they were.

She tucked the knife into the back of her jeans, then descended the steps to the great hall. It was still early, but she was surprised to find the hall empty. Surely, though, Ian's household would be up by now.

She stepped out into the crisp December chill and found herself enormously grateful for the warm clothes Thomas had bought her. She toyed with the idea of repaying him for them, then discarded it. He had done it out of love for her. She would take some of the money Jamie had given her for an inheritance and buy him something that pleased him.

Or she would hoard it for their children. They would need things along the way. Or perhaps she would save it for an inheritance for them when she was gone. That she actually had something of value to leave anyone was a miracle. She was grateful to Jamie for it.

She walked around the castle and through the east forest. Ian's house was past the little lake and over the field. Jamie had drawn her a careful map and bade her be wary of where she stepped. She had almost laughed, then she had realized how serious he was. Judging by the fact that she was now a mortal and not a ghost, and *that* thanks to the little gates in his forest, she knew she had cause to believe he knew of what he spoke. Traveling through time was not a matter for jesting.

So she carefully avoided medieval England—she had been there and had no desire to return—skirted Barbados and Ancient Rome, and made her way across the far meadow to

Ian's house. Her heart lifted with every step she took. Not that it was a particularly beautiful morning, for it wasn't. It was cold and threatened rain. But to her mind, the sun was shining and the flowers were a blaze of color. Her heart was light. What else could she have asked for?

Ian's house was grand enough, she supposed, though certainly smaller than Jamie's keep. It seemed a cozy place, and she was happy to be going there. She walked around to the back door. It felt comfortable, as if she'd done it a number of times. Then she realized it was the Boar's Head Inn's kitchen door she was thinking of. As she'd only entered it a time or two after walking in the garden, she couldn't credit herself with that memory.

Or could she?

After reading her own tale, she could credit herself with quite a few new things.

She opened the door to find two women sitting at the kitchen table with cups of something steaming in their hands. Iolanthe paused and smiled.

"Sorry to interrupt," she said in her best modern English. "Is Thomas here?"

"And why," one of the women asked, scraping her chair back as she stood, "would *you* want to know that?"

Iolanthe faltered for a moment. She'd never been faced with this kind of creature before. She was petite, fair-haired, and radiated a crispness that Iolanthe had to admire. Surely not even a single crease in her blouse dared disobey by flattening itself where it shouldn't. As she watched, the woman looked down at the black trousers she was wearing, espied a speck of lint, and screeched in horror as she hastily picked it off.

"This country is filthy!" the woman exclaimed. "Dirt everywhere!"

"Actually, it's not dirt, it's wool," Jane said, walking into the kitchen. "Very fine wool that I make into very expensive sweaters." She looked at Iolanthe and smiled. "Good morning, Io. It's good to see you. How are you?"

Iolanthe found herself surprisingly grateful for Ian's lady's friendly greeting.

"I am well, Jane. And you?"

"Couldn't be better. Girls, did you introduce yourselves? No, well, this is Thomas's sister, Victoria. And this is Cartier—"

"That's Tiffany," the little screecher growled.

"Sorry, wrong jeweler," Jane said, looking anything but repentant. "This is Tiffany. Victoria's friend."

"Thomas's *fiancée*," Tiffany corrected, turning to look at Iolanthe. "And just who might you be?"

Iolanthe considered the women facing her and just what mischief or not they were about. First, there was Tiffany, who looked as if her fondest wish would have been to bury a dagger in Iolanthe's chest—assuming, of course, that she could have done so without mussing her clothes. Then there was Thomas's sister, Victoria, who was staring at her with such a piercing gaze that Iolanthe wondered just what she suspected.

And then there was, the saints bless her, Jane Fergusson MacLeod, who stood there and looked at Iolanthe with a serene smile that Iolanthe couldn't interpret any other way but as one of friendship and affection.

"I am," Iolanthe said finally, "Thomas's cousin."

"See?" Tiffany said, brushing off her chair and sitting back down. "Thomas's cousin, not his girlfriend. I told you Megan had it wrong. Evidently your means of getting information out of your little sister aren't as good as you claimed."

Iolanthe looked at Victoria sharply. "You harmed Megan?"

"Just a little sisterly tussle," Victoria said smoothly.

Iolanthe favored Victoria with the coldest look she could muster. "If you harmed her, you will regret it."

Victoria looked at her assessingly. Iolanthe stood firm under the scrutiny. Then Victoria looked at Tiffany, and there was ice in those blue eyes.

"I'm beginning to think, Tiffany, that perhaps you haven't been as genuine as you've led me to believe," she said slowly.

"I told you that Thomas loves me. He didn't want to leave the States to come over here. He just felt obligated to come over and look at Megan's stupid inn."

Iolanthe snorted in disgust.

Tiffany glared at her. "What would you know, Miss Hayseed?"

Iolanthe wasn't sure what she meant by the title, but she had no trouble understanding that it wasn't complimentary. Tiffany cast her a final look of disdain before she turned back to Victoria.

"Thomas loves me. He's just forgotten."

"Thomas has an excellent memory," Victoria countered. "I doubt he's forgotten much at all."

"I can think of something he hasn't forgotten," Jane put in.

Tiffany looked up at her expectantly. "What?"

"You boinking his buddy thirty seconds before Thomas had a meeting with him this past summer," Jane said with a sweet smile. "I know for a fact he hasn't forgotten that."

Iolanthe made herself a mental note to discover the definition of *boinking* at her earliest opportunity. By the way Tiffany's ears turned red, she suspected that the activity was one the woman shouldn't have engaged in.

"How did you know that?" Tiffany gasped. "It wasn't that way at all!"

Victoria stood up and slapped her hands on the table. "I've been bamboozled. I cannot believe you convinced me that Thomas had gone off the deep end. I think you'd better pack your bags."

"I will *not!*" Tiffany said, stamping her foot.

The sound was so strange, Iolanthe bent to peer under the table. Why, the wench had spikes pointing down from her heels. How did she walk about in those things?

"What are you looking at?" Tiffany snapped. "Haven't you ever seen a pair of stilettoes?" She raked Iolanthe with a contemptuous look. "I doubt it. Look at you in those unfashionable clothes."

"Thomas bought these for me," Iolanthe said stiffly. "And I find them much to my liking."

"Ah-*ha!*" Tiffany said, pouncing on that like a cat on a hapless mouse. "I *knew* it. Are you some country bumpkin he knocked up? You'll never have him, you know. I'll make sure of it."

Iolanthe acted before she thought. She pulled Duncan's

knife from the back of her jeans. She flipped it and caught it several times in silence, then caught it a final time by the hilt and looked at Tiffany in feigned puzzlement.

"You'll stop me from what?" she asked. "I fear I didn't hear you."

Tiffany stood up so swiftly that her chair fell over backward and met the floor with a mighty crash. She backed away with a look of horror on her face.

"I'm being assaulted!" she screeched. "Call the police!"

"Shut up, Tiffany," Victoria said wearily. "Go pack your bags. I'll drive you down to the hotel. You can stay there until I can find someone to take you to the airport."

"She'll murder me!" Tiffany said, pointing a trembling finger at Iolanthe. "I need protection!"

"Your tongue ought to serve you well enough," Iolanthe said pleasantly. "Not even a banshee would dare accost you when you screech out your commands."

Tiffany began to stomp her feet in frustration. Iolanthe watched in fascination, marveling at the sound of Tiffany's shoes on the flagstones of Jane's kitchen. Then she watched as Tiffany threw up her hands and stormed from the kitchen.

Iolanthe looked at Jane. "Thomas is not here?"

"He went climbing," Jane said. "I think he needed the distraction."

Iolanthe nodded. "I understand. When did he leave?"

"Yesterday. He'll probably be back in a day or two."

"A bit of a climb sounds like a fine idea, actually." Iolanthe smiled at Victoria. "Good day to you, Victoria McKinnon."

Victoria watched her with her mouth slightly open. "You're Iolanthe."

"I am."

Victoria seemed to be incapable of intelligible speech. Iolanthe merely smiled at her, then looked at Jane.

"Will you let him know I came?"

"He'll be overjoyed."

"One could hope," Iolanthe said. She waved to Jane, looked a final time at Thomas's sister, then turned and left the kitchen. Perhaps Thomas had it aright, and getting out in the wilderness was the thing to clear one's head. She pulled

the door shut behind her, tucked her knife back into the
waistband of her jeans, then shoved her hands into the pockets of her coat.

She smiled to herself as she walked up the meadow. Poor
Thomas, to have such a one as Tiffany hunting him. That he
might want to be hunted by her wasn't a thought that bore
entertaining. The woman was definitely not for Thomas. Iolanthe couldn't have stood more than a handful of moments
in her presence. She sincerely doubted Thomas could have
borne a lifetime with her.

Perhaps she would tease him about it when he came to
find her. That she was certain he would was likely something
that should have given her pause, but she didn't stop to consider it. He would come for her. Hadn't he said as much?

She wandered higher up behind the keep. She'd done so
often in her youth and always found peace there. That she
was doing so in jeans and boots was almost odd enough to
make her uneasy.

How would she have known if she'd suddenly been
slipped back to her time? It wasn't as if she could have
merely looked about her and told the difference. Trees were
trees, and these resembled to a great degree the same kind
of trees she'd grown to womanhood with.

She found, quite suddenly, that the thought of what she
would leave behind was enough to steal her breath from her.
That she should have acquired so many things dear to her
heart in such a short time was frightening. Jamie, Elizabeth,
and their little boy Ian? All the rest of her kin and kith?

And Thomas?

She wrapped her arms around herself and stared into the
sun hanging so low in the southern sky. Nay, she had come
too far to lose what she'd found.

She heard a footstep behind her and stiffened in surprise.
Had Thomas changed his mind and come home? The moment the thought crossed her mind, she found the idea of it
irresistible. Maybe he'd had one of his fey fits come over
him to tell him to end his climb. Maybe he'd known she
would be here, and he had come to pledge his heart to her
and ask for her hand.

But how quietly he had come! She would have to commend him on his tracking skills. Duncan would have been impressed.

She turned, a compliment at the ready.

Only it wasn't Thomas she was looking at.

Chapter 42

T*homas, turn around and go home.*

"I know, I know!" Thomas exclaimed, stomping on the accelerator.

"You know what?" Ian said, gripping the armrests and cursing fluently.

"I'm hurrying!"

"I'm not asking ye to!" Ian exclaimed. "Thomas, ye'll kill us both!"

Thomas pulled his foot back off the gas and took a deep breath. "Sorry. I just keep hearing voices telling me to hurry." He slid a look at Ian. "And what is it with you MacLeods that you lapse into dialect when you're stressed?"

"Habit. Be grateful I haven't started swearing at you in Gaelic yet."

"You already have. Several times."

Ian cursed as Thomas screeched around a corner. "Can you blame me?" he gasped.

Thomas managed a smile, but it was a weak one. He concentrated on the road in front of him. It was just barely dawn, and he'd been driving like a maniac for a good two hours already.

Ian hadn't appreciated being woken in the middle of the night, but he hadn't complained overmuch. Thomas hadn't told him that he'd woken to the sound of a voice in his head repeating the same words over and over again. *Thomas, go home.* He'd just said they had to go back. Ian had studied him briefly in silence, then risen and helped Thomas break camp in record time.

"I think I would have enjoyed that climb," Ian said. "Maybe another time."

"We have to get back to your house."

"Trouble?"

"I can't imagine whàt else it would be.".

"I have a mobile phone. Jane would have called me if aught had gone amiss."

"I don't think it's Jane." Thomas paused, then shook his head. "No, I know it's not Jane. I just know I have to get back."

"Hmmm," Ian said thoughtfully, then fell silent.

Thomas was content with lack of talk, though it gave him more opportunity for thought than he perhaps would have liked. So he focused all his energies on keeping his car on the road and not in a ditch or plowing into a field full of sheep.

Voices again. It just figured.

It took two more hours, two hours longer than he wanted, but finally they were pulling into Ian's driveway. Thomas leaped from the car, stumbling over Ian to get around to the back door. Ian opened the kitchen door, and Thomas pushed past him to come to an abrupt halt in the kitchen.

There was his sister, Victoria, sitting calmly at the table, sipping some sort of beverage from a cup.

"Vic," Thomas said weakly.

She only looked at him appraisingly.

"Who is this?" Ian asked in Gaelic.

"My sister."

"She's fetching enough."

"Maybe, but she's miserable to live with." He managed a smile at Ian. "I think I've found her perfect match. You remember Connor MacDougal?"

"The one with the powerfully foul temper?"

"That's him. I think I'll give her the castle and watch her make the rest of his unlife hell."

"Will you two please speak in English?" Victoria asked crisply. "Thomas, introduce us."

Thomas looked at his sister. "Ian MacLeod," he said, pointing to his host. "Our cousin. And he's married, Vikki."

She threw a dish towel at him with enough force to sting as it whipped him across the face.

"I was only being polite," she said frostily.

"I'm just sure you were," Thomas said. "What are you doing here?"

"Tiffany was devastated by your fly-by-night departure from the States. I brought her here so you could make it up to her. Believe me when I tell you it wasn't easy to track you down."

"Tiffany?" Thomas asked weakly.

"Your former fiancée, remember?"

Thomas let that pass. "Who told you where I was?"

"Megan."

"She wouldn't have given in willingly. What'd you use? Thumbscrews?"

"Chinese water torture," Victoria said.

And Thomas didn't for a moment doubt her. He wondered where his parents had been, or Gideon for that matter, but Victoria wasn't above subterfuge when it came to going after what she wanted. Torturing their baby sister was just par for the course.

But that didn't solve the greater dilemma, which was the fact that apparently his sister had brought to his very doorstep Tiffany Amber Davidson, who was currently peg-legging it into the kitchen on impossibly high heels.

"Thomas!" she exclaimed. The tears began to flow. "Oh, Thomas, I knew you'd come back for me!"

"Who's this?" Ian asked, reverting to the native tongue. "Frightening wench, that."

"My former fiancée," Thomas said with a sigh.

"You almost wed with this one?" Ian asked incredulously. "Amazing, isn't it?"

"English!" Victoria bellowed in frustration.

"I've missed you, Thomas," Tiffany said, producing a few more tears for the occasion.

Thomas looked at his sister. "Did she join your theater company, Vic?"

"I *mean* it, Thomas," Tiffany said, wringing her hands. "I can't live without you! It's been killing me not knowing where you were."

"Lost me at the airport?" Thomas asked politely.

Tiffany gasped, her hand flying to her throat. "What are you talking about?" she asked.

"Yes, what are you talking about?" Victoria asked.

Thomas ignored his sister. "How's your dad's little re-model coming, Tiffany?"

"Terribly," Tiffany said, looking pitifully grateful for a change of topic. "There are all these horrible picketers harassing him all day."

"Awful," Thomas agreed. "I guess he really needs those offices, doesn't he? Now that he has a new company to find room for."

Tiffany blanched. "Now, Thomas, you know I didn't have anything to do with that."

"I never said you did, did I? How nice of you to suggest the possibility."

Victoria cleared her throat with an imperiousness that would have done credit to her namesake. "Will you two cease with this useless bickering? Tiffany, go pack your bags. Thomas doesn't want you, and I don't have time for any more of this stupidity. I've got a production to start rehearsing. I need to get back to the States."

Ian turned to Thomas. "She's a player?"

"Runs her own theater troupe," Thomas said. "Off-off-off-off-off Broadway. It's so far off, there's no traffic stopping you from getting there. But," he added, staving off what he was sure would have been a colossal barb thrown from his sister, "it's actually really good theater." He smiled at his sister. "How'd you like a change of scenery? I've got a great backdrop for you."

Her ears perked up. He actually saw them do it. When it came to anything remotely connected with her passion, she was very willing to listen.

"A backdrop?"

"My castle. It's yours. I'd even fund your entire cast's trip over here for a month to do your play. By the way, what are you doing?"

"*Hamlet*," she said, sounding rather breathless.

"Perfect."

"But what about me?" Tiffany screeched. "What about me?"

Victoria gave Tiffany a look that should have put a heavy layer of frost on her. "Your luggage, Tiffany."

"I'm not going anywhere!"

Thomas looked at Tiffany. "Go back to New York, Tiffany."

"I will not!"

"I'm paying the protestors to picket your dad," he said curtly.

She gaped at him.

"It's payback for him taking over my company."

"You were ignoring me," she whined. "I had to get your attention somehow."

Thomas looked at his sister. "Get her back to the airport, please. I consider this entirely your fault."

"I agree," she said crisply. "I was taken in by her charming ways, but I've seen the light. I'll make sure she gets on a plane."

"You will not!" Tiffany protested.

"Don't mess with me, Tiffany," Victoria said, steel lacing her tone. "I know personally most of your favorite designers. I'll tell them you're recycling their clothes in consignment shops. Cheap consignment shops."

Tiffany made inarticulate sounds of horror. Thomas grunted, then left Tiffany in the capable hands of his sister, who really had missed her calling in life. She should have been running someone's army, not keeping two dozen jumpy actors in line. Well, if anyone could get Tiffany out of the country, it would be Victoria. Thomas didn't give her another thought.

He brushed past the women, then trotted up the stairs to the guest room. He grabbed his sword, then made his way back down the stairs and back through the kitchen before he realized what he held in his hand.

What did he need a sword for?

To prod Tiffany into the car with it?

"And just where do you think you're going with that?" Victoria asked, washing up her mug. "Are you going to stab your little girlfriend in apology?"

Thomas stopped abruptly. "What did you say?"

"Your girlfriend. Iolanthe. She was just here a few minutes ago. I'm surprised you didn't see her on your way in."

"Iolanthe was here?" he asked. He could hardly believe

how lousy that timing was. "She met Tiffany?"

"I wouldn't worry about it," Victoria said, turning and leaning back against the sink. "Iolanthe pulled a knife on your former fiancée. She can hold her own."

"Where did she go?"

"To take a hike. Literally," Victoria added quickly. "I'm not making that up."

Thomas grunted at her. "Come back when Tiffany's gone, and I'll give you the whole story. I'm sure it will be quite different from the one you brutalized from your helpless little sister."

"You'd be surprised . . ."

He left the kitchen and slammed the door shut on the rest of her words. He'd heard more than enough. He could only hope Iolanthe hadn't hiked into his life to hike right back out of it. He stood in Ian's back meadow and wondered where the best place was to start looking for her.

And then, quite suddenly, Duncan was standing in front of him.

"She's in the high meadow," he said quickly. "Lord Charles is there as well."

"What?" Thomas asked incredulously.

Duncan waved away any more questions. "Just follow me and make haste. She can't see me—or anyone else who's there trying to aid her."

Thomas sprinted after Duncan, praying he would arrive in time. How had Charles found the time gates? The very thought of it boggled his mind. How could he possibly have stumbled upon them on his own? Had he been spying on them?

They should have been more cautious. Charles had probably followed them all the way up the road from Artane. Iolanthe had tried to convince him not to go that way. He should have listened.

How, though, had the man gotten all the way to Scotland? Had he used the gate at Falconberg? Jamie had said that was the only gate in England that would transport a person not only through time, but straight to Jamie's backyard. Thomas couldn't believe that Charles had walked all the way from twenty-first century England to Scotland over the past three weeks.

Then again, maybe he had.

Well, the particulars were unimportant. What was important was stopping the man before he finished the job he'd set out to do. Thomas suspected that he wouldn't have another chance to save Iolanthe's life. That was Jamie's other caveat. In all the times he'd used his gates, he'd never once gone to exactly the same spot in time. It was, according to him, a one-time thing.

Thomas didn't want to test the theory.

He blessed Ian silently as he ran all the way to the meadow and arrived there unwinded. Maybe all those endless, brutal hours of training had been worth it. He was in better shape than he had been before Everest. He burst through a little grouping of trees and came to a teetering halt twenty paces from where Charles stood waiting.

With his sword across Iolanthe's throat.

Thomas looked around to see not only Ambrose, Fulbert, Hugh, and Duncan, but every member of Iolanthe's garrison from Thorpewold there as well. Even Connor MacDougal stood there, a ferocious frown on his face.

"So," Charles said conversationally, "you decided to come fetch your little wench yet again."

"So it seems," Thomas agreed. He looked Iolanthe over quickly and decided that she hadn't been harmed.

Yet.

"This time," Charles snarled suddenly, "I have the advantage."

"Do you?" Thomas asked.

Iolanthe flinched as Charles pressed his blade more firmly against her neck.

"Yes, I can see that you do," Thomas conceded quickly. "What do you want?"

"Since I've already discovered the secret of traveling through time, I'll now have the jewels in the fireplace."

Thomas smiled grimly. "So you heard us."

"Aye, talking like a pair of babbling fools," Charles said. "Now, get me the cache in the fireplace, and let me be on my way."

"I will when you let her go. You don't need her now."

"Don't I?" Charles asked with an ugly smile on his face. "My pride has been mightily wounded. Fetch me the jewels. And while you're at your task, I'll be taking my revenge here."

Iolanthe made a sound of protest but quickly stifled it at Charles's renewed pressure on her throat.

"I was too hasty the last time," Charles said. "I could take my pleasure of her and not count myself sullied, I think." He looked at Thomas and shrugged. "If I find the act distasteful, I'll kill her afterward. That should alleviate any affront to my sensibilities she might have caused."

Thomas stood there and wondered just what in the hell he was supposed to do now. He was trained to fight a man coming at him with a sword. He knew how to climb mountains and negotiate inanimate rocks and ledges. He could survive in the wilderness for weeks at a time with nothing but a knife.

But he didn't have a clue how to barter for his love's life with a man who obviously thought nothing of killing when he felt like it.

Thomas grasped his sword and prayed for help.

It came, amazingly enough, in the form of Connor MacDougal.

The MacDougal came up behind Charles and clapped him smartly on the shoulder. The man had to have felt it, because Thomas heard it from where he was standing.

Charles jumped in surprise. Thomas started to call out to Iolanthe, but she wrenched away as Charles spun around to see who he faced.

Iolanthe bolted clear of him. Thomas grabbed her and jerked her over to him.

"Are you all right?" he asked, not taking his eyes from a very unsettled Charles.

"Nicked myself on his damned sword," she groused. "One finger bleeding, but 'tis not a mortal wound. I should have poked him with my dirk. I would have, had he not snuck . . . up . . . on—"

Thomas felt her freeze at his side.

Her stillness almost immediately became his stillness. He

realized that he hadn't felt that kind of quiet coming from her in quite a long time. For at least a month.

Since he'd gone back to save her.

He realized she was groping for his hand. His fingers met hers and she held on to him so tightly it was almost painful. He looked at her to find she was staring at Lord Charles. He suspected, though, that Charles wasn't really what she was looking at.

"Merciful saints above," she breathed.

She looked around the circle of men, never releasing Thomas's hand. Then she looked up at him.

"Merciful saints above," she repeated, sounding stunned.

"See them?"

"Aye."

Apparently, so did Lord Charles. He held his sword up, turning himself around a time or two, glaring at one and all.

"This is unfair," he said. "Are you such women that you must needs pit yourselves two score against one?"

Duncan cleared his throat. "Ach, but we've no mind to fight ye, ye wee fiend. We'll leave that to the laddie there. He'll see to ye right proper."

Well, no time like the present to either prove his mettle or get himself killed. He smiled briefly at Iolanthe, then released her hand to get down to his own business. He shrugged out of his coat and tossed it aside. He pulled his sword from its sheath, then felt hands take the leather from him.

"I'll hold that," Iolanthe said.

Thomas smiled briefly, then turned back to consider his situation. The men around him weren't heckling him. He looked at Iolanthe. She didn't look uneasy. She hadn't made any derogatory comments about his past displays of sword-play so far. Things were looking up.

The downside was, of course, that he was going to have to kill the man facing him, and that was enough to give him pause. It was one thing to do in a bunch of thugs in the Middle Ages. Somehow, the century just seemed to demand that kind of thing. But this was the twenty-first century, and he knew for certain that murder was severely frowned upon.

"He would have slain me, Thomas," Iolanthe said quietly.

"Indeed, he did once. You've no need to fear that you shed innocent blood."

She had a point there. This could definitely be called self-defense.

"She's right, Tommy lad," Ian said from the sidelines. "Do the bastard in. He deserves it."

Thomas looked to his left to find not only Ian there, but Jamie, Patrick, Zachary, and Jamie's minstrel Joshua as well.

Great, an audience.

Well, it wasn't as if he hadn't had one before during his training. But his cousins and Iolanthe's garrison at the same time? At least none of the mortals were making any comments. They were too busy gaping at the ghosts. All except Jamie, who only folded his arms across his chest and put on the frown he usually wore when assessing Thomas's skill. It felt comforting somehow.

Thomas wondered how he should begin the . . . well, duel, for lack of a better word. His contemplation was cut short by Charles bellowing out his rage and rushing toward him.

Thomas realized, idly, that he had improved since last they'd met. Charles, however, was angrier than he had been the time before, so perhaps they were still unevenly matched, with Thomas still being on the short end.

He shoved aside any concern for repercussions. It was clear even to him that the man who was angrily hacking at him with a broadsword had every intention of killing him if he could. There were half a dozen mortal witnesses to the fact, should it have come down to an inquest.

And Iolanthe had a point. Charles had murdered her in cold blood once. If that didn't demand some kind of redress, he wasn't sure what did.

"Thomas, quit thinking!" Ian yelled. "You've your lady's life to fight for!"

Thomas nodded curtly, then turned his mind to the task at hand, namely ridding Charles of his sword and using his own to end the other man's life. He emptied his mind of all thought and concentrated on watching the other man's eyes. His sword became a sharp extension of his arm. It sang through the air like faint pipes.

He frowned, then locked blades with Charles.

"Are those bagpipes?" he asked.

"Damned if I know," Charles panted.

Thomas shoved the other man away with a foot in his belly. He stood there, chest heaving, and listened to what sounded remarkably like Scottish bagpipes.

"Ach, Duncan, do ye hear?" Iolanthe asked in surprise. " 'Tis Robert!"

"It is, my girl. Come to play for your love."

Thomas wasn't sure what he was more surprised by: Iolanthe talking to Duncan, or that their clan's bagpiper was serenading him. He had to admit, though, that the music was very stirring. He looked to his right, past the men standing there, and saw a lone piper on the side of the hill, his plaid stirred by the breeze.

And then he realized that if he didn't let the sound stir him some more, he was going to find himself without his head. He ducked, rolled, and came up on the other side of Charles's flashing blade. He tuned everything else out. Full concentration came readily to him, and he supposed he would have to thank Ian for it later. He fought as if his life depended on it. His and Iolanthe's. His future and hers.

The battle felt as if it dragged on for an eternity. There came a point where he couldn't feel himself anymore. He was nothing but a lethal blade flashing through the air and the drone of the pipes winding its way through the grass and the descending twilight. He felt a part of the land, a part of his clan, a part of a connection that couldn't be severed. His ancestors stood around him in a circle, and he felt them willing him to fight harder, to stand up against the strain, to be victorious.

He could tell the precise moment when the tide turned for him. Charles looked just the slightest bit indecisive, then he fell back. Thomas pressed him mercilessly, the song of the piper and the murmuring of the men driving him, giving him strength, reminding him of what he fought for.

Charles's guard slipped, and Thomas drove his sword into the man's belly. He'd meant to skewer him straight through, but Charles twisted aside at the last possible moment. He watched Charles fall as if in slow motion.

Charles dropped his sword, then clutched his side. He staggered back, reeling, then slipped to the ground. Thomas pulled his blade free of Charles's side just as the man—

Disappeared.

Thomas was so surprised, he almost overbalanced and fell onto the precise spot where Iolanthe's one-time murderer had fallen. Hands grabbed him and pulled him back.

"Don't," Iolanthe gasped.

"Aye," Jamie agreed, giving Thomas a sure tug. "You won't want to follow him there."

Thomas looked at him with wide eyes. "Where is there?"

"The Inquisition," Jamie said with a twinkle in his eye. "Almost makes you glad you'd just nicked him, aye?"

"I did more than nick him," Thomas said. "He'll die from that."

"I suppose he'll survive long enough to wish you'd finished him," Jamie said with a grin.

Thomas rolled his shoulders. "Well, I wouldn't want to do that every day."

"No one ever does," Jamie said, clapping Thomas on the shoulder. "But you made a fine showing."

High praise from his laird. Thomas acknowledged the same with a nod, then found Iolanthe prying his sword from his fingers. She sheathed it, then handed it to Jamie. Thomas noticed absently that one of her fingers was wrapped in some kind of material that looked to have been torn from somebody's T-shirt. It was bloody.

Then she wrapped her arms around him and hugged him, and he didn't notice anything besides Iolanthe MacLeod in his arms.

"I hope that finished him," Thomas said with a sigh.

"Oh, aye," she agreed. "I daresay it did. He'll not trouble us again. Think you?"

"What I think is it was a helluva way to get you into my arms," he said. "Let's not do that again."

"I'm for that," she agreed, turning to rest her cheek against his chest.

He closed his eyes, unable to decide what he was more grateful for: that the battle was over or that Iolanthe was standing willingly in his embrace. At this point, he thought it might just be a toss-up.

"I thought," he said finally, "I honestly thought I wouldn't get to you in time."

" 'Twas a close thing."

"Duncan came and got me. I don't know if I would have found you otherwise."

"Weren't the pipes lovely?" she asked, her voice muffled against his sweater. "Robert always could play a tune to stir the dead."

Thomas snorted out a laugh before he could stop himself. He met her eyes as she lifted her head.

"You've found your sight then, I see," he said with a smile.

"Apparently so," she said.

Then she smiled up at him, and it was all he could do not to bend his head and kiss her. The thought had crossed his mind so many times over the past few months, but he'd never been able to do anything about it. Well, there was no time like the present, especially when the lady seemed willing.

He started to kiss her, then realized they had a very large audience, and likely one that they wouldn't get away from any time soon.

"We should go fix your finger," he said. That would be enough reason to get her into a bathroom small enough to exclude this cluster of Highlanders.

"But . . ." she said, hesitating, looking around her.

He had no trouble understanding her hesitation. He looked around him as well at all the men who were looking at her with smiles on their faces. He touched her cheek.

"Greet your kin. And your garrison. I can wait."

"You're a very patient man, Thomas McKinnon."

When compared to all the patience she'd had in waiting for him to show up and put into motion things souls had counted on for centuries, he considered himself rather hasty. But he'd tell her that later. For now, it was enough to watch her receive the garrison of Highlanders she had known either in life or death.

And to watch her weep as, to a man, they knelt before her and again offered her their fealty.

Well, all except Connor MacDougal, of course, who informed her in no uncertain terms that he had no intentions of giving his fealty to a mere woman.

Thomas clasped his hands behind his back and smiled to himself. Apparently some things never changed.

Except the woman who was now turning to him, her cheeks wet with her tears. He held out his arms, then gathered her close.

And he was grateful to be able to.

Life was, he decided as he stood with his love in his arms in a meadow surrounded by Highlanders both mortal and not-so-mortal, nothing short of miraculous.

He closed his eyes and smiled.

Could things get any better?

Chapter 43

Could life get any worse?

Iolanthe stood in Jamie's thinking chamber for yet another morning and scowled down at the book in her hands. This wasn't where she wanted to be. It wasn't so much just being at Jamie's hall that disturbed her. It was being at Jamie's hall still unbetrothed.

She wasn't sure at whose feet to lay that blame. Thomas's? It wasn't as if he hadn't tried to get her alone. But it had been a little difficult when Ian's house had been filled with Highlanders of all sorts, living and dead. Perhaps 'twas at their feet she should lay the blame. She'd managed to sit next to Thomas for the better part of the day on that day he'd saved her life yet again, but that had been the extent of her success. She'd returned to Jamie's keep, accompanied, but unbetrothed.

Damn all those men, anyway.

Which left her again that morning in Jamie's thinking chamber, looking for aught to do. She'd pulled her book from Jamie's desk, opened it up, and read a page or two, smiling a bittersweet smile at what was written there. By now, she'd come to terms with the truth of it. She'd also come to think that perhaps it hadn't been an existence completely without merit. She had certainly met many people she wouldn't have any other way.

But then again, when compared to what her future held, that former existence was certainly best left as something kept between the covers of a book.

Assuming, of course, that she had a future that held something besides haunting Jamie's keep.

"Good day to you, granddaughter."

Iolanthe looked up to see Jamie standing at the doorway. She smiled.

"And to you, my laird."

"Thomas sent word that he'd like to come fetch you, if you were willing."

Her heart sang so suddenly that she felt a blush come to her cheeks. "Did he?" she asked faintly.

"Aye. You can ring him, if you like."

She shook her head. "I think I can find my way there."

"If you will," he said doubtfully. "See that Thomas brings you home before the evening is out."

She looked at him blankly. "Does it matter?"

"I'd say it does. He has no business keeping you at Ian's all night till he weds with you."

"He hasn't asked me to wed with him, my laird," she said quietly.

"Well," Jamie said, folding his arms over his chest, "I should think that would be his first task."

"Am I to prod him about it, then?" she asked crossly. "I can't force the man!"

Jamie uncrossed his arms, walked across the chamber, and kissed her soundly on the forehead.

"He'll ask soon enough, I'll warrant. But until he has and you're wed, you'll sleep under my roof. I'll take my blade to him otherwise. You'll remember that I'm the one who taught your love most of his swordplay. Should we need to settle our arguments either with blades or a wrestle, he'll not come away victorious."

"Aye, my laird."

"I don't suppose you need men to see you to Ian's, what with that garrison of yours cluttering up my hall."

Iolanthe was still a little stunned by the fact that she now held the fealty of forty Highlanders.

"Aye," she managed. "I suppose I'll be safe enough."

"Then off with you, my girl. Mind your step."

"Perhaps a few signposts wouldn't be planted amiss on those particular parts of your land, my laird."

"Ah," he said with a twinkle in his eye, " but where's the sport in that?"

Sport wasn't exactly what she would call suddenly finding

oneself in another century, but perhaps Jamie had a different perspective on it. He certainly had more practice at it than she did.

She bid her laird good-bye, tucked her book under her jacket, and made her way from his hall, collecting a mighty guard on her way. She felt quite safe surrounded by the fierce men who had chosen to accompany her. Her only regret was that her father couldn't have seen the like. She felt an echo of that sentiment in her soul and suspected that she'd passed a great many years thinking the same thing.

Her self-appointed personal guard walked into Ian's kitchen with her and would have continued on into his great room had she not looked at them with a frown.

"I'm safe," she said.

"We're sworn to ye, lady," one of the fiercer of the lads said. "We'll protect ye at any cost."

Iolanthe looked at Thomas sitting rather harmlessly in front of the fire.

"I daresay I'll be safe enough with him," she said.

The men grumbled a little but retreated to the kitchen. She scowled at them, but they, to a man, folded their arms across their chests and scowled back at her. So, they were refusing to retreat any further.

"Oh, you came," Thomas said, looking enormously pleased. "I would have come for you."

"The walk served me," she said with a smile.

"And you did have your army accompanying you," he agreed. He rose and took her hand. "What's the deal? Don't they trust me?"

She shrugged helplessly. "I've no idea. They seemed determined to fulfill their obligation quite thoroughly."

Thomas led her over to the couch and sat down with her. "It has to be flattering. You'll notice they didn't go down on bended knee to me. They like you. And they respect you, which probably means more."

"I don't know what I did."

"I'm sure they'll tell you if you ask."

She wasn't sure she wanted to know. She was beginning to suspect that what she really wanted was some privacy so

Thomas could ask her any questions that might be burning inside him at present.

Damnation, but would these ghosts never give her any peace?

And now more of them! She scowled as Ambrose MacLeod, Hugh McKinnon, and Fulbert de Piaget came strolling into the great room as if they had a right to. Duncan came as well, but she couldn't fault him for it. After all, he was her closest kinsman.

Chairs appeared as if they had conjured them up out of thin air, tankards of ale were hefted in a spirited manner, and talk revolved for quite some time around Thomas's performance two days before. By the saints, hadn't they discussed that enough already? The men criticized, complimented, and considered Thomas's showing until Iolanthe was heartily sick of ghosts, swordplay, and ancestors who should have known when to take their leave so that Thomas might be about the business of asking her to be his wife.

Assuming he wanted her to be his wife.

Fulbert stood up with a grumble. "I can tell we're no longer wanted." He scowled at her. "Mind yer thoughts, missy. Yer shoutin' 'em at me."

Iolanthe felt her jaw slide down of its own accord.

Fulbert tossed his mug into the fire and disappeared.

Hugh stood up and made her a low bow.

"Don't mind him," the former laird of the clan McKinnon said kindly. "He's a sour sort. I'll see to him for ye, if ye like."

She could only nod as she made a valiant attempt to retrieve the lower half of her face from where it currently rested on her chest.

Ambrose stood finally and looked at her. "Too much talk of warring does become tedious, daughter. But I thank you kindly for sharing your man with us this morning. He showed himself very well, didn't you think?"

"Aye," she managed in a strangled voice.

"Good afternoon to you then, Iolanthe, my dear," he said, as he turned and walked through the wall.

The illusionary chairs vanished. Well, all except the one that still contained Duncan MacLeod. He looked primed to leave as well, but Thomas held up his hand.

"Duncan, please stay."

Iolanthe would have protested, but for the look in Thomas's eye. And his tone. There was a seriousness in his voice she'd never heard, and she wondered if it could but betide something foul. She felt herself grow unaccountably nervous.

"Thomas," she began, "perhaps 'tis I who should leave—"

"Why?" he asked, looking at her with surprise. "Do you want to go?"

"Nay," she said slowly, "but perhaps my wishes should not matter."

"They matter most of all," he said. "They always have. Well," he added quickly, "except for when I said I was going to use the time-travel gate in Jamie's forest. You were hopping mad about that, and I ignored you." He smiled at her. "I'm sorry."

"You aren't," she said with pursed lips.

He smiled. "You're right, I'm not." His smile faded, and he wiped his hands on his jeans.

Iolanthe could hardly believe it, but he looked nervous.

"I need to talk to you," he said. "And Duncan needs to stay and hear it."

Was he going to tell her he was leaving? That he'd changed his mind and didn't love her? That killing to save her had left such a bad taste in his mouth that he couldn't look at her anymore?

He stood.

And she thought she might be ill.

He fished about in his pocket for something, then knelt down in front of her.

Well, that was promising.

"I hope," he began, "that I'm not being too hasty about this."

He stopped.

She frowned. "Be hasty," she said. "I think I've waited long enough."

"Hey," he said, sounding aggrieved. "You haven't been the one Ian's been grinding into the dust every day over here for almost a month."

"Nay. I was the one haunting the walls of Thorpewold for six centuries."

"All right," he conceded, "you win." He took her hand in
his and looked at her with affection shining in his eyes. "I
love you, Iolanthe MacLeod. I loved you from the moment
I saw you, and there hasn't been a day since where I haven't
either wallowed in it or fought it." He smiled. "I didn't fight
it for very long."

That was romantic enough, she supposed. Her great-
grandmother would have approved.

"I am willing to give my life for yours, if need be," he
continued. "But more than that, I want to live my life forever
intertwined with yours. I will protect you with my body, I
will shelter you with my name, and I will work to see you
never lack for your needs."

She wished somehow that she'd had a pen to write that
down. They were surely the finest words ever said to her.

"I'd like," Thomas finished, "to ask you to marry me."

Aye had almost rolled off her tongue when he interrupted
her.

"But I should ask your father first."

"My sire?" she said, in surprise. "My sire? Why in the
bloody hell would ye ask that damned fool?"

A romantic? Why, the man was an idiot!

Thomas only smiled faintly. She had the intense desire to
slap him quite smartly across the face.

"I'd ask him," Thomas said quietly, "because he's sitting
right there, waiting for me to."

And then he quite slowly and deliberately turned to look
at the other man in the chamber.

Duncan MacLeod.

Iolanthe looked at her cousin. Nay, she was quite sure she
wasn't looking at him, she was gaping at him. And he was
looking none too pleased with Thomas.

"Lad," he said, blustering about indignantly, "this was
hardly the time—"

"I would like," Thomas said, "to ask you, Duncan
MacLeod, for Iolanthe's hand in marriage."

"Father?" Iolanthe repeated. "Why did you call him my
father—"

She found, quite suddenly, that she couldn't find the words

to say anything else. Duncan squirmed and looked as if he
wished quite desperately to bolt.

Iolanthe sat back, speechless. She looked at Duncan and,
as she did so, memory after memory washed over her. Duncan standing two paces behind her for centuries, comforting
her with a quiet word, a brief touch, a ready ear. Duncan
defending her against others who had tried to take her keep
from her. Duncan watching over her as she puttered in her
illusionary garden. Duncan skewering Roderick on his sword
innumerable times to rid her of his annoying presence.

"Where is Roderick?" she asked suddenly.

"Won't set foot in Scotland," Duncan answered promptly,
then clamped his lips shut.

"Well," she said. "I suppose there are lines a man cannot
cross."

She looked at Duncan, who currently stared down at his
scarred hands and felt the memories of when she'd known
him in life and in death layer themselves over each other
until she realized that she knew him more thoroughly than
anyone else, even Thomas. She knew his skills, knew of his
learning, knew of the sacrifice of his own life that Thomas
might save hers. And it occurred to her, in a blinding flash,
that were she to have the choice of a father, it would have
been this man.

For he had loved her.

And Malcolm MacLeod certainly had not.

As for how it had all come about—him being her sire in
truth and not Malcolm—perhaps that was better saved for
another time. Now, there were more pressing matters to be
seen to.

She looked at Thomas to find him regarding her with a gentle expression. "Well?" she asked briskly. "There's my sire,
and I'm proud to call him such. Be about your business."

Duncan looked up in surprise, and his eyes grew quite
bright, as if they were filled with tears.

Thomas's eyes were just as suspiciously bright. Then he
blinked and turned to Duncan. He spoke in Gaelic.

"Duncan MacLeod, I've known you in two lifetimes, and
you've known me. You know I love your daughter, that I
would give my life for her, that I would raise my sword in

her defense. I will care for her as if for myself, put her comfort before my own, give her children, and see her sheltered. I ask you to give her to me."

Duncan cleared his throat. "I do know ye, Thomas McKinnon, and trust ye with my life. I trust ye with my daughter's life, as well, for ye've risked yers to save her. She's yers, if she'll have ye."

Thomas turned back to her. She felt him take her hand and watched as he slipped a ring onto her finger.

"Iolanthe MacLeod, will you have me?"

She hesitated. "I have no dowry."

"You call that garrison of Highlanders no dowry?" he asked with a smile.

"I don't know that they'll pledge to you," she admitted.

"They're your men, Io," he said with a gentle smile. "I wouldn't ask them to be anything else."

There was a shuffling sound from the kitchen. "We'll pledge to him," one brave voice called.

"We will not," argued another. "I'm a MacLeod! I'll *not* place my hand in a McKinnon's!"

"He's a MacLeod as well, ye fool."

"Is he now?"

There was a bit of low grumbling.

"Aye, through his mother, that's right."

"Well," said another voice, "half of us could pledge to him and the other half pledge to her."

"We've already all pledged to her, and I'll not take back me oath!"

"Nay, we'll find others to come be his men." That voice spoke more strongly. "We're Herself's men, Thomas McKinnon. And ye'll answer to us if ye don't treat our lady proper!"

"Beggin' yer pardon, laird Thomas," added another.

Iolanthe looked at Thomas. "I could bid them—"

"No," he said with a shake of his head, then he smiled at her. "Iolanthe, what I really want is you, not your men, not your castle, and not your piper."

"Though he is a fine one."

"He is. But that's not what I want. I want you. I want you to want me. Will you?"

She put her hands in his, looked him in the eye, and spoke her oath of fealty.

It seemed the thing to do.

And it made several tears roll down his cheek, which she supposed couldn't be a bad thing.

"Well," said a resigned voice from the kitchen, "we're his in the end, it seems. Never thought I'd serve a McKinnon, but there it is."

"She seems to love him. There's something in that."

Iolanthe laughed and put her arms around Thomas's neck. "Look what you've bound to yourself. Me and my ghosts and bogles."

"It's worth it," Thomas said, pulling her off the couch and into his arms. "It's more than worth it."

Iolanthe closed her eyes as he kissed her. She realized that she'd spent the whole of her life dreaming of this moment, hoping beyond hope that this man would come for her and make her his.

And then she found that ruminating over those happy memories was simply more than she could do and concentrate on his mouth at the same time. Who would have thought that a mere kiss would undo her so thoroughly?

And then she found herself immensely grateful that he had such a tight hold on her, for when he began to kiss her more intensely, she felt as if her entire world had begun to spin. All she could feel was his mouth on hers, his hands in her hair, his finely fashioned form pressed up against hers.

It was bliss.

And then a male throat or two cleared themselves.

Iolanthe came to herself to find that she was on her knees being embraced by Thomas who was also on his knees and that they had quite a large group of spectators. Thomas looked at the garrison, who had seemingly found its way into the great room.

"Privacy?" he suggested.

"Aye," one man said.

"Assuredly so, my laird," said another.

"After ye've wed with her," stated another, the largest of the lot, whose hand caressed the hilt of his sword lovingly.

Iolanthe found herself deposited back onto the couch without haste, but with a goodly bit of reluctance. She ran her hand self-consciously over her hair and felt Duncan's gaze boring into the side of her head. She hazarded a glance his way.

"Aye?" she asked hesitantly. "Father?"

He scowled at her. "Such sweet words will not drive me from here. I can see as how ye need a chaperon to watch over ye until ye're wed."

"Chaperon?" Thomas asked with a snort. "Why do we need a chaperon? We have a bloody audience!"

"Plan the wedding," Duncan instructed, folding his arms over his chest. "Soon."

Thomas looked at Iolanthe. "My parents could be here in a couple of days. Is that too soon?"

She smiled weakly. "Is it too soon for them?"

"I very much doubt it. My mom has called a couple of times to find out how you were."

"And if I'd come to my senses?"

He laughed a little. "Yes, well, that, too. I think she was more worried I'd make an ass of myself and you'd never want to marry me."

"She knew you wouldn't."

"I wouldn't test that." He touched the ring on her finger. "That's her wedding band. She sent it with me up here, just in case. If you said yes, she wanted you to wear it until I can get you something you'll like better."

"That was kind."

"She's a MacLeod," Thomas said with a smile. "And—"

"And his sire's a McKinnon," said Hugh McKinnon, appearing out of thin air and pulling up a chair, "which makes Thomas here of fine enough stock, my girl."

"But 'tis the MacLeod blood that serves him so well," Ambrose said, appearing next to Hugh and pulling up an even finer chair and a hefty tankard of ale.

Fulbert de Piaget reappeared, dragged up his own chair, and sat down with a grumble. "And I'm not related to either of ye, but ye stayed at me nevvy's hall at Artane—several times removed, ye understand—and ye'll need me good sense plannin' the nuptials, so I'm in as well."

Thomas put his arm around her, and drew her close.

"We're doomed," he whispered.

"I heard that," Fulbert said sharply. He looked at Ambrose. "Ingratitude, that's what that was. The curse of the young ones."

"Mayhap he's of no mind to have yer suggestions," Hugh said hotly.

"I've quite a head for plannin' a weddin'!" Fulbert exclaimed.

Iolanthe leaned her head on Thomas's shoulder and closed her eyes with a smile. She suspected that Thomas might have things aright. They were doomed indeed—

To have their hall filled with grumbles, and sword fights, and arguments over which clan was superior, and the saints only knew what else. She and Thomas would add their own tales and laughter. Perhaps between the two of them, their children, and their men, they would create something quite magical.

Assuming they didn't drive each other daft, of course.

She passed the remainder of the afternoon sitting next to Thomas, holding his hand and leaning her head on his shoulder. And she wondered, as she sat, if she'd either wished for the like desperately or she'd dreamed of it, for it felt very familiar. Indeed, she felt so comfortable and at home that she closed her eyes and let her thoughts begin to wander.

She realized she'd fallen asleep only when she felt Thomas stir next to her. She lifted her head off his shoulder and looked around her.

No ghosts.

"We're alone?" she asked sleepily.

"I'm sure it won't last," he said. "Jamie invited us for dinner. Let's drive there while we have the chance to do it by ourselves."

" 'Tis likely safer than walking," she agreed with a yawn. "Wouldn't want to trudge into medieval England by mistake."

"Heaven forbid."

She let him bundle her up, put her in his car, then drive her the small distance to Jamie's keep. He walked with her to the door. She stood on the top step and looked at him standing on the step below her.

"Did I dream today?" she asked with half a smile.

"I certainly hope not. You agreed to marry me, remember?"

She put her arms around his neck and held on tightly. "Thank you," she whispered. "Thank you for my life."

"No, the thanks are mine." He hugged her and was silent for several moments. "I love you, Iolanthe."

She pulled back and looked at him. There was but faint light from the stars above, but she hoped he could see that there was no lie in her eyes.

"I love you, Thomas McKinnon. I loved you before. I just couldn't say it to you."

He was silent for a moment, but he was smiling. "Thank you," he said finally. "I wondered."

"You won't have to wonder in the future."

"Neither will you." He kissed her softly. "Let's go inside before we freeze. And then call me when you get up tomorrow if you want company. My company," he clarified. "We could go for a walk."

"Aye."

"With a map."

"It would probably be safer that way," she agreed.

"A map and a score of chaperons," he groused.

"What more could you want?" she asked with a smile.

"What indeed?" He smiled, kissed her, and ushered her inside the house.

She held him back at the door. "Thomas?" she said.

He stopped and looked down at her. "What?"

"Thank you. For the tomorrows."

He smiled, that same smile that had taken her aback the first time she'd truly seen him in the guard tower when she'd first put her hand in his.

As if he'd found what his heart had sought his whole life.

It was a smile to take into her heart and treasure.

"Let's go," he said gently. "Your family is waiting."

"My family is here," she said, squeezing his hand.

And the smile that earned her was enough to bring tears to her eyes. So she didn't protest when he kissed her, then led her through the great hall to the kitchen.

Epilogue

A month later, Thomas stood on the deck of his house and stared out over the beach in front of him. It wasn't really the kind of day that was made for standing outside. It was January, cold as hell, and blustery to boot. But he loved the sea, so there he stood.

And as he stood there, he thought back over the past month and all the things that had changed in his life.

That had changed his life.

First and foremost, of course, was finding himself married to Iolanthe MacLeod. He'd expected to have it be the best thing he'd ever done. He hadn't expected to have it rock him to the core.

Her passion had just about done him in. And it wasn't just making love to her that devastated him so. It was watching her seize up every shred of enjoyment from every moment of life that left him breathless. It didn't matter whether she was walking along the beach or praying out loud on a transatlantic flight; she never did anything halfway.

It was like seeing his entire life afresh from someone whose eyes never missed a thing and whose bone-deep satisfaction in whatever came her way left him no room to take anything for granted.

And that made him wonder what she was doing at present— and how dangerous that thing might be. With Iolanthe, one just never knew.

He turned to go back into the house, sparing a nod for the Highlanders who decorated the outside of his house.

"My laird," several said, with nods of deference.

Well, that was something else entirely, but he'd think about it later, after he'd found his wife and made certain she hadn't found herself bested by a modern invention. She usually came out on top, but it had been touch and go there for awhile. He suspected that she hadn't done all that much investigating at Jamie's. Either that or she felt more at home in his home.

Which he hoped was the case.

He found her, finally, in his study, staring up at the painting over the desk. It was the portrait he'd had done of her months ago.

"It is a beautiful picture of you," he said quietly.

She shook her head. " 'Tis haunting, Thomas. I can scarce take my eyes from her. Was she so miserable, then?"

He put his hands on her shoulders. "I can't answer that, Iolanthe. Your book would tell you more than I could. When I met that woman, she'd had centuries to grieve for what she'd lost."

"But you gave her love."

"And she gave me love in return."

Iolanthe turned and looked up at him. "And so I've loved you twice," she said with a smile. "Perhaps I am doubly blessed."

"I know I am," he said fervently.

She laughed, then turned and lifted her book from the top of his desk. She smiled at him.

"I have something to show you. Come outside with me?"

"It's January."

"It's the sea. And I can tell by your cheeks that you've already spent a goodly amount of time staring over the railing, so I daresay you can bear a bit more. Besides, I hear the sound of piping, and you know how you love a goodly bit of piping whilst you watch the sea."

"Well, you have a point there."

She led him through his own house, seemingly as comfortable in it as if she'd lived there all her life. He wasn't sure how it was possible, but it felt more like home since she'd come, as if it had been built more with her in mind than him.

"What are you going to show me?" he asked, once they'd reached the deck.

She leaned on the railing, then handed him her book.

"Look on the last page," she said.

He opened the book, which he had to admit he hadn't read very much of. It hadn't been from a lack of desire. It had been painful to read, and he'd only managed it in short doses. He was far from the end, which he supposed was why he'd never seen what he was looking at now.

A drawing of his house in Maine.

Of the ocean in front of his house.

He looked at it silently, startled.

"When did you do this?" he asked, finally.

"After I'd read the book. Jamie told me to sit and think of where I would go if I could go anywhere. And," she added, looking at him, "who I would share that anywhere with. And so I drew this from my dreams."

"My house."

"Aye, apparently."

He stared at the drawing for a moment or two more, then shut the book. He drew his wife into his arms and rested his cheek on top of her head.

"I love you," he said quietly.

"And I love you, Thomas McKinnon."

He closed his eyes and listened to the waves rolling ceaselessly against the shore. He felt as if they had been standing there together for centuries. He had an idle memory come to him of thinking that he would be wise to duck just in case Fate sent any stray arrows winging his way.

A good thing he hadn't taken his own advice.

"I can," he murmured against her hair, "hardly believe you are mine. I can still see you standing in your hall with the sun streaming down on you. I thought I'd never again take a normal breath."

She pulled back to look at him. "You came to me first in my dreams, then in my memories, then in my life. And I don't know now if I'll ever manage a normal breath again."

He laughed. "If we're dreaming, I hope we never wake up."

"We're not dreaming, Thomas." She put her arms around him and hugged him tightly. "Not anymore."

He closed his eyes and held her close. She was right.

Their dreams had come true.

ROMANTIC ROOTS

MACLEOD

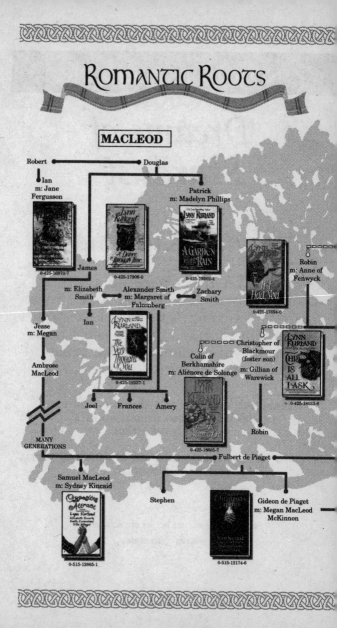

Robert ——————————— Douglas

Ian
m: Jane
Fergusson

Patrick
m: Madelyn Phillips

Robin
m: Anne of
Fenwyck

James

m: Elizabeth
Smith

Alexander Smith
m: Margaret of
Falconberg

Zachary
Smith

0-425-16970-7

0-425-17906-0

0-425-19202-4

0-425-17694-6

Jesse
m: Megan

Ian

Christopher of
Blackmour
(foster son)
m: Gillian of
Warewick

Ambrose
MacLeod

0-425-18237-1

Colin of
Berkhamshire
m: Aliénore de Solonge

0-425-18033-6

Joel   Frances   Amery

Robin

MANY
GENERATIONS

0-425-18085-7

Fulbert de Piaget

Samuel MacLeod
m: Sydney Kincaid

Stephen

Gideon de Piaget
m: Megan MacLeod
McKinnon

0-515-12865-1

0-515-12174-6

family lineage in the books of
LYNN KURLAND

DE PIAGET

Rhys de Piaget
m: Gwennelyn
of Segrave

Another Chance to Dream
0-425-16514-0

Nicholas | Amanda m: Jackson Kilchurn IV | Miles m: Abigail Garrett | Isabelle | Montgomery | John

This Is All I Ask / Dreams of Stardust
0-515-13948-3

Christmas Carol
0-425-15542-0

Phillip

Kendrick m: Genevieve Buchanan

Mary

Jason m: Lianna of Grasleigh

Richard of Burwyck-on-the-Sea (foster son) m: Jessica Blakely

William m: Julianna Nelson

A Knight's Tale — Patricia Potter, Deborah Simmons, Glynnis Campbell
0-515-13151-2

Stardust of Yesterday
0-425-18238-X

Tapestry
0-515-13362-0

The More I See You
0-425-17107-8

MANY GENERATIONS

Robin | Phillip | Jason

Thomas McKinnon m: Iolanthe MacLeod

My Heart Stood Still
0-425-18197-9

Victoria McKinnon m: Connor MacDougal
(to come)

PA-2080